Madame Dorthea

*L*EAVING the Middle Ages and the present day, Madame Undset in her latest novel makes a new departure and sets her scene in eighteenth century Norway. Revealing that she is as much at home there as elsewhere, she gives us a story kaleidoscopic in movement and peopled with a whole gallery of picturesque figures. The first chapter takes us straight into the heart of it with the disappearance of Thestrup, Madame Dorthea's husband, on which event the whole may be said to hinge. And from that point on we follow with absorbing interest the play and interplay of truly fascinating action. In its course we meet besides the title character and her sons such vivid characters as: Cold, a dissolute ex-captain of the Danish army, and his housekeeper-mistress; the gypsy woman Sibilla, noted for her gifts of soothsaying and leechcraft and for more sinister arts; old Scharlach, the German foreman of the glass-works of which Thestrup was manager; above all the domineering personality of Elisabeth, Dorthea's mother, married for the fourth time to the peasant-born Sheriff Lundo, and hiding in her remote past possible guilty secrets whose disclosure is threatened by her former satellite Madame Dabbelsteen. Re-creating in fact and spirit the whole atmosphere of a bygone age, it is all in all a novel that is a real event in Scandinavian letters.

D1158108

Sigrid Undset,
HEROINE

WHEN the year 1940 began, Sigrid Undset was living and working quietly, in the peaceful seclusion of her old Norwegian house in Lillehammer—caring for her family and household, writing by night, enjoying the fruits of a life that has brought her the very highest honors as a creative artist. This had been her way of living for years, this she expected it to be for years to come.

The fury of war has changed all that. As these lines are written Lillehammer is a ruin, in Nazi hands. Madame Undset's eldest son has died a soldier's death, defending his country against the invader. She herself is a homeless exile in Sweden; for she dared to raise her voice in protest against the rape of Norway's land, she exhorted her countrymen to fight for their liberties, she served her government in the censorship and in organizational work until such time as the coming of the Nazis to Lillehammer forced her to flee. In this fashion an unprovoked war of conquest has destroyed the outlines of a useful and peaceful life.

But the high courage which led her, at fifty-eight, to confront and defy the appalling sweep of German armed might—that is not destroyed. Nor is the fine creative flow which in the past has given us such major works as *Kristin Lavransdatter* and *The Master of Hestviken,* for even in this year of trouble it gives us a new novel, *Madame Dorthea.* Her fame for the future is secure—not only as a great novelist, but as a great patriot and a great human being.

"Her supreme achievement is in the appealing humanity and fallibility of her characters." —THE NEW YORK TIMES

The Works of

SIGRID UNDSET

Winner of the Nobel Prize for Literature *in* 1928

MODERN NOVELS

Jenny

The Winding Road
which comprises
The Wild Orchid and
The Burning Bush

Ida Elisabeth

The Longest Years

The Faithful Wife

Images in a Mirror

Madame Dorthea

MEDIÆVAL ROMANCES

Kristin Lavransdatter

A TRILOGY

The Bridal Wreath
The Mistress of Husaby
The Cross

The Master of Hestviken

A TETRALOGY

The Axe
The Snake Pit
In the Wilderness
The Son Avenger

Gunnar's Daughter

ESSAYS

Stages on the Road
Men, Women, and Places

These are BORZOI BOOKS, *published by*
ALFRED A. KNOPF

Madame Dorthea

Madame Dorthea

BY

SIGRID UNDSET

Translated from the Norwegian by

ARTHUR G. CHATER

ALFRED A. KNOPF
NEW YORK 1940

The characters and situations in this
work are wholly fictional and imaginary,
and do not portray and are not intended
to portray any actual persons or parties.

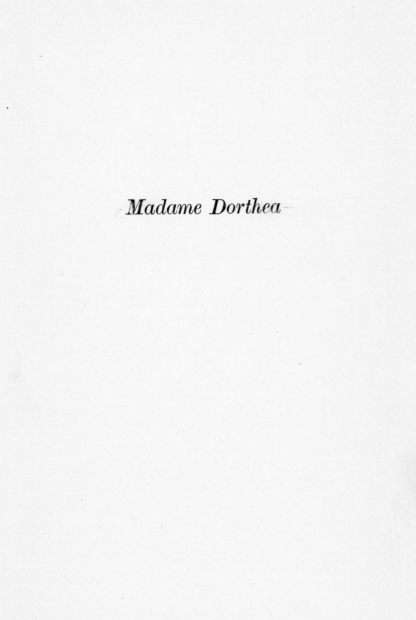

Madame Dorthea

1

As Madame Dorthea opened the front door, the force of
the wind was such that the rushlight she had set down on
the hall table was almost blown out.

She closed the door again. With her hand on the latch
she stood listening to the roar of the wind round the house.
The feeble flame recovered itself and cast its flickering
light upon a narrow space of the log walls. She quailed
with a momentary shiver. The draught moaned up the
staircase to the floor above, where a pale gleam showed
— it was the moon shining in through the passage window. She knew quite well that those black masses in the
dark corners were nothing but clothes chests and garments hanging on the walls. But she could not get over
the unreasoning start it had given her just now, on opening the door of the tutor's room, to find it empty and dark

and cold. Though of course she had known already that
Herr Dabbelsteen had not come home either.

And after all it would have been worse if she had found
him in. At any rate she could now assume that the boys
were with him. Though Herr Dabbelsteen in himself was
not the safest of companions for them — certainly not on
a day like today, when the roads had been so crowded
with farmers' carts. It had reassured her for the moment
when Lars returned with the news that no one in Lervik
had seen Dabbelsteen since early afternoon. And he had
only looked in at Else Dragoon's — and the boys had not
even gone in with him; they had spent the time toboggan-
ing on the road outside. So Else had said.

Out of doors water trickled from every roof. The gusts
roared among the old ash-trees. This would spoil the
roads for Thestrup's sledges, thought Madame Dorthea
sympathetically. The thaw had set in so suddenly. All
round the house the window-shutters rattled as the wind
caught them.

She became aware of the hushed buzz of voices in the
kitchen. They must be left to take their meal in peace. If
the children had not come home by the time the servants
had finished supper, all the men would have to go out and
search. Lars must take the sledge and drive down to Fenstad. If he had turned in at the Captain's, Dabbelsteen
would scarcely be in a fit state to reach home on his feet.

All the same, this was a thing he had never done yet —
absenting himself in this way when he had the boys with
him. Madame Dorthea had held a protecting hand over
him, though she had to admit Thestrup was right in what
he said — that even if Dabbelsteen was undoubtedly a talented young man, he was an extremely untrustworthy

mentor. No doubt it was true that she felt a certain maternal liking for the unfortunate youth; but her chief reason for insisting on their engaging him for another year had been her reluctance to send Vilhelm and Claus away from home as early as last year. And to send them to Christence.

Of course she could let Haakon or one of the maids go down to Scharlach's. But she preferred to go herself. In her heart she was sure they were not with Scharlach. But at any rate it would do her good to have a talk with the old German. Everybody at the works appealed to the foreman blower when at a loss. And now she really *was* anxious, though she tried to assure herself that, late as it was, it had happened before that the boys had forgotten their afternoon meal and come in late for supper, if they had anything special on hand.

And supposing for instance they had been run over, or had got caught among the sledges, she would have had word of it long ago.

Madame Dorthea put on her hooded cloak, spat on her fingers, and pinched out the rushlight.

As she opened the door a gust of wind tore it out of her hand and flung it inwards with a crash, nearly throwing her off her feet; she heard something rattle to the floor within the hall. In a sweat of terror she got hold of the latch and managed to pull the door to behind her. And no sooner had she put her foot on the doorstep than she slipped and nearly fell — the drip from the roof had coated the stone with ice. Her heart sank within her — what a night! What *could* have become of the boys!

The wind shrieked and whistled, it howled in the old trees. The moon, nearly full, appeared to be falling from one abyss to another among the driving clouds, now veiled, now clear again. Across the valley, on the bare black and white ridges, there was a gleam as of mica from the ice-clad rocks.

For a moment Dorthea stood hesitating. Then she drew down her hood more firmly, picked up her skirt, and bent to the wind, which splashed her face with icy drops.

The swept-up banks of snow beside the tracks in the yard were greatly shrunken even since the morning, she could see, and the surface was wet and slippery. The out-houses were asleep, with coal-black shadows before them and splashes of moonlight on their roof-tiles — nearly all the snow had slipped off. Here under the lee of the houses it was not so bad; but when she came to the gate, a gust of wind caught her and she had to stop.

At that moment the moon came out from under a cloud and sparkled on the ice in the fields, where the stubble showed up — the snow had already run off to that extent. Again Dorthea thought of her husband — he so badly wanted the winter surface to hold out a little longer. And this storm of wind — it always put him in dread of a fire in the works; in weather like this he often spent the whole night in his office. And he had had a tiring day, she knew.

What if she were forced to send him a message that the boys had not come home, nor Herr Dabbelsteen either? And if anything had happened it would be her fault for keeping on that untrustworthy person.

The wind was hushed for a moment. Dorthea hurried across. The road was slippery too; rubbish and horse-dung had been washed down and lay in little drifts with smooth patches of ice between.

the yard, which was full of black shadows. The
ms fell full on the grey, weather-worn façade of
building. There was a light in one of the kitchen
which they had forgotten to shutter. Dorthea
t heart: something in the old man's voice filled
lire and anxious expectation. The wind roared
-tops, a loose board rattled somewhere in a wall,
ld drops flying through the air made her shiver
uck her in the face.

e's an unfortunate creature, Madame Thestrup.
one of the men from Skaardal — it was Anders
was bringing a load of quartz from Kindli —
ving today, down at Else Dragoon's, that last
is girl presented herself at her parish priest's
ed that she had made away with her twin chil-
she had given birth to secretly at Christmas-

ul God, Scharlach, what are you telling me! "
e girl has declared that it's her stepfather who
of them. Margit Johansdatter Klokkhaugen,
ame. He's her mother's second husband; he
daughter must be about the same age."

y people! And poor Dabblesteen — if he is
girl! For she has forfeited her life — "
not speak of it till we came outside. Mutter
to hear of such things."

hought for a moment. Then she took courage

think we ought to search along the river —
may be traces? "

we ought to search everywhere, madame. I
down to the sawmill myself, get men from

Below the slope, on the other side of the highroad, lay
the two long barracks. In the moonlight they looked like
two strange lizards resting with their bellies on the ground
and their feet drawn up — there was a high flight of steps
and a covered porch in front of each entrance, leading to
the kitchens. Scharlach's chimney still showed signs of
life — the wind pressed down the column of smoke and
whirled it round.

Behind the barracks the river made a bend across the
level ground, before losing itself among the thickets at
the point on which the works stood. There was a glimmer
of moonlight on black water between the floes, and the
snow covering the ice was sodden in the thaw. — They
were always good, obedient children, Vilhelm and Claus.
— But supposing Dabbelsteen had had some business on
the other side and then discovered that they were late. He
was not to be relied on. He might have taken it into his
head that they should cut straight across the river, at a
place where the ice looked fairly sound, to save going
round by the bridge.

But where *could* they be? And what a wind!

She breathed with relief on reaching the highroad. Her
feet and skirts were as wet as they could possibly be; still,
she tried to avoid the worst puddles of melting ice in the
horribly churned-up road.

A faint light showed at the edge of Scharlach's window-
shutters. Thank God, she thought, as she stood in the
porch and heard the old man answer her knocking:
" Come in! "

Scharlach sat crouched in the chimney corner with a
book which he was studying by the light of the embers.
On seeing who the visitor was, he started up:

"Madame Thestrup! *Ei du lieber Gott* — are you abroad in this weather?"

Mother Scharlach had been nodding over her spinning-wheel; she got up and pushed forward a chair for Dorthea. There was a pleasant cosy feeling in here, at any rate for one coming from outside; an odour of humanity and of newly boiled milk. Finchen's two little children lay fast asleep in their grandparents' bed. This usually meant that the son-in-law, Wagner, who had his quarters next door to the kitchen, had taken a drop too much.

"It's Claus and Vilhelm, Scharlach — they have not come home. They went out with Herr Dabbelsteen this afternoon. And since then no one has seen them. So I wondered if they might be here. Scharlach, can you tell me nothing about them?"

"What of that student — has he not come home either?" Scharlach wrinkled his bushy black eyebrows.

The foreman blower was a square-built man, short in the neck and very broad-shouldered. His round face with its prominent cheek-bones and deep-set dark eyes was a leathery yellow, streaked with a network of red veins. His black hair, tinged with grey, bristled untidily about his head, so that the ribbon of his pigtail was usually left dangling on a few shreds at the back.

"Have you made enquiries at Lervik, madame? The tutor was in at Else's this afternoon, Hans Wagner told me." Scharlach's eyes were fixed in a sombre gaze.

Dorthea told him of Lars's fruitless enquiries at the dragoon's and at the schoolmaster's. "I am so afraid the manager will be much upset when he hears of it. As Scharlach knows, Thestrup will have worries enough already, in this weather."

"Madame Thestrup
send men out to mak
too —" He began to
had not noticed till no

"But, Scharlach, it

Scharlach shook his
hauled them on. "Th
what that person may

He crammed his bi
his hair well in under
zu Bett, Mutter," he
about with a frighter
Scharlach had kept
Norwegian was not
have been at least fif

The moon was be
Scharlach took Dor
ame Thestrup — I
know if Student D
thing to do with th
up by the houses, h
mouth."

As they came up,
kennel, rattling hi
proached the Ger
down and patted

"Well then, *m*
down at the drag
there had been s
girl at home; that
away."

The moon nov

tened in
moonbea
the main
windows
felt sick a
her with
in the tre
and the c
as they st

"Yes, h
And now
Överli wh
he was sa
Sunday th
and confes
dren that
time."

"Mercif
"Ay. T
is the fathe
that's her
and his stej

"Unhap
fond of this

"I would
cannot bea

Dorthea t
to ask:

"Do you
in case there

"I think
mean to go

there to go with me; then we can search along both banks of the river. Although — you must know, in this weather and after all the traffic on a day like today — what traces can we expect to find? But above all, madame, send mounted messengers along the road, let them enquire at the houses of call if anyone has seen the tutor."

" Yes, but the children, Scharlach, the children! They must be a hindrance to him if he is in a state of desperation! "

" He may have left them behind, or told them to wait for him, at some place along the road. We must not lose heart *yet,* dear madame. We must leave it in God's hand."

It was as though Scharlach's last words had suddenly made it all clear to her — the uneasiness of the last few hours *could* be nothing but the beginning of an anxiety such as she had never known. Leave all in God's hand — well, that she had always done. But if anything had happened to Vilhelm and Claus, it would not be easy to leave all in God's hand.

Scharlach laid a hand on her shoulder.

" Come now, madame. Let us get the men away as quickly as possible."

When the men were well away, Dorthea sent all the maids to bed except the cook, Ragnhild. But Elen, the dairymaid, declared she would not go to rest till they had news of the student and the boys.

The long kitchen table was crowded with cups and dishes. Dorthea sat down by the chimney with her bowl of beer broth in her lap. It was good to get something warm, in the cold and wet state she was in; she herself grew calmer as she talked reassuringly to the two maids who set about the washing up. Probably they would have the student and the boys here before long. It was no use being too anxious, when there might be no cause for anxiety. Ragnhild and Elen could take turns lying down, so long as one of them sat up and tended the fire, for of course they must have something warm when they came in, not only the boys, but those who had been out searching.

She lighted the candle in the bedroom candlestick and took up the kettle of boiling water. Once more she exhorted the maids to keep the fire up and not to be too uneasy.

But as she entered the bedroom, candle in hand, the little clock on the desk struck ten.

It was a large room with two windows; a third window behind the four-post bed was blocked. Its log walls were bare and unpainted, but it was so arranged that the huge brick chimney of the kitchen formed the dividing wall between it and the nursery, so that these rooms were the warmest in the house. For this reason they took their meals in here in the winter.

In front of the stove the tea-table was laid for Thestrup. Dorthea put down the candlestick, filled the urn with hot water, and opened the door of the stove — but found it almost burnt out. She raked and raked with the tongs, got hold of some embers for the urn, and added charcoal. Then she laid bark and blocks of wood in the stove, knelt down, and blew it up with the bellows. But she felt her heart beating violently against her stays as she tried to be calm and attend to her duties.

The cradle by the bed began to rock on the floor —

Dorthea hurried over to it. Little Christen had stirred — but, thank God, he lay still again and went to sleep. His mother bent down and caught the warm, milky scent of the child.

Thank God for the little ones, one knew where one had them. Although — just now in the kitchen Elen had reminded her of little Ole Skrumsrudhagen, who strayed away and was lost while his mother was at the sæter. This had happened the year they came to the glassworks. All the countryfolk believed the child had been taken by the fairies. And for that matter the Germans thought so too — they were just as superstitious as the natives, which was not to be wondered at, since many of them were papists. But Dorthea had never had the heart to throw doubt on it — the truth was probably far worse. What must the poor little one have suffered, wandering alone in the wild forest, hungry and tired, calling in vain for his mother! Unless indeed he had been swallowed up in a bog, or drowned in one of the many tarns up there.

The urn was singing; the fire roared in the stove and shed a warming glow through the draught-hole. The wind rumbled in the chimney. But its force was not felt so much on this side of the house, though the window-curtains stirred and the flame of the candle flickered even as it stood on the tea-table by the stove.

Her feet were like lumps of ice; she was shivering in her heavy drenched skirts. Dorthea put first one foot, then the other on the plate before the door of the stove.

She was always ill at ease when there was a strong wind at night — how easily a fire might occur down at the works! Oh, but the boys were certain to be under a roof somewhere by now, Dorthea tried to comfort herself.

They had been kept at some place where Dabbelsteen had taken it into his head to pay a visit, and someone had promised to drive them home. And they sat there waiting while Dabbelsteen drank and forgot the time. At the Captain's at Fenstad. Or perhaps he had gone as far as Vilberg, to Attorney Hauss, to get a lawyer's opinion about the fate of his girl. *That* was quite likely. If only she had thought of it before and spoken to Lars. But perhaps it would occur to him, too, to make enquiries at Vilberg.

But Bertel could not be left sleeping by himself up in the boys' room — supposing the noise of the wind woke him and he discovered that his brothers were not there. On realizing how sorely she dreaded having to pass through the dark attics Dorthea drew herself up and shook herself. Impatient at her own weakness, she snatched up a spill from the jar on the table, held it in the flame of the candle, and went to the dressing-table to light her little hand-lamp which stood there.

Meeting her in the mirror was the image of a woman with a screw of burning paper in her hand. For an instant she felt she was looking at a strange woman — a pale face, marked by age, framed in the pointed arch of a towering, lace-trimmed cap.

She had continued to wear side-curls and to dress her hair in the fashion of her young days — she combed it high up over a pad and let a curled lock fall on each side down to her throat. She had seen of course that her hair was getting thinner — it was more difficult to make it cover the pad entirely. It was still cinder-blond, but it had lost its bright silvery lustre. It was dull and streaked with yellow, as fair hair often is when it begins to fade.

Year in, year out, she had faced her mirror, but her

casual glance had scarcely noticed the traces that age had left in her face. They had stolen on her so imperceptibly. She was still a fine-looking matron. Dorthea Thestrup had regular features, rather large; her nose was straight and delicately formed, but a trifle too long, her mouth extremely handsome. But it was long since she had instinctively left off showing her teeth when she smiled. And by degrees the flesh of her face had subsided, as it were, and gathered in a loose fullness below the charmingly rounded chin.

She had given little thought to the passage of time and the fading of her beauty — since she became Jörgen Thestrup's wife she had scarcely consulted the glass to see how she looked; she was mirrored in his eyes and they told her that to him she was always beautiful. — She did not know how it came about, but now, as she faced her own image, darkened by the anxiety she strove to conquer, it was as though she had a vision of one she had known long ago. Thus she had examined her face in the glass, in a nervous suspense which she scarcely dared to confess to herself, years and years ago when the flight of time made her heart quail, since she was Dorthea Bisgaard, an old man's young and blooming wife.

It was what she had heard about the unhappy young people at Skaardal that had revived the memory of those days, of which she never thought if she could avoid it.

Fifteen years by the side of a good husband whom she loved. A fruitful, active, and useful existence, sweetened by the joys of sincere love. Oh God, this trepidation which had just made her recall her joyless youth, did it mean that now their happiness was ended? All the trouble and adversity they had gone through together — how easy it had been to accept it all as trials laid upon them by the fatherly hand of an all-loving God! Their sorrows no less than their joys had served to strengthen the bond between her Jörgen and her. But if anything had happened to Vilhelm and Claus — God, she thought not even her Thestrup could console her, and she herself would be powerless to assuage his grief.

Her eye fell on the little picture which hung beside the mirror. It was a copperplate, evidently cut out of a book. A nymph with flowing hair and drapery stood leaning against an altar with a torch in her hand. Behind her was a classical temple in a grove. But Peter Andreas had coloured it so nicely, and on the front of the altar he had inscribed some lines of his own enclosed in a medallion:

Be thou aye a joy to husband
And to friends, my Sister blest,
And as in the past, so ever,
Cherish Virtue in thy breast.

Then shall Fortune smile upon thee
Wheresoe'er thy footsteps lead,
And as year to year succeedeth
Blessings still shall be thy meed.

Dedicated to my amiable Sister, Madame Dorothea Thestrup, by her faithful Brother Peter Andreas Hiorth Eckelöff.

This had been enclosed with the letter in which he congratulated her on the birth of Vilhelm Adolf. Dear brother! In good and evil days alike his sympathies had always been with her. Twenty years of separation had not been able to cool his affection for the sister in his far-off native land — each year still brought a letter from him. It had been a consolation to her, in reflecting on the approaching separation from her two eldest sons, that in Copenhagen they would meet Peter Andreas. Her brother would be able to see them; possibly they might even shed a few rays of sunshine upon his melancholy existence.

The frame around the little picture was Vilhelm's work. He had seen how she prized this brotherly greeting. And one year, when Vilhelm was not more than nine, he had been to the pressing-house and begged a few strips of coach-glass, joined them to make a frame, and painted the back of it with marbling, very neatly. Scharlach no doubt had helped him in his work. But it was the child's own charming idea.

No, no, it would not do to stand here woolgathering. Dorthea took up the lamp and passed through the nursery. Deep breathing from the great bed told her that they were asleep, both the nursemaid and the nurse with little Rikke in her arm. By the other wall lay her two elder girls in a wicker cot. Dorthea let the light shine on them for a moment. They slept back to back, their fair curls intertwined on the pillow. They were charming, with their warm red cheeks shaded by long dark eyelashes. As usual fat little Birgitte had pulled the whole of the down quilt over herself, so that Elisabeth lay with her thin limbs exposed. Their mother put the bedclothes straight, tucked in the quilt and went on.

Draughts swept through the dark passage. The stairs creaked under her feet, and the noise was transmitted to the beams and logs of the groaning old timber building.

On the floor of the attic the light lay in uncanny white squares — the moon was now right above the house and shone down through the skylights.

The schoolroom was pitch-dark. Holding the lamp before her, Dorthea went straight to the truckle-bed — her eyes avoided the empty bed in the alcove. But she started in alarm on meeting Bertel's wide-open eyes.

" But haven't you gone to sleep yet? Or did Mother wake you, my dear? You are not afraid of anything, are you? "

Bertel made no answer. But as Dorthea stroked the hair off his clammy forehead he seized her hand and held it fast.

" Listen, Bertel, I think you had better come downstairs with Mother. It is so stormy. I'm sure you will sleep better in Father's and Mother's bed tonight."

Bertel sat up suddenly in his bed. " Mother — where are Claus and Ville? "

" They are out with Herr Dabbelsteen. Now put on your jacket and stick your shoes into your feet — "

She noticed it as soon as the words were out of her mouth: putting things the wrong way about was supposed to mean bad luck. Well, one ought not to believe that sort of thing. All the same, she hurried the boy rather impatiently, as he gave a shrill laugh of relief and repeated her words: " Stick my shoes into my feet — "

Bertel clung close to her and stumbled over things that lay scattered over the floor. It was very evident from the wild disorder that Dorthea had not been up here this evening. — Thestrup was often so tired when he came in that he preferred to take his tea alone with her, and then to sit in peace for a while, reading. On these evenings she

would herself take up supper for the tutor and the boys,
and then she would sit up here for a time with her knitting. Ah, that Dabbelsteen, she could not help liking him
a little — how eloquent he was when she let him tell her
and the boys about Snorre and the old kings of Norway,
or show them his experiments and his collections of plants
and minerals! And he would speak with enthusiasm of
all the remarkable things that were happening out in the
great world, in America and in France. Thestrup, it was
true, did not approve of all the student's ideas; he was
afraid all this might turn the boys' heads. But she could
not help it — she was glad her growing sons should have
these evening hours with the zealous young enthusiast.
Thestrup himself had enjoyed a free and happy youth,
and that was why he did not understand so well as she did
how precious are the joys of youth.

As she and Bertel came down the stairs the watchdog
barked and was answered by the rougher voice of Feierfax. — Heavens, what would he say!

Thestrup with the sporting dog at his heels burst in at
the front door so violently that he almost collided with
his wife.

"What is it now? The boy there isn't — there's nothing wrong with *Bertel,* is there? " he whispered excitedly.
He laid his hand on Dorthea's shoulder and pushed her
before him into the bedroom. " Can you find my riding-
boots — and pack some food in the bag — they've driven
northward. Early this afternoon in a peasant's sledge.
Scharlach heard it down at the dam. With one of the
quartz-carriers from the north, they didn't know which —
hadn't noticed. They thought he had just given them a
lift for their pleasure." Thestrup flung hat and greatcoat

over the end of the bed, let himself drop heavily into the armchair by the tea-table.

" Thea, Thea — why didn't you send word to me at once! Then we could have set out after them immediately. Now God alone knows — "

" Slip into bed and cover yourself up," whispered Dorthea to Bertel; the boy was shaking with excitement and cold, in nothing but his nightshirt under his little jacket. "Well, but then you *have* some sort of trace of them? " She handed the cup of tea to her husband, who lay doubled up in the chair — a tall, bony, angular figure. He looked tired, and slovenly dressed — his neckcloth was not clean and was carelessly tied, his myrtle-green redingote was faded and stained, his light-grey breeches were worn shiny at the knees, his stockings and buckled shoes were wet and muddy.

Jörgen Thestrup had never been really handsome. His face was round and thin, with a prominent nose, bony and shiny over the bridge, and a large, narrow-lipped, and very sensitive mouth. But his appearance had been attractive, with its great gleaming light-brown eyes. They were now bloodshot, and his fine ruddy complexion had become brown and weather-beaten with age. He still disdained to hide his light-brown hair under a wig, but it had retreated a long way from his round forehead — his Trönder skull, as he called it himself — and behind the ears it was ragged and streaked with grey; he seldom gave himself time to curl it.

Strangely reassured, almost elated, Dorthea stood watching him as he gulped the tea and stuffed the bread and butter, a whole piece at a time, into the range of his great yellow horse's teeth.

" At any rate you must rest a little, Thestrup my dear, before you set out."

" Rest! What do you say? " He laughed with his mouth full of bread and butter. " When I know they are out on the highroad at night-time? Or sitting at some posting-station among drunken drivers and our friend Dabbelsteen. They are nice customers, these drivers from Kindlia, many of them."

" I dare say, but — " Now that she knew at least where the boys had gone she did not feel so anxious about them. " Do you think it can do any good to ride after them to-night? They must be under a roof somewhere long before this. You cannot very well ride about rousing people at all the houses and farms along the road. What if you were to start the first thing in the morning, taking a man with you? And by that time perhaps the wind will have dropped."

Thestrup shook his head.

" Time, time, Thea dear! How long do you suppose I can be away from the works? Scharlach will stay in the office tonight. Besides, you have heard of this horrid business at Klokkhaugen. I suppose Dabbelsteen's idea was to get home to Skaardal immediately. The man is a hare-brained fellow, as we know. We cannot tell either what part he has really played in the affair — in any case he went home to his mother's twice last year. — Upon my word, this is a nice business for two half-grown youngsters to be mixed up in — to see at close quarters. No, little Thea. And if they stay the night somewhere on the way, you may be sure Dabbelsteen will be off again at an un-earthly hour in the morning. And the chase will be so much the longer."

Dorthea said no more. She went out to the kitchen and gave orders for the food, then fetched her husband's riding-gear from the dark passage. When she returned to the bedroom with her arms full of clothes, he was standing at the bureau overhauling his pistols.

" Are you taking *those* with you? "

Without turning round Thestrup said curtly: " The Sibilla crew are said to be abroad in the dale. Besides — you know there has been talk of attacks on travellers several times this winter — up in the forests. So even if I don't meet the vagabonds — "

Dorthea kept silence. But she felt herself turning pale. If only her Thestrup had not been so headstrong. — Last year he had had an encounter with the Sibilla gang. When the gypsies had interfered too much with the people at the works, he and Captain Cold had got together some of the younger men, mostly chosen from the foreigners, and had driven the band away from the neighbourhood of the glassworks. The peasants on the farms round about had not liked this; they were afraid of the gypsies' vengeance.

Thestrup slipped a flask into his pocket, put on his heavy caped coat. " My cloak — what are you thinking of, in this wind! No, hang it up again."

" I thought — can't you roll it and strap it on behind? In case you should need it, for yourself or one of the others. I'm sure Dabbelsteen was very thinly clad — "

"You and your Dabbelsteen! Do you think he deserves — " Her husband broke into a loud laugh. " Well, well, come on with it then. Oh, you Thea! "

Seeing how pale his wife was, he laid his hands on her shoulders.

" Cheer up, my dear! You'll see, tomorrow at this time we'll all be sitting here together laughing at our worries." He let his hands slip down her arms till he held her hands in his. Quickly he raised them, kissed first one and then the other.

It brought a smile to her face. Although she thought to herself: " Not Dabbelsteen — at any rate *he* will not be sitting here with us and laughing at his worries." But she knew, if only she could have her own boys home again safe and sound — well, then the young stranger's misfortunes would not be able to mar her joy very profoundly. It needed only a little unexpected mark of kindness like this — something beyond the habitual signs of the good connubial understanding between them — to assure her that no misfortune, not even if something had happened to the children, could make her so unhappy that her deepest and most intimate feeling would not be one of happiness. So long as she had her Thestrup.

" No, no, don't go outside. Elen can come with me and show a light."

So Dorthea stood on the doorstep holding Feierfax by the collar. The moon was now so high in the heavens that it looked quite small. The sky had become quite clear and the wind had dropped. Dorthea waited shivering till she saw them come out of the stable, the dairymaid with the lantern and Thestrup leading Reveille. The mare was restless, she had been short of exercise lately. Dorthea conquered her impulse to run out into the yard, say good-bye once more, and beg him to be careful — Thestrup would not like her to do so. She stayed where she was, holding the dog, who struggled and barked madly — he would have liked to run with his master. Thestrup turned in the saddle, waving to her, and Elen set off at a run, sliding and splashing through the puddles, to open the gate for him.

The watchdog in the yard silently retired to his kennel, rattling his chain, but Feierfax was still straining and barking. Dorthea stood still, listening to the sound of the hoof-beats and thinking how good it would be to change into slippers when she came in; her feet were like ice. Then came the lantern and Elen carrying it up again, and she could hear that Thestrup had reached the muddy highroad. The sound of his horse's hoofs grew fainter and fainter.

2

FLUNG headlong out of a dream that had ended with the thunder of cannon, Vilhelm awoke in thick, stifling darkness. He freed his sweaty, tickling face from some heavy woollen cloth that smelt of stables, felt the chill night air against his skin, and discovered that he was lying in the middle of a forest and that it was moonlight.

The last traces of his dream faded as he sat up, confused and chilled to the bone — only his head was hot. His brother's shoulders had been lying across his chest; now Claus sank heavily into his lap. In their sleep they had pulled the rug up over their heads, so that Claus lay on his side with his back exposed and his long booted legs crooked against the battered side of the vehicle.

Vilhelm saw that he was sitting in a sledge which stood stock-still, and there was snow on which the moon was shining and dark fir forest on both sides of the road. A swollen stream roared beneath them — they had stopped on a little bridge over it. The stream came down through a narrow cleft on the higher side of the road, ran under the bridge and spread out over an ice-covered surface with brushwood here and there — a swamp where the moonlight glistened on the water and twinkled among the bushes.

Vilhelm wriggled himself free of his brother and got on his knees. Mechanically he covered Claus with the rug and bits of sacking. He had no idea where they were, and it was evidently the middle of the night.

He had a horrible taste in his mouth and his chest was on fire. In the forward part of the sledge under the driver's seat lay two bodies in a state of collapse. They were snoring, otherwise they were as still as corpses. The boy fought against a growing sense of fear — struggled to collect his thoughts.

They were at the bottom of a deep ravine, and high above the cleft was the moon, quite small and nearly full, so that the air was both light and dark at the same time. Behind them the road descended sharply, and before them it ran up a steep slope into the forest. Vilhelm saw now that he had been waked by the horse stopping suddenly — the thunder of cannon in his dream was the noise of the sledge on the bridge.

The ragged dun horse stood panting with bent knees, its sides going in and out. Vilhelm climbed out and went up to it, stretching himself. He began patting the horse and talking kindly to it.

So this was what came of drinking brandy.

He seemed to remember having seen the sky full of racing reddish-brown clouds — there was a coppery reflection over the roughened surface of the frozen lake, where pools of water were caught by the wind. The sun must have set when they came out of the house at Sandtangen. But they had been told they would be driven home again by somebody or other, Dabbelsteen had said so. But he did not recognize this narrow side valley; he was almost sure there was no place like this on the road between Sandtangen and the glassworks. And he had a feeling that the horse's head was pointing more or less to the northward.

Nor was this the sledge that had brought them from the Dragoon's tavern to Sandtangen; that had been bigger, and it was drawn by a sorrel mare. Vilhelm turned in bewilderment to the mass of huddled humanity in the fore-part of the sledge; but it was impossible to see their faces and he did not like to touch them. Nor would that have been of any use, they were certainly too sound asleep in their drunkenness. He could see all the same that one of them was Dabbelsteen. But who was the other — and how had they come here? He could make nothing of it.

Perhaps it was the man that Dabbelsteen wanted to meet at Sandtangen. Vilhelm had a vague notion that they had gone outside once, while they were there, and they had been standing by a sledge, and he had patted a little ragged dun nag like this one. Then, he supposed, Dabbelsteen had got into the sledge and been driven off in his drunken state, and he and Claus had been so fuddled that they did not know what they were doing. Now he thought he remembered too that on leaving Sandtangen they had

driven into a forest — but of course they should have
gone south over the lake to get home. But in that case
they might now have come a long way north in the dale
— the sun set at seven and it was now about midnight, he
could see by the moon.

For a moment the boy felt a tightening in his throat and
a smarting under his eyelids. He was tempted to wake
Claus. Claus Hartvig who was always so bumptious — let
us see what this bold brother would say when he discovered the situation they were in — let us hear if Claus
knew what was to be done now.

But he was ashamed, for it was he who was the elder.
And besides, it braced him with a welcome dash of energy
to feel that this time it was he who had to do the thinking
and get them all out of the mess — not only his brother,
but the two drunkards in the sledge behind him as well.
For the matter of that Claus must be too sound asleep, he
had drunk more deeply. When Dabbelsteen had insisted
on their taking a stiffener with him, as they had been so
buffeted by the wind on the long drive, it was Claus who
without hesitation had swallowed the first dram straight
off. He himself had not been equal to draining the glass
of stinking, scorching raw spirit in one gulp — it made
him cough till the tears ran down his cheeks. And while
those who sat round laughed at him, somebody praised
Claus — he had already taken his second dram like a real
man.

The wind was not nearly so high now. Or was it merely
calmer down in this hollow?

The anxiety and confusion of his mind were so painful
that the boy instinctively tried to repel all the feelings that
pressed upon him and turn aside all thoughts but the one

— what was he to do now! Dabbelsteen's mysterious affairs that had led to their finding themselves here in the depth of the forest, he himself the only live person with a sledge-load of men dead drunk — he tried not to think of this. Because it filled him with shame, for one reason; he had gathered enough to know that in one way or another their tutor was mixed up with an ugly business of adultery and murder somewhere to the north along the dale. But he had not got the hang of the story, and that made him shy whenever his thoughts touched on the fringe of this mystery.

At any rate they would have to see about getting out of this forest. Home. What were they thinking at home of their disappearing like this? Mother — oh, she must be terribly frightened at this moment. And Father angry. What would he say and do when they saw him again?

But he did not know how far they were from home — certainly a very long way. He could not even guess where they were now. And so tired the horse was; it was no use thinking of turning back. It was an old horse, he would be sure to make for his stable. If they once reached some habitation they would find help.

To see what he could do Vilhelm took the reins and clicked his tongue: " Gee up, Dobbin! " The horse actually set his hoofs on the planks of the bridge, shook himself and went on.

Vilhelm walked by the side of the sledge up the slope of the ravine, encouraging the horse with a word or two. He found it calmed him to talk. Earlier in the winter, when the cold was severe, there had been many wolves about. Robbers too he had heard of — several peasants had reached home penniless, plundered on the way, when they had been drinking or were travelling alone.

Every sound that the boy imagined he could distinguish through the murmur of the trees and the scraping and bumping of the sledge made him start. Then he thought with vindictive pleasure of the reception his father would give Herr Dabbelsteen, when once they came home. Perhaps he would turn him out of doors. But then Vilhelm's heart sank — no, he did not want that at all, it would be too hard on Herr Dabbelsteen. And he certainly did not wish to be rid of their dear preceptor. There was no one who had given them so much amusement.

But now and again, when the horse stopped and he had to give it time to get its wind — This fearful solitude, the uncanny moonlight and the soughing of the dark forest, the steep hill rising straight before him into a hidden infinity — Vilhelm panted, listening and fighting against the impulse to behave like a child, burst into tears, throw himself upon the sleepers in the sledge, shake them and bump them and shout in their ears till they woke. He was hungry, his feet were cold and wet, his mouth was nasty and dry, and a scorching sourness was trying to come up in his throat all the time. He was furious with Dabbelsteen. Of those at home, his mother, his little brothers and sisters, he simply dared not think. But he kept on his feet, supporting the sledge with his frail strength, sucking a lump of ice — and then he clicked his tongue again: " Gee up, Dobbin! "

At last they reached the high ground. As far as Vilhelm could see the road now stretched level before him through a thick forest — and the surface was good here in the shelter of the trees. He climbed into the sledge, straddled

over the two lifeless bodies and found a place for himself
on the driver's seat. In spite of all he began to feel on
top again as he sat and drove on. The horse went ahead
quite well; in places the road went a little downhill.

Mother — now she would be going about the house
wringing her hands, perfectly miserable. And here he
was, driving farther and farther away from her. But he
could not help that. Though to be sure, he need not
have drunk spirits at Sandtangen. But then Herr Dabbelsteen had insisted so strongly; they would be ill without it, he said. But that they *had* been drinking, *that* he
would admit to his mother. For he felt that the other
thing, the ugly business about which Dabbelsteen had
talked with Anders Överli — he simply could not utter
a word about that. It made him quite sick merely to
think that they might have heard something about it at
home. If they had he would feign complete ignorance.

He found a rug and spread it over his knees. His feet
too were beginning to thaw, he could warm them against
the bodies of the two sleepers. But his hands were horribly cold. Dabbelsteen's muff! he suddenly thought of
it — the tutor had his muff with him when he went out
at midday. It seemed an age since then — a fresh wave of
pain swept over the boy as he thought of the sunshine on
the fields at home, he and Claus jumping on their bob-
sleigh and rushing down the hill, while Dabbelsteen came
dancing after on his long shanks. How ridiculously dandified he had looked, dandified and threadbare in their
father's old coat and three-cornered hat with the fur trim-
ming on its turned-up brims; he had waved to them with
his muff. They were only going to run down to Else
Dragoon's with a letter — Dabbelsteen wanted to see if

he could get any of the carriers to take it up the dale; it was to his mother. " So he's trying to strike her for money again," whispered Claus, and that had made him angry. One must not *say* a thing like that. But Claus Hartvig could never see when he ought to hold his tongue.

Perhaps they would be landed at Madame Dabbelsteen's, he thought, and that cheered him. He had heard so much about her. They said she used to write her husband's sermons. And she had the power of discovering stolen goods and staunching blood. He would be very glad to have a sight of this queer person some time.

And that brought him back to the thought of his own mother and how alarmed she must be about them. All of a sudden he felt he could not bear this any longer — here he was driving he knew not whither, and the night was so dismal, and he could not bear any more.

Vilhelm bent down and felt over the two sleepers with his feet. What the devil! — the stranger had a beard, wet and sticky, and Dabbelsteen was wet too, he seemed to be slobbering in his sleep. The boy quickly withdrew his hand and wiped it on the rug — better to let them sleep after all. But he could not refrain from trampling on them a little as he got into his seat again. It helped to stiffen his courage. The swine! It was clear he was the one who had to get them out of this.

He had found the muff down at the bottom of the sledge. He could drive just as well if he kept his hands in it. The horse went as it pleased anyhow.

The road led over a white plain which glistened under the moon. Stunted birches and osiers threw short shadows — it was a bog. On its edge lay some little houses with a field on the south side bare and black; a cottar's.

Over the roof of the barn a spruce-tree spread its tufted top, pale against the light sky and the few far-off stars. The horse jogged along — and then the road took them up into the forest again. Once more Vilhelm was on the brink of tears. And he was so tired, and cold.

Then he gave a start. He must have been in a doze, for how long he did not know. But the sledge was jolting and swaying and the horse was holding back. Now they were going downhill, sliding, jolting, sliding again. The forest came to an end, and below him Vilhelm saw a broad valley with many signs of habitation. He got off the sledge at once, took hold of it to keep it from overturning. Soon he felt it did him good to use his muscles.

They were high up on a ridge. The moon was now sinking to the northward, shining over wooded slopes and distant snowy mountains, filling the deep bowl of the valley with hazy light. There were white stretches of level ground in the bottom of the valley with the dark course of a river running through them, and far to the north the valley divided into two. There was something familiar about the dark wooded hill that parted them. On the shady side the slopes were dark with forest, with white patches here and there round little farms. But on the sunny side the fields were bare and dark far up the hills, and he could make out the bright threads of watercourses which were already free of ice.

The horse, and Vilhelm with it, halted before a short stretch of uphill work. The boy was now wide awake with excitement. This must be the main Dale itself they were coming to. Then they would soon reach a house — and that would be the end of this horrible night journey. There was not a cloud in the sky and the wind had almost dropped; he had not noticed this till now, when he stood still and heard the distant purling of water down in the sleeping valley.

It was freezing though — he could see his breath and the steam from the horse's flanks in the moonlight. And there was a crackling of new ice under the sledge-runners. They were passing a wooden fence — to the north of the road lay fields, and there was a big farm-house which caught the moonlight in its many windows; the log walls showed up pale brown. A yard dog from the farm began to bark and was answered by another dog farther off. There were snow-drifts along the fence, making the sledge heel over and swerve — Vilhelm heard the sleeping bodies slip and bump against the side — but who cared, it would do them good. Then the sledge righted itself again — they were driving through a birch copse where soft shadows glided over the snow. And the road swung round into the shade of a hillock covered with birches, and high above their gauzy frosted branches towered a steep-pitched shingle roof with a tower and a slender spire.

His heart leapt within him. But this was Herberg church, it was one of the Herberg farms that the moon was shining on just now — and there lay Lunde straight ahead, just south of the bridge. He knew where he was now, and warm thrills of joy shot through his stiff and weary frame. He swung himself up on to the driver's seat — the rest of the way was not so steep, he seemed to remember. What would their grandmother say when he came driving into Lunde like this in the small hours of the morning and told of his adventures? Upon my soul you're a stout fellow! that's what she would say. Vilhelm was already beginning to make up his story of the night's exploits.

On reaching the high road the little nag too seemed to take fresh heart — he broke into a smarter trot. But when Vilhelm turned him into the road that led to the bridge he was inclined to jib — this was evidently not his way home. Up and down the Lunde hills he went, holding back as well as he could — it was hard going. The horse was tired out, the sledge-runners grated on bare mud in many places. Vilhelm looked in fury at his load of flesh — the proper thing would be to shake up the whole lot of them, give them a piece of his mind, force them to crawl out and walk. But Vilhelm let them be — just gave a few cracks of the whip he had dug out of the mess at the bottom of the sledge. When he drove up to the front door at Lunde he would bang on it with the butt of his whip and rouse the people of the house. What a surprise it would give them! And then the Sheriff himself would appear, and grandmother would come down.

But when he came to the last turn of the road he saw lights in the windows of the main building. Sledges stood harnessed in the yard. And as he swung in between the big gate-posts somebody called to him. Vilhelm could not quite catch what was said, but it seemed they thought he had come to drive someone home. There must be a party at the house tonight.

"Not this time." He tried to shout it cheerily, but found that his voice was hoarse and rusty. "We thought of begging a night's lodging here."

A door opened; black figures showed up against the ' firelight behind them. Vilhelm stood by the sledge, saluting with the handle of his whip: "We are from the glassworks — it's Vilhelm Adolf Thestrup, Madame's grand-son " — and he gave his sleeping freight a few digs with the whip.

Someone came out and helped him to shake them up. First an unknown, thickset, grey-bearded countryman was lifted out and set upright in the glare from the kitchen door. Then they got Dabbelsteen propped on his feet — hatless, with his dark hair straggling in wild disorder about his pale discoloured face. They stood blinking like owls, not yet awake, utterly bewildered. Somebody laughed: " My word! these fellows haven't gone thirsty on the road! "

" Drunk as owls," said Vilhelm briskly, but there was a crack in his voice. He began to unpack Claus from his scraps of rug and sacking: " Wake up, mon frère, we've arrived! Hey, wake up, can't you — " and a man lent a hand, got the boy out and stood him up with the other two.

Sheriff Haagen Lunde appeared in the doorway at that moment. His clothes were hanging unbuttoned about his giant frame, and he was not very steady on his feet as he came down from the doorstep. He made some passes with the long pipe in his hand — pointing at one or another of the four figures in front of him, as though uncertain which of them might be his wife's grandsons. Vilhelm stepped forward and held out his hand:

" Good evening, my dear Sheriff — or good morning rather! Well, this is an odd time to come on a visit — to drop people — drop in on people all of a sudden like this " — in spite of his affected cheeriness he could not get his voice to sound right. " Yes, it's a funny story, as you shall hear."

" Ye're welcome! Ye'll please to step inside." The Sheriff's voice was rather thick. " It's you that is Vilhelm Adolf, eh? Come you in, come you in."

Vilhelm was about to follow the Sheriff when he saw that they had unharnessed the horse. He ran up, patted the sweaty neck and stroked the muzzle of this faithful comrade who alone had shared the emotions of the night with him. " There, there, poor old Dobbin." The horse snuggled his head against the boy's chest, puffed into his hands. " He's brought us without a break all the way from Sandtangen " — and suddenly the tears burst from his eyes, from relief and from sympathy with the good old horse.

The man took the little dun and led him away — so gently and kindly, Vilhelm thought, that he would have liked to be left in peace to cry awhile, now that this miserable journey was over and done with. But Haagen Halvorsen was waiting for him at the door. And at the head of his lamentable and utterly dazed company Vilhelm followed him in.

The atmosphere of the parlour was thick with tobacco smoke and there was a smell of punch. Red faces glowed through the blue-grey clouds that lazily drifted about the candles on the long table. Only one of them was known to Vilhelm — his mother's young half-brother Ole Haagensen.

" Well, ye'll please to seat yourselves," said the Sheriff, but he addressed himself to Vilhelm. The other three stood still in a bunch by the door, but Vilhelm went up to the hearth and held out his freezing hands to the fire.

" Ye'd better sit down." Haagen's big handsome face

was red and glistening with perspiration. He beckoned
to the girl who was clearing the table; she placed a chair
for Vilhelm by the hearth. Then the other three dropped
down on a little bench by the door. They evidently did
not know where they were. Claus however was beginning
to wake up; he looked about him with wondering glances.

" It was a hard drive ye had? " the Sheriff opened the
conversation. " The snow's mostly gone, I'm told — bare
all the way from Torstad south to Bergum hill. So maybe
there was not much left this way either."

" It was fine going up on the hills. We came another
way. We came by the Herberg farms, past the church."

The Sheriff nodded. " That was rightly done, ay. That
ye took the high ground. Nay, I doubt the main road's
scarcely fit for driving, some parts."

" I'm sure I don't know! " Vilhelm could not resist
talking in a loud and jaunty tone, but his voice would not
quite support him. " For at any rate it was no merit of
mine that we chose the better road. We came from Sandtangen on the Krok lake, and there our driver turned into
a logging track. But you must know, we had all had a
drop. Enough said — " he began to laugh, and saw there
was a smile on some of the red faces of the strangers; but
the Sheriff stared at him, gravely surprised. " When I
woke up I saw it was late at night and we were in the
middle of a forest, I don't know where. The others were
fast asleep, each of them well sewed up. So there was
nothing else for it, I seized the reins and left the horse to
find the way out of the forest. When we came in sight of
the Gullaug mountain I knew where I was at once. So
I decided to drive here and ask you and grandmother to
give us shelter for the night " — he gave a little mean-

ingless laugh of triumph, and one or two of the strangers
joined in the merriment.

At this point a door opened and there she stood, his
grandmother. Vilhelm gave a start — it was so long since
he had seen her; he remembered of course what she looked
like, but all the same she was quite different, now that he
actually saw her. His laughter was cut short by terror as
he met her extraordinary eyes: they were like great dark
globes rolling round within the puffy old eyelids. There
was something about her face that reminded one of dogs
— both of pugs and mastiffs. The colour of her big face
was yellowish like the nightcap in which it was framed;
her little flat nose with its black open nostrils gave one the
idea that she could *see* with them too, or pick up a scent
with them like an animal. Her cheeks sagged, heavy and
flat, around the little mouth, where the under lip projected, round as a cherry, and the corners were drawn
down, in ill-humour or derision.

Age had rendered her body shapeless — it put Vilhelm
in mind of a mountain. She had on a wadded green silk
gown over a blue and white striped petticoat, and big
Lapp brogues of reindeer skin with bright-coloured laces
and tufts on the toecaps. The boy felt quite embarrassed
as he went up and kissed the hand she held out to him.
Madame Elisabeth's hands were tiny, perfectly round
with fat, with many knobs and dimples at the joints,
covered with rings and fairly dirty: the plump fingers
ended in a point of oval nails, shiny and pink with coal-
black borders.

"Well, I never — but how *big* you've got, my boy!
How you *have* grown since I saw you last. So you are
Vilhelm Adolf. And there we have Claus Hartvig —

welcome to you, Claus! " Vilhelm noticed that his grandmother's wheezy voice became a trifle warmer, as though
the sight of Claus lit up a kind of inward smile in the old
woman. When he too had kissed her hand she patted him
on the cheek. " There — there. A fine pair of lads you've
turned out, the two of you, and no mistake." So saying
she gave Vilhelm in his turn a little dab on his bushy red
hair. " But to be sure — Claus has quite outgrown you,
little Vilhelm! Didn't I say so — Claus will be a head
taller than his brother I said, last time I saw you."

Vilhelm himself felt how small and thin and scraggy he
looked by the side of his handsome well-grown brother.
From his earliest childhood he had been teased because he
had green eyes and red hair — what made it worse was
that it was so curly, with an irrepressible tendency to stick
up over his forehead, that when people wanted to be
funny at his expense they blew at him, as if he was a
candle. Or else they called him fox-face — he had a little
three-cornered face with a pointed nose which jutted out,
inquisitively as it were, from his delicate little features.
And his soft red and white skin was covered with freckles
which winter only made a little paler. He suspected,
rather than knew, that there was at the same time something in his face that was attractive: when now and again
his mother took him under the chin and looked at him he
felt there must be something about him that she regarded
with heartfelt joy.

Nevertheless it had been one of the basic certainties of
his childhood that he was not good-looking, but that
Claus Hartvig was. And that Claus was a handsome boy
was a fact of quite another category than, for instance,
that their two little sisters, Birgitte and Elisabeth, were

charming children who were admired by visitors, and spoilt by their father and the servants. He himself was proud of them, except just when they did something that annoyed him. And it cut him to the heart whenever it was forced on his consciousness that Bertel was far too small for his age, almost deformed — then he was seized with a burning desire that his pale, delicate brother with the fine dark eyes and brown curls might grow big and strong, and in his evening prayers he had begged God to cure Bertel of his humpback. And as for Rikke and little Christen, they were sweet — there was no protest in his soul when he heard the women's outbursts of rapture over the two little innocents.

With Claus it was another matter. The difference in their ages was hardly a year, and then there were four whole years between Claus and Bertel, and Bertel had always been weakly. So that he and Claus had always had to go in double harness as it were. But at the same time it was always impressed on him that he was the elder. All orders and prohibitions were given to him to pass on, since he ought to have more sense and was expected to be an example to his younger brother. They had always done the same lessons, but it was assumed that he should learn them more readily than Claus. When they quarrelled he was reminded that he was the elder and therefore must give in. If they had to share any sweetmeats he ought to let the younger have the best ones. And now he had even had to forgo the privilege he had enjoyed when they were small — of being the first to have new clothes, while Claus sometimes had to wear out his old ones, or at any rate rate the boots and shoes he had outgrown. First it was Claus's hands and feet that had grown bigger than his; then his brother grew broader — and now he was half a head taller into the bargain. Now it was he who inherited Claus's clothes.

But because it was his mother in particular who always reminded him of all these responsibilities that he had to bear as the elder brother, and because he felt, vaguely but with unerring certainty, that although no doubt she was equally fond of all her children, yet in some way or other he was nearer her heart than the rest — Vilhelm bore the burdens of his birthright without any great resentment. Bertel occupied a position of his own — had a peculiar right to his mother's solicitude. Their father had little time to devote to his sons; their attitude towards him was affectionate, but marked more by reliance and respect than by intimacy. When he came home their father was usually tired; he found rest in his little daughters' innocent merriment. Birgitte especially, who was named after his idolized mother, was the object of his tenderest affection; her naive babbling and droll conceits were a source of the keenest delight to him. Their mother and the nurses vied with one another in looking after the two smallest of all. His own place was with Claus.

And in a way Claus was everyone's favourite. Vilhelm saw that his parents were proud of the robust, good-looking boy — as they well might be: he himself was proud of this brother of his. But all the same — in this teeming family group Claus stood curiously independent of all the others, and close behind himself. Yes, he stood in front of Claus; with his sharp and lively nose and his flaming head of hair, his inferior strength but more robust health — for Claus was more muscular, but far more apt to catch any kind of illness or infection, whereas he himself, Vilhelm, was as tough as the devil and had scarcely had a day's sickness in his life — he always had to act as a pioneer for his brother, a sort of battering-ram to force a way by which Claus with his greater weight could advance.

But they must sit down to the table and have something to keep them alive, the Sheriff suggested. A servant-girl laid for them at the end of the long table. They had flintware plates in this house, and big silver spoons. Another maid brought in a pewter tureen and served out steaming soup with grease floating on the top, cabbage and lumps of meat swimming below. Usually this was the best thing Vilhelm could think of, but now it seemed as if his entrails turned against it — he had a burning sensation in his chest and that nasty taste in his mouth. Then young Ole Haagensen came in carrying a big silver tankard with a head of froth and drank to him.

Never had Vilhelm tasted anything so good as that cold foaming beer. He buried his face in the tankard and gulped draught after draught of the bitter, satisfying drink. Ole looked at him with a little smile, and over the rim of the tankard Vilhelm smiled back at his mother's brother. Come on now, soup, meat and cabbage, here was the lad to do them justice! He shook his foxy forelock and greeted the other three with a fatuous smile of superiority as they dragged themselves up to the table, forlorn and half asleep.

He knew none of the Sheriff's guests, but they were peasants every one — warm men, he could see. He guessed that the tall thin one whom the Sheriff addressed as Lars was Lars Gullaug, father of Uncle Ole's betrothed, Ingebjörg Larsdatter. It was a strange thing, when he came to think of it, that his grandmother was married to a peasant, even if that peasant was a sheriff and a corporal, and that his mother had a half-brother in that class. Ole had not even wished to alter his position — Vilhelm knew it was the lad himself who had opposed his mother's plans of having him educated for the Church. But at this moment Vilhelm thought he could understand Ole's view of the matter. There was a wonderful sense of comfort in this room. Everything spoke of a spacious life on the great farm — even the sleeping forms which he had discovered after a while on the benches and in a bed inside the door of the bedroom. Great carved cupboards bulged out from the brown log walls, gay with painted and carved arabesques — they were gorgeous in a curiously barbaric way.

She preferred a live sheriff to a dead dean, and a warm corporal in his bed to an embalmed major in a leaden coffin, his grandmother was reported to have said when she married Haagen Lunde. Haagen Halvorsen Lunde had served in the Lifeguards in Copenhagen and afterwards in the second Southern regiment of Norwegian Dragoons as a non-commissioned officer. He was about to go home to take over Lunde and the office of sheriff on the death of his elder brother, when the widow of Dean de Theilemann caught sight of him and decided that *he* was the man for her. Such was the story of his grandmother's fourth marriage, as Vilhelm had heard it from the servant-girls at home. And she had her way, although the children of her first marriage and particularly the friends and relations of her third husband protested acrimoniously.

Vilhelm could not tell why he should be thinking just

now of the old lady's eventful matrimonial career; but
there was something in the way she had first patted Claus
on the cheek, with lingering enjoyment, and then had
given him a playful smack on the noddle. There was a
likeness between Claus and Sheriff Lunde. Or not a likeness exactly — the Sheriff had fair hair, a high bald forehead, and his eyes were blue and his face very red. But
Claus had light brown hair which fell softly in loose
curls about the full oval of his face; his complexion was
slightly brownish and his skin was soft as velvet. He
chatted with his grandmother as he ate, and looked up
at her with his big eyes, which were like those of an ox,
dark, but coated as it were with a dark bluish film. Yes,
now Claus was to the fore, he had taken over the conversation with their grandmother and gave ready answers
to her questions about their mother and how things were
going at home — far more detailed answers than seemed
necessary to Vilhelm. Dabbelsteen and the strange peasant sat bending over their plates with humped-up shoulders, eating eagerly. But Claus held himself upright,
looked up into his grandmother's face and smiled, taking
a spoonful of soup now and again when he could spare
the time from talking. He was like that at times — a
chatterbox. At other times he might take a fit of saying
scarcely a word for days together.

Yes, Claus was like Haagen Lunde after all, and his
young uncle Ole was like both of them. They were all
of them fleshy in the same way; there was a heavy, solid
well-being about their bodies: all three had rounded
limbs with plenty of muscle, a fine, well-nourished skin
and moist eyes.

The Sheriff had visited them a few times when his

journey took him past the glassworks, Ole Haagensen too, but their grandmother had never been there. It must be about three years since he last saw her, for he remembered that when they came home his mother had said to his father that the old lady had hinted at coming over this time to be with her daughter during her confinement. This was when she was expecting Rikke. And their father had laughingly remarked that it was not the first time Madame Elisabeth had threatened them with a visit, but thank God she had never yet carried it out. There was no love lost between their father and grandmother.

Uncle Peter Andreas had declined to take the portraits of his father, Major Eckelöff, and of their grandmother as she looked when she married him. Vilhelm's parents had offered to send the pictures to him in Copenhagen, but Uncle Peter Andreas had replied that they really must not put themselves to this expense. So now the two portraits were hanging over the sofa in the parlour at home. And now he could see it — there was after all a certain sameness between the huge, stout old woman before him and the handsome young lady of the portrait. In the picture she had the same rolling round eyes, but they were as blue as violets. And the pug-nose with its greedy round nostrils was enthroned in a round and firm little face, dewy white and rosy as a wax apple. The young lady of the portrait had fair powdered hair which lay close against the head in curly locks and waves — when he was small this curious style of hairdressing had always reminded him of whipped cream that had been thrown into rings by the whisk. A rose was inserted by the left temple, and long chains of beads and yellow stones set off the provokingly attractive femininity of the face, whose pouting lips vied with the red rose in her hair. She was portrayed in a triangular bodice of sky-blue silk, which was cut so low that her ample breasts were bursting from their prison, firm and round as though turned in a lathe. Surmounting the left breast was a bunch of red roses and green leaves. He had always been impressed by the lady's elegance, but until now he had not realized that she must have been pretty — in spite of the pug-nose and the bared breasts which had always given rise in his childish soul to vague notions of sucklings and wet nurses, diapers and powder-puffs. But *now* he could see that his grandmother must have been an extremely attractive person, in that far-away past when she was the wife of Major Eckelöff.

So it was easy to understand that Uncle Peter Andreas and Uncle Caspar had considered that she was guilty of a mésalliance in marrying a non-commissioned officer. The Major in his portrait undoubtedly looked very distinguished with his long dyed moustache against his dark complexion, his three-cornered hat over his white wig and his martial red, blue and yellow uniform. But — in that case she had already made a mésalliance in marrying their real grandfather, David Frazer. He had been clerk to her first husband. Below the two big paintings in gilt frames hung a little pastel portrait of him — a narrow, blond head in profile, somewhat obliterated, through soapy water having got under the glass during a spring cleaning. Vilhelm knew that he came from Helgeland, but of course the family was of Scottish origin. They were supposed to own a great deal of property in Nordland, but David had fallen out with his relatives, as his grandmother had induced him to bring an action against a brother-in-law. Bertel was named after him — his full name had been

Bertel David Alexandersön Frazer. Vilhelm's mother remembered nothing of her father except that he had been kind to her and was an agreeable performer on the flute.

Grandmother Elisabeth herself was the daughter of a skipper from the neighbourhood of Fredrikshald. She had made a good match and followed it by a mésalliance. Then another good match, when she married the wealthy old Dean de Theilemann; but by him she had no children, so that the greater part of his fortune went to his children by his first wife. After that the Dean's widow went and married the young Sheriff. It was indeed a fairly chequered career, Vilhelm was bound to say. Actually their grandmother was just as queer a character as Madame Dabbelsteen, for instance. Perhaps people talked about his grandmother too. He had never thought of that before.

" You keep looking at me so," said his grandmother. " Was there anything you wanted to say, little Vilhelm? "

The boy's embarrassment increased on finding she had been aware of his stolen glances. He quickly turned his eyes on his plate and shook his head.

" — but my good Augustin Dabbelsteen — so it appears you have actually *abducted* these children? " Madame Elisabeth's calm voice had a threatening undertone. " Do you mean to tell me that you have unceremoniously absconded from your situation with my son-in-law? With two of his young sons who were committed to your charge? And without anyone at his house knowing what has become of you all? "

" That was never my intention, dear madam. I thought we should meet someone at Sandtangen who could conduct them home."

" Yes, but why in the world should you drag Claus and Vilhelm with you up to Sandtangen? "

" They were themselves so intent upon the drive. And I could not well explain to such young persons what was the object of my going there. Oh, I cannot remember what was in my thoughts! " Dabbelsteen pressed his long narrow hands against his temples so that his dark curls twined like snakes about his thin fingers, and shook his head. Then he flung himself back and looked his tormentor straight in the face — for Vilhelm saw in a flash that his grandmother was purposely tormenting him. The sweat came out in drops on his pale narrow forehead. The tutor's face did not look so well in profile, in spite of his Roman nose, for the jaw was rather prominent, but the chin receded. It gave the impression that the man was forward, not to say aggressive, in order to stifle an inner anxiety. " You can surely understand, madam — I was shaken, disturbed in my innermost soul — "

" — and fuddled in your head by the dragoon woman's firewater."

Dabbelsteen's head sank between his humped shoulders. " In my state of mind — I assure you, I was near swooning. Yes, I had been drinking. In order to recover my self-possession. I was faced by the necessity of acting, and acting swiftly. I had to rally my spirits — what was I to do? "

" Well, what had you actually thought of doing? "

Dabbelsteen flung out his hand in a wild gesture:

" What had I thought of doing? My God, Madame Lunde, that was just what I could not tell." His voice broke, on the brink of tears. " My only thought was for her, my unhappy Margit. I was constrained to go home, to be near her. If possible to speak words of comfort to her, to assure her of my unalterable devotion — how can I tell! To plead her cause, draw up a petition for mercy and hasten with it to our gracious Crown Prince. For she has fallen a victim to unhappy circumstances, to the most terrible temptation. Was it then so unnatural, when I met Ansten here, our faithful friend from childhood's days " — he pointed to the old bearded peasant — " that in my flurry I forgot to see about the boys' return? "

Madame Elisabeth shook her ponderous head. In no unfriendly tone she answered:

" It is no use, Dabbelsteen, you must surely see that yourself. She has confessed of her own free will that for more than three years she and her stepfather have — I say no more. And that during this time she has given birth to and made away with three children."

Dabbelsteen wailed aloud:

" Madame Elisabeth, help us! Cannot you help us? "

" No one on earth can help in such a case," replied the lady in the same tone as before.

" Oh yes, yes! If anyone can find a way it must be you! Assuredly it is Providence that has guided us to your house tonight."

" It was the drink, little Dabbelsteen. And the fact that Vilhelm here slept less soundly than the rest of you, and that the lad has some brains in his head."

Some of the visitors had drawn nearer. They stood gazing with their strangely wooden red faces at this pale youth who wept, beating the air with his long arms — manifestly still under the influence of drink. Vilhelm was seized with a sudden fit of anger. The stout Norse yeomen of whom Dabbelsteen was so fond of boasting, they were none other than these old-world men who stood here staring in mute disapproval at the student as he screamed and made an exhibition of himself. Before he knew what he was doing he was at the tutor's side, grasping his shoulder in his skinny boy's claws and shaking it:

"Herr Dabbelsteen — you must not! Control yourself, Herr Dabbelsteen. Come, let us go — you can speak to the Sheriff tomorrow."

"That was truly spoken." Haagen Lunde nodded. "Ye'd be better in bed now, Dabbelsteen. That was right of you, Vilhelm — get him along."

"Away with you, urchin!" Dabbelsteen shook off the boy's hand. "You think you can give yourself airs because it was you that — away, I say. I wish to speak to the mistress here. You can do what you will — I *know* it! You who know everything about everybody — I know that you know such things about your neighbouring Sheriff, about Simen Byrsting I mean, that you could force him to open the door of my Margit's prison."

The blood shot up into Vilhelm's cheeks. Angrily he clutched the other's shoulder again. He was *not* giving himself airs — *he* could not help it if he had some sense left and was trying to save his tutor from disgracing himself completely. "Herr Dabbelsteen, I beg you, come!" He looked about him, as though he would ask help of the grown-ups —

Then it struck him that their faces had undergone a change that frightened him, for it was all beyond him and he could only feel the painful discomfort of the scene. His grandmother had risen. Huge and threatening she looked with her great sallow head surmounting the green

pyramid of her night robe. "Come!" Vilhelm tugged at
Herr Dabbelsteen. "Come," he implored almost whim-
peringly, for he saw that the other had no idea of the danger in the air — but he had been saying the most shocking
things, the boy could see that. And Claus just sat there
looking sheepish, but availed himself of the opportunity
to empty a glass of punch. For a moment Vilhelm felt that
he too was going to lose control of himself — he was furious, and he despaired of these two who could grasp nothing of it all.

Dabbelsteen pushed him away with such force that
Vilhelm staggered a pace or two over the floor. And there
was Augustin Dabbelsteen on his knees before the old
lady with outstretched arms and clasped hands.

"Madam! You are acquainted with the aberrations of
the human heart. Madam! you yourself have experienced
the power of the god! Have pity on us. Oh, you have a
power over your fellow-creatures, over men. Go there!
Say that you wish to visit your old friend, my mother."

"Dabbelsteen, you must indeed be mad! I cannot help
your girl to escape — for I suppose that is what you mean.
She has denounced herself as a murderess."

"Remember, remember, Madame Elisabeth — my
mother was once in your confidence."

"Now we can have no more of this." The old woman's
whole being was suddenly one single threat. Then her
manner changed again — exactly as before; she turned to
her husband: "We must see to getting this person put to
bed now. He is so drunk he does not know what he is
saying."

The Sheriff nodded. "Ay — it is time someone took
and helped him out. The boy can't manage it. And

Claus there looks as if he might have trouble enough with himself," he added with a smile.

" I proposed that the student and Ansten should sleep in the loft of the old house," said his wife shortly. " You must take hold of Dabbelsteen, Ansten — and you, Ole, call Einar, he must come here and help. Those two can manage him."

Dabbelsteen had leapt to his feet. He flung the old peasant aside and stood swaying, tall and solemn:

" Madame Elisabeth, do you remember, in the holy scripture, how Adonijah came to Bathsheba and begged her intercession — that she would help him and Abishag the Shunammite? She interceded for them, for she had a feeling heart for lovers in distress. A feeling heart — that had Bathsheba, David's wife — Bathsheba! " He set up a howl and fell on his knees again: " Madam, show that you have a feeling heart — " and now he was sobbing wildly.

Frightened out of his wits, Vilhelm stared at the crazy fellow. It was as though he had been dreaming, and the dream now culminated in a sheer nightmare. And there stood Claus beside him, glaring stupidly with his big ox-eyes — and then the beginning of a smile stole over his handsome boyish face. O Lord, yes — Dabbelsteen *was* comic with it all, as he knelt and gesticulated like this. *That* was the most dreadful part of it.

Their grandmother stood staring down at him. Then she jerked her shoulders as though chilled at the sight — the gesture seemed to ripple down through the overflowing lines of her figure. Her dark eyeballs rolled back under their baggy lids. " He'll never be able to get to bed alone. You'll have to carry the creature."

Ole Haagensen and a lad — Einar, no doubt — and the old peasant hoisted him up among them. Dabbelsteen shrieked horribly and tried in vain to resist, but they soon had him out of doors.

Madame Elisabeth shivered again, shaking like a jelly within her gown. Then she turned to her grandsons as though waking up:

" Now I think it is time you went to bed too. A room is prepared for you in the royal lodge. You understand, every room here is occupied. You are not afraid to sleep alone in the lodge? It is daylight already," she added reassuringly. " The servants are up long ago. You are not afraid to sleep in the royal lodge, are you, Vilhelm? "

Vilhelm shook his head. But it gave him the creeps to think of sleeping there. The lodge stood out in the field a good way from the other houses of the farm. Although — he probably would not have thought of being afraid if his grandmother had not suggested it.

" Afraid? no. But, grandmother, would it not be better if Herr Dabbelsteen slept there too? There are two beds. And then we could keep an eye on him."

But his grandmother ignored him. " As I told you, the servants are up already. There is nothing to be afraid of, little Vilhelm."

" No, of course not. Well, come along, Claus, we must say good-night. And then you will send word to Mother the first thing in the morning? So that they may not be anxious about us any longer than necessary."

Madame Elisabeth gave him a kindly nod.

" The man is riding there now." She laid her hand on his shoulder. " I am glad to see you have turned out such a thoughtful, sensible boy." Again she stroked Claus

Hartvig's cheek, took hold of his chin and raised his face a little: " You must be sleepy, my dear — well, good-night to you both."

Outside there was already daylight enough to show up the houses of the farm, dark against a pale greenish blue sky, and in the south-east, where the valley closed in at the bend of the river, the sky was a yellowish white over the mountains. The upper half of the stable-door stood open and there were men inside with a lighted lantern.

Claus kept falling over his own feet, till Vilhelm took him by the arm. The mud in the yard had frozen stiff, it crunched stickily under their feet — the frost had come with the early morning and the wind had dropped almost entirely. Vilhelm dragged his brother out through the gate. The path to the lodge was grass-grown, it rustled with rime as they walked on it. There was a light in the little bow-window of the gable — a great relief to Vilhelm.

Why was their grandmother unwilling that Dabbelsteen should sleep here with them? With a terrible sense of loss Vilhelm reflected that perhaps they would never again have Dabbelsteen's companionship in the old way. He guessed that there was much in Dabbelsteen's life which was unknown to them. Oh, he had made everything so enjoyable for them; he knew so much, he was so clever and so enthusiastic — but now Vilhelm realized that it was not the whole Dabbelsteen, what they had seen of the man. *His* portrait of the dear tutor had tonight been shattered so thoroughly that Vilhelm would never be able to put it together again. And now Augustin Dabbelsteen was about to pass from their field of vision. Their father would never forgive him this escapade, that was clear enough to Vilhelm.

The royal lodge loomed dark and fantastic, with an upper storey leaning over far beyond the lower. It was so ancient that rumour said King Haagen Haagensen had once passed the night there. With much difficulty Vilhelm managed to pilot his brother up the steep flight of steps and along a dark gallery which ran round the side of the lodge. The door was so low and the threshold so high that he knocked his skull although he remembered to duck. Getting Claus lugged in after him was quite a job, and Vilhelm was not sorry for the bumps and bruises his brother received in the course of the proceeding.

On the slab under the little window stood a lighted candle, and by one of the beds he could distinguish the back of a young girl with long fair plaits of hair. It was bitingly cold in here, much colder than outside, so Vilhelm was glad to see she was passing a long-handled warming-pan between the sheets. She turned round, and her face was wonderfully bright and pretty, with a broad, clear forehead.

" It's late for you," she smiled, herself yawning as she spoke. " You must be pretty tired now? "

" It's late for you too, isn't it? " Vilhelm followed her nimble movements with interest — she poured water from a can into a basin which she set on the table, laying a towel beside it.

" Oh, it's no more than three hours since I got up," she laughed. She collected her things to go. " Then I hope you may sleep well! "

" What's your name? " asked Vilhelm gaily. She seemed to be about the same age as they, but grown up of course, as she was a girl.

" Tora."

" Good-night, Tora, and a thousand thanks! "

He stood listening to her steps as she descended the stairs. The can she carried knocked against the wall. He had grown calm all at once and cheerful. All the impressions of the night gave way to the proud consciousness that for the first time he had been up a *whole* night. The people on the farm were up and about, and now *they* were going to bed. And all the things he had gone through!

Outside he heard the clear metallic notes of a bird — the spring note of a titmouse, te-te-te, te-te-te. Against the back wall were two built-in bedsteads, separated by a narrow carved cupboard. And the room had a fine ceiling, panelled with mouldings that formed a kind of star. And there were two chairs upholstered in stamped leather. It was all handsome — the lodge had been refitted in the late sheriff's time. As to the old kings and warriors that haunted the place, according to Dabbelsteen's romantic stories — that was all nonsense. In the mountain ash outside the titmouse kept on with his gay matutinal te-te-te, te-te-te.

" Do see about getting to bed," he tried to coax Claus, who was hanging about half-asleep. He himself had his clothes off in a moment, took his neckcloth and tied a knot in each corner — he had seen his father do this once when they spent the night way from home and his father had forgotten to bring his nightcap. Then he was in his bare shirt, ready to jump into bed. Not till then did it occur to him that he had forgotten to say his evening prayers. Or perhaps he ought rather to take his morning prayers? He came to the conclusion that a morning prayer would meet the occasion surprisingly well; kneeling down he began rapidly:

" O almighty and everlasting God, merciful heavenly Father! I glorify thee in this morning hour with my inmost soul and mind, for that in the darkness of the past night thou hast been a sun and a shield over me and averted all danger and harm from my body and soul." He spoke in a rapid whisper, for he was horribly cold; but at the same time he had a wonderfully vivid sense of the meaning of the old words, to which he usually attached no definite thought; they were simply part of his morning prayer which he *had* to say: " — save my poor soul from temptation, my body from sickness, my eye from weeping and my foot from falling. But since sin is the greatest of evils, help me, O God, before all things to resist it " — but this was really *true*, he reflected, thinking of Dabbelsteen's sweetheart and Dabbelsteen writhing on the floor. Instinctively he went on more rapidly: " Let thy hand be over me, thy Spirit within me, thy peace surrounding me," he prayed with relief — it was like turning into a kind of spiritual highway where the journey was safer, now that he had finished with that about sin and misery. " Let me not live in myself, but in the faith of the Son of God."

By this time Claus too was undressed to his shirt and kneeling beside him — moving his lips so fast that he seemed trying to catch up his brother. " Have you nothing to put on your head? " whispered Vilhelm disapprovingly. Claus gave a little shake of his curls and Vilhelm went on: " O all-loving Father, have also my good parents in thy safe keeping " — with a pang of remorse Vilhelm acknowledged that he had scarcely had a thought for their anxieties at home, since he himself had arrived safe and sound under the roof of Lunde. It had been so — well, it had been terrible too, seeing Dabbelsteen behave as he did — but there had been something else in it — something exciting. In any case, he had been entirely taken up with the whole adventure.

He rattled through the conclusion of his prayer without taking in what he was saying — overwhelmed by the newly discovered fact that in a way he had enjoyed the events of the night, and that his feeling of sympathy for his parents had been most intense at moments when his own fears were at their height. As soon as he knew he was in safety it seemed to fade away.

He climbed into bed. It was rather clammy between the sheets; the warming-pan had drawn the moisture out of the raw linen. But it felt delightfully cosy all the same to stretch his cold feet down into the warmed nest. And luxurious feather quilts and pillows — oh, they were well off here; at home they only had a straw mattress. Again the sense of well-being folded him round, compelling his mind to relax its feeling of anxiety, sorrow and sympathy with the fate of others. Something within him, stronger than the will to open his heart to his fellow-creatures, bade him wrap himself up in enjoyment of the comfort he was in.

Claus pattered with bare feet to the cupboard between the beds and opened its lower door. " Look, Ville — do you remember this? " He stood laughing in his white shirt, with his long brown hair hanging loosely over his back, and showed his brother the chamber-pot he held in his hand.

Vilhelm could not tell what made him flare up in such a burst of shame and indignation. Then he remembered — he too had allowed himself to make merry over this piece of furniture the last time he was here, had found it inconceivably witty and piquant. At the bottom of it were depicted the severed heads of the two counts, Struensee and Brandt, surrounded by a couplet which invited every loyal Dane to show his contempt for this pair of traitors in the obvious way.

" Put it back! " With immense surprise he noticed that his voice was almost stifled with rage. " Go out on the balcony if you want to do it. You shan't do it in that."

Claus looked at him in astonishment. But he replaced the pot and obediently shuffled out.

They were dead; they had atoned for their crime with their lives. It was low — yes, now he saw what a low thing it was to dog the fallen with unreasoning scorn.

3

DORTHEA started up, deeply disturbed. She must have fallen asleep as she was lying, supported on her left arm, with her bosom and shoulders bare. She was freezing and her arm was quite numb. But little Christen was sleeping warm and sound against her hip — he had slipped down between the bedclothes. The candle on the bedside table was flickering deep in its socket, giving a smell of hot brass and melted tallow. And through the peep-holes in the shutters the grey dawn made its way.

With intense relief Dorthea recognized her bedroom. She blew out the smoking wick and huddled under the eiderdown — straightened out the arm that was asleep. Thank God, it had only been a dream. But at the same time she felt the deception and shame of it as a hand on her throat. She had dreamt that she lay in bed with Bisgaard.

It had been cold in the room last night when she had to attend to Christen, so she lay down in bed with him when she had to give him the breast. And then she must have fallen asleep in spite of her deep anxiety. To awake unrefreshed and frozen, her back aching from the uncomfortable position. Her troubles came full upon her in a flash. And to make them worse the dream had conjured up a bygone epoch of her life and overwhelmed her with an old, half-forgotten inquietude.

It had happened before — at rare intervals — that she dreamt of her first husband. But never so vividly — with such detestable intimacy. Shuddering she buried her head in the pillows, took the baby in her arm, which pricked and tickled now that the blood was returning. Behind her back she felt the warmth of Bertel's body — and a suspicion which she tried to suppress told her that it was his sharp bony elbows that had revived the memory of the old man.

The outlines of objects in the room began to take shape. So this terrible night was now at an end. And at any rate they could resume the search with renewed strength. They would get help from the neighbouring farms. There had been talk of the gypsies last night in the kitchen, among the men who came home and the maids. For the extra refreshment with coffee that she had ordered for Lars and the other searchers had brought them together in a swarm, all the servants of the house, even the nursemaid and the nurse with Rikke in her arms. Well, well, no doubt their anxiety and sympathy was honestly meant — it was not their fault if this nocturnal coffee

parliament served also as an enlivening change from their
daily duties, or that with a certain blend of horror and
gratification they had discussed every possible explanation of the tutor's and the boys' disappearance.

One would suppose that the poor gypsies must have
more than enough trouble with rearing their own children. That they should make a business of stealing other
people's children had always appeared to her scarcely
credible. She was much more afraid that Thestrup might
encounter the vagabonds, as he called them. He was so
violent when provoked.

It was hopeless to think that this state of uncertainty
might continue, and *she* could do nothing to put an end
to it. When everything was done that lay in human
power, the only thing left was to wait, to try to be patient, and hope.

Dorthea felt racked with tiredness. Now the house was
awakening to a new day's work. She usually lay down
again, when Johanne had been in to fetch Christen to the
nursery — then she had a nap till she had to get up at six.
Through her light dozing she was aware of the wide-awake
chirping of the two youngest in the next room, and the
screams of the little girls when they got soapy water in
their eyes or Gunhild the nursemaid pulled their hair
while combing it. Then they laughed, and then they
squabbled a little — and then it was time to get up. Even
while she sat at her dressing-table the maids came running
in for orders. Gradually, as she felt the threads of her
household management beginning to run through her
capable hands, the blood began to circulate more briskly
in her veins; her brain felt refreshed.

But with old and ailing people the vital force seems unable to rise again, after having ebbed to its lowest point in the small hours between night and morning. Most people die during these hours. Bisgaard died at half-past four in the morning, on the twentieth of March. And she had felt, when hovering between life and death after the birth of the first little still-born Bertel, that to the weakened it is a temptation to step out of the ranks, to lie down and sleep the last long sleep, just at the time when the healthy enjoy their awakening to another day's activity.

For her too that morning hour would come one day, when she would close her eyes for good and let the others go on without her. She had never thought of death as a thing which concerned her immediately — not even that time, twelve years ago. Yet she had always felt how soul and body summoned up hidden resources which carried her once more over the point where Death steps in and gathers his harvest of those who are ready for him. But she was not ready: she had her dear little ones who could not do without her, and she had her Thestrup. They had lived together for so few years — were only at the beginning of all they might be to each other.

They had now been married for sixteen years. Happy years they had been, since she had had the companionship of her dear husband, and he had been able to confide in her his hopes and his disappointments, his plans, both those that had failed and those that he had been able to carry out. But in the ordinary way Thestrup was not given to talking; he was somewhat obstinate and distrustful, especially of his superiors. Many a time she had almost wished they had stayed where they were, at the ironworks in the south. Time after time Thestrup had been tempted to throw up the whole thing, such was his irritation with the members of the commission, their interference and their worrying. How many difficulties he had had to encounter before he could carry out the improvements and alterations in the working which he saw to be necessary! Though it was true that even at the ironworks there had been friction between Thestrup and the Chamberlain.

When he took up the appointment of manager here he had found the woods felled, the warehouses filled with inferior products. The most capable of the older workmen had left the glassworks, through dissatisfaction with the irregular payment of their wages and the stoppage of the allowances in kind to which they were entitled. The book-keeping had been irregular — for a number of years the actual loss had been greater than what was officially announced. In spite of all difficulties her Jörgen had succeeded in putting the works on their feet. In the first place he had got the Scharlachs, with the son-in-law Wagner, to return from Sweden. From that time the quality of the output was better and the rejections less frequent. He had reconstructed and rearranged the buildings and had made advantageous contracts for raw materials and the transport of the glass. In four of the last five years the works had shown a considerable profit. He had started a school for the children of the workpeople and improved their living quarters. Jörgen Thestrup, kind, critical and hard to please, had often been *well* satisfied.

She wished indeed that he could have spared more time for the children. But the main thing was that he was worthy of their respect and trust. So it had been left to her to attend to their other needs. And thank God, it looked as if she had done so. They did not seem to lack anything. Even Bertel had really grown stronger of late. And for many subjects he showed a quick apprehension — those were Herr Dabbelsteen's words. He was slow enough at arithmetic and Latin grammar; but he could draw charmingly and was very musical. And the four that had been born since they came to Brovold were healthy, happy and handsome children — and his little daughters had been a great joy to Thestrup.

She had paid for every child she brought into the world with a part of her youthful beauty — the smoothness of her rosy cheeks, the pearly whiteness of her smile, the lustre of her glance, which Winther had belauded in his birthday verses. Her breasts were sunken, her figure had spread. But it had often given her a curious satisfaction to notice how the life she was living left its traces on her. In her first marriage her charms had been preserved, barren, fading almost imperceptibly — as flowers wither slowly when kept in a cold room. Oh, how vain she had been — and full of hopes! — when it dawned on her that she promised to be a pretty girl. The servants at the Deanery had encouraged her to look in the glass, had fired her imagination: one fine day a young and handsome, charming and wealthy wooer was certain to come and carry her off from the home where her place was that of the poor stepdaughter, the fruit of the mistress's ill-advised marriage with a young man of no fortune.

In place of that Dean de Theilemann went and died. And the friend, the neighbour who succeeded to his office — whom she had looked up to in her childhood with reverence as a noble old man, whose twenty-year-old daughter's dark beauty she had admired! No doubt she had half hoped that her mother would now marry Dean

Bisgaard; she had dreamed of finding a sister in the lovely Christence. It had fallen on her like a bolt from the blue when one day her mother informed her that Bisgaard had sued for her hand. It was of no use to think of resistance. With her father's family she had never had any communication; her half-brothers were far away, Caspar in the West Indies and Peter Andreas in Copenhagen. And the consciousness that she had never been able to muster any warmer feelings for her mother than the dutiful desires for health and happiness prescribed by virtue and religion, made her despair. Her mother's sons by Major Eckelöff had felt even less devotion for her — she had perceived even as a child that behind their formally courteous behaviour towards Mamma her big brothers concealed feelings which were not far from hostile. But at the same time she could see that their mother did not regard her children with any great maternal affection. Even at that time she had known in her heart that her sympathy for her mother was somewhat misplaced — but nevertheless she was unable to set herself up against her with any force and energy. And yet this was due, at any rate in part, to her feeling pity for her mother, who was now left a widow for the third time, abandoned by her sons, disappointed in her hope of having children by the Dean, the bulk of whose fortune now went to his children by his first wife. And old — for that she was in the eyes of her young daughter. And even at that time she had had sense enough to guess that for a woman of her mother's temperament it must be terrible to grow old and to see that a man whom she herself had doubtless thought of marrying preferred her daughter.

This last concern indeed she might well have spared

herself. Scarcely six months after she herself had become Fru Bisgaard her mother married young Haagen Lunde. As no doubt she had intended even before marrying off her daughter. For otherwise she would not have been so set on Dorthea's accepting Bisgaard.

She was in her sixteenth year when she had to go to the altar with him.

"L'amour c'est un plaisir, l'honneur c'est le devoir." These words her mother had written to her when Bisgaard had had his first seizure. In looking back upon those days it surprised her that her mother's letters at the time had aroused no other emotion in her but a certain chilly ironical gaiety. Did Mamma, who could not possibly lack experience in such matters, imagine that the *plaisir* in her marriage with Bisgaard had been on her side? But two years had passed since she was a bride. It must have been as a kind of self-defence that she had developed a certain cynicism.

And yet, as she grew older, she had gradually become more and more convinced that this maxim was beneficently sound and true — although from her mother's pen it had a rather droll look.

Her youthful inexperience had preserved her from a full understanding of the frightfulness of all those years during which she and Christence had been occupied with the old invalid who had to be tended like an infant, carried from his bed to the armchair by the window and back again to his bed. To tell the truth, in the beginning she herself had not been sorry that things took such a turn as to render her relations with Bisgaard purely filial. The possession of a girlish wife had awakened in the old gentleman an unnatural ardour to which she had never learnt to reconcile herself, and which at the same time had destroyed the respect she had felt for Bisgaard so long as she knew him only as her stepfather's honoured friend and her own paternal well-wisher. Long after the disorder had paralysed his body Bisgaard retained much of his mental clarity. He laid upon his wife and daughter the task of feeding him intellectually as well as physically, by reading aloud such books as for the most part were far beyond the comprehension of the two young women. But in those first two years of her husband's malady she often felt almost happy, as she sat opposite him by the window, reading aloud and listening to his explanations of what she had read. Although in her girlhood her education had been much neglected, she had acquired a good deal of desultory information, partly on her own account and partly through her brother Peter Andreas's interest in her. And she was still so young and full of curiosity that she was glad to be instructed by her old husband. He still had hopes of being able to complete the great work on which he had laboured for many years, a physical and economic description of Lower Thellemarken. She had to read out to him the parts that were written, to correct and rewrite from his dictation; the drawings she executed after his sketches — of implements, animals and plants — met with Bisgaard's approval. She owed him the deepest gratitude for having initiated her into the glorious poems of Ossian. Her memory of the father she had so early lost was revived in a strange way when she submitted herself to the enchantment of Morven's royal bard. Oscar, Calthon, Shilric assumed her father's pleasant, half-forgotten form; his flute-playing in the twilight, which was what she remembered most clearly, now seemed akin

to the spirit of those melancholy lays — his family too had
its origin in the same far-off misty Highlands. And she
herself lived in fancy with the white-bosomed heroines
with flowing locks, Malvina, Minona, Vinvela, whose
lovers were snatched from them before they had tasted
the joys of love to the full, and who sang of their sorrows,
bending over the harp in deserted royal halls, or wandered by night in misty moonshine among the ancient
cromlechs on the moor.

In later years she had smiled at these youthful fantasies
of hers, through which she sought compensation in the
luxury of imagined grief for the losses fate had laid upon
her. Bisgaard's mind became blunted with the years —
the teacher gave place to the cross and tyrannical old man
who was no longer interested in anything but his bodily
needs. And meanwhile her womanliness was maturing.
Denied the joys of love and motherhood, her dreaming
turned to a sweet poison, which occasioned her, now a dull
loathing, now a painful desire for all the things of which
she had been defrauded.

She shuddered when she looked back upon the pitfalls
which had beset her ignorant steps. In those days perhaps
it would merely have filled her with horror and disgust,
if she had heard of an intrigue such as that between
Margit Klokkhaugen and her stepfather. Now she was
scarcely capable of being scandalized by it — so shockingly natural were such results of unnatural marriages
between youth and infirm old age.

The first of Bisgaard's curates to awaken feelings in
her bosom of which she was ashamed, was Snæbjörn
Gislason. Inexperienced as she was, she nevertheless divined that it was the force of circumstances rather than

Gislason's person which made him a danger to her peace
of mind. Ardently she had desired that it might come to
a match between him and Christence — Gislason's was a
violent nature, his inclination seemed to embrace both
her and her stepdaughter at the same time. But she was
never able to understand Christence. They shared a bed
at that time; it stood in Bisgaard's room, for it was better
they should both be there to help him at night. Although
indeed *she* had never been able to see the necessity. Bisgaard was small and light, she was young and strong — she
could quite well have undertaken the nursing of him as
well as the housekeeping, with paid help. And Bisgaard
was by no means insusceptible of reason; on the contrary,
he quite agreed with her when she suggested that at
Christence's age it was high time she saw about getting
married soon, and that it was desirable the wedding
should take place from the paternal roof.

But the fact was, Christence had exaggerated ideas of
her duty as a daughter. And that she was very unwilling
to relinquish the reins of housekeeping to her younger
stepmother, Dorthea had discovered from the day she
entered the house. Although in other ways Christence
had met her with a warmth which was positively embar-
rassing: in her own home Dorthea had been so little accustomed to being kissed and hugged and coddled. The
sisterly friend she had wished for was far too affectionate,
and moreover insisted on treating her as her little sister,
a mere child.

While Snæbjörn was with them as curate things went
very badly. The long tearful scenes at night, when Christence clung to her, declaring that she had the highest
esteem for Gislason, but that she would not desert her

father and her precious Thea — these were, to put it plainly, excessively disagreeable. When Gislason's stay with them came to a sad end through his getting a girl of the parish into trouble, Christence could not find words hard enough in which to condemn him. It was not Christence's fault that the affair did not assume such dimensions as to render its results irreparable for Gislason. Dorthea was certain the calamity would never have occurred if Christence had accepted the curate. She had heard that Gislason was afterwards married at home in his native Iceland and by all accounts had turned out a particularly good and worthy clergyman. And the girl had married a pewterer in Christiania and was now living very happily with him. How much sorrow and shame people could save themselves and others if they would listen to the voice of nature and use their common sense!

In Dahlgreen's time there had been peace. His betrothed had lately died and he sought consolation in zealous work. Christence did not like him — Dorthea could not see why. When he was given a living in the Trondhjem district and married, it was not without bitterness that Christence indulged in comments on eternal fidelity.

But it was worst of all when Winther came to them. This was the last thing she would have imagined when the little Jutlander with the bushy red eyebrows and horn spectacles made his entry into their house. He was the most peaceable of men, amiable, helpful, besides being musical and gifted with a vein of poetry. In the beginning he was a real acquisition to their cheerless home. And when his cousin obtained his appointment at the ironworks and became a constant visitor at the house, she

had really felt as if some flowers of joyfulness might bloom
even upon her path.

She had not begun to reflect upon the nature of her
feelings for Jörgen Thestrup; but she looked forward to
his visits, was happy while he was with them, and thought
a good deal of him when he had ridden away. She was
stricken with dismay when Bisgaard suddenly informed
her of his desire that she should marry Winther after his
own early demise. To his curate he had once expressed
his concern for her future, when she became a widow —
with a mother married into the peasant class and brothers
abroad, in straitened circumstances. Winther had then
declared that it would signify the fulfilment of his dearest
wish, if Fru Bisgaard would accept his hand and his heart,
when the time came. Bisgaard considered this an excellent plan — especially if at the same time a marriage were
arranged between Christence and Thestrup.

She had replied, after expressing her gratitude for
Winther's offer, that so long as Bisgaard was alive she
would come to no decision regarding another matrimonial engagement. And privately she had given Winther
to understand that she did not intend to allow her hand
to be disposed of a second time, she would now choose for
herself. She blushed as she said it — for she saw that
Winther understood what she had in mind. But she
blushed still more from the knowledge that six months
previously she had regarded the amiable Winther with a
dreamy sympathy, since she hoped that — possibly — he
might be the one who was to make her what she longed
to be: a contented wife and mother in the home of an
upright man.

She knew now that her feelings for Thestrup had been

of a different nature from those which hitherto had disturbed her soul and senses and which had had for their
object now one and now another of the young men of
her acquaintance. If she had failed to get Thestrup she
would doubtless in the end have married another. But
the natural, modest contentment which a female may
achieve in a marriage sensibly contracted would no longer
have been capable of gratifying her. She would have been
ill fitted to make a respectable husband — Winther or another — as happy as he deserved to be.

To be sure, she did not know *how* happy Winther had
been with Christence.

Ah no, she had come to see that love is a dangerous
power. And if it has been vouchsafed to one to taste the
joys of love while at the same time complying with the
dictates of duty and virtue, one can never be sufficiently
grateful to Providence for this rare mercy.

The tears ran slowly down Dorthea's cheeks. She had
been so happy. If it was now at an end — O God, she
dared not complain. *Les délices d'amour,* which drove
women to deceive their husbands, men to corrupt innocence, friends to be false to one another, had to her been
the delicious warmth which was the driving force in all
she undertook.

Dorthea threw the quilt aside, fumbled with a naked
foot for her slipper. She felt tumbled and untidy, stiff
and tired after passing the night in her clothes. The
morning light seemed to her mockingly grey and cold,
though she saw that the clear pale southern sky promised
a fine day.

Many, many hours she would have to wait in any case
before she could hope to hear anything at all — before

any of the different parties who were now setting out could be expected to return with news — and even then they might have nothing to report.

Leave all in God's hand, perform her round of duties — the thought of having to do so now seemed so dreadful. *If* anything had happened to her husband or her sons. With her, happiness had become an ingrained habit — ingrained was the very word: one day Thestrup had brought home a piece of wood, sawn from an ancient fir. Within the bark which had entirely grown over it was fixed an iron arrowhead of ancient type. Like such an arrow, shot from the bow of the god of love, she now thought she had borne happiness in her heart, sweetly and securely encased in her manifold wifely duties. Not without mortal pain could it be torn out of her being. The joyless fulfilment of duty which she had nevertheless been able to accomplish in her first marriage — this now seemed to her so unlovely, nay, repellent. Was that to be once more her lot!

Alas, at times she had wondered why it was that virtuous and estimable people were often so unattractive. They were spoilt by an ill-concealed self-sufficiency, a certain sourness or a kind of suppressed envy of their more cheerful and frivolous fellow-creatures. Never again would she condemn them for this — it is a bitter thing to have to perform joylessly the tasks that must be done. He who must constantly overcome his natural propensities in order to act rightly is easily tempted to feel too pleased with himself — what other source of contentment has he, poor man? This lesson she had learnt, however, at the price of seven years of her youth in slavery: we must fill the position in which we are placed as well as we are able — otherwise the world would be too terrible to live in. Even though, from the frailty of human nature, only great and noble souls are equal to the effort without incurring some degree of moral curvature of the spine.

Nor was it possible that her own life could ever again resemble that of those who must be resigned to regulate their conduct merely by love of chilly virtue and reverence for far-off Heaven. Whatever losses she might be called upon to bewail, the goal of all her efforts must always be the welfare of her beloved children.

But the children themselves had been precious to her as pledges of love before all else. Devotedly as she was attached to her Thestrup, in the early days of their married life she had not been able to reciprocate his ardour to the full. She honestly strove to repay her husband's fervour with affectionate friendship — but she had been so thoroughly chilled by her first marriage that she often asked herself with secret misgiving, had she become unfitted to make a loving spouse really happy? When a change occurred in her physical and mental condition and she noticed with joyful surprise that this frigidity was loosening its grip on her, she discovered at the same time that she was pregnant. It was like a miracle — the warmth of the new life in her womb seemed to thaw the unnatural frost within her, so that she felt that she was ripening, being filled with strength and sweetness, as the hard, sour apple ripens at last, even if the fine weather is late in coming and the summer has been cold and grey.

Afterwards she had found out that other women had had the same experience. If so many mothers love their first-born with peculiar partiality it is because motherhood alone has brought their womanliness to full ma-

turity. To their husband they pretend that he alone has
brought it about by his kindling passion — since one is
so prone to believe that love is exalted above the laws of
physical nature, one would persuade oneself and the beloved that it is exclusively the feelings of the heart and
not physical changes that cause the blood-stream to circulate at a more lively rate, the nerves to quiver more
briskly and vigorously. No doubt all her children were
equally dear to her, each had a special claim to her care.
But she knew why it was that Vilhelm nevertheless was
in a way her favourite.

Madame Dorthea had seen the various search parties
well away.

The bedroom looked towards the north-west; no ray of
sunshine ever fell upon it at this time of year. But from
the raised floor by the window where she had seated herself with her well-filled darning basket Dorthea looked
out upon the bright day of early spring. Where the
shadow of the house fell across the garden the snow still
lay in heaps, but farther away the grass was bare, over-
spread with rime, and up by the fence the twigs and
branches of the young apple-trees glimmered in the sunshine. Thestrup had always been fond of expressing his
loud contempt for the former manager, who at heavy cost
had laid out a garden on the north side of the house. But
there was obviously no other place to put it, and it had
been a source of much pleasure and usefulness to Dorthea
of late years, since the trees and bushes had begun to bear
fruit.

Birgitte and Elisabeth were at school today — it was

their father's wish that they should receive their first in-
struction at the works school; if it was not good enough
to provide his children with the first elements of knowledge, then it was no good at all. Then Birgitte could
begin to take lessons at home in French, drawing and
music, when she had completed her seventh year this
spring. But Bertel sat on the footstool at her feet, grind-
ing away at his Latin lesson half-aloud — the last that
Dabbelsteen had set him. He had left off asking for his
father, his brothers and the tutor. But when Dorthea
suggested that he might sit over by the stove he shook
his head: " If Mother will give me leave I would rather
sit by you."

The two little ones were in the nursery with the maids.
It would soon be time for her to fetch Christen and feed
him. But it was so painful after a while to listen to
Johanne's and Gunhild's cogitations and to their tales of
all the mysterious and disastrous events that had occurred
in their native districts.

It was one of Dabbelsteen's stockings that she picked
up on dipping into the basket. With some hesitation she
drew it over her left hand — then took up her darning-
needle with something of a superstitious feeling that if
she behaved as though nothing was changed, perhaps it
would help to make this true. *Three* people could not
possibly disappear entirely without a trace. The ice, the
gypsies, a sudden access of madness in Dabbelsteen —
there was not much more to guess at. But of course what
really had happened would be the last thing one could
imagine. She found nothing at all on which to base her
fancies when she tried to picture to herself some situation
or other in which Vilhelm and Claus might now be

placed. It was like peering into the mist. In her state of profound depression, being utterly unable to imagine where they were, what they were doing, what state they were in, it seemed at last that their very forms and faces became indistinct; it was as though she had already begun to forget what they looked like.

Were they safe, had they come to grief, were they calling to her, in their hearts if not in words? She did not really believe they were. The maids had raised a great to-do, calling upon God to save the poor creatures. She *knew* that they might have met with an accident, but she could not believe it. Probably they had had to go through a good deal, in such weather as had raged during the night, and they had not been clothed for any long journey. But there was nevertheless something within her which said that perhaps they were not so excessively miserable either — unless they had met with an adventure which was too sinister altogether. She possessed a sort of insight into her boys' nature. Neither of them was really timid. She had dreaded having to *send* them away. Often, when she reflected that soon they would be among strangers, far from home, she had felt a shrinking of the heart: she knew how bitterly they would miss her and their father, how homesick they would be for everything at Brovold. But that was if they were *sent* away.

She let her work sink into her lap — turned rigid at the thought. What if Dabbelsteen had got them to run away with him — out into the wide world, to enlist — or go to sea? He had stuffed their heads with enthusiasm for the champions of liberty in America and France: they had raved about their uncle Caspar's marvellous life under the glowing sun of the West Indies, about Tranquebar and the China merchantmen. Supposing he had had the idea in a moment of desperation that they should turn their backs on their native land, seek their fortune out in the great world? They were good children, she knew that they loved her devotedly. But Dabbelsteen was dangerously persuasive at times — and boys, boys. She had heard of so many who had run away to sea, although they were genuinely fond of their parents. When the thirst for adventure overcame them they smothered the voice of conscience by romancing about the joys of home-coming and all the fine things they would bring back for father, mother, brothers and sisters.

But in that case of course they would be overtaken and brought home, she reassured herself. Thank God, it was a long way from here, far inland, to any sea-port. Had they still been living at the ironworks — well, then she would not have known what to think. Though this was not the time of year to find a ship in a hurry. They could not have had any money either.

Ah, she remembered how Thestrup had teased her when she was so unwilling that he should accept the post here at the glassworks. " Just think of all the alarms you would have to go through when Ville and Klunsen are old enough to manage a boat." She had often been anxious when Thestrup was sailing in his yacht among the outer skerries. Though she always began looking forward to his return the moment he was outside the door. Those had been lovely days.

The years had not failed to leave their mark on Thestrup either. The ardent lover had become a considerate spouse; passion had yielded to tender confidence. But she could not help looking back upon those days, sometimes,

with a sigh. Her youth: it had been late in coming, in the
nature of things it could not last so many years. It had
been all the sweeter for that. In light summer nights they
had strolled in the grounds of the ironworks, in close
embrace, intoxicating themselves with the balmy scent of
the leaves and the trills of birds — till Jörgen with
brusque impetuosity tore the fichu from her shoulders,
covered her cool bosom with red-hot kisses and drew her,
with his arm tightly clasped about her waist, through the
avenues up to their quiet rooms in the creeper-clad house.
Well tucked in she sat in the seat of the sledge; Thestrup
stood behind her driving — with loud cries he urged on
the horse till its pace was such that she had to shut her eyes
against the biting snow and chips of ice that flew up under
the horse's hoofs as they dashed over the frozen surface
of the creek on their way home from a party in town.
Then, late at night, when at last she reached their bedroom — where she hastened to pluck the ornaments out
of her hair and take off her silk gown, laughingly afraid
lest Jörgen should burst in on her. Under the excitement
of wine and music and the rapid sledge drive he might
insist on forcing on her his services as lady's maid — a
proceeding which was by no means to the advantage of her
only party dress.

She had to go and see to the dinner. There was barley
gruel and salt sea-perch, Jörgen's favourite dish. True,
he was the only one who cared for the fish — and now it
had gone very rancid into the bargain. But Thestrup received his kegs of sea-perch from the cousin in Trondhjem regularly year after year. He had said he could not

be absent from the office for long — perhaps he might be back by dinner-time?

She decided to lay for Thestrup in any case. Even so it was a strangely small table, with one wing down, since at any rate three were missing. Dorthea thought it would have been more comfortable after all to dine with the servants in the kitchen — as she usually did when it chanced that all her menfolk were out. But it seemed to keep up her courage if she laid the meal in the bedroom and said to herself she expected her husband home to dinner. And as soon as Elisabeth and Birgitte came in, with strangely wide eyes and a look of perplexity on their little faces, their mother summoned them to table.

" Now can you say grace, Lise — I think it is your turn today? "

Elisabeth stammered and faltered badly; she was never very good at saying prayers — was a little backward altogether. And all at once her eyes and her sister's flew to the empty chair at the head of the table, with their father's dram-bottle, glass and beer-tankard, two empty plates, the deep one on top, and the massive silver spoon and fork. They all looked so curiously imposing as they lay thus at rest. The little girls seemed never to have noticed before how big and heavy they were, the spoon, fork and knife which usually darted backwards and forwards between the dish and their father's big mouth with its gleaming teeth — Thestrup, the ever-busy man, was in the habit of bolting his food so carelessly that their mother had to remind them that Father had work to do, but *they* must please eat slowly and nicely, *they* had plenty of time.

Naturally Birgitte and Elisabeth had heard gossip in the school about the mysterious disappearance of their brothers and the tutor, but they dared not say anything or ask any questions; the expression of their mother's face absolutely forbade it. Bertel had jerked his chair as close to Dorthea's as he could, but he did not say anything either. So the meal passed in deep silence.

The sunshine was obscured and the light outside turned to a sullen greyish yellow while they sat at table. At last they were done with the stale, rancid sea-perch and Dorthea allowed the three children to share the sugared small beer in their father's tankard: " It will be cold anyhow; I had better make it fresh for him when he comes in." Then Bertel said grace. Dorthea saw that an occasional flake of snow floated past the windows.

She went out into the hall with the two little girls, helped them on with their outdoor things. She was stooping down to tie Elisabeth's mob-cap when the child seized her wrist: " Mother — must we go back to school *today?* " And Birgitte burst into tears: " Mother — can't we be let off today? "

" Your father would not be pleased." She kissed them both reassuringly: " You must just take no notice of it — of what they say down there."

" Oh but, Mother — do you know what they are saying? "

" You are not to take any notice of it, I tell you. When you come home they will be back here, all of them, you may be sure. Then you'll be able to laugh at the croakings of these gossipers." But when she opened the hall door the air outside was a whirling flurry of huge snow-flakes.

If only she had persuaded him to take Feierfax with him, she thought as she entered the bedroom. If anything had happened to him —

Bertel stood at the window looking out. " It's snowing now, Mother! "

" I've seen that, Bertel. That will please your father — if we have a proper snowfall. Then they can go on using the sledges for a while. Have you learnt your lessons? "

" Yes, Mother."

" Perhaps you would like to borrow a book to amuse you? You may take the picture Bible if you like."

" Thank you." But his voice was low, without enthusiasm, and he received the little book mutely when Dorthea took it from the drawer of the escritoire. At other times her children were never tired of poring over it with delight — though actually it was intended for the very young and the children knew it by heart long ago. Each page had a saying from the Bible, but all the nouns were replaced by woodcuts representing the object or idea in question. Very easy to understand — except that there might be some trouble in guessing what the figures were meant for; they were not exactly masterpieces.

Not a sound from the nursery — Johanne and Gunhild must be sitting in the kitchen, chatting with the others. " Oh, Bertel, run and tell Hanne to bring in Christen — he must be hungry. Rikke can come in too for a little while."

Little Christen howled wildly as the maids brought in him and his sister — he was sweaty and blubbering, and sticky about the mouth: they must have given him a scrap of something in the kitchen to stop his crying, so that they need not break off their gossiping. " I thought Madame would prefer to be left in peace for a while," was Johanne's excuse.

The baby sucked greedily when she gave him the breast. Still panting after his fit of crying he swallowed the milk the wrong way, shrieked, and drank again — but then he calmed down. He would soon fall asleep again, she could see.

Dorthea sent the maids into the nursery. A moment later the two spinning-wheels were whirring one against the other. Rikke crawled about the floor, got up and stood by her father's chair. "Puss," she said gleefully, pulling the cat's tail — it must have slipped in unnoticed; now it curled itself up in the armchair. The good-natured animal was purring, it showed no resentment at Rikke's teasing.

It was good to have a few moments' peace with the two little ones who suspected nothing. For it was so painful to read in the eyes of all the others that they were thinking of the same thing — and to know that *their* anxiety was blended, in the case of the grown-ups with a certain pleasurable excitement in this game of guessing at all imaginable possibilities, in that of the children with dread of what they were unable to understand. In her profound trouble she was quite alone. Thestrup, Thestrup, would he not soon come back! Did he not say he could not be absent from the works so long? — and now it was already afternoon.

Rikke came padding up, laid a fat little hand on her knee: "Ma — ," and then she slipped her whole little person into her mother's lap. She was such a friendly, peaceful little child.

Ah yes, at this time last year, when she was obliged to engage a wet-nurse for Rikke, as she could no longer doubt that Christen was on the way, she had reflected with a certain longing that in six or seven years she would be beyond *that* age, and that too would be good. Not that she was not happy and proud of her fine flock of children. But she nevertheless looked forward to the time when they would all have grown bigger — a little less trouble-some to their mother. They were so lovable, while still in their babyhood — but they were also amusing when they grew a little bigger, it was so enjoyable to see their intelligence and thirst for knowledge asserting themselves in earnest. Now she shuddered at the thought of all the anxiety and uneasiness children may cause their parents when they grow up and want to follow their own devices. Dorthea pressed Christen's head in its moist cap closer against her breast, making the child give a little grunt; with her other hand she sought Rikke's podgy little paw which lay on her knee.

" Mother — may I ask you something? "

" You know, Bertel dear, you can find the explanations at the beginning of the book, there's a key to all the pictures."

" It's not that." He came up and laid the open book on the table before her. " Mother — " he pointed to the picture in the middle of the page. " That means Life, it says in the key. Why is Life like that, Mother? "

Dorthea read: " He that followeth after Righteousness and Mercy findeth — " and below was depicted a fat genie, or a child, or whatever it was meant to be, sitting astride on a skull and blowing soap-bubbles.

Bertel turned on to one of the last pages: " Look, there he is again. It means Life there too. Why does it, Mother? "

" I don't know, my child."

Bertel shut the book with a smack. " May I stop looking at it, Mother? "

Dorthea nodded.

Soon after she thought she heard someone come riding
into the yard. A faint flush coloured her pale cheeks.
With Rikke on her arm — the sweet little doll was smiling so delightedly — Madame Dorthea hurried out to
meet the rider.

Outside in the falling snow stood a strange young peasant lad beside a smart little horse — its light forelock was
matted in wet little curls. The lad shook off the fresh
snow in showers.

" Good day — it's the mistress herself, I'm thinking? I
was to tell you from your mother, your sons got to Lunde
last night."

She had seen the messenger comfortably settled in the
warm kitchen before an ample spread of food and drink,
before she opened the little note that he had dug out from
under his cap. But there was no more in her mother's
words than the lad had told her.

Their grandmother would keep Vilhelm and Claus till
the next day — they might need a day's rest before she
had them driven home to the works. Compliments for
Vilhelm's presence of mind. What was it the messenger
had said? — " that Vilhelm's a smart lad, he is; it was he
that pulled them through." A warming wave of pride
surged through his mother's fear-chilled heart — Vilhelm, Vilhelm, her brave, sensible boy. Dorthea seized
the dram-bottle, poured out another glass for the lad
from Lunde.

" You did not see anything of the manager along the road? He rode north late yesterday evening to search for Dabbelsteen and the boys. You have heard no news of his movements, whether anyone has seen him? "

No, the lad had heard nothing.

Well, perhaps it was scarcely to be expected. He could not possibly have gone as far as Lunde by the time the lad here had left the farm. Nor was it easy to guess which road up the valley he might have taken.

At dusk, as Dorthea was in the kitchen spreading bread-and-butter, Scharlach arrived. She went out into the porch, where he stood stamping the snow from his feet. But he seemed calm — and that reassured her immensely. It was already known all over the works that the boys were in safety. And Scharlach's words echoed her own thoughts: Thestrup must also have arrived at Lunde by now and would return with his sons next day.

In this calm wet weather the works were in no danger, so Scharlach intended to go home to bed. But he was easily persuaded to come into the kitchen, where Dorthea provided beer posset, bread-and-butter and meat for all who had taken part in the search, besides anyone else who chose to take advantage of her hospitality.

The kitchen was crowded with people after a time — they sat round the table, on boxes and upturned tubs, and in the chimney-corner, so that Madame Dorthea and Ragnhild could hardly make their way to the milk-pan and the beer-keg. Birgitte helped the maids, running with cups into which her mother poured the grateful steaming posset, but Elisabeth had taken refuge on Scharlach's lap. Women and children had come from the farms whose men had been out; the housekeeper from the parsonage had looked in to ask for news, and so she too joined the rest. Ragnhild had to go out to the storehouse for more bacon and sausages.

And it was late before the last of the visitors had taken their leave and the mistress and her maids had finished clearing up after them. Dorthea remained seated before her mirror after she had arranged her hair for the night and put it in curl-papers. She was so tired that she did not feel equal to getting up and undressing.

But anyhow the good people had enjoyed themselves. How curious it was, this taste for horrors among the common people. Their conversation had turned on hardly anything else but murders and executions, witchcraft and witch-burnings, ghosts and warnings — it was like a rivalry among them, who should contribute the most uncanny tale. And no one doubted that the two boys who had been killed under a stack of wood ten years before still haunted the place — more than one man declared that he had seen them floating about the spot at night. As to Heinrich Mahler, who was said to have been the cause of the accident through flinging the boy from him in a rage, so that the wood-pile fell on him, and who was afterwards drowned below the bridge, Scharlach asserted that he had met him in the avenue by the churchyard one night as he came home from shooting. For that matter, Thestrup had admitted that he too had had some inexplicable experiences both in the churchyard avenue and by the works at night-time.

When one thought of it, this same predilection for the horrible — did it not lie dormant in most people? All children prefer to hear uncanny tales of horror. If, of all forms of poetry, tragedy is that which enjoys most favour with the cultivated public, does not this show the same taste, only a little more polished?

Dorthea turned the pages of the little book of Biblical rebuses which Bertel had left behind. In fact many of its pictures were by no means pleasant. Swords and scourges — and Death was always represented as a skeleton. And the Heart — the heart which occurs in almost every other saying from the Bible — as it was depicted here, heavily shaded to make it appear round and full, with a snick in the middle as of a severed artery, was really just like a heart in a butcher's shop. It had never affected her when she was a child — she had prized this little book as a precious sign of her stepfather's favour; it was not so often that he surprised her with a present. Dean de Theilemann had never been unkindly disposed towards her, nor was he nearly so strict with her as with Caspar and Peter Andreas. But all the same her respect for him had been mixed with a certain fear.

But Bertel's was a sensitive nature — perhaps the gruesome pictures made a different impression on him. Her children had grown up in a far more gentle, more affectionate atmosphere. No doubt instinctively she had striven to give them all that she had to dispense with in her own childhood.

Dorthea cautiously snuffed the smoking tallow candle on her dressing-table. No, she must really see about getting to bed now.

But it was strange, all that people said about Sibilla's gifts of prophecy and her powers of healing sickness in man and beast. Probably the old gypsy woman was a good deal wiser than most people and knew many old and tried receipts, which enabled her to practise physic with success — in cases of injury or ailment doubtless brought about by herself, sometimes at any rate. And then there was this animal magnetism of which one had heard so much talk. One could not really believe in magic and witchcraft, surely? But would to heaven Thestrup had not encountered her band — Sibilla's sons were an ugly set of fellows, very ready with their knives.

No use being anxious — had she not learnt now that her agony of fear for her boys had been quite unreasonable?

Dorthea turned over and over, trying to find the most comfortable position among the soft pillows and quilts of the bed. Bertel had curled himself up by the wall and was sleeping like a stone — his thin little body gave out a pleasant little warmth. Christen was well fed and dry and it might be hoped that he would keep quiet at any rate till about midnight. She drew the cradle close to the four-post bed, so that she could reach the child when he woke without having to get up.

If only one could avoid frightening oneself with one's own fancies, then people might spare themselves much suffering. But that was just what they would not do — it was as though one found some enjoyment in exciting oneself to the point of terror.

Tomorrow evening — Dorthea folded her arms over her bosom and pressed her hot cheek against the cool skin of her shoulder — tomorrow evening she would certainly clasp her good loved one in her arms.

She remembered, the moment she awoke next morning, that she had dreamt of Thestrup — she closed her eyes again, trying to retain some of the scenes of her dream. And all at once it came back to her that she had seen her father too — quite plainly his handsome, youthful figure, which in her waking hours she had never been able to conjure out of the mists of oblivion, had appeared to her vision. And Major Eckelöff — she knew him from the engraving in the parlour. The three men seemed to have been sitting together in a large room; it was and was not her own parlour here at Brovold. Then someone she could not see came in, beckoned to them from the door, and all three went out together.

She brushed aside the impression as she proceeded to dress — it vanished like swept-up cobwebs. Outside the snow was still falling heavily; the trees in the garden swelled out in a light burden of white, and on the far side of the field's white expanse the white spruces merged in the snow-filled air. It was useless to expect them before evening with the roads in this state.

Dorthea profited by the good quiet day. She found time to cut out the new chemises for Birgitte — the child had outgrown all her underclothes this winter. And she inspected the weaving-room upstairs — the weather would soon be mild enough for her to set the maids to work up there. And she herself could spend her leisure hours at the loom — she looked forward to that.

When darkness fell Dorthea opened the door of the stove and seated herself with her knitting in Thestrup's armchair; she would indulge herself with a good long blindman's holiday, while the maids were in the kitchen with the little ones and Bertel and his sisters were building a snow castle in the yard —

— Then she was startled out of her slumber by dark

figures bursting in heavily shod upon her darkness, and
her sons' eager, joyous voices calling for Mother. Behind
them came Johanne with two lighted candles which she
set down on the table.

" Vilhelm — Claus! " — she started up, and the boys
flung themselves into her outstretched arms. " Dearest
children, what a fright you gave me —

" — But where is your father? "

" Father? " asked the boys together.

" Isn't your father with *you?* "

Vilhelm raised his head, looked quickly and pierc-
ingly into his mother's face: " No — ? Isn't Father at
home? "

Johanne clapped her hands together with a scream:

" Then don't you know it — that the master started off
after you as soon as he heard you were lost? "

Dorthea stood rigid, as though stunned. Without
knowing it she pressed Claus Hartvig once more to her
breast — the boy clung closer to his mother and dropped
his head as he began to suspect that something was
wrong.

Vilhelm had instinctively drawn himself up, he stood
tense, looking straight into his mother's face with the same
expression of eager enquiry. On seeing her falter he
seized her by the shoulder.

Dorthea sank into the armchair. She vaguely wished
she might fall into a swoon, slip away for a time, escape
having to think. But she could not faint away: that was
not to be, much as she would have wished it.

Claus, whom she had drawn down with her as she
dropped into the chair, began to cry softly, in a frightened
way — he was now on his knees with his head buried in

his mother's lap. Dorthea stroked his wet, dark hair, without knowing she did so, as she reached out her other hand and grasped Vilhelm's:

" Vilhelm, Vilhelm — Vilhelm, Vilhelm, what are we to do? "

4

AFTERWARDS it seemed to Dorthea that she had known it from the first. The moment she saw that the boys had neither seen nor heard anything of their father she understood — an accident must have happened.

In the first long nights she lay thinking out explanations. It might have occurred to Thestrup that the fugitives had taken the south road after all, making for the capital and the coast, and so he had turned after them. Or he was lying injured at some out-of-the-way farm or cottage. A fall with his horse perhaps; Reveille had always been apt to shy, and this winter she had had far too little exercise. Although Jörgen was a good horseman. And in her heart she was certain that Thestrup, if he was alive and not altogether unconscious, would have seen that a message was sent, both to Thommesen, the chief clerk at the works, and to her.

The snow continued to fall. Were he and the mare lying buried somewhere under the drifts? Oh, if only she had persuaded him to let Feierfax run with him.

But she got up every morning, firmly determined to appear composed. The people of the house positively devoured the reassuring words with which she sought to comfort them. Now that they had gulped down such a feast of terror on the boys' account they were satiated and would gladly fall back into their old ways again.

Claus Hartvig too was more than ready to accept his mother's assurances that they would soon have an explanation of his father's absence. One must not begin by thinking the worst, that was all. And besides, the boy had a mass of things about which he was burning to talk to his mother. There was the approaching big wedding at Lunde — Uncle Ole wanted Vilhelm and him to be pages, and their grandmother had said that she, their mother, must come and make her famous apple fritters. Dorthea saw that Claus was extremely intent on going to this entertainment; he refused to harbour the thought that something might have happened which made it impossible for him to attend the feast.

Only Vilhelm understood. Every time she met her eldest son's eyes she read in them that he was thinking — well, much the same as herself. It was perfectly clear to him that things looked sinister.

After dinner the first day Claus came and offered to hold a skein for her. And while she wound the wool he talked about Dabbelsteen. When they went up to the house in the forenoon they found that the tutor had dis-

appeared. Their grandmother would say nothing. But
Tora, one of the maids at Lunde, thought that Dabbelsteen had gone on to the northward to his mother's. Tora,
by the way, was related to the Sheriff's family, Claus said,
so she was not a regular servant girl, but she was staying
with them.

Dabbelsteen, thought Madame Dorthea. So Thestrup
had been right. If only they had got rid of him last autumn. And to all her other anxieties this fresh one was
added, that her two eldest boys would be going about here
with nothing to do — and that meant that she would have
to control her desperate fear even more, would never be
able for a single moment to surrender herself to tears —
for which she felt an uncontrollable longing.

Ah — for if the worst had happened she knew that her
thoughts of the beloved, her tenderest longing, her very
grief for her incomparable spouse — all this would be
forced aside, to the inmost corner of her soul, while she
would be constrained to busy her thoughts with the future. What was to be her fate with seven children under
age, if they had been made fatherless? Merely in caring
for them she could still nurse her affection for their father.
Oh, but her whole being rose in the most impetuous longing to be able to mourn him with her full heart, to lament
the inconceivable loss of her lover and friend.

Little Christen screamed and screamed the whole of
the second night — his stomach was in a very bad state.
It must have been her milk that had turned sour from
emotion. When she changed him in the early dawn she
saw that the child had already failed a great deal — his
limbs had become thin and flaccid, his face was sunken
and blue under the little eyes. " Oh, my poor little mite,

poor little darling." Her tears gushed out, and it was a relief to let her overcharged heart shed some of its overflowing store. But she got up, with the thought that she must make the day pass somehow.

She was already seated at the window sewing Birgitte's chemises in tiny backstitch when Vilhelm came in. The other children were still at their morning porridge in the kitchen.

" Mother — we've been talking it over, Scharlach and I. If we hear nothing about Father again today, ought we not to send word to Christiania, to the office? "

Dorthea looked up from her sewing.

" Well, Mother, what I mean is, couldn't I go there? For there's nobody else that can be spared here because of the work. You understand, Mother, don't you," he said impetuously, " I can't just stay here and do nothing at all."

" It cannot be necessary *yet,* Vilhelm. And besides, it will be for Thommesen."

" He's much worse today," Vilhelm broke in hurriedly. " Madame Thommesen says this alarm about Father has given him such a shock that she can't tell when he'll be well again."

" No, no, but in any case — if your father is lying somewhere up the valley with a broken leg it may take some time before we get word of it." Even as she said it she saw how unlikely this was — so many people had been out searching that they must have heard of it by now. And it was impossible that he had strayed far from the common highways. She felt as if her fear tightened its hold on her heart. But she said in the same tone as before: " I thought of proposing that you and Claus should continue to pre-

pare your lessons by yourselves, as well as you are able —
and then you, Vilhelm, could undertake to teach Bertel,
until we see — "

" As you will, Mother."

But when she had heard the boys' footsteps die away on
the floor above, she went out to the kitchen. Birgitte's and
Elisabeth's laughter stopped abruptly when they caught
sight of their mother. They were running about flicking
at each other with the washing-up cloths — were supposed to be helping Ragnhild, but they treated it as play.
Absently Dorthea stroked the head of the nearest child —
it happened to be Elisabeth: " You're making yourselves
quite useful. And when you have done you may go out
with your hand-sleighs. And Hanne and Gunhild can
stay here in the kitchen with Rikke — Baby's asleep, he
was so restless last night."

Then she could be left undisturbed in the bedroom.
With her arms crossed among the heap of linen on the
work-table and her head buried in them she wept, almost
noiselessly so as not to wake the child in the cradle. At
last she scarcely thought why she was weeping; it was such
a relief to be able to give way.

Johanne opened a crack of the door: " Captain Cold is
without and asks leave to pay his respects to Madame."

" One moment." Instinctively she went to the mirror,
thrust straggling hairs under her cap and arranged her
fichu. She could scarcely recognize herself, so red was she
about the eyes and nose. Hurriedly she moistened her
handkerchief and tried to cool her tearstained face.

" Madame Thestrup! " Captain Cold seized her hand
and pressed his moustache upon it. " You must not, no,
you must not despair — not yet. My dear good friend,

come and be seated! " He led her across to Thestrup's armchair by the stove and forced her into it, snatched the bottle of sal volatile from the dressing-table and held it under her nose. " There, there, if you feel stronger now — permit me " — he drew up the footstool with a booted foot and sat down on it close against her knee. " Dear Madame Thestrup, if you are strong enough to hear the news I can bring you — we must consider it good news, that is my view in any case."

His skin was rough and reddened by an open-air life and by drink and dissipation and he was beginning to be rather corpulent, but the Captain was still an extremely handsome man. Now that she looked down straight into his eyes it struck Dorthea that they actually reminded her of Thestrup's — they were full of fire, large and dark blue, with a glimmer of little yellow and brown specks sprinkled over the blue. Cold's eyes too were those of an elderly man — the whites were yellowish and bloodshot. Her Jörgen's had gone like this from excessive work; those of this much younger man from — well, from excess in other directions. But was there not perhaps a certain kinship in their natures — might not this be the reason why the relations between these two had so often been strained? If Thestrup's career had been abruptly checked while he was still in the full force of his young manhood, who knows where Jörgen's passionate nature might have led him?

Captain Cold was able to tell her that they had now traced the movements of the Sibilla band " and it appears to be out of the question that they can have had anything to do with your husband's fate." It could not even be described as a band at present, for the sons and all the younger members, except a daughter whose husband was in prison in Christiania, had moved northward before Christmas. The worst of them, Rasmus Tjuril, had been arrested somewhere in the Trondhjem district on a charge of stabbing at a fair. The two old ones had been lodging for several months at a summer dairy in Björgedal, but their behaviour appeared to have been irreproachable on the whole — the women and children had gone about begging, of course, and Sibilla had practised her customary arts. But her husband, Leivardo-Johan, who by the way had always been reputed a decent person, for a gypsy, was mortally sick with cancer: " it looks as if his case was beyond the reach of his spouse's famous remedies — well, well, no herb that grows can cure a man of death, as they say." Of course the whole company would be closely examined for any evidence that might contribute to the solution of the mystery. " But as I say, it appears that we may entirely disregard the possibility of your husband having been attacked by gypsies."

All the time he was speaking he held her cold hand in his big warm one, and Dorthea had no thought of withdrawing it. There was something consoling in sitting thus and allowing his eager sympathy to enfold her. He was the first person she had been able to talk to, to consult even, in her anxiety, as one who might be expected to possess greater insight and judgment. Thommesen was sick, Scharlach she did not care to trouble, knowing that the whole responsibility of the works rested on him — for Wagner was as unreliable as he was capable; he and many of the others would be sure to avail themselves of the general confusion to relax and waste time in gossip and drinking, if Scharlach did not keep them in order.

"You may be sure I am grateful to you for coming, Captain. You see, I am sitting here quite alone " — alas, she was more alone among all these people to whom she had to exhibit a calm countenance than if she had been in complete solitude. " If only I dared to share your opinion that it is a good sign that the gypsies — But can you imagine what *can* have happened to him? Both man and horse cannot have disappeared without leaving any trace."

Cold shook his head: " If this unfortunate fall of snow had not come and destroyed all tracks. But I shall have enquiries made, whether anything has been seen of the mare; for every child round about knows Reveille." He squeezed her fingers: " You must not lose heart yet, dear madam. And I am entirely at your service in anything you may wish me to do for you."

"You are very kind " — she withdrew her hand and rose to her feet. All the time her inmost thought had been that Thestrup would have disapproved if he had seen her sitting tête à tête like this with Captain Cold. But it had been a solace to have him to talk to.

He too had risen. " And my young friend Bertel? I'll tell you what, Madame Thestrup; would it not be a relief for you to be rid of one of the children, at any rate just now? Bertel could come home with me to Fenstad; it would be a kindness to my poor Carl to be given his company. And Claus is welcome too, if he cares to come — I assume that you may have some use for Vilhelm."

Dorthea blushed, was embarrassed when she felt it — and so blushed more deeply: " My dear Captain, I am touched by your thoughtfulness — but I cannot accept the offer, I am sure it would cause too much disturbance of your household — but I am grateful to you for your generosity."

A mocking smile passed over the Captain's face: " It would certainly cause no disturbance in my household. Jomfru Langseth would do her best to make the boys comfortable, and would be glad to do so. But if you do not wish to send them from home " — he shrugged his shoulders with a haughty little grimace.

" I am convinced she would do so; Jomfru Langseth is a kind person, I know. But I do not feel that I can part with any of my children at this time." Little Christen actually saved the situation, by setting up a miserable howl, and Dorthea hurried to the cradle. She bent over the child to conceal her confusion.

" Very well, my dear friend, I will take my leave. But remember, if I can serve you in any way, it will give me genuine pleasure." He kissed her hand in farewell. " I met Pastor Muus down by the church," he said as he was about to go. " He intended to pay you a visit later in the day, he said."

" Oh no! " Involuntarily she laid her hand on Cold's sleeve as though trying to stop something.

" How now? Would you rather be spared a visit from our worthy pastor? "

" Alas, my dear Captain — I fear I am in no state to receive the consolations of religion just now — it is no doubt my fault, but — Well, you know the pastor."

" Damme, I do — your pardon, madam. Yes, I know him."

" You understand, I could not bear to listen to his pious platitudes, when I am so full of anxiety — my baby here is not well either, and — Captain Cold, I keep thinking

of — thinking of the river. Of the lakes, the unsafe ice."
Her tears began to flow again.

The Captain said nothing.

" That would explain how both Thestrup and the mare
could disappear in this way. Answer me, Captain Cold,
do you think *that* is what happened? "

" It is a thought which naturally suggests itself," he
replied in a low tone, as though reluctantly. " But, Madame Thestrup, we must console ourselves by the reflection that the most obvious explanation often turns out to
be — not the right one."

Dorthea shook her head in despair: " O God! Can you
do nothing, nothing to comfort us? Cannot you think
what may have made it impossible for him to give any
sign — if he is alive? "

" One may think of so many things." Again he hesitated. " When we arrive at the issue it always proves to
be that which had eluded the thoughts of all. At present
no great length of time has elapsed."

" It was late on Tuesday evening that he rode from
here. Today we have Saturday."

" Yes, yes, dear madam. But do try nevertheless to
keep a good heart. In any case I will call at the parsonage
and say that you are unwell and unable to receive more
visitors. And that you will not be present at church
tomorrow."

" Yes. I shall be grateful if you will do that."

He seized her left hand, which was hanging loosely —
with the right she was rocking the cradle continually.
" Believe me," he begged her earnestly, " it cuts me to the
heart to see you so despondent. Would there were more
I could do for you — to prove in action my sympathy, my

friendship for a noble woman like you." Once more he
pressed his lips to her hand.

Dorthea was busily occupied with the baby. Alas, the
little thing had come to look quite peaked and shrunken
even since the day before. But she could not help being
annoyed with herself for blushing. Now of course Cold
would think she had joined the chorus of the virtuously
indignant who discussed the relations between him and
his housekeeper. That it was for this reason she was unwilling to send the boys to Fenstad — which in fact was
true in a way.

For one thing, the Captain's ménage was no concern of
other people — she had always maintained this when the
tattlers broached the subject. And Jomfru Langseth was
an affectionate and devoted stepmother to little Carl —
she had nursed him through diphtheria, becoming infected herself and nearly losing her life over it. But of
course what Jörgen said was true — it would have been
no more than right and proper if Cold had redeemed his
debt of gratitude by marrying her. Whatever might be
the truth about Cold's supposed — and bastard — noble
birth, *now* at any rate he was nothing but a discharged
officer, with no prospect of being able to resume his interrupted career. Presumably he would have to stay at Fenstad till the day of his death — if indeed he were not
compelled to give up the place long before that. A calamity which possibly the capable and industrious Marie
Langseth might be able to avert, if the man had sense
enough to make her Marie Cold.

But Dorthea had obeyed her first impulse — declin-
ing his well-meant offer to relieve her temporarily of the

care of two of her children — because she knew that
Thestrup would have disliked her sending the boys to
Fenstad. Not that she believed they would be exposed to
any injurious influence there. Cold no doubt drank fairly
hard when he was at home. But she knew that he concealed his excesses as well as he could from Carl's eyes,
and in the boy's presence he and the housekeeper preserved decorum. He loved his only — or only legitimate
— child with all his heart. And he would certainly have
shown the same regard for her sons. Claus would have
been overjoyed at the chance of escaping from home now
— he was ill at ease in the midst of all this sorrow and
anxiety. And Bertel, poor Bertel with his sensitive nature, he suffered from the same cause in a far more dangerous way. For him the visit to Fenstad would have been
beneficial and the company of a friend of his own age
would have been a relief in this sad time.

For both these lonely little boys had really found an
intense pleasure in each other's company during the six
months when Carl Cold had also been a pupil of Dabbelsteen. It was hard on Bertel that his father had put an end
to the arrangement. And his reason for doing so was that
it gave Captain Cold a pretext for the frequent visits to
Brovold which had aroused Jörgen's jealousy. That she
found the Captain's visits agreeable she could not deny —
it was true that there was in his manner towards women
a certain something, she would call it a kind of enthusiastic benevolence, a warm and cordial feeling for their
welfare, which no doubt justified the reputation he enjoyed of having been an impassioned votary of the sex.
True, she had also heard, from people who were acquainted with his life in Copenhagen and Rendsborg,

that so long as his wife was alive he had been an exemplary husband. It might be supposed too that anyone could have seen that the handsome Captain's gallantry towards her was of an entirely innocent nature: after all, she was a woman of mature age, happily married — and moreover an expectant mother just at the time when his visits were most frequent. But the fact was, Thestrup was altogether unamenable to reason on this point.

Everything about Johannes Cold seemed to irritate him. His mysterious origin, which in most people's eyes endowed the Captain's person with an attractive mystical nimbus — Jörgen would have it that Cold coquetted with it in a way that was undignified and unmanly. Rumour asserted that he was a natural son of Count St. Germain by a very exalted Danish lady, but that was obviously nonsense — the Count did not visit Denmark before 1760 or 61, and at that time Cold must have been five or six years old; it was not likely that the famous soldier brought a youngster with him in his baggage. Nor did he resemble the Count in the least — so said Sheriff Lunde, who had seen the Count several times both in Copenhagen and on the Trave. Moreover Cold himself had admitted to her in a moment of confidence — one evening when he was sitting here in the dusk waiting for Carl to have finished with Dabbelsteen — that he had no idea who were the authors of his existence. But he dimly remembered that before he was adopted by Judge Cold he had lived at a farm-house which was situated in a forest, and that he had been visited there at times by a beautiful lady, thickly veiled, who had kissed and hugged him. He believed she was his mother.

Dorthea had understood that the want of parents, whose

very names he did not know, and his ruminations as to
who he really was, had cast a shadow over Johannes Cold's
childhood and youth. It did not appear to her altogether
unnatural that he should have snatched eagerly at the idea
that his unknown father was St. Germain — he was a
great admirer of the Field-marshal's exploits. Cold himself had given early proof of being an unusually promising
engineer officer, an accomplished mathematician and
trainer of young cadets — he must have felt himself spir-
itually akin to the famous reformer of the dual monarchy's
military forces. Some casual remarks addressed to the
youth had then conveyed to him the idea that he was
actually St. Germain's natural son. His adoptive father
had informed him that he was destined for a military
career — though the lad was never told who had decided
this, it was reasonable to suppose that it was his mysterious
relative, of whose influence he had often been sensible.
For, talented as he had shown himself to be in his profession, it was nevertheless inconceivable that he should
have been given such rapid promotion without powerful
patronage; at the age of two-and-twenty he was already
a captain and had been entrusted with important work
in connection with the fortifications of Copenhagen. And
the same hidden forces must have favoured his audacious
wooing of the beautiful Helle Skeel. For although her
father might be considered a poor man and the young
Countess herself a rustic innocent who felt out of place
and unhappy in the dazzling social life of the capital, she
was well provided with relations who might easily have
found her a vastly more brilliant match than the young
officer of obscure origin — even though Cold at that time
still possessed a very tidy private fortune and excellent

prospects. That he was also somewhat given to dissipation was probably not taken too seriously in those circles — Cold had told her, by the way, that in his bachelor days he had not gone to any great length in that direction. Presumably he had tippled, gambled and frequented the minor lights of the theatre and the frail nymphs of the town because it was good tone to do so. But his work and his studies had simply left him very little time for amusements of that sort — as a young man he had not been nearly so wild as he was reputed to be. " And believe me, Madame Dorthea, at that time I cherished the deepest veneration for innocence. The purity of a young girl, the peace of mind of an honest woman were far too sacred for me to wish to cause a virtuous woman an instant's agitation." Only when his matrimonial felicity ended after scarcely four years with Fru Helle's death, and their newborn daughter followed her mother to the grave, did the change come over him. To deaden his pain, and his bitterness — for it filled his soul with a kind of bitterness that he was evidently to be denied any enjoyment of the sweets of family life — he plunged wildly into the life of pleasure which before his marriage he had only tasted in an occasional flutter of frivolity.

It ended in the unfortunate duel which put a stop to his military career and obliged him to bury himself and his ruined fortunes far away in " Norre." Whether the facts were as Cold liked to think — that the rigour with which he was treated was due to secret forces which had a grudge against him on account of his unknown origin — or, as Dorthea privately believed, the real reason was that the victim was closely related to the powerful Minister and that influential persons were deeply interested in the fair one who was the cause of the duel. Not to mention the fact that in the eyes of the world Johannes Cold must have appeared a favourite of fortune and on that account must have been envied by not a few. There were also those who said that the duellist had not been treated with any inhuman rigour, since he was permitted to remain in the King's dominions and to take up his residence at a farm which he had inherited from his adoptive father.

Dorthea had never denied, either to herself or to Thestrup, that she found Captain Cold sympathetic. His agreeable manner, as well as the way in which he had been the sport of capricious fortune, his loneliness with his charming motherless child on the melancholy neglected farm — though indeed Fenstad had been no more melancholy or neglected than other farms until Cold took up his residence there — all this was bound to make a direct appeal to her woman's heart. But then Jörgen had refused to be touched by it, and he had not liked her being friendly with the Captain.

But now, in this time of distress, when she had such need of a friend's advice, who else was there that she could consult? Of course it was quite clear to her that, had not Cold been situated as he was, expelled from his career, alone in a strange land, it was improbable that he would have courted her friendship so assiduously: she was a middle-aged matron of the bourgeoisie, he a Count's son, at least in his own imagination — and as he had once for all got it into his head that he was that, it mattered little whether it was true or not. In any case it was certain that in Copenhagen and Rendsborg he had moved in distinguished society. But now he was her friend, and she had no others.

She had been more than ready to acquiesce in Jörgen's disinclination to maintain any very active intercourse with the other gentlefolks of the neighbourhood; she recognized that her husband had neither time nor energy to spare for social distractions, so tirelessly was he devoted to the work which was his whole life. It had certainly been different when they were living at the ironworks; at that time one might have called Jörgen Thestrup a born society man. But then the Chamberlain had kept a tight rein on him — only when he came here was he able to work in conditions which permitted him to realize his own ideas. Besides, he had got on much better with the livelier inhabitants of the coast town — he did not mix nearly so well with the rather stolid natives of this inland district. So it happened that his relations were somewhat strained with several of their nearest neighbours. With their parish clergyman they were positively hostile — it began with a disagreement about sittings in church for the workmen at the glassworks. And in addition to that Pastor Muus was greatly scandalized when it came to his ears that Thestrup had sent a proposal to the Trading Company in Copenhagen for the provision of religious ministration for the foreign workmen in the Company's establishments in Norway — and that a Calvinist minister and a Papist priest were sent to Christiania year and year about, to remain in the town for some weeks. Finally a conflict arose between Muus and Thestrup concerning the boundary between the parsonage woods and the property of the glassworks — and then the fat was in the fire.

It was true that with Procurator Hauss of Vilberg Thestrup was on a relatively friendly footing; from time to time Thestrup employed him as his legal adviser. But he had no very high opinion of the man's moral worth. On the other hand he had a great esteem for his amiable wife and enjoyed a joke with her charming little girls.

For Captain Cold, then, he had a decided aversion, and he was jealous of him into the bargain.

And she had taken her husband's unsociability lightly — so long as she had him by her side. Her large family of children, the cares of her extensive household occupied her so fully that she had not even time to regret the absence of social intercourse. The management of the farm also fell upon her. Jörgen had imagined, when he insisted on farming Brovold himself, that he would be able to undertake this in addition to his other work, it would merely afford him a pleasant change. But even her dear Thestrup was not able to accomplish *everything*.

Now that she was obliged to face the possibility that she had been deprived of her only friend and support, she could only reflect with deep dejection that in truth he *had* been her only one. And that she had never had any refuge but her Jörgen.

Her brothers — ah, but they were no more than her half-brothers. And Caspar and Peter Andreas were so far away — besides, even if she had had them near her, would they have been such valuable helpers? Poor Peter Andreas had himself suffered the blows of fortune, and she was not sure that the accounts of Caspar's opulence were much to be relied on. Ole she was very fond of — there was something so genuinely kind about him, something which inspired confidence. But he was so young, and he belonged to a different class, whose ways and ideas were not those to which she had been brought up. With all the affection and respect she felt for Brother Ole — feelings which she could see the young man reciprocated — confidential relations between them were nevertheless out of the question.

It was in particular her mother's chameleon-like capacity for accommodating herself to the most various circumstances and social positions which gave Dorthea a hopeless feeling of estrangement in her relations with her. In reality the old lady had not sufficient respect for manners and customs and opinions, either in one class or the other, to make her care to be loyal to them any further than was compatible with her own plans and necessary for her welfare. But she had remained all through her life the same Elisabeth Andersdatter Hjort who did what she pleased and got what she wanted — whether she appeared in the part of a major's lady, a dean's lady or a sheriff's madam. Her daughter had learnt to regard this with serenity so long as she herself was married to a man who made her happy. But if the worst had happened — oh, then she shuddered with repugnance at the thought of having to meet her mother and accept her consolation or advice.

Sheriff Lunde — well, of course he was her stepfather, though she seldom thought of him in that capacity. He was a man of sense and an upright man. But Dorthea could not entirely avoid feeling a certain disdain for this peasant who had allowed himself to be caught by a much older woman, three times a widow, and a stranger in his social surroundings. She knew very well that in doing so Haagen Lunde had exposed himself to the criticism of his fellows — for it would have been more fitting if he had married a daughter from one of the other big farms in the dale. A prime reason for Dorthea's sympathy with her brother Ole was that he had chosen, in preference to all that his mother had proposed, to stay on his farm and marry the daughter of Lars Gullaug.

Nor had she anyone on Thestrup's side to whom she could turn in her difficulties. She had not seen Iver Thestrup's widow since they moved to Brovold, and both Jörgen's sisters had settled so far to the north that she had never met them or their husbands.

Such then was her solitary position — if she had been left alone with all her many children.

5

A WEEK's rain changed the fresh snow to grey slush, so that no one ventured out on the almost impassable roads unless it was absolutely necessary.

Dorthea felt worn out with inactivity, for the household duties with which she attempted to fill her days brought her but little satisfaction. She was not in a state to fix her attention on them, and when she tried to concentrate her thoughts on a piece of work she found herself thinking instead: what is the use of it — now? Soon they would have to go away from here, whither she did not know — she knew nothing about the future; as yet she had not been equal to making any plans. The only thing certain was that they could not stay here at Brovold.

She had lost all hope of seeing her husband alive. All she dared wish for was that his body might soon be found.

So that the last dying embers of an uncertainty which was now nothing but pain might be quenched. It would be a sort of consolation to be able to lay his mortal remains to rest in a befitting way, and to invest herself and her children with the mourning garments which proclaim that bleeding hearts have bowed to the irrevocable blow of fate.

In long sleepless nights she wept bitterly, tossing on her lonely couch. The cradle had been moved into the nursery — she had been obliged to resign little Christen to Johanne's care. With her nursing the poor little thing seemed to be a trifle better, though his stomach was still disturbed, he cried a great deal and was not putting on flesh. Dorthea listened to every sound from the next room. When Christen whimpered she was tempted to rush in and take him — it would have been a relief to put him to her hard and heated breasts, which ached so that she could not fall asleep, even when tired to death with grief and brooding. But her milk had turned to poison for the little one. Never again would she feel the sweet lips of an infant enclosing her nipples, the warm, light pressure of a baby's head in the bend of her arm. And never again would her beloved rest here by her side in the bed, never again, quivering with tender desire, would she be able to embrace his dear form, never again lie down to sleep securely locked in the arm of a faithful husband.

The skin under her eyes was scalded by her salt tears; it scaled off in dry shreds. She seemed not to recognize the ghastly, blotched and red-nosed face which she saw in her mirror each morning. It made little difference when she rubbed on cooling ointments and dabbed her face with almond powder.

It was vaguely in her thoughts that she ought no doubt to speak to Procurator Hauss — but she shrank so from taking this step, it would look as if she were in a hurry to establish her husband's death. But she could say to herself that when the Company's Christiania house came to the conclusion that Thestrup must be regarded as having disappeared they would immediately take steps to appoint a successor, at any rate a temporary one. She would have to try if possible to get some idea of her financial position, if the worst had happened.

She guessed that this position was far from brilliant. Thestrup had invested his not inconsiderable patrimony in some of the then newly established Norwegian factories which would never show a profit and finally languished away altogether. This was before she became acquainted with him; he had then already lost the greater part of his fortune. But nine years ago he had had another legacy from an aunt — the amount indeed was not very large, but it would have been good to have that money now. She was afraid however that he had been unfortunate in its investment, since he was so unwilling to talk to her about it.

In any case, when she married Jörgen Thestrup she quite understood that in all probability he would never be a rich man — though it was unlikely that he himself had given up his dreams of one day making a lucrative business of one or other of his undertakings. But he was far too ready to venture all the means at his disposal in new projects, preferably out of the common. Money was to Thestrup — she would not go so far as to say a plaything, but in any case it was like a handful of counters; it amused him to gamble with it. But what then? She was far from having any ambitions in the way of an elegant mode of life, any longing for indolent well-being or social pleasures and idleness. She had allowed the modest inheritance left her by Bisgaard to remain in her brother-in-law's, Julius Bisgaard's business; the interest on it afforded her at any rate sufficient pin-money. And for the rest she relied on Thestrup being always able to support her and the children whom it might please Heaven to give them, seeing how capable and industrious he was. She knew that she would be able to perform the duties entailed on her by marriage carefully and well. It would all go well. And it had gone well, she had been perfectly happy in her lot. While she could share it with her Thestrup.

But what life would be like without him — to this she had never given a thought. Jörgen was so healthy and full of vigour, their ages were so equal — she had taken it for granted that they would walk hand in hand till the evening of life. Nay, she had often dreamed with sweet sensibility of the old age which they would enjoy together, when the children were off their hands, had perhaps founded families of their own. Then they could retire to a modest but comfortable dwelling — a little house surrounded by a strip of garden, on the coast for choice. Possibly one of the girls would choose to stay with them and devote herself to the care of her aged parents. Or Bertel might prefer to remain unmarried, as he was not too strong.

She had experienced the state of widowhood once already. But it would be untrue to pretend that she had known a widow's sorrow. With gentle melancholy she had closed Bisgaard's eyes and followed him to the grave, but in her heart there burgeoned the hope of the new and happy life on which she would enter, as soon as a becoming time had elapsed after the old man's death. Never had it occurred to her that one day *she* would be left a sorrowing widow.

One day after dinner she got Vilhelm to drive her to Vilberg. But the Procurator could not tell her much more than she knew herself. That plans were on foot according to which the King would lease all the Norwegian glassworks to Counsellor Wexels, who in his turn intended to lease each one separately to men who would carry them on independently. But Thestrup had himself confided this to her — he had thought that now at last his dearest wish would be fulfilled and he would be able to work entirely according to his own devices, without that interference on the part of superiors which he had always detested. It appeared then that he had also discussed the matter with Hauss, but he had told the Procurator frankly that he had not the necessary capital to put into the undertaking; he would have to borrow the funds for the further improvements which he intended to introduce.

Dorthea sat in silence, depressed and preoccupied, as they drove home in the mild spring evening. In the west the dark tops of the pine forest were outlined against a clear space of golden sky — there was a prospect of dry fine weather. The afterglow of the sunset cast a gentle yellow light upon the bare, dark banks of clay; the snow had run off the slopes. But it was still lying grey and watery on the edge of the thickets which filled every fold in the banks through which a beck found its way down to the river, and the narrow strip of level ground along the river bank was still covered with snow.

These meadows were rich with lush grass and gaily coloured flowers in summer — ah, how lovely they were then, thought Dorthea. How delightful it had been to take a walk over these banks, with the children picking flowers and berries! In one of the little spruce copses by the side of a beck she would then collect her merry flock around the picnic baskets which their nurse Gunhild had packed. And once or twice every summer she had succeeded in getting Thestrup to tear himself away from his work and join them down by the river. On those occasions he always insisted that Gunhild should sing; she had such a fine voice. And if it was a song that Jörgen knew, he would join in — finally they all sang together.

She would have to part with Gunhild too, she supposed, if she were obliged to leave Brovold. That was a pity, for she was an unusually sensible and amiable girl and all the children were fond of her. Johanne on the other hand — poor thing, she was a fool and quite lost her head the moment she thought anyone of the male sex was taking notice of her. Actually Johanne was the only one of her maids for whom she did not care very much. But she would be obliged to take her with them; Christen could not do without his nurse.

The spring birds chirruped and sang everywhere in the thickets along the river. The chaffinch had come long ago, the robin and redwing too. The afterglow had faded, the banks loomed dark in the misty blue dusk, and against what light was left on the edge of the sky the spires of the forest stood out black as coal.

The murmur and rippling of running water filled the air, and through the gentle hum of spring the creaking of the carriage, the grating of the wheels against stones, the splashing and spurting from puddles as the horse plunged into them, jarred with a disagreeable noise. Dorthea was splashed all over with mud — wet right up to her face.

Between the black and white banks it looked as if the water of the river stood quite still; only if one fixed one's eyes on one of the dark yellow patches of foam or a drifting piece of ice could it be seen that a rapid current was running under the dark surface, which was of the colour of the opaque brown glass of the preserve-jars they made at the works. It was terrible to think that perhaps this dark ice-cold water had flowed over *his* lifeless body. She simply could not imagine it. And yet it was more probable than anything else — that he had gone through the ice and been drowned.

Vilhelm kept as quiet as his mother. Dorthea had asked him to drive her, chiefly because she hoped that perhaps a visit to Vilberg would cheer up the boy a little. " Mother Vilberg," as Karen Hauss liked to call herself, was such a warm, companionable creature, and Dorthea thought she had detected that Vilhelm had taken a fancy — no doubt the lad's first love — to the merry brunette Mathilde. While she was closeted with the Procurator Vilhelm had taken coffee with Madame Hauss and her daughters in the adjoining room. But even that rare treat, coffee, did not appear to have raised his spirits to any extent.

It was almost dark when they reached the works. The endless rows of wood stacks showed up dimly and gave off a sharp, acrid scent. A lad who passed them in the dark murmured a greeting. And as they drove round the corner of the works the glare of the furnace shone through the open door, throwing a curious light on the figures moving within.

Vilhelm jumped down and led the horse up the slope of Brovold.

"You had better take out the Junker and put him in. I'm sure Hans will be in bed by now. Afterwards you can come indoors and have something warm."

Out in the kitchen Dorthea found the jug of milk; it was half buried in a heap of cinders to keep it warm. She poured the milk over the cold porridge in the dish, took out the butter crock and some biscuits. Ragnhild was snoring away in her bed. As she was taking the candle from the long table Dorthea saw there was somebody in the bed besides the cook — a little boy. Frikk — how did she come to forget him! Of course, it was today he was to come here as herd-boy for the summer, and she had forgotten it. At any rate he ought to have had sweet porridge and gingerbread to welcome him. Well, it was to be hoped Ragnhild had seen that he was well looked after.

Alas, that arrangement too would be upset. Poor Ragnhild had been looking forward all the winter to having her boy here; he was not happy with his grandparents where he spent the winter. They were very poor, and his grandmother was an ill-natured woman of hasty temper; she was always after her daughter's bastard, abusing him, beating him and pulling his hair. Though little Frikk was such a bright and attractive child. But the old woman could not forgive Ragnhild for having yielded to a married man, nor the boy for having survived all his grandmother's attempts to make away with him in his mother's womb.

Ragnhild's home was distant a seven hours' walk in the forest, so she could hardly ever go there. And now Dorthea had promised her that Frikk should stay at Brovold for the winter as well. He could certainly make himself useful there and still have time to attend the glassworks school. With the brains the boy possessed he deserved an education, so that he could get on in the world. The question was, would the new people at Brovold agree to such an arrangement?

Vilhelm stood in front of the stove warming his hands when she came into the bedroom with the food.

" We must help ourselves from the dish, Ville; I did not bring any plates. You can sit in the armchair there. You were not long in the stable? "

" Hans woke up when I came." The boy looked shrunk and lost in his father's chair. The eldest son. His mother breathed a little sigh. They would feel the change, all the children, by degrees. But first it was Vilhelm's turn. Some of the family responsibility would inevitably fall on those narrow shoulders.

His nose seemed more prominent and pointed than ever — his face had grown thin. After the drive in the moist evening air his carroty hair was more ruffled than usual; even the little queue at the back was rebellious, as if it would wriggle out of its ribbon. And he had on the old skirted coat he wore every day — it had once been blue, but the front and the outer side of the sleeves were now so faded as to be almost grey, and it was tight across the chest and so short in the sleeves that a length of bony wrist projected from the cuffs.

" He's so sorry about Reveille. And about Father too, he says — but he's much more sorry about Reveille."

Dorthea nodded: " Hans is very fond of the horses. It is natural that they should be nearest his heart, as they are under his care. You might have put on your brown coat to go to Vilberg — you might have known you would meet Madame Hauss and the girls."

" In this weather — when one gets splashed right through one's greatcoat! I'm sure *they* don't care how I look! "

" But Vilhelm! They have always been so kind to you both — to you and Claus. I thought you and Mathilde were particularly good friends? "

The boy made a grimace: " Mathilde looks on me as a youngster just out of the nursery. Well, of course she's a good deal older than I."

" Naturally." Dorthea suppressed a smile. Mathilde Hauss was sixteen.

" And now they say she's to marry her cousin Nymoen of Aas."

" O-oh? Who says so? "

" Madame Hauss hinted as much. Well, anyhow I could have wished her something better than that scarecrow. Oh no, Mother, you needn't think people look on me as they used to, I've been made to feel that already. Because my prospects are not the same as they were " — his voice sank to a whisper — " when we had a father."

Oh, poor boy, his mother thought. Had he been dreaming that Mathilde Hauss would wait for him, the school-boy, till he was grown up and ready for her? It was comical of course — when it is a question of marriage a girl of sixteen is much, much older than a boy of fifteen.

Vilhelm would have found that out in any event. But that did not make it any less painful that he had come by this experience in such a way that he connected it with the change in his prospects resulting from his being fatherless.

" But it is no more than I have deserved! " His hands clutched the arms of the chair, he looked up into his mother's face, and Dorthea read the most intense despair in her son's features and voice. " For it is *my* fault! Mother must not think I don't see that — I am alone to blame. If Father is dead — if Mother and my brothers and sisters are forlorn and ruined — *I* am to blame, for *I* at any rate ought to have known better. Than to have gone off that day — without a thought — with such a jackanapes. And to drink my wits away in his company at Sandtangen." He let his head drop over the table and buried his face in his arms.

Dorthea had risen very quietly, and quietly she moved the empty dish to one side, lest he should knock against it as he lay weeping over the table. She laid a light and gentle hand on Vilhelm's neck under the oddly twisted little queue:

" My darling child — you must not think anything like that! My own Vilhelm, my own boy! " Cautiously she stroked and stroked his shaking shoulders, his narrow back. " Vilhelm, listen to your mother — what am *I* to say? For it was I who wished to keep Dabbelsteen another year — your father would have let him go last autumn, but it was I who kept him here. So it is far more my fault. It will never do to think such things, Vilhelm. It was very wrong of him to take himself off as he did, it was very wrong of you both to go with him — but no one could guess that it would lead to — "

She knew she ought to talk to him about the inscrutable will of Providence or something of that sort. But she was not equal to it — she who had actually avoided meeting Scharlach of late, for fear he might attempt such words of consolation as would seem natural to the pious old man. Instead she preferred to say:

" It was to be, Vilhelm. You know what the country people say — when a man's time has come. It must have been that." And she went on cautiously stroking the boy's hair and back, till little by little he grew calmer.

" That damned Dabbelsteen! " he whispered, clenching his teeth.

" Hush — hush — we shall not make things any better by swearing."

Vilhelm looked up:

" And so he might just as well have left last autumn! As things have turned out. For anyhow I shall have no use now for all that Latin and Greek — because you may be sure I see *that* well enough — we can't afford any more studies for me. When Mother goes to Christiania I shall go too; I will try to get something to do — as junior clerk in an office, or I might take commercial training. Mother's hands will be full in looking after the children. You must not be troubled with me too."

" But my dear, dear child." Dorthea looked down into the boy's thin face, so tearstained and so flushed with eagerness. His eyes glistened under the fair lashes which his tears had darkened and stuck together. " We do not yet know whether it will be necessary. But your father would have been pleased if he had seen you show such consideration. But as yet we do not know how things will turn out. And you know it was your father's wish that you should go to the university."

" Claus can go there — if we can afford it."

" You have more brains than Claus, you know."

" Oh, Claus has brains enough for a clergyman — or a lawyer."

" But your taste for natural science — your idea of being a doctor."

" Pooh — *now* I would much rather begin to earn money at once. So Mother won't have to keep me."

" Here, drink your tea! " Dorthea poured out a cup and handed it to him. " And eat some biscuits." Thank God, he had stopped crying for this time. And it must have eased his heart to confide his remorse to her — and his plans for the future.

Dorthea sank back in her own chair and swallowed some of the warming beverage. " Now you shall hear what I have been thinking — if we have to leave here. I must find some means of earning bread for so many mouths. A dame's school — I could quite well undertake to educate young children, you know that — as well as bigger girls in needlework and painting in water-colours. Well, that is what I had in mind. But if you went to the university, and we joined forces — we could keep a school for older children too."

" Yes — we could of course — " but he did not look particularly enthusiastic. Perhaps he had been relishing the idea of trying his own fortune in the world.

" But — you haven't eaten any biscuits, have you, Mother? " Vilhelm glanced shyly at the last two which lay forlorn in the dish.

" I don't want any — you can take them. But then you had better go upstairs to bed."

Vilhelm had said thanks and got up to go. " By the way," said his mother, " Frikk has come."

" Yes, he got here in the forenoon. He slept at Mid-forest last night and then he was given a lift by one of the sons who was riding down to the village this morning."

" It would be a sad thing if Ragnhild were to be disappointed. If the farm is to be taken over by new people — and they are peasants. Even if they keep Ragnhild on — or if she gets a place where she can have the boy with her — it is very doubtful whether they will allow him to have much schooling. Unfortunately it seems that the peasants find it hard to understand that poor people's children ought to have a proper education the same as others."

" That is just what Scharlach was saying. He told Ragnhild she had better let Frikk begin now in the works. Then he would be sure of his schooling and would get three rix-dollars a month. There will be many who will miss Manager Thestrup and Madame, Scharlach said " — and all at once the boy's tears were flowing again.

As Dorthea put her arm about his shoulder he flung himself into his mother's embrace, nearly making her cry out with the pain in her tense breasts. But she only pressed her son closer: " My good, my precious boy! "

For the first time in more than a week she knelt beside her bed and said her evening prayer. It was like an evil memory to reflect how bitterly she had implored Heaven that her beloved husband might be restored to her. But this evening hour with Vilhelm had consoled and cheered her so much — she could not neglect to pray that God would protect her children, great and small — and Frikk and the maids and all the good people from whom she was soon to part.

Thestrup — she dared no longer pray that he might come back to them. For she no longer believed him to be among the living.

6

Madame Dorthea postponed her contemplated journey to Christiania, waiting till the roads were in a better state. Lars could not spare any of the men on account of spring work on the farm, and so Vilhelm would have to drive her.

Six weeks had passed since Thestrup's disappearance. The little girls brought her bunches of short-stalked spring flowers — blue and yellow anemones, and the first tiny white ones tinted with red on buds and leaves. Their cheeks were warmly flushed by the fresh air and their hair was damp with perspiration under their hoods. Now and again their mother would notice as it were the shadow of a cloud passing over their faces — they had chanced to think of their father. But then it was gone again. Out of doors the meadow was green, the alder thickets along the river were hung with brownish-red buds — and there were new-born calves in the calfpen, and Elisabeth's sheep had twin lambs. How could they be expected to mourn?

Even Vilhelm — he seemed so serious and full of thought that Dorthea often regarded him with anxiety; but he was looking forward to the trip to town nevertheless, she could see. One evening he began to question her about the Bisgaard ladies with whom they were to stay in Christiania: " Wasn't there one of them who was very small, and lame? "

" Cecilie, yes — the youngest daughter. She is quite a cripple, poor thing — it is a great pity, for she had the most charming face. But can you really remember our going to visit them? You were no more than six."

" That was when we moved and came here. I remember quite well they had a big room with such funny chairs. Claus and I climbed up on them to see if we were as high as the backs — they were very straight with some scroll-work at the top. But then you came in and said we mustn't do that. They were bright red, with gilding."

" Fancy your remembering that! " Dorthea smiled. " Antonette's husband had the old furniture from Sol-holm — it is upholstered in pigskin, bright red and gilt — you are quite right. I believe my first husband envied his brother for getting it. I never thought it pretty — old-fashioned and gaudy. But it had been a long time in the family."

" It is after him I am named? " said Vilhelm thought-fully. " Dean Bisgaard, I mean."

" You know that is the custom. But I am sure you may be quite content to be called after Vilhelm Adolf Bisgaard. He was a man of some mark, a noble character."

" But he was much older than you, wasn't he? And the Fru Bisgaard whom we visited in Christiania, she was an old lady? "

" My sister-in-law Antonette was a good deal older than — well, her daughter Ottilie, Fru Meijersted, is about my age. Let me see — yes, she will be an old lady too soon. Like your mother, little Vilhelm."

" I can well remember them all three." Vilhelm paused for a moment." Mother — don't you think Fru Bisgaard might help me to get into their business if you spoke to her about it? "

There, it was out! So his mind was still running on his plans of starting something for himself. Aloud she said: " Antonette disposed of the business when her husband died. I don't know whether she has any say in it now. I have been told that she is not on the best of terms with the new owners. But of course we can think about it. And you would have to get up at four every morning, my friend, if you mean to learn shopkeeping."

" Doesn't Mother think I could manage that? " Vilhelm was evidently a little piqued.

Well, well. They would all have to do something. She too. Even if she continued to live in her sorrow — to carry it with her as a snail carries its shell, at once a home, a protection and a burden — it was not the same for the young. And thank God for that!

But there might be good reason for taking Vilhelm's idea into consideration in present circumstances. In replying to her enquiry whether she could take in Vilhelm and herself, Ottilie Meijersted had mentioned among other things that Laurids Winther and Christence would be leaving Copenhagen some time in the early summer; he had been given a living in the country not far from Viborg. Thus the plan that Vilhelm and Claus should live with them and go up for their matriculation in Denmark came to nothing.

This had been one of Jörgen's favourite projects. He himself had been sent to Copenhagen, to his aunt and her husband, when at last old Thestrup found his son's pranks more than he could bear. He and his cousin Laurids then became inseparable. And when Father Winther was given a living in his native town, Viborg, the two young men moved into a garret in Rigens-street, where they shared bed and board — they even had the only full-dress peruke available in common. It was not often in use — Jörgen had laughingly told his children how one day Cousin Laurids wished to adorn himself with it, as he had to wait on a distinguished personage with a petition, and they discovered that a mouse had been brought to bed in their wig!

But Claus and Vilhelm were not such madcaps as their father had been in his time. For that matter the problem might have been solved by their going to the grammar school in Christiania. Dorthea was very fond of Winther; she was also genuinely attached to Christence. But not many things in her life had given her such a surprise as the news that these two had married. After Bisgaard's death Christence had moved to her aunt's in Christiania — very sensibly, Dorthea thought. With such private means as she possessed her stepdaughter could live very comfortably and free from care, if she joined them. And the thought of marriage appeared to have no attraction for Christence;

where could she find more congenial surroundings than with Aunt Bisgaard and her cousins — two widows and a girl destined by nature to remain unmarried? However, Christence soon had enough of living with them — she was so peculiar and fantastical, as Antonette had also found out. After a year or so she moved to Copenhagen, though she had hardly any acquaintance in that city; she even had to hire a lodging with perfect strangers — the lady with whom she lived had been an acquaintance of her mother's, that was all. But in Copenhagen Christence had chanced to meet Laurids Winther again.

With the knowledge Dorthea possessed of her former step-daughter's peculiar temperament she was rather inclined to be sorry for Winther. But Thestrup thought it an excellent thing that his dear Laurids, who by then was really entitled to be called an elderly bachelor, had been brought safely into the haven of matrimony. And when in due course his cousin was able to announce that Christence had presented him with a daughter, he was positively jubilant. And in expounding his pet idea, that his two eldest sons should complete their education under Winther's guidance, he would often conclude playfully — who could tell, perhaps one of them would seal the bond of kinship and friendship by bringing home little Minona as his bride?

On the day when they smoked the hams and sides of bacon from the winter's salt-tubs it was the custom at Brovold that the wives of the workpeople should come up and smoke their meat and bacon at the same time. Dorthea's eyes were smarting and she was both tired and sooty when she came back from the brewhouse in the afternoon

and saw a carriage turn into the yard. She knew the horses
— they were Procurator Hauss's blacks with a white blaze.

With the thought which was always latent behind all
else in her head, Madame Dorthea hurried to meet the
visitors — instinctively she wiped her hands on her apron
as she went. But the Procurator had brought others besides his lady; in the back seat Dorthea discovered not only
Jomfru Sofie and little Mathilde but also the nephew —
whom Vilhelm had so unkindly alluded to as the scare-
.crow.

So their coming could not mean that they had found
him.

But when Procurator Hauss had climbed down from
the carriage he composed his face in such funereal lines
and took her hand in both his and held it with such tender
sympathy that for an instant she thought — had he come
after all to announce — ? Her heart sank in terror.

Mother Vilberg kissed her on both cheeks as she embraced her. But then she laughed quite gaily, when Dorthea remembered that she must look horribly untidy and
excused herself; and then the two matrons had a lively chat
about their household stores, while Dorthea conducted
her guests into the parlour.

Then she had to ask them to excuse her for a moment,
but Madame Hauss followed her into the bedroom almost
at once. She wanted to hear whether her dear Thea had
quite got over the troubles of weaning the baby — and the
darling little angel, was he thriving on the nurse's milk
— and poor Bertel, how was he doing now? She was not
at all like herself today, Mother Vilberg — so fussily and
overpoweringly cordial. She who was usually so pleasant
and natural.

But Dorthea could not bring herself to ask anything. She was afraid. There had been one thought of late against which she could not defend herself — when they did find him, he would certainly be very much changed. She wished of course with all her soul that his mortal remains might be laid to rest in consecrated ground — she wished too that there might be an end of this terrible uncertainty which no longer left room for hope. But she had an unspeakable horror of seeing that body which had been so dear to her — when dissolution had already set its mark on it.

" Well, little children, little troubles — if they are well, that is," sighed Madame Hauss; " and big children, big troubles. Though I ought to be grateful for my girls, *they* have not brought me any troubles to speak of *yet* in any case. But it will be strange to part with little Mathilde. Though she will not be going so very far from us either."

" Oh! What is that you say — is Mathilde leaving you! " Dorthea smiled. " That must mean she is going to be married? "

" I thought perhaps you had heard a little bird sing of it. Yes, now it is all settled between her and Esten Nymoen." Madame Hauss wiped away a tear or two. " He is such a good fellow, you know he is, Thea; if there is any man to whom I can safely confide my little one, it is Esten. But it gives one a strange feeling for all that. Well, her position will be secure." Madame Hauss shed another tear.

" It will indeed." Dorthea was holding a clean neckerchief in her hands — now she put it down: " But then I must congratulate you, dear Karen! " She embraced the other and gave her a kiss. " You will have a son-in-law whom you know and esteem. And Tilken will still be so near to you that you will be able to see her as often as you wish. I am sure you ought to be glad." He *is* a very presentable person, and Aas is an excellent farm; no doubt there is money in the stocking too. But I could have wished that nice girl Mathilde a bridegroom who was better-looking and not so dull and taciturn. And who had not such a dreadful lisp. Aloud she said: " But we must be prepared to see our girls leave the nest. And I am sure we should not wish anything else. It might be pleasant enough to be allowed to keep them and to have them about us in our old age. But when we are no more — and they have grown into old maids. You must remember that, Karen."

" Yes. Yes. That is very true, Thea. And I am *very* pleased about it, you may be sure."

" And that is what you came to tell me — indeed it was very kind of you! Now I will be ready in a moment. I must go and congratulate my little friend Tilken — and we will drink a glass to the health of the engaged couple."

" Wait a moment! " Madame Hauss had got up; her whole affected manner seemed to have dropped from her. The fine brown eyes were serious and distressed. " I have something to say to you — that was why I came in here. I thought perhaps you would rather hear it before Hauss speaks to you.

" He was in Christiania last week. Come, sit down here, my dear." She laid her great soft hand on Dorthea's arm. " And so he talked to them at the office — well, he went to see the Counsellor too. You must not take it that we do not feel the deepest sympathy for you, for the blow that has fallen on you and the children." Mother Vilberg's pleasant round face showed an expression of intense embarrassment. " But the hope that Thestrup may be found alive — ah, Dorthea, even you must have abandoned that long ago! The Counsellor is obliged to çonsider the future of the works. Well, Martin also took the opportunity of pleading your cause — about your pension, you understand. It appears that Thestrup had come to no agreement upon the amount — but the Counsellor will prove generous, he promised Martin that."

" I understand. The Counsellor has consulted your husband about a successor to Thestrup at the works here? "

" There must be someone to manage them, you see." Madame Hauss was twisting her handkerchief. " Ah, Dorthea, I do feel for you, you must never doubt that. But it is no use burying one's head in the sand."

" I am not doing that, my dear Karen. For a good while I have seen clearly that we shall have to leave here. Does your husband know who is to be appointed to succeed Thestrup? "

" It will be Esten," said Karen Hauss with some embarrassment. " You know, he is used to buying and selling and calculations, and then he has taken the Danish degree in law. But Hauss intends to supervise himself. You see, if the works are to be leased out, he may consider — "

Dorthea nodded. " That was Jörgen's idea too. He thought it might turn out a very good business, if he was able to realize his plans."

" Yes, in fact I think it was your late husband who gave him the idea."

My late husband. It was the first time anyone had referred to Jörgen in these terms. My late husband, she had said on the rare occasions when she mentioned Dean Bisgaard. But now it meant Jörgen Thestrup as well. She had a sudden and terrible desire to laugh as the thought struck her — what would the meeting between her two husbands in heaven be like — the frail old man, small and bent and white with study and sickness, and her hale and weatherbeaten Jörgen who would come storming in, armed and in riding-boots, fresh from his last fatal ride? Ah God, but one did not enter the abodes of the blest in the body and clothes in which one walked here below. In Heaven there shall be neither marrying nor giving in marriage. It was brought home to her with glaring clearness that now she was again a widow, and that this time it was for ever.

" You are not angry with us? " said Madame Hauss pleadingly. She dabbed her handkerchief to her eyes. " Someone *had* to take over the post in any case. You say yourself that you had had it in your mind. I thought at any rate you would rather *I* broke it to you, instead of hearing it from Martin. When you were quite unprepared."

" Thank you for thinking of it. It was — it was — very considerate of you, my dear Karen. You have always been a good friend to me." Dorthea kissed her on the cheek. " Believe me, I understand."

She went over to the mirror, arranged her fichu over her shoulders and fastened it with her Sunday brooch of rose-diamonds. " You may be sure," she said, facing her own image in the glass, " I understand quite well how natural it is that the Procurator should have taken steps to prevent anyone forestalling him. And Mathilde! " She

turned round to Karen Hauss. " Never should I have imagined — that that child should be my successor here at
Brovold! "

It was only natural that the Procurator had taken steps
to prevent anyone forestalling him — she repeated the
words to herself as she sat alone on the sofa in her parlour.
She had seen the Vilberg party off in their carriage and had
returned to the room to clear away her best glasses herself.

She gave a little shiver. It was as though the walls of the
room had preserved some of the chills of winter, though
the sun shone on it in the forenoon and she had the shutters taken down every day now, so that the damp air
should not harm the furniture.

It was in brown lacquer, with gilding on the carved
scalloping and scroll-work; Jörgen had had it made by a
joiner in Trondhjem on the model of some chairs his
brother had brought home from abroad. The furniture
took up very little room in this big parlour; there were
only two console mirrors, and Jörgen had always talked
of having another made to fit the space between the middle
windows — as late as last Christmas he mentioned it again.
She would try to take these things with her; *they* at all
events should not be put up to auction. But of course she
would have to hold an auction before moving. The Procurator had said Mathilde and Nymoen might buy many
of her things. But it would certainly pay her much better
to dispose of them by auction.

She could not in decency allow the two big portraits of
her mother and her first husband to be auctioned — her
mother lived far too near, it would be reported at Lunde,
and besides, the people round about would criticize her

for doing it. But God knew, she had little desire to drag them about with her. She might ask if Brother Ole would like to have them — though what should he want with the portrait of the Major?

Vilhelm and Claus had gone shooting with Hans Wagner; they were not likely to be home before early morning. Dorthea felt she was utterly alone, as she sat, shivering a little, in the great empty room.

Nothing else was to be expected. It is an ill wind that blows good to no man — she must often have quoted the proverb herself. But now it was Thestrup's death that had opened up the prospect of a livelihood for Esten Nymoen. Not that he could be called badly off by any means — but both he and the Procurator would no doubt be glad of a little extra butter on their bread. Provided they succeeded in carrying on the glassworks at a profit. If she should hear one day that they were not doing so, she was not the one who would grieve for it — such is the nature of the human heart. Though the step they had taken was perfectly fair and aboveboard. And though she knew that the old working staff would suffer for it, if from inexperience and failure to grasp the nature of the business the new men ruined what her husband had built up. And that such a result would make Thestrup turn in his grave.

But of course it would also recoil on herself — it would be incumbent on the works to provide her pension. The Counsellor would certainly see to this in drawing up the lease. And that being so, why, she could only wish them success. Every man for himself, that was another old saying. Alas — it is a depressing occupation, learning to know oneself, as Bisgaard used to say.

The pungent smell of smoke still hung about her

clothes, reminding her that she had no time to sit here and ruminate. Dorthea got up and replaced the decanter and glasses on the tray. Yes, she had been round with Karen, Mathilde and the future son-in-law — they had inspected the house, which as a matter of fact they knew quite well before, with fresh interest, and while Hauss paid a visit to the works office they had been through the outhouses. Nymoen informed her that he intended to farm Brovold himself; his brother-in-law was to take a lease of Aas.

Dorthea was satisfied that she had kept her countenance the whole time. Ah yes, she had always known that it is not given to many people to be particularly noble and lofty in their sentiments. It had been easy for her in all the years she was married to her Jörgen. So long as virtue and duty and inclination are in unison there is no difficulty. Now she could feel how weak and ignoble impulses were continually springing up in her soul — impulses which she would have to suppress if she was to act as she ought.

The afterglow was gilding the sky to the northward and sent a warm yellow light into the bedroom, where Dorthea sat giving Rikke her gruel, while Bertel undressed beside the great four-post bed. She had the little girl with her at night now, so as not to sleep entirely alone, and tonight Bertel too was to sleep here, as his brothers were in the forest.

On this side of the house it was not so easy to hear the arrival of visitors — she did not always notice the barking of the dogs. So she was taken quite by surprise when the door opened and Ole Haagensen appeared.

Why, how well he is looking, she thought, cheered at

the sight of him — the evening light fell full on his
healthy, red-cheeked face and well-knit figure. To think
that on this of all evenings she should have a visit from
one who really did belong to her!

" But my dear Ole — are you in these parts! It's a
pleasure to see you! "

" I am so, ay. And you're thinking I might have come
sooner, eh? The way things are here."

" Your father has been here — twice. But sit down, sit
down — Bertel, run and ask Ragnhild to bring up a jug
of beer for Uncle Ole. No, if the Sheriff has not been
able to do anything, how should you? But what news of
Mamma? "

" Oh ay. Well, you see, she's been that busy, bustling
about for the feast and all. Anyway, I've just come from
Christiania, I have. Brought a load of stuff. No no, you
shouldn't have given yourself any bother for me."

" Nonsense, Ole, you must have something to eat. Let
me see, you like a cup of tea, don't you? I remember that."
He had removed his cap and placed it on the floor between
his feet; Dorthea could not resist stroking his shoulder
lightly as she passed with the table-cloth over her arm.
She knew very well that her little caresses always made him
bashful; he was a real peasant in that way. And indeed
their mother had scarcely contributed to change his ideas
on that point; she had never been lavish of caresses with
her children. But it was so tempting to pass her hand over
the light yellow hair which fell about his handsome youthful face almost to the collar of his coat. " Poached eggs, I
know you're fond of them; yes, of course you shall have
poached eggs! " Mamma had always been so stingy with
her eggs.

The dear, handsome boy! It was no use trying to worm things out of him; if he had anything to say to her he would have to bring it out in his own good time. So she only asked about the roads, were they dry now and in a good state? And had he had any company on the way? She knew the farmers liked to arrange it so that they travelled in a body when they had to go to the capital. But Ole laughed at her — no, this time the country people were far too busy to be roving along the roads; he had had to make the journey alone. " But I was thinking I'd take my groomsmen with me when I go off home."

" Vilhelm and Claus? But my dear Ole, nobody from here can attend a wedding now. What do you think people would say if I allowed my sons from a house of mourning, as this is, to take part in a big festivity with dancing and all sorts of merriment? "

" You mean *you* can't come either? " asked her brother in a low voice.

Dorthea shook her head.

" Ah but, you know, they don't *have* to dance, if that's it — if they'd just ride to church with us and sit at table with their uncle. That couldn't make folks talk, could it now? Well, I don't see why you can't come too and help your mother with the kitchen and that — they can't say that's any more than right. Besides, I haven't any kinsfolk on Mother's side but you and your young 'uns."

" Ah, Ole, you can understand how glad I should have been. The boys have looked forward to this festivity, immensely. And it was my most heartfelt wish to be present when you lead your Ingeborg to the altar, to invoke the blessing of Heaven upon your union. She is so pretty, Dabbelsteen told me."

Instantly the young peasant's face took on an expression of embarrassment. "*I* am quite pleased with my choice — she's kind and she's useful, is Ömbjör. It's too bad you can't be there; you had a right to know your sister-in-law, I should say! "

" Yes, you may well say that, Ole. All the more as it seems very uncertain when I shall have an opportunity of making your bride's acquaintance, if it cannot be this spring. Before long we shall have to leave Brovold, as you can understand."

" Ay, maybe you will. But I thought you needn't be worrying about that — just yet. Seeing they haven't found your husband. I don't see they can put in anybody in Thestrup's place till it's proved he's dead. So they'll have to leave you alone here meantime? "

Ragnhild came in with the food and Dorthea poured a dram from the hour-glass bottle: " There, Ole, help yourself, you must be hungry and tired too. Go on, my dear — " and while seeing that her brother had all he wanted she told him about the Procurator's visit.

The tot of spirit had made the young man a trifle less reserved. He expressed his opinion of Hauss with some warmth, denouncing his conduct as shabby.

" Ah, my dear brother — it is quite natural that the man should have an eye to his own interest and that of his future son-in-law. Even if his behaviour betrays a certain, what shall I call it, lack of delicacy — which after all no one, I think, suspected to be one of his qualities. But in any case I shall never agree to let him take over the stock of cattle, and such of the furniture and effects that I shall be obliged to part with — at a valuation made by his puppets, or men who have reason to fear him. Do not you agree that I ought rather to hold an auction before we leave here? "

It had not occurred to either of them that Bertel might be lying awake — till suddenly the sound of his crying reached them from the great bed. Dorthea hurried across: " Hush, hush, my own angel, you must not wake Rikke — my dear child! " She took him on her lap, seated herself on the edge of the bed, and with his arms flung round his mother's waist Bertel hid his head in her ample skirts, where the sound of his sobbing was almost stifled.

Ole Haagensen put down his knife and fork. With an air of placid sympathy he sat waiting till the boy's crying had quieted down. " Look you here, Dorthea — I was thinking you'd do best to have a talk with Father, get his advice about it all. I don't believe you can hold an auction at Bruvoll straight away, you see — you must first get a paper from the authorities to say your husband has been missing such and such a time, so it must be presumed lawful to dispose of his estate. Ay, you'll have a monstrous heap of papers to get, I'm afraid. Far too much for you to bother with alone. But you know, Father'll be glad to help you the best he can. Whether you want him to come here or you come to Lunde."

" Oh no, Mother! " Bertel set up a loud wailing. " Oh, you mustn't do that."

" *What* mustn't I do, my boy? Kind Sheriff Lunde, he is my stepfather — he has only our welfare at heart, you must see that."

" Mustn't get paper about it," sobbed the boy. " No, Mother, you mustn't do that. For that will make it *certain* — that our father is dead! "

Dorthea pressed Bertel to her: " Ah, my child! Do you

think your father would have let us remain so long in anxious uncertainty if he were still alive? He would never have had the heart to do that."

Bertel rubbed the tears from his face with the back of his hand, looked up at his mother with a strangely penetrating glance: " No. No, Father could never do *that*," he said, as though there were something reassuring in the thought.

A suspicion seized Dorthea. Had the child heard gossip, conjectures? That rumours were in circulation — must be in circulation — regarding the manager's mysterious disappearance — what inconceivable lethargy had prevented her from thinking of this before? She stroked Bertel's tear-stained cheeks affectionately: " My big, sensible boy! We must try to bear it as well as we can, Bertel! The good God will not desert the fatherless, you may be sure of that — " she said, rather weakly. Ah, she herself was far from feeling reconciled to God's inscrutable providence.

" Are they going to sell everything — the Junker and Snerla and Old Brownie and all the other horses — and — and everything here — and Elisabeth's sheep and my calf and all? "

" There there there, my child! You hear what Uncle Ole says — it won't be either today or tomorrow." She turned to her brother, who had been listening to the boy's complaint with an expression of bashful sympathy:

" Well you see, Ole — don't think I do not appreciate the offers of assistance your father has made me when he was here. But Mamma — her health is not what it has been, from what he told me. And now she has been busy for a long time with preparations for the wedding. I am not sure that it would be opportune for me to burden her with my troubles."

" Mother — Scharlach says it's such a pity you don't seek consolation with your mother — as she lives no farther off than two days' journey from here."

Yes — people who knew nothing of the relations between her and her mother were bound to think so. That she was a strange daughter not to hasten to throw herself into her mother's arms with her affliction. Although might one not with equal justice have expected the mother to hurry to the side of her afflicted daughter? But she said gently: " Bertel, I do not wish to scold you this evening. But you must not be always interrupting your uncle and mother." She arranged the pillows under the boy's head, tucked up him and Rikke well and drew the curtains of the bed: " Now try to go to sleep."

She went back to the table, was just going to ask Ole to help himself to the fourth poached egg — he had to be pressed for each one.

" Mother is your mother too, you know that, Dorthea," said Ole in a hushed voice.

His sister nodded. For a moment she paused, feeling almost put to shame. " Yes, Ole, you are right. But help yourself — oh yes, to please me, do take the last egg! "

Next morning she accompanied her brother to the open cartshed and watched his struggles to get the portraits of their mother and her first husband strapped on to the load — Ole had accepted them gladly. She would really have liked to give him Feierfax too — the dog knew him and got on with him; he had borrowed him more than once for a bitch he owned. The good faithful animal would

be quite at home at Lunde. But she had seen what a
shock it gave Vilhelm and Claus when she suggested it
that morning at breakfast — they were very fond of the
dog, and they did a little shooting when they had a chance.
So the question of Feierfax's future was postponed for the
time being. But she was now able to form a clearer idea
of what it must mean to the children to say good-bye to
their four-legged friends — and indeed to the whole of
their dear old home and everything, living or dead, that
belonged to it. She was almost glad that Ole had reminded
her of the many formalities that would have to be gone
through before the break-up could become a reality. It
was anyhow a postponement.

" And Dabbelsteen," asked Madame Dorthea, " has no
one heard any more of him? "

" They were saying at church the other day, he's got
across to Sweden — Gunder Ophus and his son Elland
heard that tale when they were in town a few weeks since."

A couple of nights after leaving Lunde in the spring
Dabbelsteen had been caught by the sheriff of his home
parish in the act of attempting — very clumsily, by the
way — to release the murderess Margit Klokkhaugen,
who was under detention in a cottage on the sheriff's farm,
as the lock-up consisted of a single room, and in that her
stepfather and accomplice was confined. After that, when
Sheriff Byrsting lodged the unfortunate student in the
same lock-up, there were such scenes between the two men
that Byrsting, who did not care to handcuff a son of Madame Dabbelsteen, moved him to a bedroom in his house.
From there he had had no difficulty in escaping. But how
the poor fellow had managed after that, penniless and
insufficiently clad, during the sharp thaw that had set in

just then, rendering the roads along the valley almost impassable — was indeed a riddle. Even though his mother, the curate's widow, was feared by the common people of many parishes round on account of the occult gifts she was reputed to possess.

To get across into Sweden was a very common desire among Norwegian lawbreakers.

" Ole — will you answer me frankly like a true brother? Have you heard anyone hint that Thestrup's disappearance might — well, that it might be interpreted otherwise than as an accident? "

Ole Haagensen had finished rearranging and strapping his load. He turned to his sister and together they made their way back to the house.

" That he went through a lead in the ice, that's what they think, most all of them. Ay, some folks guess he was robbed and killed by that band that was seen about here last winter, or by gypsies maybe. But you know, there's always a deal of idle talk when a thing like this happens."

" I see. And what is it they are saying, Ole? " she asked in a low voice.

He hesitated: " Oh — it's just one thing and another."

" Do they say that Thestrup has also — gone to Sweden? "

" No, I've never heard that," said Ole decisively.

Ole had to buy some glass to take home, and Dorthea went with him down to the warehouse.

In the dimly lighted room between the office and the warehouse a ray of sunshine came through the only window, gilding the dust that hung thick in the air and lighting up Vilhelm's tuft of red hair as he stood at his high desk — he had to have a box to stand on in order to reach it comfortably. With his quill stuck behind his ear — it had left traces of ink on his cheek and on his hair — and with a sort of apron of sacking tied round him he seemed equipped to assist the old clerk, Thommesen, either in the warehouse or in the office. It was a fortnight already since he had taken up these duties.

The reason was that Pastor Muus had paid a call accompanied by his wife. With genuine goodwill they had made an offer to Madame Thestrup that her boys should come to the parsonage and take lessons from the tutor there. Of course the parson's children were much younger, the eldest girl was of the same age as Bertel, but that need not stand in the way. However, both Vilhelm and Claus protested against her entertaining this well-intentioned offer — honestly, said Vilhelm, he thought he was at least as well grounded in all grammar-school subjects as that Student Mikkelsen, God help him! And Claus Hartvig informed her that he had met Captain Cold, and that the latter had offered to give him lessons in mathematics and drawing until his mother had made other arrangements.

The end of it was that Vilhelm was allowed to start in the glassworks, while Claus rode to Fenstad three times a week, and according to his own account learnt more from the Captain in a morning than Dabbelsteen had been able to instil into him in three months. Well, mathematics had not been Dabbelsteen's forte exactly, and she had no doubt the Captain was more capable as a teacher of French. The weakly Bertel could not possibly walk the whole long way to the parsonage and back by himself — though the real reason for Dorthea's unwillingness to send him there alone was that she did not know what tricks the "little mice," the Pastor's naughty and much spoilt little girls, might play upon him. So now she gave Bertel part of his lessons and let Claus give him the rest. And found to her surprise that Claus acquitted himself of the task far better than Vilhelm had done when he tried. In his dreamy, not to say drawling, way Claus seemed to exercise a beneficent influence on Bertel's sensitive, easily agitated nature, and even to stimulate in him a thirst for knowledge and an interest in his lessons.

Old Thommesen came out of the office and met Madame Thestrup and Ole Haagensen with a cordial greeting. He went on to enlarge with much enthusiasm on Vilhelm's ability.

"How glad I am to hear you say that, my dear Thommesen! But now I have come to ask you to give Vilhelm Adolf a week's holiday. My brother here is very desirous of seeing his two nephews among the groomsmen at his approaching wedding, and, as you may suppose, I should not like to refuse him. For there is no one in these parts except my boys to represent his mother's family on this occasion."

She studied the old man's face closely as she spoke, but he showed no surprise; on the contrary, it was only right and proper, he said.

Dorthea had made up her mind to let the boys attend the wedding. Everyone was at liberty to see that Jörgen Thestrup's family had no reason to fear any disgraceful revelations. It had not occurred to her till now that her secluded attitude since the abandonment of the search might be interpreted as a desire to conceal something besides her tears.

Now, before the boys went away, she would assume

widow's weeds and dress the girls and Bertel in mourning. And now she would have to do what she had shrunk from hitherto — write to Thestrup's relatives and her own to announce the tragic event.

What a strange thing, it struck her as she thought of her sister-in-law Maren Sabine — she too had experienced the same soul-devouring expectation, the same slow death of hope, her husband's disappearance without a trace. Though in Bina's case it must have seemed less unnatural; every time a sailor sets out on a long voyage there is a possibility that he may never return. Moreover Jörgen was of opinion that the relations between Iver Thestrup and his wife were not of the best, even though she did mourn his loss. In any case she had not married again.

The sisters had not seen their brother Jörgen for many years. Fredrikke, Fru Devle, was tied to her bedroom armchair in the Captain's house in Namdal; Karen Anna, Madame Jæger, had not been so far south as Trondhjem even for years. So it was hardly to be expected that they would be crushed by the news — although undoubtedly they would be strangely impressed on learning that their second brother had also disappeared, swallowed up by an element which seemed determined to retain its prey and its secrets.

7

DORTHEA decided that this afternoon she would drive to
Fenstad and fetch Claus Hartvig. The weather was so
warm, and now the poor boy had had to walk there and
back every day for more than a week. All the same Lars
put on a rather sour face when she said she would want
one of the horses today, and she had to put up with Old
Brownie.

As a sort of pretext for the visit she put all her potatoes
into a basket. Jomfru Langseth had said one day last winter that she would like to try a few beds of this new kind,
and Dorthea had then promised her a few dozen seed
potatoes. But now she was welcome to the whole lot.
Dorthea had thought of sowing and planting her garden
as usual — it was one of Jörgen's hobbies that they ought

to do something to spread a knowledge of gardening among the peasants of the neighbourhood. Dorthea could not help smiling: Jörgen had never had time to attend to the matter, so it was another of the things he wanted her to do. And indeed she would have been glad that those who came after her at Brovold should find a well-stocked kitchen-garden, with potato beds and the rest. But as it was to be the Nymoens — Mathilde could easily get seed potatoes either from Aas or from her mother.

Bertel's dejected little face brightened up when she proposed that he might go with her and see his friend Carl.

She had to leave the pace to Brownie. At a slow jog-trot they went along the rough forest road. It was quite cool here under the trees, which were still hung with catkins, giving out a fresh and powerful scent. In a hollow Bertel discovered with delight that there was still a little dirty snow lying under the spruces on the northern slope.

" Look — look, Mother, a magpie — isn't she pretty! " He seemed to know all the birds they saw or heard. He could mimic them too — he whistled like the blackbird up on the ridge and cooed to the wood-pigeons in the thicket.

" Bless my heart, where did you learn all this about birds, little Bertel? "

The boy blushed. " From Vilhelm," he said, hesitating. And in an even lower tone " — and from Dabbelsteen."

They came out on the level ground. Really the situation of Fenstad was beautiful, at the foot of a dark wooded knoll. The fields sloped down to a stretch of bog, in which bright little tarns mirrored the blue sky. The houses were now old-fashioned and out of repair; their shingle roofs and unpainted walls were grey with weather and moisture — some of the outhouses were only roofed with turf. But at one time it must have been an imposing place, in the taste of bygone days. And surely it could be made so again — if only its owner were at all interested in agriculture. And had means enough to repair the buildings.

" Here, Bertel, can you take the reins? " She knew how pleased the child would be if he were allowed to drive as they came up to the house. But she made a show of having enough to do with brushing off dust and horsehair, re-tying her hat-ribbons and smoothing out her gloves.

But there was no sign of life in the yard as they swung in through the gate. Only a black and white cat sat by the cellar entrance licking its tail. The sun beat down, littered straw and chips of wood showed yellow on the grass, and not so much as a dog broke the afternoon stillness. In some surprise Dorthea descended from the carriage, took Bertel by the hand and approached the main building.

All the doors in the balcony stood wide open. On entering the hall Dorthea heard short sharp exclamations and a metallic clinking from within the parlour. Astonished so that she forgot to knock, she paused in the doorway.

Claus flung himself forward, with flashing foil he made a lunge at the Captain, whose back was turned to her. The hair hung in wild disorder about the boy's scarlet, perspiring face, his shirt bagged loosely over his belt. With sullen fury he made lunge after lunge which the other parried — the dust whirled about the fencers in the great sunny room, which was almost empty of furniture.

Then with a sharp ring the slender weapon flew out of

Claus Hartvig's hand. The boy stood agape, panting for breath, and Cold lowered his foil and burst into a peal of laughter: " Bravo, bravissimo, my son — you're getting on! Upon my soul, this time you were — " and he wiped his face with the sleeve of his shirt.

" Bravo! " shrilled Carl's childish voice exultingly. Dorthea discovered him, squatting cross-legged on the red-lacquered tea-table by the middle window. In the sun-shine which poured in behind him the child's fair curls stood out like a transparent golden cloud round his little head. " Bravo, papa! You won after all."

The Captain laughed more uproariously than ever: " Papa won after all — do you hear that, Claus! Gad, you're getting to be a respectable opponent, boy! If only you'd learn to keep cool — but, my faith, you have the right style — now then, pick up your foil."

At that moment Claus caught sight of the couple in the doorway. He gave a cry of dismay: " Mother — is Mother here! "

Cold turned round sharply. He too was very red in the face and his shirt was drenched under the armpits. He saluted with his foil: " Madame Thestrup — what a de-lightful surprise! " His voice was still bubbling with laughter. " And Bertel! Hurrah, Carl, a visitor for you, my boy! Well, madame — you must excuse our toilet — we have just had a fencing lesson. A relaxation after mathematics."

He was not actually intoxicated, but not altogether sober either. On the big table by the far wall was a medley of school-books, maps, writing materials and drawings, surrounding a spirit decanter, glasses, tankards and cups. Claus had been drinking brandy too; Dorthea could smell it as she helped him on with his jacket. With repeated excuses Cold also put on his waistcoat and coat.

Carl had jumped down from his table — he and Bertel now stood surveying each other in bashful silence. Through Claus they had constantly exchanged messages, had even sent little notes, and now that they were face to face they found not a word to say.

"But do be seated, dear Madame Thestrup — Claus — " Captain Cold looked about him helplessly. Claus moved a violin-case and a French horn from the nearest armchair and wiped its stamped leather seat with his hand. "Will you not loosen your mantle? — ah, the warm weather has come now in all conscience — oh, Claus, see if you can find her, what's her name, the maid."

The parlour was a dreadful sight — the floor befouled with spittle and the tramping of muddy boots, litter and confusion everywhere. Clothes hanging over the chairs, folios and fishing-tackle on the floor, clay pipes, twine, knives and powder-flasks on the window-ledges. The scanty furniture was oldfashioned and clumsy — Cold had picked it up at auctions, and much of it came from peasants' houses. The red tea-table with its china top and a clavichord in a gilt lacquered case evinced however the gentility of their owner. And while the grey log walls were otherwise merely adorned, or rather encumbered, with fowling-pieces, hunting-knives, elks' heads whose points supported fishing-lines, travelling flasks and shooting bags, there hung on the fireplace wall above the sofa a life-size portrait of Cold's deceased wife.

It was a remarkably lifelike portrait, painted the year before her marriage to him. Waving fair hair, adorned with a wreath of wild flowers, set off the young lady's delicate complexion; her pale blue eyes bore witness to her birth, in their air of gentleness and composure. The fine shoulders and bosom were half veiled by a fichu of white lace, greyish blue satin enclosed the slender bust and fell in rich folds over the rounded hips. And indeed the Juel who had painted her was according to Cold one of the most esteemed portrait-painters in Copenhagen.

Dorthea had never been able to regard without emotion this memorial of Johannes Cold's lost happiness, which surveyed so significantly his present unhappy state. But on the few previous occasions when she had been here the parlour had always been clean and tidy. Dorthea began to wonder — did it mean another temporary withdrawal on the part of Marie Langseth? Although, if anything of that sort had been in sight, Cold would hardly have thought of inviting the two boys to visit Fenstad this spring.

Claus Hartvig came in again, accompanied by a young female in peasant dress who stopped in the doorway and looked about as though bewildered.

" Oh, you, see and tidy things up a little — no, stop a moment. I should offer you some refreshment, ma'am, but I don't know — beer, I'm afraid, is all the house affords for the moment, and you do not care for beer, I remember."

" I beg you, Captain Cold, no trouble for my sake. We have only come to fetch Claus. But I wished also to thank you personally for your kindness in giving him lessons, it is so extraordinarily obliging of you."

" Oh, pray — it has been a gratification to myself." He laughed. " There is something of the schoolmaster in many an old officer, as you know. And he is really a delightful pupil, your Claus — he has a turn for the very subjects of which I can teach him most."

"He will now have to be absent for a time, however — " and she told him of her brother's approaching wedding.

The Captain pitched a pile of books and papers into the open drawer of the table. It was one of those massive old tables with bulbous legs that were to be seen in many of the farmhouses. Meanwhile the girl collected tankards and cups, and Claus replaced the decanter and glasses in the sideboard. Poor boy, how he is sweating, thought Dorthea between laughter and annoyance — fencing lessons and dram-drinking on an afternoon like this were enough to make anyone perspire.

"A wedding, eh? — so you're going to a wedding, Claus! It's a pity though, for we were getting on so well with our studies" — he laughed again and clapped his hand to his mouth to stifle a hiccup. Then he winked at Claus: "What do you say, shall we initiate madame votre mère into our plans? Well, you must know — " at that moment the maid came in with a pewter jug and three pewter tankards. "Ah yes, here comes the beer."

Dorthea accepted the mug and sipped at it. Cold emptied his, but Claus affected to be unaware that the Captain had filled one for him. The education he was getting here at Fenstad was evidently more comprehensive than she had supposed — even if he was really being well grounded in mathematics he seemed to be acquiring other less profitable arts.

"Well, Madame Thestrup, as you see, we live on a war footing in this house. My housekeeper is rather unwell, she is keeping her bed just now."

" How tiresome — you see, I had also something for Jomfru Langseth. I hope her indisposition is nothing serious."

" God knows! " Captain Cold passed his hand over his flushed forehead. " To tell the truth, since you happened to come here today " — he seemed to be nervous and hesitating — " I could almost wish that you would take a look at her, Madame Dorthea — that old ass, Mother Fallet, is drunk day and night."

Dorthea intercepted the glance her young son shot at the Captain. She was acquainted with that expression of disapproval from one man to another, when one of them forgets himself and reveals to a female something which in the opinion of the other is unmentionable in the presence of her sex. Instinctively she looked round, but the two little boys had vanished.

" I should be very glad to do so, if you think I could be of any service to your excellent housekeeper."

Claus looked as if he wished to raise some objection, but the Captain cut the ground from under his feet: " See if you can get the dogs in, will you? " He threw the boy their collars and leashes. " I believe I heard them outside the fence just now. They got out this morning — that bitch Belinde, I shall have to shoot her — I can't cure her of hunting sheep and she draws the others on. Everything goes wrong here," he burst out. " I'm inclined to — pardon me, madame, I will lead the way."

A stairway, narrow as a henroost and very rickety, led from the hall into the open gallery outside the first floor: " This is where she fell," explained Cold; " it was slippery after the rain — I am afraid she hurt herself pretty badly."

With her eyebrows raised in incredulity Dorthea surveyed the Captain. His irrelevant burst of laughter, the worried look that settled on his flushed face whenever for a moment he stopped babbling and smiling, betrayed the fact that he was not only half intoxicated, but also a prey to anxiety.

Johannes Cold conducted her through a big room which contained looms and spinning-wheels; hanks of various kinds of wool hung from the beams of the roof. Without knocking he opened the door of an attic. " This is Madame Thestrup, Marie, who has come to see you — how are you now — a little better, eh? "

The loathsome stench of impure blood confirmed Dorthea's suspicions. The bed stood in the shadow under the sloping roof, but Marie Langseth's face showed almost as yellow as the hair which protruded in a tangle from under her nightcap. Her nose was sharp, her face had fallen in under the eyes and at the temples, making Dorthea think with horror: But surely this is a dying woman.

On the floor beside Marie's bed sat little Margrethe hushing her rag dolls to sleep on a footstool where she had made their beds.

" How are you feeling? " repeated Cold, assuming a fatuous air of sympathy. " A little better, are you not, Marie? At any rate you have no fever? — you are not so hot." Jomfru Langseth was shivering with throes of cold.

Dorthea flared up: " Oh, do go away, Cold, I can do nothing with you standing there staring — and get the child away — take your brat with you and go."

The big man still hung there, looking miserably chap-fallen.

" Oh, Cold, Cold, I'm in such pain — I think I'm going

to die," wailed Jomfru Langseth. She wriggled her head
into the pillows. " Do go — oh, can't you go, Cold —
when Madame Thestrup asks you to? "

" Yes, go now, Captain Cold, and take Margrethe with
you."

" Eh bien — come along, my lamb — you and I seem to
be de trop " — with a silly laugh the Captain lifted the
little girl on his arm. The child seemed quite at home
there; she abandoned herself trustfully to her father.
" Your dolls — don't you think your dolls ought to come
too, Grethe? " With a touch of fellow-feeling Dorthea
noted that Cold had some affection for his illegitimate
child.

As soon as the two had disappeared Dorthea flung aside
the bedclothes. The stench of putrid blood was absolutely
stifling. She cautiously felt the sick woman's abdomen —
it was swollen, the thighs and calves were puffy and had a
whitish gloss: " But, my God, Marie, this is puerperal
fever, my girl."

" I knew it." Jomfru Langseth moaned; a shudder ran
through her frame. Dorthea made haste to cover her up
again. " It was so far gone this time that — oh, Jesus, I'm
in such pain." Her voice was worn quite thin with suffering.

" And no one to nurse you but that slovenly old Mother
Fallet? "

" I didn't want people to poke their noses into — anyhow Marthe Fallet doesn't talk."

" Yes but, my good woman — you are risking your life
in this way."

" What does that matter, I was going to say. Oh no,
never mind " — the sick woman whimpered, almost in

tears; " God forgive me, I didn't mean that — I daren't die either, seeing what my life has been — I should go straight into Hell."

" O-oh." Dorthea had taken off her outdoor things; she rolled up her sleeves to the elbow. " Have you any sort of apron here, Marie — in that chest of drawers? Good. Bless me, my dear Marie, the Almighty knows very well it's not so easy for a lonely female, especially when it's one's housemate that — " Meanwhile she was cudgelling her brains to remember what treatment Doctor Lange-mack had given her when she had puerperal fever after the birth of Bertel. They had rubbed her with dry wool-len cloths when the perspiration was excessive — but she was sure Jomfru Langseth was in no state to endure such drastic methods. And while these shivering fits continued she dared not leave the door of the weaving room open — though this dreadfully close atmosphere must aggravate the patient's headache.

" Will you tell me where I can find clean sheets? — and then I must fetch water. At any rate I can change your bedclothes and then you'll feel a little better."

" Change — isn't that dangerous? Marthe says — "

" Old wives' talk! " Dorthea tried to talk cheerfully and with authority. In her heart she was in the utmost alarm — what in the world was she to do? Send for Mads Olsen and get him to bleed the patient? — although pre-sumably she had already lost a great quantity of blood, this was probably the only way to relieve the pressure in her poor swollen legs.

Jomfru Langseth muttered something to the effect that she did not think there was any clean linen — the Cap-tain's house was ill provided in that way. She had often

had to use her own. Yes, that was her chest there by the
door. She spoke all the time in a pitiful whimpering
tone.

Underneath a mass of chemises, nightgowns and neck-
cloths, rolls of ticking and neatly folded blankets Dorthea
found at last a pile of huckaback towels and a set of fine
embroidered linen sheets. She spread them out over a
couple of chairs, to air them.

" My bridal sheets," sobbed the sick woman. " Heavens, they were to have been my bridal sheets. I little
thought when I was making them that I should end like
this."

" But they can be washed, Marie, and they'll be as good
as ever. We must use what we have; you cannot lie in
this horrible mess any longer."

One has to do what one can. Dorthea drew out the
article from under the bed and hid it under her apron.
" Oh no, Madame Thestrup, that is no work for you."

" It looks as if there was no one else to do it." Bridling
with disgust Madame Dorthea passed out of the room.

Cold stood leaning over the balcony. He turned as if to
ask a question, but on seeing that the lady was carrying an
object under her apron he flushed deeply and looked aside
as she went by.

In the empty kitchen Marthe Fallet sat huddled up in
the chimney corner. She was fast asleep and snoring.
Dorthea gave the horrible old mass of obesity a shake.
" Here, go and empty this. And then fetch me a couple
of pails of water."

Marthe replied gruffly that the lad was down in the
field.

" Then you'll have to carry them up yourself."

The biggest kettle was half full of water and it was at least lukewarm. Dorthea swung it over the fire and added more fuel. As she squatted down and blew up the dying embers she suddenly recalled having seen a fire on the fringe of the woods, black figures hovering round it, a woman blowing into the smoke of green wood — and then there came back to her the name that had been so often in her mind of late. She was said to be in the next parish at this very time.

As she returned to the balcony with the bucket of hot water in her hand she ran into the Captain: " Tell me, Cold, do you know if Sibilla is still at Aaserud? So that we can get hold of her? "

" Sibilla — ? " he looked at her in sheer horror.

" Yes. This is really an occasion for testing the truth of all that is said about her miraculous powers of healing."

" I did not think " — the man was visibly worried. " You have always expressed yourself so slightingly of — of the superstitions of the common people."

" Yes, but in this case I really do not know what other resource we have. Our midwife " — Dorthea gave a little shudder — " I'm sure she has tortured to death as many women as she has helped in the course of years. I had her myself *once,* and that was enough! Olsen, the surgeon, can draw a tooth and open a vein — not much more " — she shrugged her shoulders. " As to getting a doctor from Christiania, that would take at least two days with the best of luck, and by then it may be too late. If you ride off to Aaserud at once and she is still there, you may bring her back with you by midnight. And believe me, there is no time to lose."

" Is it as bad as all that? "

" I am going home, as soon as I have done what I can for Marie — I must fetch a number of things and leave word that I shall be staying here tonight. Then Carl can come with us, and Grethe — it is too bad that Marie has had the child in bed with her all this time, ill as she is. Now do as I ask you, Captain Cold — for you are the cause of the poor girl's sufferings."

He was evidently on the point of returning a rough answer, but Dorthea took up the bucket and went in.

She had done what she could for the sick woman with the means at her disposal and had asked the girl whom she had seen downstairs to sit with Jomfru Langseth till she came back. Then she hurried down to get the children.

Claus Hartvig arrived with a bag full of books which he wanted to stow in the back of the gig. " But what has Mother got here? "

The basket of potatoes. " Just let it be, my boy." The sight of it gave her a quite unwarranted emotion. Those wretched seed potatoes which were to be of no use to anybody assumed in her agitated imagination an image of all the good things — health and well-being, order and security, even peace of mind, happiness and life itself, which were hazarded by inordinate human passions. She picked up her skirts and ran across the yard, calling aloud in a scream that saved her from bursting into tears: " Bertel — Carl, Bertel — Carl — where are you? "

At last she came across the boys. On the slope below the smithy they were lying on their stomachs over the little spring which bubbled up here. When they heard that Carl was to go to Brovold and sleep there that night they jumped and clapped their hands with delight. Dorthea made them come with her and got them seated at the back of the gig.

Grethe was nowhere to be found. Well, it could not be helped.

She left the reins to Claus. The boy did not utter a syllable all the way, he was evidently put out and sorry for himself. But his mother was in no mood to help him. Though it was really not his fault that he was mixed up in this painful and unsavoury business. But Dorthea was so angry — and at the same time not merely angry: the necessity of doing something had in a way taken her thoughts off her own sorrows and troubles and thus brought her relief — her very annoyance was beneficent after the last weeks of enervating helplessness.

So mother and son drove homeward in profound silence.

The sun had gone down behind the hills as she drove back to Fenstad. A white mist rose from the bog and drifted over the low-lying fields. Down in the south-west the young moon shed its honey-coloured light on the edge of the forest.

There was now a crowd of people in the kitchen. The fire was burning briskly, and Marthe Fallet was actually wide awake, as far as that was possible for her; she was holding forth to the people of the farm about this and that — or, as Dorthea guessed, about the housekeeper's condition. Dorthea drove them out, kindly but firmly, and set about the preparation of her medicines.

It was fairly dark up in Jomfru Langseth's room — it had only one little window in the gable. But Dorthea saw at once that the sick woman was now in a high fever.

She lay with a dark glint in her open eyes, groaning and mumbling at intervals. The girl whom Dorthea had set to attend on her explained that the fever had returned shortly after Madame Thestrup had left. The girl — her name was Magnille — appeared to have some sense. Dorthea could see that she was the only person in the house from whom she could expect much assistance.

Little Margrethe had found her way back into her mother's bed. She was sleeping sweetly in that clammy, evil-smelling nest. "Here, Magnille — I think you could make her up a bed in the biggest of the wool-baskets in the weaving-room." Dorthea carefully lifted out the child.

Marie Langseth seemed not to be aware of what was being done to her. Dorthea managed to get some dry towels underneath the patient and placed two big pillows under her swollen legs. Then she laid the heated bags of herbs on the sick woman's abdomen and thighs, raised her slightly and tried to give her the warm tea of milfoil and sage. Some of it ran down her chin, but she managed to swallow a good deal.

Magnille had come in and was following Dorthea's actions attentively. "You must see that she is well covered right up to the throat. And whenever this cloth that I have put on her forehead gets too warm you must dip it in cold water — you may also moisten her lips with a wet cloth, but she must not have anything cold to drink, however piteously she may beg for it. You may then give her a little of this tea, it purifies the blood. But wrap up the tea-pot again each time, to keep it warm. Best to get her to perspire very freely, so that the unhealthy humours may be expelled as quickly as possible. But her head must not get too hot — that may be positively dangerous to her reason, you understand."

Dorthea opened the door of the weaving-room wide to get rid of some of the noisome air that filled the sick-room. She tried the windows, but it seemed there was not a single one in the whole house that was contrived to open. So she had to throw open the door to the balcony.

She then had to rig up a kind of screen around the child's basket, to keep off the draught. Dear me, thought Dorthea compassionately, here she was lying asleep like little Moses in his ark of bulrushes. And, like Moses, little Grethe had to submit to being called a foundling by his own mother — no, by the way, she remembered with a touch of shame, we were told in scripture that Moses was really the son of the Hebrew woman and not of Pharaoh's daughter. The other version was only an irreverent fancy that had occurred to her when she was a child — one Sunday in church when her stepfather had held forth at unconscionable length on the finding of Moses in the river Nile, little Dorthe had had the idea of asking him when they came home how we could tell that he was not really the son of the Egyptian princess? But of course she never dared to do so.

Let us see, it was three years last Christmas since Jomfru Langseth's stay in Christiania. Poor wee thing, then she was a year older than Rikke. But at any rate both " Aunt Marie," as she called her mother, and the Captain were fond of the child.

Dorthea could not refrain from taking a look at the fabric Jomfru Langseth had on her loom. Woollen stuff — the light was not good enough for her to see the pattern properly, but it seemed to be charming, and the stuff was

so firm and even to the feel. Again Madame Thestrup
had that sense of profound and sorrowful indignation —
why *must* people make such a mess of their lives! A good-
looking, capable girl — of decent family too, it was said
— takes the situation of housekeeper to a widower still
in his most ardent age. She must know what is likely to
happen in such cases — and how improbable it is that he
will marry her. And here lies poor little Margrethe, and
in there her mother, in danger of a hideously painful
death.

She had gone out on the balcony for a mouthful of
fresh air. Just as well to look in at the wash-house while
she was about it, to see if Marthe had done as she was told
and put the dirty linen in water.

As Madame Dorthea returned over the dewy grass the
Captain happened to ride into the yard. She stopped on
the doorstep and waited for him. " You are alone — was
the woman not at Aaserud? "

" No, the bird had flown. But they promised to send
word. So she will come right enough. Since you seem to
think that evil is to be cured by evil." As Dorthea said
nothing he asked in a rather more civil tone: " And your
patient — how goes it with her? "

" Not well, Captain Cold."

He shuffled his feet slightly. " You must not think,
Madame Thestrup — you must not doubt my gratitude.
Upon my honour, you *must* believe me when I say that if
anything should happen to Marie, I should be deeply
grieved."

" Then I am afraid " — she shrugged her shoulders —
" that you must prepare yourself to *be* deeply grieved,
Captain Cold."

He affected to misapprehend her gesture. "You are cold, Dorthea, you're shivering with cold." That was true, as it happened; her clothes were wet through as the result of her nursing efforts. "Come indoors, come into the parlour and have something to warm you."

The atmosphere in the parlour was cosy between its sunbaked log walls, but there was a close smell of dust and stale tobacco-smoke. By night the room seemed even more cheerless and poor — the naked gaping windows let in the pale light from outside deadened by the dim coarse glass of the panes. The objects on the walls and in the corners were now mere darker masses of the dusk. But over the fireplace the bright figure of the portrait glimmered almost like a ghost.

The Captain made a dash for the sideboard, but Dorthea stopped him: "Thank you, *I* will not take any brandy. And *you* can put off drinking at any rate till I have gone upstairs."

He stopped short, with a little laugh of embarrassment: "As your ladyship pleases — but will you at least accept what my poor house affords?" He waved his hand in the direction of the china-topped table under the middle window, on which food was set out, then drew a couple of the old stamped leather chairs up to it. "Do me the honour?"

All at once Dorthea discovered how hungry she was. She had had so much to do in the short time she was at Brovold that she had simply forgotten to take any food. So she seated herself and took a hunk of pease-bread and a slice of sausage. The Captain poured out a glass from the pewter flagon, but the beer was now quite flat, and lukewarm too.

" Of course I understand quite well — you are offended on behalf of your sex, if I may be permitted to say so! " He made a grimace as he washed down a mouthful with a draught of the stale beer. " Il y a un esprit de corps aussi entre les femmes, n'est-ce pas? And now you are enraged on Marie's behalf with the wicked libertine — oh yes, you are; God bless my merry heart, I know what thoughts you have of me. Well well, devil take me, nobody can ask that you should see these things from the man's side."

" My good Captain, you need not swear so persistently — I understand."

. " No, upon my soul and salvation, you do not, Dorthea! You are a very lovely lady, your friendship has been to me an oasis in this desert — an oasis which, I'm bound to say, I have not been permitted to visit too often! Nay, be assured that I respect you highly, dearest friend — I esteem you, am sincerely devoted to you. But, God in Heaven, how should you know what it means to be exiled, banished to a desert such as this, condemned to languish away years of one's life, a man's best years, in this frightful place? "

Dorthea looked around the gloomy room:

" Even this place need not have been *so* frightful, Captain Cold — if you had tried to make something out of your property. You well know how many of our Norwegian officers manage their farms in a model fashion, setting an example to the generality of plain countrymen. And Fenstad is in reality a very valuable property, it might be — "

" Fenstad! " he interrupted her, and there was a hiss in his voice as of hatred. " Do you know what Fen means in

Old Norse? I have it from Student Dabbelsteen — it means swamp, bog, quagmire."

" I dare say, it sounds quite likely — here you have the great bog just below you. But by ditching a good part of it might be turned into excellent meadow land."

He burst out laughing:

" I'll *give* you the whole of Fenstad — in fee simple — if you'll sleep with me a single night."

" *That* is a good deal more than *I* can afford to give for an estate," said Madame Thestrup dryly.

As Cold remained silent, obviously somewhat abashed, she continued quietly:

" It appears to me that according to that valuation Marie Langseth has acquired a right to Fenstad long ere this."

In spite of the dusk she noticed that he was regarding her with a penetrating look:

" No, dear friend — there are *many* things which so wise. a woman as yourself can never understand." He laughed bitterly. " Which Marie does understand — no doubt just because she is *not* wise."

" Dear me, Cold, there is certainly nothing difficult about it. A housekeeper who is engaged to undertake a part of the duties of a mistress of the house. Until the domestic atmosphere results in her undertaking more of them than was bargained for in the original agreement. As everyone knows, this happens every day."

" Ah, there we have it, there we have it! " He laughed again — that unpleasant grating laugh. " *That* is all you understand, Dorthea. You have always been secure — have insisted on a clear understanding as to your position. Your first husband, the reverend old man into whose

arms you were flung when you were but a half-blown
maid. Did you not resign yourself, did you not stifle every
wayward thought, every fickle desire, rather than risk
your peace of mind and your clear conscience? It was
fine, it was worthy of admiration — but how should it
enable you to understand the hearts which are not capable of rising to such heights of resignation? And your
second spouse — you loved him, I know — loved each of
his peculiarities, against which a weaker woman would
have rebelled — no, no, do not be angry with me, it is not
my intention to try to disparage Thestrup; he had good,
nay, great qualities, he was honour itself. And I doubt
not he was a charming husband in all the main attributes
of the term " — again Cold's disagreeable laugh. " You
took the rough with the smooth — his restless temperament, his exacting and experimenting nature, the un-
sociable and laborious life in difficult financial circumstances to which he condemned you. You renounced
the triumphs which are the right of a beautiful woman
of sense; nay, you even renounced the preservation of
your beauty — I respect you for it, my wise and good
friend! But what does your strong and resolute soul
know of the pangs of despair, of uncertainty, of hopes
deceived? "

" *Those* at any rate I should have learnt to know by
now," she whispered in bitter protest.

" You have learnt to know them, yes, but you have already given them their congé. Soon you will have forgotten them — oh no, Dorthea, you need not be angry.
It is not your lost husband that you will forget, I know
that. But if you are to be honest — you no longer believe
that Thestrup is alive. You have liberated your soul of

uncertainty long ere this and have dedicated your heart as a temple to the memory of a deceased beloved."

" But Cold! " she exclaimed hotly, " what else can I do? How could I still cherish the faintest hope — "

" No! But thereby you have freed yourself from the worst of torments — the death-struggle of hope! "

Overwhelmed by the truth of his words Dorthea stared at Cold — in the dim light she could not make out the expression of his face at all clearly.

" Marie, you see — " he laughed as before. " At times I am sure she has hoped that it would end in my marrying her in spite of all. Well yes, sometimes I have hoped the same. For I am very fond of the good girl — God knows I am."

" Oh yes? " said Dorthea expectantly.

" But I shall not do it! If her recovery depended on my going up and saying to her, Marie, we are to be married — I tell you, I could not do it! *I cannot* condemn myself to pass all the rest of my life in this damned, detestable place of exile. Never have I been able to abandon the hope of being allowed to return to Denmark, to the army — to the work to which I am attached body and soul! And Marie would not believe me if I came and made her such a proposal. For Marie is not to be fooled by me — she knows me even better than I know myself.

" But of *this* I can assure you nevertheless — I take God to witness, Dorthea — *I* have had no hand in this — horrible affair. You *must* believe me, never to all eternity would I have advised Marie to rid herself of her unborn child — but I did not even know that she was in this condition again."

Dorthea was too overcome by abhorrence to be able to

get out a word. Although she was well aware that she had
known it all the time.

" No — you must believe me. In this frightful business — I have had no share."

The terrible agitation in his voice recalled her to calm
consideration. Actually, was it not illogical that people
— herself included — should feel it as something more
horrible to destroy an embryo than to murder a child
already born? But every woman who had not a heart of
stone pitied an infanticide. And shrank in horror at the
thought of the other thing.

" Yes but, Cold — she was in her fifth month — how
could you avoid noticing? "

" I noticed that she was depressed, melancholy. But I
thought she understood what my recent lively correspond-
ence with friends in Copenhagen might imply — and that
it was on that account. And when I informed her the
other day that Carl's uncle had offered the boy a home at
his place, Aunsögaard, she was in sheer despair."

" Carl — are you sending little Carl away? "

" I hope to be able to make the journey with him
myself — some time in the course of the summer. Yes,
Dorthea! " She saw that the whole man was trembling
with emotion. " Thanks to our beloved Crown Prince's
zealous solicitude for the army — not to mention that of
the Prince of Hesse. You know, I dare say, that these
fertile brains hatch out a new plan for the reform and
improvement — or otherwise — of the army every day of
the year, so to speak. But now amongst other things the
artillery corps is to be strengthened — the number of
officers increased. And, wonder of wonders, the Crown
Prince seems actually to consider it desirable to appoint

an occasional Dane among all the Holsteiners and Germans. And my former brother-in-law, Count Chresten Skeel, and several of my old brother officers — above all my paternal well-wisher, General Roepsdorff — have put in a word for me. I am to be graciously permitted to enter the service again. Yes, yes, yes. I wonder if you can realize what it means to a man, after years of hellish inactivity, to return to all that makes life worth living! "

" Yes, Cold, *that* I can understand. I ought indeed to know the passion with which an active man regards his calling. Ah, I could congratulate you with all my heart, dear friend. But for the thought of that unhappy Marie Langseth. For that she can accompany you to Denmark is perhaps out of the question? "

" Out of the question — even if my prospects were more secure than they are." He was silent for a moment. " Three years ago I could still have made her a suitable dowry. And an acceptable, an excellent person was ready to marry her. To tell the truth, I had expected her to seize the chance with both hands. I was aware that she really entertained deeper feelings for myself. But you know how stories of this kind usually end — when a decent and capable girl had been for some time — deputy wife — of a man to whom she cannot expect to be married. Sooner or later there comes a day when she prefers his valet, his coachman, his barber — and an honest and regular position. Rather than her dubious situation with a man who perhaps has a greater personal attraction for her."

Madame Dorthea nodded. Of course, that was how it usually turned out — and as a rule it was best so. A brief pain, and when that was past a toilsome life in an honourable condition, often ending in calm and contentment.

"But Marie would not have it. And *now* I cannot do much for her. I shall need all my resources — God knows they are wretched enough — and even the support of my friends, in order to rehabilitate myself at home."

Dorthea sat in silence for a while. The summer night was now at its darkest; she looked aside, out of the window, and said very quietly:

"I know of course, Captain Cold, that an officer cannot marry whom he will; he must have the approval of his superiors. But you have not yet entered the service, I think? Would it be a hindrance to your future career if you *were* married when you came to Denmark? Since you have just assured me of the warmth of your feelings towards her. And she is a girl of great intelligence — so capable that in any circumstances she would be a true helpmate to her partner in marriage. With engaging manners, and very well brought-up, for her condition. And, I doubt not, in a high degree susceptible of improvement."

"What you say is true enough, Dorthea. But I cannot begin life over again, after all these wasted years, with such a millstone round my neck as a — a marriage of inclination with my housekeeper would be. I must have my hands free. If not for my own sake, for Carl's."

"Then it would almost be a fortunate thing, for Marie in any case, if she were never to rise again from her sickbed," said Dorthea bitterly.

"Dorthea! You must not say such a thing!" whispered Cold, and she guessed that she had given expression to an idea which he dared not acknowledge to himself.

" Well, but what is to become of her when you have gone away? "

" There must be some way out of it," he said in a low voice.

" And little Margrethe? — she is your child as well as hers."

" We shall have to find some way out," he repeated as before.

In the weaving-room Dorthea found an old armchair which she moved inside the door of Marie's bedroom. This enabled her to breathe a slightly better air in the intervals of attending to the patient, and at the same time to keep an eye on Grethe.

Sometimes Marie Langseth lay with open eyes, at other times she kept them closed; but she was never fully conscious, and she moaned almost incessantly. Occasionally she muttered something, but it was not easy to catch what she was saying. Dorthea did not think any change in her condition could be expected for the present — she herself dozed off now and again, as she sat there in her chair.

And then she was wrenched out of her light slumber by loud, heart-rending cries of pain from the sickbed. When Dorthea rushed up and bent over her, Jomfru Langseth seized hold of her arms so violently that it hurt her. The sick body seemed trying to writhe, but each sudden, involuntary movement increased the pain. And all the time she continued to utter those terrible shrieks.

Dorthea fought with her. The exhalations from the bed of sweat and blood and tainted matter were almost unbearable. Marie had perspired so that not only her nightcap, but the pillow under her was quite dark. If only she had not sent Magnille to bed, if only she had got the barber-surgeon here last evening, if only she had some red wine to give her, but there was none in the house, nor was there any at Brovold — she ought to have let Claus ride to Vilberg or to the parsonage to borrow a couple of bottles. And get a doctor here — it was just possible he might arrive in time to do something.

When at last the sick woman had calmed down sufficiently to admit of her leaving her, Dorthea found that her legs were trembling beneath her. She herself was sweating almost as much as the patient — she scratched her head under the toupee, and her side-curls fell in a sticky tangle down over her neck.

It was daylight already, she saw, as she stepped out on the balcony. Little pink shreds of cloud floated high up in the pale sky, and the cold morning air was gratefully pure. Oh, thank God, in an hour or an hour and a half the people of the farm would be up, her terrible lonely night watch would be at an end. Two brown horses had come into the yard — there was a dull thudding now and again as they moved about and grazed with a tearing sound at the lush grass along a trickle of water from the leaky well.

In the kitchen the maids were sleeping in the dark within closed shutters. Dorthea woke Magnille and sent her up to the sickroom with the warm water and a jug of freshly made herb-tea. She would have to get Marie Langseth to swallow a little brandy — it might dull the pains a little and stimulate her failing vitality.

On tiptoe Madame Dorthea stole into the parlour. It was as she had thought — Cold had not gone to bed at all. The wan morning light showed up his sprawling figure

— with arms and·head resting on the table he snored, surrounded by bottles, books and papers.

As quietly as she could Dorthea lifted bottle after bottle — looked through them against the light. Here was one which was at any rate half-full.

The man woke up, made a grab after her waist — " my good angel — ministering to me so faithfully," he babbled, dazed and maundering, " — Dorthea, Dorthea — weisst wohl, mein feines Lieb, wie du mir teuer bist."

" You must try to collect yourself, Cold, collect your thoughts. Good God, man, I don't know where to turn, she is so ill. You must send to Christiania, get hold of a doctor — do you hear! "

But he was already asleep again. Dorthea shook him, stamped on the floor. Then she shook her head in despair, kicked away some books that had fallen on the floor, and went off with the bottle. At any rate it was good French brandy, by the smell.

When Marie Langseth had got down a fresh dose of Dorthea's tea with cognac in it, she seemed after a while to fall into a kind of doze. Madame Dorthea could not determine whether it was due to the drink or to sheer exhaustion, and to the morning hour, when sick people so often sink into a kind of deathlike torpor. But it looked as if the poor creature would at last enjoy a few hours' sleep.

So she would have to see about getting home, thought Madame Thestrup. She was now so tired that she moved as in a trance. But she believed she had given Magnille sufficient orders when at last she was ready to leave.

The Captain had gone to bed, the servants told her when she enquired after him. Well well, in puerperal

fever, if the truth were told, the doctors could do no more
than any experienced woman could do just as well. In
such cases she trusted in spite of all more to such people
as that gypsy woman — it was quite conceivable that she
knew of some old remedy.

— What kind of spring work would be done on this
farm of Fenstad — when the master was sleeping off his
debauch and she who should be mistress lay mortally sick
— Dorthea shook her head, as she drove down towards the
bog, where the little water-holes lay blinking so brightly
and charmingly in the morning sun.

There was so much that had to be done when she came
home. She had to get out the boys' best clothes and look
them over, see whether she had the necessary ingredients
for the contribution they would take with them to Lunde
— apple fritters and an iced cake with the initials of the
bride and bridegroom in red sugar, she had thought of.
And then she had to pack a clothesbasket full of linen and
other necessary things to take with her when she drove
back to Fenstad that evening.

After dinner she felt she must lie down for a while. As
she drew the bed-curtains and stretched her weary body
in their dark green shade it occurred to her that for the
last twenty-four hours she had scarcely bestowed a thought
on her own sorrows. Jörgen, my beloved, my lost one, she
tried to whisper. But she could feel nothing now but a
void in her soul, no pain. She had grown accustomed to
his loss. As sleep descended upon her this discovery of
hers shaped itself into an image — something she had
often seen as she worked in her garden: the way in which
many plants went out was by dying in the centre, so that

a few dry stalks on a patch of bare mould was all that was left of the flower she had tended. But in a ring outside it there came up suckers and seedlings. In the same way her interests and cares were beginning to be absorbed by all the things that lived outside the withered fellowship with her dear one. Alas, she had long been certain that he was dead. But only now did she become aware that she was already well on the way to living without him.

It was late before she was ready to set out for Fenstad. The evening sun filled the bedroom with a piercing yellow light which dazzled Dorthea as she went up to the glass to tie on her hood. Am I really so cadaverous, she thought, or is it the yellow light that makes my face look so wan? And brings out every wrinkle so sharply.

It is not pleasant to discover how much one has gone off. And one likes to know that there are still some who find one sympathetic, even when one's looks have faded. Captain Cold's lively sympathy had been agreeable; she had to admit that to herself, since it flattered her feminine feelings that this handsome younger man showed so frankly that he was attracted by the matron with the pallid cheeks. Her knowledge of the many weak sides in his character made no breach in her sympathy for him. Even now her feeling for him and for the victim of his conduct — which was no different from that of so many other men in his position — was rather one of compassion. He drank, neglected his own welfare — and now he had made up his mind to leave his mistress and their child in the lurch. This revolted her at the moment, when Marie's misery was actually present to her eyes. But when Cold had left the country she would remember him as an amiable and unfortunate man and forget his faults. Nor was it he who had prompted Jomfru Langseth to this desperate step — and if it should cost her life, Cold would feel a passing shock of pain. But it would facilitate his departure from Fenstad. The thought was not a palatable one, but so it *was*.

Even if one knows oneself loved by one's spouse, with the solid affection which is built up on mutual contentment in many years of married life, one is not displeased to find that one can still make a certain impression — in all honesty, of course — on a man who did not know one in the flower of one's youth. In all honesty, ah yes — but is it not only one step farther, and then another, and another — and one finds oneself among the coquettes, the frivolous, the shameless women who themselves run after men in search of renewed satisfaction of their senses and their vanity? Dorthea suddenly felt something resembling longing as she thought that soon she would see her mother again. Now she would be able to meet her without feeling that unfilial censorious coldness which had always pained her like a sort of cramp whenever she found herself face to face with her mother. Poor mother — though Dorthea had never remarked that her mother was hurt by the lukewarm feelings which her children, with the possible exception of Ole, entertained for her. This had certainly been a matter of some indifference to her, so long as she had proofs of her power to make conquests of the men she had picked out for one reason or another.

Dorthea dared now to confess to herself — she had hated her mother during the years in which she had dragged out her youth in her marriage with Bisgaard; she had regarded her with tolerant contempt while she herself was living happily by the side of her Thestrup. When she had experienced the joy of receiving the living pledges of her husband's affection, she felt a half disdainful compassion for a woman who had thrown away the pure joys of motherhood in order to capture, first a husband in prosperous circumstances, then one whose chief attraction was youth and good looks. Now that grief and loss had taught Dorthea to realize how strong and how weak are a person's most sacred feelings, when they are bereft of the physical, tangible elements that nourished them — now it seemed she must be able to meet her mother in true sympathy. In spite of all — poor mother! Time after time she must have experienced this emptiness, when she had won the object of her desire only to be deprived of it again. What was it she had read the other day in one of the boys' school-books? *Afflictio dat intellectum.*

She gave a start as the door opened — in the mirror she saw it was Claus who entered. Positively she felt as if she had been surprised by her son in something illicit. " What do you want, my boy? " She turned round to him. He was in outdoor clothes.

" The horse is in. And the things are lashed on to the cart."

" Thank you. Then I had better be starting. Will you see that Bertel and Carl go to bed in good time — and you and Vilhelm must not stay up too late either."

" But am I not to drive Mother? "

" No, my dear boy, you shall not be asked to do that. I am staying there tonight. It is a *very* bad gastric fever Jomfru Langseth has got; you had better not go there for the present."

She saw that the boy suppressed a kind of smile. He knew very well what sort of gastric fever Jomfru Langseth's was, Dorthea could see, and she was not pleased. But Claus was serious again in a moment. An expression of tense expectation came into his dark sleepy eyes. "Well — is anything the matter? — you are looking at me so strangely, dear child."

"No — oh no. I was only wondering — has the Captain spoken to you? About me, I mean."

"About you, little Claus? Yes, he said he was very pleased with the progress you have made these last weeks. But with all this illness in the house — I had so much to see to — I had no time to talk much to our good Captain."

"Then he has said nothing to you about — about what he would propose — about my future? That he will try to get me into the artillery cadet institute — he wants me to go with him to Copenhagen, he says he is convinced he can do something for me, when once I'm there."

"Merciful God, Claus! What ideas are these?" Dorthea sank back in the armchair, with a terrified look at her son. "Have you and Captain Cold behind my back" — her alarm was so intense that she grew angry — "have you and he been hatching plans for your future that I am to know nothing about?"

"No, no, Mother, but let me tell you." Claus talked as fast as if he had to take his mother by storm. "Captain Cold is sure I have a turn for engineering and, Mother, that's what I want to take up. But I didn't think it was any use asking you if I might go to the mathematical school in Christiania. And here in Norway we have no connections who might interest themselves for me — but in Denmark, if I go there in Captain Cold's company —

And it wouldn't cost Mother anything — not so much anyhow. The Captain says I know enough — he would give me lessons himself so that I could get into the top class almost at once, then I should be a non-commisioned officer — and it's much easier, there's a far better chance of promotion in the artillery or the engineers than in the other arms. For it means hard work, Captain Cold says, so they have no appetite for that, the young gentlemen who are only after uniforms and rank and want to play the dandy."

Dorthea checked his torrent of words with a raised hand: " But child! Never did we imagine, your father and I, that any of our sons should enter the military profession."

" Well but, Mother — ! "

Memories crowded into her brain of all the times Thestrup had expressed his dislike of everything connected with the military. From his student days he could tell stories of the German officers' brutality and stupidity, of their Danish comrades' absurd conceit. The Norwegian students in Copenhagen had taken a prominent part in the endless feud between the university and the garrison. Coarse brutes was what Thestrup called the non-commisioned officers — and they had to be so, between their tyrannical superiors and the rank and file, of whom the enlisted men were mostly criminals and the militiamen reluctant country louts. Ill-treatment of soldiers, bullying of respectable and industrious citizens, drunkenness and gambling and the spreading of loathsome diseases, these were the most notable exploits of the gallant warriors.

" Your father would never have given his consent to such a fantastic scheme, Claus! "

" Yes but, Mother — now that we have lost our father. I know *he* would have intended me for another career. I never had much fancy for being a student — but if Father had lived, of course I should have had to do as he wished."

" Claus! " Dorthea raised her hand in deprecation. " What a way to talk, boy! One would almost think you did not mourn the loss of your father."

" *That* I do! But " — he shot a sidelong glance at his mother. More than ever his dark eyes looked like those of a pondering, sullen bull-calf. " Now that he *is* gone, we have got to make the best of it. No, if Father had lived, the Captain would never have thought of making us an offer like this. Then it would have been for Father to help me on in the world, and so of course he would have had to decide for me.

" — Well, Mother mustn't think I don't know that Father was " — he searched for the unaccustomed grown-up word — " prejudiced against the officer class. But that's no reason why I should throw away such a splendid chance. When for one thing Mother would be let off having to provide for me — after a little while, anyhow."

" Claus, Claus — I really have no great liking for that career myself. It is a path that is beset with temptations and dangers."

" Prr." He looked a little frightened by his own disrespectful snort. " Mother doesn't know so much about these things," he went on, with scarcely concealed defiance. "You surely understand, if one wants to shine in one's profession, to have a chance of promotion, then upon my word one has to study, read, work."

"Ah, promotion, child — for that the first thing need-ful is to have birth and connections — or powerful in-fluence. So capability rarely counts for much."

"Yes, that was what Father always said; but I can assure you, Mother, that does not always hold good now — and besides, it holds good just as much in every service. We are going to feel the want of distinguished patronage, whatever we take up — and here, *here* Captain Cold could introduce me to —

" — and as to those temptations and dangers that Mother is thinking of," his voice was rapid and trium-phant, as though the boy had just been struck by this acute idea — "you surely don't think that a *student's* life in the capital always follows the paths of virtue and industry? Oh no" — he laughed scornfully. "Mother need only think of Dabbelsteen. And you should have heard too the tales *he* had to tell. About things that I have never heard the Captain *mention* — except that he is always saying a young man who wants to get on in the world and has nothing to depend on but his own good parts and his integrity must steer his course as wide as he can from the temples of Bacchus and Venus."

"Claus, I trust you all to do that, whatever you may take up."

Claus tossed his head impatiently: "Yes, of course. But I think all parents do that, and it happens sometimes that they're mistaken on that score. Does Mother believe for instance that Pastor Muus in his student days was so much more virtuous than Cold when he was young? The only difference was that the divinity student had to take mighty good care to pay his visits to the wenches in the narrow alleys behind Green Street when nobody was looking — and even then the fat was in the fire once or twice, Dabbelsteen knew that well enough. But the young second lieutenants have only to take their meals at an eating-house where they're waited on by girls and everybody thinks — you know what. And which of them does Mother think is best informed — even in Latin and philosophy — which do you think has got most out of his education, our Pastor or the Captain? "

" Hush, hush, hush. I am shocked at you, Claus — how could it enter Herr Dabbelsteen's head to speak of such things to children who were committed to his charge! "

" Because Dabbelsteen never wanted to go to the university either. It was only because he couldn't offend his mother, and she was set on his being a parson, so that she could come and live with him some day. But Dabbelsteen only wanted to go out into the wide world and look around him — to the West Indies — he was always talking about Uncle Caspar, don't you remember, Mother? And he talked to the Captain about enlisting, in some foreign service for choice. Yes, he said so many times — and that was before he heard about that business at home. But the Captain advised him not to do it — he said he'd be sworn that Herr Dabbelsteen with his weak character would never get anything out of soldiering but a stirrup-leather or the cat. And now I expect he's gone and done it all the same."

Dorthea sprang up: " There, that's enough! I will hear no more of it. I have no time — do you see, the sun is almost down, it will be night before I get to Fenstad.

Her heart was beating wildly with agitation and she was quite weak in the knees. The sight of the boy's sulky mien, as he stood holding the door open for his mother, filled her once more with the terror that had come upon her just now. What unforeseeable misfortunes had the immediate future in store for her?

" Had I not better drive, Mother, as it is so late? " They had reached the waiting cart, with old Brownie standing over in the shafts. The highest tree-tops on the ridge glimmered with a fitful band of gold where the sun had just slipped down behind them.

" No, I told you. You had better go and find Bertel and Carl and get them in — it's their bed-time — where can they be? "

" They are down at Scharlach's." Claus was fingering the knots that lashed the throne-like piece of furniture to the back of the cart. Its back towered high above the sides of the cart, it stretched its curving arms hospitably to the rear and exhibited its stuffing and its cushion of blue lustrine. On discovering that no such convenience was to be found anywhere at Fenstad, Dorthea decided to take with her the biggest *chaise percée* they had at Brovold.

" But it isn't anything infectious that they have."

Quick as lightning Madame Dorthea whirled round and gave the boy a sound smack on the mouth, making Brownie start out of his doze. She climbed hurriedly into the cart: " Run and open the gate for me. And then you can go down to Scharlach's and fetch the children."

*

8

MADAME DORTHEA actually succeeded in driving Brownie
at a brisk trot down the Brovold slopes, past the glassworks and over the bridge. Then the horse fell back into
his usual jog-trot and her trembling limbs relaxed and
settled down, while by degrees her thoughts emerged
from the first chaos of unhappiness.

At first it had almost paralysed her soul when she realized the dissolution of her world — like a house which
the spring floods lift from its foundations and break up,
till scattered beams and planks are whirled away by the
current, out of sight. He who had held it all together was
gone — and again she was agitated by a violent longing
for the first days of her mourning, when the place he had
left was still warm in her heart and mind. But so much
had already intervened between that time and the present.

Every day she found herself obliged to take up burdens and cares which it was hard for a woman to bear alone. She had already journeyed a good way since the hour of parting, and the empty space her husband had left in her life had grown cold and desolate.

She had not understood, when Vilhelm came forward with the plans he had made of casting off from the family circle and seeking his own fortune — the dear boy had shown so much filial devotion, so affectionate a zeal to lessen the burden of the flock of children for whose future she had to provide. But in Claus Hartvig, when he disclosed this evening that he too had made his plans for the future without asking her advice, she had discerned an attitude which seemed to say: if Mother tries to stop me, now that my father is gone, he who might have deterred me from the path I wish to follow, then Mother must be made to feel that I can meet force with force and we shall not be friends.

Nonsense! A boy of fourteen is really only a child. And Claus is not even confirmed yet. It is Cold who has put these notions into his head. The worthy Captain is pleased to find so apt a pupil, it amuses him to talk to the boy about the ins and outs of his profession, to teach him to fence and shoot. Then it occurs to him that this talented, handsome and strongly built youth would certainly cut a good figure as an officer — and he blurts out his fanciful idea, and the child at once takes it seriously and is enthusiastic.

Dorthea was really angry with her friend Captain Cold when she thought of it. It was too bad to stir up such fancies in other folks' children. The fact that *she* had felt sympathy for him did not entitle him to imagine she would approve of one of their children being ready to ignore his deceased father's wishes; and he knew very well with how little favour Thestrup regarded the whole military profession. Besides which, her feelings towards Johannes Cold had cooled considerably since she had seen how lightly he intended to break with his mistress. Even if Marie Langseth's conduct could not be called blameless, her loyal devotion to him and his welfare had nevertheless deserved a different reward. That the story was as old as the hills — that housekeeper-mistresses all over the wide world suffered every day the same fate as Marie, that thousands of fathers light-heartedly abandoned their natural children to an ill-starred fortune, if it was too inconvenient to them to secure their future — did that really make the matter more morally defensible?

She would tell Captain Cold what she thought of his attempt to entice the boy away from her in this manner — yes, indeed she would.

Claus, she thought, Claus. Was it reserved for her to encounter in one of her own children the spiteful opposition to following the path laid down by parents which she herself had felt when her mother gave her to Bisgaard. Not because they were hindrances which she desired to remove from her path, but because their happiness in life was now the only goal she had left, she would stand out for her right to lead their footsteps into the grown-up world.

Jörgen Thestrup — he was lost to her here on earth, ah, far more effectually than if she had been able to close his dear eyes in the sleep of death and receive his last farewell and advice. Soon she would be leaving this place which for so many years had been his and her home. She would have painful legal and financial difficulties to face unaided, before she could think of building anew her reduced existence within narrower lines. But the children, the flock of his and her children, the whole responsibility for whom had now been left to her — this flock she would take with her undivided when she departed from Brovold.

But she acknowledged with a quaking heart that the elder boys were far less children than she had imagined. She seethed with anger at the thought that Dabbelsteen's sense of propriety had fallen so far short of anything she had conceived to be possible. " Wenches in the alleys behind Green Street " — it was incredible that this person should have thought of entertaining his charges with such talk. And about Pastor Muus's infelicitous conduct in his student days. For of course Claus was not the only one he had regaled with this gossip. Vilhelm had certainly heard it too — only Vilhelm would not for the world let his mother know that he had been initiated into subjects of indecency. A tender heart and a sense of propriety seemed innate in him. Why, even little Bertel — she could not even be sure that the thoughtless tutor had always respected the child's innocence. If he refused so flatly to go to the parsonage for lessons, perhaps it was not merely because he was afraid of the ill-mannered little girls — possibly it was because he felt he could not look Pastor Muus in the face without blushing.

Of course, in her childhood she herself had received fairly extensive information, from the servants at her stepfather's, from old women and children in the cottages, on subjects a knowledge of which she would not have admitted at any price to her grown-up relatives. And it had done her no harm — she could not absolve herself of a certain curiosity about these matters, but the talk of the kitchen and outhouses had nevertheless inspired her with disgust and fear of vice more than anything else. She remembered an old dairywoman's description of the victims of disease — ah, how many sleepless hours it had cost her! She felt certain that Vilhelm had felt the same profound abhorrence when Dabbelsteen served up gossip about the shady side of life in the capital. And poor Bertel — how it must have pained and frightened him, if he had been listening.

But Claus Hartvig was different — his nature was not so clear to her as that of Vilhelm or Bertel, but she knew that he was different. She recalled his burning face and sparkling eyes when she surprised him fencing with the Captain. With a pang she remembered how the bright blade seemed almost to form part of the splendid, lightly clad youthful frame. And his breath had smelt of brandy when she helped him on with his jacket afterwards. And there had been no sign of either fear or shame in his manner, as he let her know that he was pretty well informed about the salacious ways of the grown-up world. Far from it — there was a covert challenge, and something like a secret chuckle in his voice and mien. As though he would say to her, it's no use for the hen to try to teach the egg. Or the young cockerel either.

Alas, alas, the hen who can gather her chickens under her wings, she is to be envied. A wife who is left a widow, with a flock of children of all ages, from nearly grown-up to a babe in the cradle — how is she to keep hers together?

One moment she thought she would ask Cold for an explanation — how could he encourage another person's child in such wilfulness? The next moment she thought — best to leave it alone. Supposing it had been nothing but a few careless words of the Captain's which Claus had taken too seriously. Then it would be putting the poor boy in a ridiculous light if in this connection she demanded a solemn elucidation of the Captain.

The jagged line of firs along the ridge stood out black against the sky and the meadows were shrouded in a dusky green as Madame Thestrup swung into the yard at Fenstad. All at once the steady old horse shied violently — as though he were going to bolt. A tall shadow of a woman with a forward stoop detached itself from the darkness between the main building and the storehouse.

Dorthea tugged at the reins, as her heart gave a leap in her breast with fright. In an instant she knew that this was the mysterious creature who had been so often in her thoughts during the last months — and the gypsy woman greeted her in a deep voice from out of the darkness: " God's peace! "

Dorthea turned the scared horse in a great curve round half the yard and with a wo-back! managed to halt him by the stable-door. In a moment the other was there — noiselessly as a ghost she appeared by the side of Brownie. The old horse started again, but the gypsy laid her hand on his neck, made a soft whinnying sound, and then proceeded to unharness the animal, which was manifestly only half quieted.

" Good evening," said Madame Dorthea. " Is nobody awake in the house? " There was not a light to be seen anywhere, and the whole place was as silent as the grave.

As though from the outskirts of this stillness came the mocking, exuberant trills of the song-thrush up on the hill.

" No, the kind lady will have to put up with me to-night." The stranger's voice was deep and not unpleasant. The wheedling tone which gypsy women are fond of adopting seemed to have been smoothed into a kind of submissive friendliness. " I'll take the horse and slip him into the paddock."

Woman and horse merged into one shadow, as she led it between the outhouses. A gate swung to with a dull thud.

Although the sky above was so light it was murky down here on the ground. Dorthea stayed by the cart, listening — somewhere near the leaves rustled in the tops of the aspens. The air was so cool that it refreshed her to breathe it — it was moist and full of grateful scents. Suddenly the shadowy black figure reappeared close beside her.

She had seemed almost uncannily tall at first sight, but now Dorthea saw that the gypsy scarcely came above her shoulders. She walked with a very marked stoop, it was true. A kerchief was bound across her forehead, so that Dorthea could not see much of the woman's face.

" But surely they can't all be asleep in this house? " Dorthea asked. " They can't have left you all alone to keep watch here tonight, mother? "

" Oh yes, they can that." The woman's voice became even more silky. " For it's well known to all, let me tell you, there's no need to keep watch or ward, bolt or bar, where Sibilla comes to cure the ills of man or beast. There's no need to distrust me, my good lady. They well know, both gentle and simple in all the country round, that it's only good and never evil that springs up in *my* footsteps."

" Well well, mother, no offence — I did not mean it in that way. But you must have someone to help you attend to the patient? And *I* should have been glad of some help in getting these things into the house and up to her bedroom."

" We'll soon manage that." Sibilla had dexterously untied all the lashings in spite of the dim light. Now she lowered first the clothes basket and then the night-chair down on to the ground. " If my fine lady can so lower herself as to take hold of the basket " — she lifted the cushion and the brass bowl out of the seat of the chair, then stuck her head through the aperture, so that the unwieldy object was poised on her shoulders. With one hand she supported the chair, with the other she took one handle of the clothes basket. Dorthea took the other. A remarkable sight — Dorthea was glad there was no one to see them, as this procession made its way across the yard and into the house.

How Sibilla managed to wind her way through the doors and up the steep and narrow stairway to the upper storey, almost without bumping against a wall or making any noise, was beyond Dorthea's comprehension. All the movements of the gypsy woman were so rapid and so silent that they gave Dorthea the creeps — though she said to herself that she ought rather to admire the other; her power of moving about almost noiselessly was indeed remarkable and certainly very useful in her profession.

On the table under the little window in the gable stood a tallow candle which had burnt so low that it gave out a smell of scorched grease and heated brass; otherwise the air of the room was not nearly so bad as it had been on the previous evening. Dorthea dug out a packet of candles from the basket — she had brought with her everything for which she could imagine there might be a use; it was evident that nobody at Fenstad knew where to find anything when Jomfru Langseth herself was not about. She lighted a fresh candle by the flickering wick and took up the candlestick — the handle was quite hot.

Marie Langseth was sleeping, quietly enough to all appearance. But her face was yellow and sunken, her skin dewy with perspiration. And she was so hot, when Dorthea felt her chest under the bedclothes, that she must still be in a fever. Dorthea raised the coverlets — there was a mass of blood and matter on the sheets under her, but it was mostly dark and coagulated. And its smell was mingled with that of aromatic herbs and mixture which Dorthea did not recognize. But whatever the nature of the gypsy woman's remedies, they seemed to have had a beneficial effect; the patient's abdomen and legs were less swollen than yesterday. Dorthea cautiously pressed the swollen parts — the flesh had a curious doughy feel, and the depressions made in it by her fingers did not fill up at once. But no twitching of Marie's face betrayed any sensation.

" I see you have put leeches on her, mother? "

" Ehey. The bad blood must come out; no use trying tricks with drinks and drams while that's there. Nor with those bags of yours either," she said quickly, as Dorthea took up the bag of herbs that lay on the chair by the bed.

" At any rate it can do no harm."

" Oh, but it can do harm — it can turn back what has to come out, turn it into the flesh and blood, so that the matter goes to the heart and the head, and that means death, let me tell you, lady." The gypsy evidently meant to have sole command of the sickbed. " If they've sent for Sibilla they'll have to leave the remedies to me. They may safely do that; I've learnt many things that the doctors and midwives won't find in their books, that time I was seven years in Nordland and learnt the art from the wise Lapps."

Dorthea surveyed the other. Under the shade of the black kerchief the gypsy's face was almost broader than it was long, with markedly prominent cheekbones and wide eye-sockets, in whose depths glowed little coal-black eyes. For all that, she could not be called ugly, wrinkled and yellow as was her skin. In spite of the sly, self-satisfied smile that played about her narrow lips as she boasted of her wisdom acquired among the Lapps, a certain dignity was diffused over the tall, somewhat bent figure. Her movements were easy and silent, and Dorthea remarked that the yellow, not too clean hands with their many rings of silver and brass were small and had the smoothness of youth.

Sibilla had set down the night-chair at the foot of the bed and replaced its accessories. She now lowered herself into this throne-like seat; leaning forward, with her hands on her knees, she followed the lady's every movement with keen eyes.

Dorthea could not help it — her feeling, if not exactly eerie, was nevertheless one of uneasy discomfort beneath the stranger's persistent stare. It was after all a curious situation — it must be about midnight, and here she was alone, in a strange house, with this enigmatical vagabond by the bedside of a woman sick to death. The tallow candle she had chanced on was not a good one; there was a thief in it already, it was burning awry and running down in a horrible way.

She looked about for the snuffers — there were none on the table, and she went over to Marie's chest of drawers to see if they might be there. But she felt even less at her ease as she stood with her back to the gypsy woman. To calm herself she took up the glass jar that was on the chest of drawers, held it up to the light and examined the black leeches in it; they looked so strangely distorted as the light was refracted in the water. She put down the jar and was about to look at the brass box which lay beside it, when the other stopped her with a sharp cry:

"Take care you don't go near my box — there are strong things inside. There may be trouble if you go meddling with what has the hidden powers in it, when you don't know the right way to go to work."

"O-oh." Dorthea turned half round to the woman, but did not remove her hand which rested on the lid of the box. It must have been imagination, that faint pricking she felt in her finger-tips. "It cannot be so dangerous as that? I am quite ready to believe, Mother Sibilla, that you have great cunning — it looks as though Jomfru Langseth has already profited by your treatment. But surely the things you have in this box are not powerful enough to act through a closed lid?"

"Dangerous enough for you!" she answered glibly. A rapid, scornful smile flitted over the woman's dark face. "If you had had faith I could have done good to you and yours with what I have in that box. But I know well

enough, you great folks have little faith in the wayfarers'
wisdom — it seems like you don't believe either in almighty God or the other man whose name I will not utter
in this place " — her black eyes rolled round in her head
for an instant, as though sending a glance to the wan sick
woman in the bed behind her. " But that makes it hard
to come by what you don't know. And how should the
great and mighty ones of this world know of those things
that are hidden from the wise and revealed to the outcasts,
as the scripture says."

Madame Dorthea crossed the room and seated herself in
the ragged leather chair that stood by the door of the
weaving-room since her last night of watching. She tried
to remind herself that this queer bookish talk of the
gypsy's was if anything rather absurd — it was only the
time and place and the woman's outlandish sing-song in-
tonation that lent a certain solemnity to her rigmaroles.
She kept on with her mystifying recitations:

" — he who lies asleep under roof, behind locked door
and bolted shutter, he does not see what we see, no, for
we lie out under the sky at night and listen to what is out
and on the move, we do — and trust me, that makes a big
difference. You *kvanting* lady, you dancer in gilded halls
with mirrors and fine chairs — it was to another measure
that I stepped barefoot into the snakes' dance to catch the
white snake."

There was really a sort of prophetess-like dignity about
her, as she sat there in the chair, lighted from the side by
the single candle on the chest of drawers. Half hidden by
the dark chequered silk shawl which she wore over her
shoulders, hooks and eyes of silver gleamed on her black
bodice; where it opened a strip of flaming scarlet under-

garment showed through. About her waist she wore a broad leather belt ornamented with studs and stars of brass; a well-filled pouch with copper fastening hung by her side. Otherwise her dress was of peasant fashion, quite dark, but it looked decent and serviceable. When she pushed back her black kerchief Dorthea saw that her forehead was low and broad — though not so broad as her face across the cheek-bones — and furrowed by three deep wrinkles. She wore a black cap like those of older peasant women, and round it she had tied a silk handkerchief in glaring colours. The little that could be seen of her hair under this head-dress was jet-black.

She was certainly calculated to make an impression on the superstitious among the people and she had a right to her name Sibilla — Dorthea could not help wondering if it was not a professional name which she had adopted at a mature age, since it suited her so well.

" Well well, mother, there may be something in what you say. I am willing to believe it. But what ails the patient here is an illness which has nothing to do with witchcraft. And you will cure it best by natural remedies, without any kind of magic. That it was beneficial to put leeches on her is no secret, even to my poor comprehension."

" I borrowed them from a woman out at Aaserud." Sibilla smiled scornfully. " That is so, I know many a cure of those that are revealed to your folk as well as to mine. And since 'tis not malice nor gusts of breath that have brought the Jomfru to this, but just what they call natural causes, we must use natural means too. Not but what it was Sibilla and not you that drew out the rotten blood and staunched the living blood and saved the life of this here captain's trollop. Fie on them!" The gypsy spat. "Ay, 'tis nice ways the great folks have, say I! You never heard of a Romany killing the babe in her womb with a knitting-needle — oh, fie on their beastliness!"

Dorthea shuddered involuntarily. Deeply as she had been disgusted at the thought of Marie Langseth's desperate act, it was as though the whole horror of the crime were only revealed to her by the gypsy's words and by the abhorrence displayed even by a woman of the despised race of vagabonds. She had a sudden sense of nausea — the bad air and the heat of the room seemed more than she could bear.

She got up hurriedly — there was little Margrethe in the weaving-room to be seen to. But she had a strange sensation of discomfort as she imagined she could feel the old woman's piercing eyes in her back.

Little Grethe was sleeping sweetly in her wool-basket. But she had kicked off the coverlet, and even in the faint light that came through the window Madame Dorthea could see that the little legs and feet were frightfully dirty. She was wet too, an acrid smell rose from her basket, and now she scratched her head violently, but without waking up. Poor little creature — was there no one to take care of her now? She would have to attend to Grethe and see about getting her clean, the first thing in the morning. This thought seemed to deaden the nervous uneasiness with which the gypsy's presence inspired her and of which her reason did not suffice to free her.

She started violently on seeing that the sibyl had followed her into the weaving-room. The stealing, cat-like footsteps stopped behind her. Dorthea guessed that the other was also looking down at the sleeping child.

" What do you think will become of this little one? "
the question escaped her without reflection. Then she
collected herself and said in a lighter tone: " They say
that you people can read human destinies, past and
future? "

" And that is no lie either." There was a strange authority in the vagabond's low-voiced answer; against her
will Madame Dorthea was thrilled by a shiver of excitement. " 'Tis a gift the great God gives to the pious that
have to suffer unjustly the wickedness of the children of
this world. It were well if he knew what I know, the
father of the little girl here, then maybe he would not have
been so hard on my daughter and her children, that time
he tried to force us to speak of things we knew nothing of.
Could he have seen what I see at this moment, I warrant
he'd not have been so harsh. I saw it in his eyes, the same
sickness that's eating up the liver and lungs of my old man,
it lies in wait for my brave Herr Kaftein — soon 'twill
bite him in the belly, ay ay, so it is! And this daughter of
his, I see her stand before the sheriff to answer for crimes
she never has done, as we had to, many a time. She shall
go on the gypsy trail, and 'tis a rogue of a man she takes
up with — Romany he is not, a scamp from the country-
side that has cast in his lot with the travellers will be her
man. *Buro* and sheriff drive her from pillar to post — ai
ai — 'tis a bad job. The sweet little angel, here she lies
sleeping so prettily, she little knows she has lost both
father and mother before the new year's dawn lights up
the sky, poor child."

Again it seemed to Dorthea that the old woman was like
a shadow that had detached itself from the shadows in the
dark corners of the room — but now she had become a

threatening, fateful shadow of misfortunes to come. She was breathing audibly, and Dorthea could catch the faint chink of the silver chain which expanded and contracted with the heaving of the soothsayer's bosom. She divined in the other a hatred of everything and everybody that did not belong to the roving folk, a hatred so fierce that it made her quite afraid. But then her anger flared up: these evil predictions of the fate of the innocent little creature — fie, they were too odious — and what were they but idle breath, evoked by the desire to see the ruin of an enemy's child?

" I thought you said, mother, that you were sure of getting Jomfru Langseth well again with your doctoring. Now you tell me that both she and the Captain are to die before the new year? "

" Cured of *this* trouble she will be, I know what I'm saying. Fit as a fiddle she shall be the day she gets up from her bed, but beyond that my power does not reach. For I have no hold on him that waits to be revenged on his mother. Had he been buried alive, then I could conjure him out of scree or bog, with steel and with strong prayers. But the steel has gone through him already, and so there's nothing to be done. She'd better mind herself, the Jomfru, when she gets on her feet again, not trip on the stairs after it's dark. There might be one waiting for her there, and then it's all up with her. And the Captain — I don't know whether he's dead or what's happened to him. But he's not here at new year, I see that plainly. I know what I'm saying."

The dismal voice uttering these prophecies in the darkness acted on Dorthea with a strange excitation:

" Since you can see all this, perhaps you can see more,"

she whispered. " Can you see where my husband is now? "

The shadowy woman was seen to rock her head, but no answer came. " Try if you can see him! " Dorthea begged in a low and earnest tone. And all at once it was borne in upon her that this was what she had been waiting for all the evening — for the chance of putting this question to the gypsy woman — nay, that it was really for this she had insisted on bringing her here. " Where *is* my husband? Cannot you see where he is lying? Shall I ever find him again? "

" Your husband I cannot see. A darkness comes over my eyes, 'tis just as if the power runs out of me, as soon as I try to find him. Oh, never will you find what you're seeking."

Dorthea sighed deeply. Involuntarily she supported herself against the loom beside her. The gypsy went on speaking, but gradually her chanting voice rose into solemn accusation:

" He was a hard man to me and mine, your husband, when he forbad our menfolk to fake in the smithy and trade with the works-folk. He would not allow the poor women of the place to profit by the wisdom of the travellers. Sibilla knew of many a cure for sickness and all other ills, both of man and beast, but he forbad them to use them, for he had no faith in such things, your husband. That is why I cannot see him now — for he lacked faith in my powers. You have got this faith now, I see that, and that gives me power to see your future, Madame Thestrup. Yes, I see there's many a good thing awaits you yet, my dear madame. I see you living beside a great smooth water, I think it must be the sea, but I don't know how you come there, I only know you are to travel a long way from here, and much awaits you, both good and ill, where you are going. But what you most desire will not be yours, and what you seek for most you will never find! " The soothsayer drew a long, sad breath, making the silver chain on her bosom chink faintly.

But during this last harangue of hers Dorthea had begun to recover her senses. Hot with shame at the ease with which she had allowed herself to be taken off her guard, she bethought herself — of course she ought to have given the woman a substantial gratuity before asking her for any prediction. Then undoubtedly she would have piped to another tune. But she had actually allowed herself to be taken in, for a moment she had believed in the sibyl and had thus given her an opportunity of pouring out her hatred and her vindictiveness, which was directed against the gentry no less than against the peasants, perhaps rather more, since these *kvantings,* as the gypsy called them, often did not regard them even with a superstitious awe. And it struck her now that the woman's manner and way of speaking had differed considerably from the customary demeanour of the gypsies when they visited the farms. Did the woman herself feel unsure of her ground when facing a person to whom she bore a grudge and whom at the same time she wished to impress?

Aloud she said: " Well, my good woman, these were not very favourable prospects you disclosed for any of us. But since you do promise me some measure of success, I must no doubt reward your benevolence. Here " — she unfastened the little brooch that held her shawl together. " I have not my purse with me, but I have always heard that your women are fond of gewgaws and finery."

The gypsy snatched the brooch, hurried into the bedroom with it and examined it carefully under the light, even biting it. It was a charming little thing, a milk-white agate surrounded by garnets and set in silver-gilt. All the same the old woman seemed only moderately pleased — Dorthea had heard of the exaggerated generosity with which simple-minded peasant women sometimes rewarded Sibilla's supposed cures effected on their cattle, loading her with heirlooms, food, silver spoons. " You know," said Dorthea carelessly, " if you succeed in making Jomfru Langseth well again, the Captain will certainly pay you well for your trouble."

Sibilla sat weighing the brooch in her hand:

" It is a moonstone, I see — ay ay, there is great power in them, and garnets too — they have power over the blood in the hearts of men. Perhaps I might try to see for you once more. You had this brooch of your husband, I think? " It had been a present from Dorthea's first husband; she nodded. Her belief in the soothsayer's supernatural gifts had vanished. It might easily have come to her ears that Captain Cold was planning to leave Norway; that she herself would soon have to give up Brovold was no secret either, and it was natural to conclude that she would then settle in Christiania, which lies on the sea. Such parts of the prediction as were certain to be fulfilled might have been foretold by anyone. And now she knew what the smell was that had hung round Marie Langseth — it was laudanum. So it was natural that the poor girl should sleep fairly peacefully tonight.

She got out the knitting she had brought with her and settled herself comfortably in the armchair. It was really comical after all that the old impostor had been able to make so strong an impression on her. No doubt she was quite a commanding figure as she sat in the high-backed padded throne with her hands in her lap and her feet close together on the blue cover of the foot-board — and yet it was only Bisgaard's old night-chair that had attained to such honour and dignity. Dorthea was almost inclined to laugh.

Nevertheless she shuddered as she drew out her knitting-needle and was reminded in a flash of what the gypsy had told her about the injury Marie had inflicted on herself. And against her will she could not but follow the preparations for performing the art of soothsaying with some fluttering of the heart.

Sibilla fetched the brass box, drew a chair up to the little table and announced, as she opened the casket of strange objects: " Have you ever seen one like this? "

Dorthea glanced at the object lying in the gypsy's brown beringed hand. It looked like the root of a plant, shaped something like a manikin doll. What else she had in the box Dorthea could not see very clearly — there was what looked like the skeleton of a small deaf-adder, a silver pouncet-box, some lumps of tin, seed-pods of plants and a variety of rubbish besides.

" I dug him up on the gallows hill north of the old town in Christiania thirty years ago. Yes, I remember it as if 'twas yesterday, believe me. You must have oil of beaver and crossed steel on your breast as you do it. And then you must have a dog to pull up the root when you've dug away the mould."

" A brownie to help you, is that it? " said Dorthea over her knitting.

" No, no, we don't own any such nastiness, we are honest folk, we are, don't use brownies to get our remedies

— no, this is what tells me fortunes." But Dorthea's interest grew less and less — this was just ordinary hocus-pocus. And as the woman drew from a pocket in the recesses of her gown a pack of cards, horribly greasy and black, and solemnly announced that these were her fortune-telling cards and they would first see whether they had anything to say about Thestrup's fate — Dorthea could hardly restrain a smile of incredulity: it was an incomplete pack of taroc cards that the other was dealing out over the table with weird antics.

But in spite of her incredulity Dorthea could not help following all the old woman's gestures with a certain intentness and listening to her mumblings as she turned up one card after another — some were in Norwegian and some in her gypsy language.

She let her knitting sink into her lap and took out her snuff-box. "This is the thing to keep one awake," she remarked as she arranged a pinch on the back of her hand and sniffed it up. "Perhaps you would like a pinch, mother?" Was this in order to soften the other a little more before she proceeded to interpret what the cards revealed?

The gypsy stuffed her nostrils full of snuff. "Did you ever see the like! It's just as if the cards won't out with anything either — but they'll have to give in" — she shuffled the cards and dealt them again. "You might let me have another pinch, it clears the brain — hey! Now it's coming!" And again she uttered a rigmarole in her own tongue. "Ah, now I'm beginning to see some light. Look here now — "

Dorthea bent forward eagerly. She did not know the game, but remembered the pictures from her childhood

at the deanery, and instinctively she tried to follow Sibilla's train of thought, as the woman drew conclusions
from the situation of the cards. By the side of the king of
hearts lay the wheel of Fortune " — that's your husband's
fortune, and Death is not far off; no, it don't much look
as if he's alive — but the Sun and the Wain are in between — " she glanced up at Dorthea with a queer sly
look. " I don't believe he died the same day as he went
south — for south he went, you see that yourself — you
couldn't tell me if he had business in that part, something
he didn't want talked about? no, no " — as Dorthea shook
her head. " And the maiden here, I wonder what she had
to do with Thestrup " — it was the World card she was
pointing at. " That he's lying in the river I'll never believe — he's a long way from water — but look you
here! " With a triumphant smile she put her finger on
the Tower with the flash of lightning. " Ay, now I call to
mind, he was lost the same night as the great snow-storm
about Lady Day. Look you here — there's a strong wind
comes out of the sky and throws him down. The Tower
here, that means the mountain — look, there's stones
falling off it. I should say *that's* what happened to him
— he's ridden under a shelf of rock just as the slide
came. And there he lies, somewhere, buried under the
scree."

Oh, it was foolish, foolish to take this old fortune-
teller's words to heart — guessing and idle talk such as she
had heard before now, that was all it was. And yet Dorthea felt quite childishly unhappy — it was as though,
without knowing it, she had still entertained a tiny shred
of hope in the depths of her soul, and now that had been
extinguished. Her hands shook as she picked up her

knitting again, and she waited a few moments before trusting herself to speak — she was afraid her voice might betray to the gypsy that her words had gone home.

" It was not much after all that your cards could tell you, Sibilla. That Herr Thestrup had met with an accident has long been clear to us all. But now daylight is breaking; I will go down to the kitchen and wake Magnille, then she will make coffee. You may well need a cup too, mother — it is exhausting to sit up all night, at your age."

That morning Captain Cold insisted on driving her back to Brovold himself. But this did not lead to their exchanging many words during the drive. The Captain was quite sober today, but he appeared preoccupied, almost gloomy in fact. And Madame Dorthea sat by his side, silent and abstracted. She managed to tell him that Jomfru Langseth's condition showed a really marked improvement that morning — she had taken a cup of coffee and a bowl of barley broth with a good appetite and had talked a little in a weak but natural voice — her pains were not nearly so severe, but of course her body was still very sore; Magnille had proposed that they should get her little sister to come and look after Grethe. With that the conversation came to a standstill.

All the time Dorthea was trying to think of every possible thing except the gypsy, but odds and ends of the old woman's utterances kept turning up in her memory. Why, it was quite wrong that there had been a snowstorm on the night Thestrup rode out — there had been a storm of wind of course, but the snow did not begin to fall till the next day, some hours after the wind had dropped. That he had been caught by a fall of rock — she seemed to remember that this possibility had been mentioned before, among so many others. And were there really any places along the road where such a thing was likely to happen? Not if he had taken the main road to the north. Southward it ran in many places under precipitous crags where rock-slides often took place — but this talk of the sibyl about his having ridden to the south, was it not merely meant as an insinuation, since she too had heard rumours that for some reason or other Thestrup deliberately wished to vanish? But it was too ridiculous that she should continue to occupy herself with the old impostor's gossip. That she had really been able to help Jomfru Langseth was *one* thing — she might herself have hit upon giving the patient laudanum, if she had had any in the house. And it might very well be due to her own treatment on the first night, with bags of herbs, astringent and detergent tea, that the terrible haemorrhage had given place to a natural purgation. And the hop pillow she had placed under Marie's head ought to have produced sleep, which was what the poor woman needed above all. But the old quack too was doubtless acquainted with many genuine medical remedies, since it could not be due to her spells and incantations that her cures were often notoriously successful. But in all conscience that did not oblige one to place any reliance on her claim to be able to read people's destiny in the past and future. In any case she had not found out that the brooch was a present, not from Thestrup, but from quite another consort — indeed it appeared from something she had said that she had no idea Dorthea had already been widowed once before. But it was silly to be deliberating like this about what this hag had known or not known, and she was angry with herself for having actually allowed the gypsy woman to make so strong an impression on her during the night.

The Captain would not come into the house. But when the little boys rushed out to meet him as soon as he got out of the cart, he took Carl in his arms and embraced him warmly. And he greeted Bertel cordially.

"I will see if I can come over to Fenstad again this evening," said Dorthea, as he gave her his hand at parting.

"If only you would! I cannot bear her having to lie there with only that horrible female to handle her," exclaimed Cold hotly.

"She is not an attractive person, I grant you. But one must admit that hitherto her treatment has been beneficial."

"Yes, and the devil thank her for it, the cursed old harridan. I should think she has every right to make good the mischief she herself has brought about."

"She herself?" whispered Dorthea, horrified.

"Yes, didn't you know that? Marie went to Aaserud while the woman was there and came home " — he shrugged his shoulders. "She looked as if she had got her death — and that night, and next day — to cut it short, she confessed to me what was the matter with her. Who else but Sibilla can have done it? I thought you knew that, and that was why you absolutely insisted that I should bring this odious iniquitous individual to Fenstad. On the principle of healing with the weapon that gave the wound."

Dorthea checked him with a gesture. She felt herself turn white in the face with disgust and horror: "Stop, man, stop! It is impossible — the gypsy herself expressed her loathing of such a deed."

Cold gave an ugly laugh: " I quite believe it! She always makes her language suit her game — echoes the one she's talking to. For that matter I believe they never practise it themselves — with them the saying is, the more children the better for the begging. I'm sure the vagabonds despise us heartily for every service we pay for through the nose."

When Dorthea had finished her duties for the forenoon she crept into bed and drew the curtains. But tired as she was, she was unable to get to sleep. She could not rid herself of the thought of Sibilla — saw her in her mind's eye, kept turning the woman's utterances over and over — and she searched for reasons and excuses for not returning to Fenstad any more.

Yes — although in her inmost heart she knew it to be unworthy cowardice and a betrayal of the unfortunate Jomfru Langseth, she simply could not face the gypsy woman again, to say nothing of passing a nocturnal vigil in her company in that horrible sickroom at Fenstad.

It made her burning hot to think that she had sought the aid of this female — in order to learn her husband's fate! She was not even sure whether her motive for doing this had been a real belief in the dark, mysterious woman's possession of occult powers, or whether she had done it in spite of her conviction that it was all deception and hocus-pocus. One thing was just as bad as the other.

Ah yes — in her heart she had certainly hoped that the stranger had access to sources of knowledge which flowed in darksome depths to which the clear daylight of reason could not penetrate. And she who had believed she loved this blessed daylight with all her soul — no sooner did its rays seem to her cold and pitiless, illumining as they did a mournful present and an uncertain future — than she sought refuge in a superstitious hope that the roving people might after all possess such mysterious powers as were attributed to them by the country folk.

She had only herself and her own fatuity to thank for it — and yet it revolted her, like a horrible profanation of her grief, to think of the shadowy black figure sitting in the reddish flickering light of the tallow candle, bent over her cards, mumbling prophecies of evil, while she pretended to read Jörgen's fate in these dirty bits of paper. And, intolerable thought! — supposing she had *known* all about it the whole time, supposing it was after all she and her sons who had avenged themselves on the lonely horseman for having once challenged their hatred — for *that* indeed flowed in darksome depths and could never be brought to light.

The Captain's last words had revealed such abysmal mendacity in this creature that Dorthea *dared* not meet her again.

She was sorry for Marie Langseth — but the housekeeper had voluntarily surrendered herself into this woman's hands, so none but Sibilla herself could help her. Or a doctor — yes, of course, she would send a note over to Fenstad, earnestly representing to Cold the necessity of sending for a real doctor — but why had he not done this as soon as he found out what step the unhappy girl had taken?

Of course — it was obvious that this was a case for a doctor; such household remedies as those she knew of were quite inadequate. She would write that. In any case she had done what she could; the febrifugal and dispersive remedies she had used were at least palliative and perfectly harmless. And it looked as if Sibilla's doctoring had also had a favourable effect on the patient. She herself had seen to it that the sickroom was well supplied with clean linen, lint and the necessary appliances. She had given Magnille detailed instructions as to what the patient might be given to eat and drink. In reality there was nothing more she could do for Jomfru Langseth.

And she had her own house to look after — and all the preparations for the boys' visit to Lunde. And if she decided to go with them, as Brother Ole seemed to wish so earnestly, then there would be still more to arrange — she would have to make her own preparations for the journey and to leave things so that the maids could carry on the housekeeping and look after the smaller children while she was away. She could no longer ask Karen Hauss to come and stay for the time being — but perhaps Finchen Wagner? Oh, she had so many things to see to.

With profound surprise she discovered that now she really looked forward to going to the wedding. After all they were her nearest relations, the people up at Lunde — the dear good younger brother, the honest, kindly Sheriff, who had made it plain that he wished her to look upon him as a father. And her mother — a strange, blind feeling of expectation, or hope of assistance, a longing for her mother, arose in her soul. " Mother is your mother too, Dorthea," Brother Ole had said.

9

MADAME ELISABETH, and the Sheriff too, received Dorthea
Thestrup and her sons cordially enough. But after the
first greetings had been exchanged over a cup of coffee in
the old house Dorthea did not see much more of them.
The Sheriff disappeared, and his madam, leaning on her
silver-mounted stick, paced from house to house and room
to room, directing in person the bustling activities of the
approaching wedding.

Well, it was perfectly natural that she had no time for
much talk with her daughter. And during the few min-
utes they had sat together over the coffee Thestrup had
never been mentioned. For the journey Dorthea had put
on her church-going gown of black lustrine with white
cuffs and an armlet of black velvet. A black rosette held

her neckerchief together over the bosom, and she had edged the streamers of her cap with black ribbon. With part of her consciousness she was thinking all the time that now she had put on widow's weeds. But her mother and stepfather could not know that she had done so for the first time — they doubtless thought she had gone into mourning long ago. Dorthea guessed that to them Thestrup's death was stale news to which they no longer gave much thought. It was the eve of the wedding, and their minds were full of a hundred other things.

Women and girls arrived without cessation bearing pails of cream and baskets of provisions, and all had to be asked in and treated. Dorthea helped in receiving the things and carrying them into the storehouse. It was a lovely spring evening — for up here in the Dale it was not yet full summer; the fresh smell of trampled grass in the yard, of horse-dung and wood-pile and chimney-smoke mingled with the scent of young, moist verdure from the paddock.

Through the many cheerful sounds of activity indoors and out could be heard the roar of the mill-stream south of the farm and the distant murmur of the river at the bottom of the valley. High up the sky was covered with little clouds like tufts of wool, but in the west a subdued sunlight issued from behind the clouds and lighted up the fresh green and brown of the field around the farms, which lay in a row halfway up the slope on the sunny side. How beautiful it is here, thought Dorthea with sisterly fellow-feeling; here her dear Ole would surely live happily on the great rich farm, with his capable Ingebjörg. She was not so pretty, by the way, as Dorthea had expected, and she was a good deal older than her bridegroom

— eight-and-twenty. But she looked sensible and well brought-up and had a quiet, pleasing manner. And the sense of security that comes with easy circumstances is no mean thing.

For a moment she thought of her own future and sighed. Was not her situation almost as insecure as that of the poor people who lived in the grey cottages along the river, where in many an autumn the frost ruined the crops on their flood-ravaged scraps of cornfield between the alder-woods and the gravelly bluffs and breathed sickness upon man and beast?

The hills on the other side of the Dale rose in rounded masses, dark-blue with forest from their feet to the skyline. Only along the tributary stream which came down by Herberg church were there farms of any size with fields on the steep slopes below them, and here and there on the high ground a clearing could be seen — a croft or a sæter. As Dorthea stood gazing, absorbed in the view, the clouds in the north-west changed to copper-red, gleaming amber-yellow at the edges — the sun was about to set. Scarcely a breath of wind stirred — the great mountain-ash in the middle of the yard stood quite still with all its clusters of pale yellow blooms and tender reddish brown leaves. What would the weather be like tomorrow? Up here, she remembered, people fancied that if it rained on the bride as she went to church it was an omen of riches to come. But it would not be very pleasant if all these people were to sit in their soaked and steaming clothes, filling the rooms for the wedding feast.

She saw nothing of Vilhelm and Claus. Across the yard women were hurrying from the byre with pails full of milk; they shouted merry greetings to girls who ran from house to house with their arms full of bedclothes. Down by the King's lodge there was someone with a lantern — the bride slept there tonight with the women who were to dress her in the morning.

Dorthea took up her pail of sausages and went down to the bake-house. A pleasant smell from the great soup-kettle met her as she opened the door. Busy female figures enveloped in thick clouds of steam moved about in the glare of the stove, others were occupied at the long kitchen-table, on which stood a couple of tallow-candles in iron candlesticks among bowls, cups and baskets of eggs. In a corner of the room a woman was pounding forcemeat as hard as she could in a great stone mortar. She was wearing a great white cap with streamers which fell forward and entirely concealed her face as she stooped over her work.

Her mother had asked Dorthea to shoot these sausages into the soup-cauldron — she wanted to make the soup as strong as possible. But the woman with the big cap came up as though to stop her: " What are you doing there, mother? — it's me that's looking after the soup — eh eh," she checked herself, " why, dear me — it's never Dorthea, Madame Thestrup I mean? Well, I dare say you don't recognize me? "

There was really something about the other which seemed familiar to Dorthea, though at first she could not put a name to this face. It was long, like the face of a horse, although the cap-streamers hung right down over the forehead and in the glare from the stove the big features seemed to cast shadows over themselves — the long flat cheeks were hollow, the nose large and straight, curiously angular at the tip, the chin long and perfectly flat.

As she held herself with something of a stoop from the hips up, even after she had left her work at the mortar, she momentarily reminded Dorthea in an unpleasant way of Sibilla; but this woman wore town clothes and spoke like a person of quality. A light broke in on her:

" Why yes — surely it must be — Madame Dabbelsteen? "

" Indeed it is — fancy my sweet Dorette knowing me again! Well, you must excuse me, my dear Madame Thestrup, but I always think of you as my darling little Dorthea Frazer, my own little pet you used to be when I was living with your mamma and Dean de Theilemann."

To tell the truth Dorthea had no recollection of this; on the contrary, it had always been her feeling that she was not at all fond of Jomfru Aleth, as her mother's companion was called at that time. But then she was only a little girl when Aleth left them, as far as she could remember in order to take up a post as housekeeper to an elderly clergyman in the Kongsvinger district. It was many years later that she married the curate Dabbelsteen — she must have been already an old maid. It was true enough that in persuading her husband to engage Student Dabbelsteen Dorthea had been largely swayed by the fact that he was the son of her mother's former dependant — Dorthea believed Jomfru Aleth had been with her ever since Major Eckelöff's time and at any rate during the years of her marriage to Dorthea's father. But now that she saw her again Dorthea was quite certain that she had never liked her.

Madame Dabbelsteen skimmed the bubbling soup, talking all the while:

" Well, that was indeed an unexpected pleasure — that

I should see my dear Dorthea here — Madame did not think you were coming to the wedding. So this is truly an unexpected pleasure. And all the kindness you showed my poor son, I can never thank you enough for that! Yes, I saw your sons here just now — oh, what a delightful pair they are, especially the eldest — that's the one they call Claus, I think? "

" Vilhelm is the elder. But Claus has grown rather faster."

As time went by Dorthea had found the thought of Augustin Dabbelsteen a painful one — culpable as his absconding had been, her sense of justice nevertheless forced her to admit that it was to some extent excusable: what young man would not have lost his head on hearing such news of his beloved? One could not lightly lay the whole blame for the disaster that had resulted from his conduct upon Dabbelsteen. And yet Dorthea could not think of him without a bitterness so deep that it pained her. Nevertheless she thought she must speak a word of sympathy to his mother.

" Yes, it was they who were your son's pupils, Madame Dabbelsteen. And in many ways he was a clever teacher, my husband and I appreciated his gifts as a tutor. Do you know at all how poor Student Dabbelsteen is doing now? "

But the woman only sighed and shook her head, making all the white streamers flutter about her dark face.

Dorthea was no more than moderately pleased when Madame Dabbelsteen informed her that they were to share a bed that night. Meanwhile there was so much to be done in the kitchen that Dorthea held out to the end — she and Aleth were the last to leave.

The night was already far advanced. The weather was

still fine and calm and the sky was covered with faintly grey-blue cloudlets, but a tissue of golden lines showed where the moon shone behind them. In the light June night which was already giving way to morning the murmur of running water all round the farm and in the valley below could be plainly heard, and in the paddock there were thuds and swishing of foliage when one of the many horses that had been turned out broke through the alder thickets. All the wedding guests must have gone to bed, but work was still going on among the outhouses and there was a light in the harness-room.

The room in which Dorthea and the curate's widow had been allotted sleeping quarters was situated in the dower house. By the light of the little lantern which Madame Dabbelsteen set down on the table by the window Dorthea saw that the two women in the other bed were already fast asleep — one of them was the bride's sister-in-law, the other an elderly woman whom she did not know. Over by the little cast-iron fireplace a shakedown had been made up on the floor — three fair-haired children's heads peeped out from among the fur rugs.

"It is a great pity Madame Elisabeth should have had that annoying affair with the clergyman," remarked Madame Dabbelsteen; she was engaged in changing her big white cap for a smooth little nightcap. This made her great lean face still longer and more angular, and now Dorthea saw that her nose was red — with a strangely clear redness, as if it had once been badly frostbitten. Nor was this surprising, seeing how large and prominent it was, but it did not exactly improve the look of her pale and hollow cheeks. "Well, Dorthea must have noticed that Madame's in a real bad temper — my word, how contrary she is."

" Oh well, at mamma's age, she must be dreadfully tired. She has had so much to see to, over this wedding."

" You'll see, there'll be a lot of gossip about the parsonage folk staying away from the feast tomorrow. For you might say they were half-and-half gentry here at Lunde — Elisabeth has twice been a lady! " Aleth Dabbelsteen laughed, rather maliciously, it seemed to Dorthea. " You know, it's always the way for the parson and his wife to come home from church with the wedding party. I don't suppose Elisabeth feels very comfortable just now. If only one could be sure he won't begin to talk about it in his homily — scolding and storming about the immoral ways of the countryfolk. But you can never feel safe with Parson Struwe."

" Oh? Is he such a scolder, the new parson here? " Dorthea had taken off her gown and her upper petticoats, now she was in stocking-feet putting on her night-jacket.

" Yes, the fact is he has a strong leaning to the Evangelicals — he's a Holsteiner, by the way, is Pastor Struwe. And so he was mighty scandalized when he heard that Ingebjörg had been here staying with Ole since early spring — she came here when Lars Gullaug sent over the things she was to have for her dowry. Your mother, Dorette, answered him flatly that such was the custom " — she turned to Dorthea with an ingratiating smile — " ah, you mustn't be angry with me, but I really *cannot* bring myself to say Madame Thestrup to my own pet lamb; *may* I not call you Dorette as in old days? — well, so Madame Elisabeth said that such had always been the custom with the country people here: when you married somebody

from outside the parish and the bride's father had provided the betrothal feast and paid out the dowry, it was
for the bridegroom and his folk to take over the girl and
all further expenses for her keep and for the wedding.
And besides, when the young people have plighted their
troth before the parson the marriage is as binding as need
be, so it has been in this country from time immemorial.
Well, but then Struwe held forth about the peasants' terrible immorality, and he said to your mother that as she
came from a higher class she ought to take the lead here
and break with this sinful custom — ay, it was a *disgrace,*
he said, that she should tolerate such a scandal in her
house, she who had been the wife of a reverend clergyman.
But then Dorthea may be sure she gave him as good as she
got! " Madame Dabbelsteen chuckled with malicious
delight. " Oho, how they did abuse each other! Well,
then he wanted to know why they could not hold the
wedding when Ingebjörg Larsdatter first came to Lunde,
and Elisabeth answered him, why, it's not the same here as
at the parsonage, where folks have to bring presents, a pail
of milk or a pot of cream, if they only want to have a word
or two with the old man — we peasants have to wait with
our feasting till our cow's in milk. My word, how they
did wrangle. But if only Struwe doesn't get his own back
tomorrow in church and trounce Ole and Ingebjörg in his
address — for there he's on his own ground; even Elisabeth can't answer him there! " She laughed so loudly that
Dorthea was afraid she would wake some of the sleepers
and hushed the old woman energetically.

No, Aleth Dabbelsteen was not an attractive person —
and yet, in spite of all, Dorthea was strangely moved to
hear once more the pet name by which she had been

known in her childhood — to think there was still someone who remembered her as a little girl and called her
darling and pet lamb. It was so natural that this time her
mother was occupied with everything but her daughter's
affairs, but still it gave her a sense of disappointment,
though Dorthea did not know what else she had expected.
Madame Dabbelsteen climbed up into the bed and lay
down beside her. She did not smell good — it was that
peculiar mousy smell that hangs about old people in old
clothes. And yet her feeling was not altogether one of
displeasure when Aleth patted her cheek and wished her
Dorette good-night. No one had called her that since
Bisgaard led her home as a bride — he said Thea, when
he wanted to be affectionate. And Thestrup did the
same — he had heard the Dean and Christence call her
that.

Meanwhile Madame Dabbelsteen had clasped her
hands and begun an evening prayer so lengthy that Dorthea fell asleep while the other was still mumbling.

Dorthea saw nothing of her sons till next morning, as
she stood outside with the other women helpers to watch
the bridal procession ride off — she had not even been
able to find out where they were quartered for the night.
Now she discovered Claus and Vilhelm among the body
of mounted groomsmen who were to lead the festal procession like a guard of honour.

Not without anxiety did their mother see that they had
both been furnished with fire-arms, like all their companions; there must have been about a dozen of them, and
the restive group wheeled round and round — the horses

seemed impatient already. She saw that Claus was riding the Junker, but Vilhelm was mounted on a strange horse — a young, handsome animal that looked as if it might be very lively. She would have preferred it the other way about; that calm boy Claus had a better way with horses. Well, they were both fairly good riders — Thestrup had attached such importance to their learning to ride and shoot that in spite of all he had himself found time to train them.

It was indeed a gay sight and a fair one, this brightly clad bridal party assembled in the sunshine in the yard of this upland farm. Below them stretched the valley in its springtime verdure, down at the bottom the river flashed between its alder thickets, and from the other side, where the wooded hills were veiled in an incipient heat-haze, the bells of Herberg church began at that moment to ring their invitation.

But their gentle tones were immediately drowned in the thunder of horses' hoofs and the reports of muskets and pistols; the whole body of groomsmen made a dash for the gate, shouting and shrieking as they squeezed each other against the heavy gate-posts and waving their hats and fire-arms, while the pungent smell of powder-smoke hung in the air behind them. The drummer beat a roll on his drum and the two musicians with clarinet and fiddle struck up a lively tune, which however was somewhat disjointed owing to the difficulty they had in controlling their frightened horses.

Ingebjörg Larsdatter was a splendid sight with her high silver crown glittering in the sunshine, her fluttering silk ribbons and flowing hair, with chains and brooches on her bosom and a bright red damask skirt. Ole rode proudly by her side; with his silver-laced three-cornered hat, his sword at his hip and his high black top-boots he presented an almost military appearance. After the wedding couple came the troop of bridesmaids in their finery — some of them had boys and young men to lead their horses; they had some difficulty in guiding them from their side-saddles. And then came all the wedding guests, men and women, most of them mounted, but the rear was brought up by a few vehicles with children and old people.

Dorthea followed the others who were left behind at the farm, stood with them at the gate and watched the noisy procession disappear in clouds of dust down below where the road turned into a little coppice. The sound of hoofs and wheels and the crack of shots echoed behind them, completely drowning the notes of the bridal march. And there came the advance-guard of groomsmen into view again at another bend of the road — little white puffs of smoke still accompanied them. But now the clang of church bells could be heard more plainly from the other side of the valley, and the roar of the mill-race again became audible as the noise of the bridal procession faded away in the distance. Dorthea looked across at the slender church spire pointing up above the woods at the meeting of the rivers — then she raised her eyes to the blue summer sky and offered up a heartfelt sigh, imploring Providence to bless her beloved brother and make him happy.

But indoors the tables were waiting to be laid, the food had to be dished up. Maids ran between storehouse and kitchen, others came with baskets full of juniper and globe-flower for strewing the floors.. Dorthea turned back across the yard, where the dust and the powder-smoke were slowly drifting away, and hurried to her duties within the house.

As her contribution she had brought besides the iced cake a large basket of apple fritters — true, there was no apple in them, but they were delicious for all that. Even then her mother asked her to bake another portion so that they might have hot doughnuts, at any rate at the table where the most honoured guests were to sit. This kept Dorthea busy with her baking till far on in the day. For company she had the smallest daughter of Ingebjörg's brother; the child had eye trouble and they thought it best not to take her to church. Little Abelone Harkelsdatter consoled herself by devouring apple fritters, besides which she got scraps from the other women helpers, broken twists of cake and bits of cheese, making Dorthea regret she had not brought one of her smaller children — several of the guests had their little ones with them. And here was such abundance of good things that she wished hers could have had a share of them.

The homecoming of the newly married pair was no less noisy than their departure. The tramp of hoofs and the jingling of harness, with a volley of salutes, proclaimed the arrival of the advance-guard, the groomsmen. The women who had stayed behind poured out to listen to a parley between the horsemen and the master of the cere- monies — it was as good as a play, for although this was the bridegroom's own farm, the young people pretended they had to come to terms over board and lodging for Ole

Haagensen, his wife and their company. At long last this
was conceded by the master of the ceremonies, after a
great deal of banter which time after time sent the surrounding women and girls into transports of delight and
suppressed giggling.

Dorthea saw that the young fellows, her own boys
among them, were very elated — red in the face, dripping
with sweat under their hats or caps, many of them be-
grimed with powder-smoke. Vilhelm's coat and breeches
bore marks of his having had a tumble during the wild
ride — but he was certainly not the only one. Claus had
a blood-drenched handkerchief wound round one of his
hands. They had evidently had some stiff drinks on the
road, and now, when they had come to terms with the
master of the ceremonies, the latter produced a bottle of
spirits and a glass which he sent round among the groomsmen. After that the whole crowd wheeled about and set
off to meet the rest of the procession which was on its way
up the Lunde slopes.

The drummer drummed, the musicians played a spir-
ited march, Ole rode proudly with drawn sword, and
Ingebjörg held on to her big silver crown with one hand
as it threatened to descend over her forehead. After them
the whole company poured into the yard, dusty and ex-
cited — a little child howled pitiably, and loud cries from
the guests and a deafening hubbub from the great crowd
of people and horses greeted the bridal pair's entry into
Lunde.

In the bake-house Madame Dabbelsteen's glorious soup
was poured into tureens of blue and white delf and polished pewter. Some of it went into commoner earthen-
ware pots intended for the tables in the dower house,

where young people and guests of less importance were placed.

Dorthea and Aleth Dabbelsteen, who were to preside over the serving in the room where the bridal couple sat at table, had plenty of time to get their breath after the final efforts and to cool their heated faces. They stood waiting by the sideboard while the guests squeezed along by the wall — the master of the ceremonies had to fetch them out one by one, pushing and shoving, before he could get them to take their places at the long table. The bridal couple did not sit together, but each took an end of the table — Ingebjörg the lower. She had been able to brush herself and make herself tidy, and the bridal crown again sat straight on her fair-haired head, but she looked pretty tired already, thought Madame Dorthea. But they had yet to listen to a long grace said by the parish clerk and a speech of welcome from the master of the ceremonies, before Dorthea and Aleth could begin to serve out the soup.

The sun shone in through the brownish glass of one of the leaded windows, and the fresh scent of birch-leaves in the fireplace and juniper on the floor was soon overcome by the smell of all these people who had been in lengthy contact with sweaty horses, by the steam from food and the odour of beer. The liquor servers were assiduous in their attentions. Dorthea discovered with some uneasiness that Claus Hartvig addressed himself to the tankard like a grown man and emptied the dram glass as often as it came his way. But soon she had no time to see what her sons were doing — the steaming dishes of fish and meat made their appearance, and now the women helpers had enough to do in forcing the guests to help themselves.

It was a long, long sitting, and Dorthea was sincerely grateful to Aleth Dabbelsteen for advising her to sample the dishes freely when they tasted them in the kitchen. The country weddings she had attended among their neighbours at the works had been much simpler affairs — one reason for establishing the glassworks in that out-of-the-way forest tract had been to give the poor peasants of the neighbourhood an opportunity for increased earnings.

The absence of the parson and his family did not seem to affect the good humour of these peasants at Lunde. Dorthea thought she could even trace a certain aggressive rustic self-assertion in the company: after the toast of the royal family had been drunk and the parish clerk had sung the appropriate verses, invoking the blessing of Heaven on Christian and the Crown Prince, the master of the ceremonies got up and sang a strophe which she had not heard before:

Give peace and plenty in our day, O God,
And bless our harvest, bless our native sod!
The well-deservèd plague be pleased t'abate
And mend th' industrious peasant's sorry state!
Send men with eyes to see, whose words prevail —
Our monarch cannot see through hill and dale.
The King does wish us well, his good son too;
But may th' oppressor quickly get his due!

Dorthea could not restrain a melancholy smile — how these verses would have appealed to her dear Jörgen!

The list of toasts was a long one, and each was followed by a verse of a hymn. With deep emotion the sister joined in humming the tune when the guests had drunk the health of Ole Haagensen and Ingebjörg Larsdatter:

Jesu, who dost alway
The water of our woe
Turn into wine; we pray
Be present here below
Upon this wedding-day.
Meekly we Thee implore
Thine aid outpour
And fill the cup we bear.
To every bridal pair
Thy comfort yield;
Let the rich river of Thy grace
Their griefs efface,
Bless them and be their shield!

Passing round the plate, a pewter dish in which the guests placed their gifts of money to the bridal couple, was also a matter of some little time, since both the man who carried the plate, a cousin of Ingebjörg's, and the master of ceremonies had to comment on each gift — the former announcing its amount with thanks, the latter replying with jocular praise of the giver's generosity. And scarcely was this collection finished when another plate was sent round, in which the guests made a contribution to the parish granary — a benevolent institution which the former parson had originated and which both Sheriff Lunde and Lars Gullaug seemed to regard with an interest that bore witness to their warm feeling for the common good. The afternoon was already far advanced when at last the parish clerk was able to say grace.

And now, while the guests took a breath of fresh air out in the yard, the women helpers had to superintend the clearing of the room for dancing. Movable benches and tables were carried out, the floor was swept of its strewing, candles were produced, to be lighted as soon as darkness fell. And not till this was done could Dorthea and Aleth Dabbelsteen with the other women take their ease in the little room, where it was their turn at last to help themselves to the festal fare and taste the drinks.

Dorthea's feet ached after the hours of standing about and walking, and her throat felt rough from thirst and from all the dust she had swallowed. She found her mother's strong foaming beer delicious, and she also accepted the glass of spirits that Ole brought her, in the hope that it would have a stiffening effect. But in conjunction with her tiredness and the heat of the dimly lighted little room it made her so sleepy that when the company poured back into the parlour and the fiddler struck up a lively country dance Dorthea gave a start and discovered that she must have taken forty winks as she sat among the other women on an uncomfortably narrow bench.

Poor Ingebjörg was obliged to dance — first with the master of ceremonies, but after that with all the male guests who had a right to demand " a swing-round with the bride." Meanwhile Ole called upon the bride's women and maids. He came into the adjoining room too and invited his sister, but Dorthea had to confess with a smile that she did not know the country dances. At that moment the fiddler changed to another tune, and so she had to accompany her brother on to the dancing-floor and figure with him in a newfangled fandango.

He had changed his top-boots for shoes with silver buckles and below his myrtle-green plush breeches the tassels of his great party-coloured garters bobbed up and down. But as a sign of his dignity as a new-fledged married man he danced with his hat on his head and his sabre hanging by his side — it rattled and jingled as he stamped on the floor and swung round Dorthea bowing and clapping his hands.

" Heisan! " He took his sister by the waist and whirled her round in the dance: " You're a stunner, Dorthea! And you saying you couldn't dance! "

" It's because you're such a good partner! " With her hands on his shoulders Dorthea smiled up into the young bridegroom's flushed face. Her heart was overflowing with sincere affection for him — and she was quite dizzy with all the twirling round. Although the room was crowded with dancing couples and the noise of all their stamping feet was at its height, they managed to make the circuit quite handsomely. And when they were back again going through the figure, they made a real pantomime of it, with coquettish smiles and curvettings on her part, roguish glances and bold advances on his. Several of the guests stopped dancing to watch and encouraged them with cries of applause — and scarcely had Ole released her when her stepfather turned up at Dorthea's side and drew her with him back into the dance.

The tall and powerful Haagen Lunde swung her round so that Dorthea scarcely touched the floor with her feet. For one instant the thought struck her — why, she was in mourning — but all sad thoughts and cares seemed to have become so distant and unreal; the alluring notes of the fiddle and the whirling of couples around her irresistibly swept Dorthea away from her everyday self. A passion from long-vanished days awoke within her: how she had loved dancing; O Jörgen, what an ardent, what an enchanting partner he had been — that was when they were newly married, at the ironworks.

Lars Gullaug caught her up the moment the Sheriff let her go — or set her down. She got her breath again, more or less, while Ole's father-in-law steadily tramped through a somewhat more sedate square dance with her. In the fading light the whole company now seemed to be sucked into the dance as by a whirlpool — Dorthea caught a glimpse of her mother, twirling round with the owner of North Lunde. Madame Elisabeth was majestic in brown brocade, but she wore a linen head-band and a silk cap like the other peasant women. It was only a week since she had been in the midst of the sad and harrowing events at Fenstad — yes, Aleth Dabbelsteen did remind her in a curious way of the gypsy woman who had given her such a fright — but what of it, Aleth was really a good old creature — look, there she was dancing with the master of ceremonies so that her cap-ribbons flapped about her hollow cheeks. Captain Cold — oh yes, of course he was her friend, poor man, and so was Marie Langseth — she had been a sympathetic sharer in their troubles. But all that was so far away, so long ago — *now* she could not summon up any feeling for them. She danced — with all her heart she desired nothing but to dance — more, more. Dorthea's eyes sought among the crowd for Ingebjörg's brother — she owed him the next dance, she thought — and he was a fine-looking man and a good dancer, was Harkel Larsson.

Then it was that someone lit the candles on the long table — Aleth Dabbelsteen it was. And the flames of the candles were reflected in the dark eyes of Claus Hartvig;

he stood leaning against the sideboard, watching with a curious expression of chilly disapproval the unbridled abandonment of herself and all these elderly persons in the dance. Dorthea felt as if she had been plucked out of a dream. At that moment Claus leapt forward and seized Ingebjörg, who had just been released by Vilhelm — Dorthea understood that the boys had come in to secure the dance with the bride to which they were entitled in their capacity of groomsmen. Of course — they had never before pictured their mother in connection with anything so youthful as dancing.

She laughingly declined Harkel Gullaug's outstretched hands: " Thank you all the same! But now I must go and see about my duties." And indeed it was high time to think about the guests' supper.

It was a comparatively simple collation — all the pails of cream porridge that the neighbours had brought, besides waffles and cakes. This time it was to be served in the dower house, so that the parlour could still be used for dancing. But in the dower house the young people had kept up their dance to the music of the clarinet. So here the situation was even more difficult than in the main building; and only after a good deal of discussion and the assistance of the master of ceremonies were the women able to turn out the unruly and headstrong dancers.

After being driven out these young men and women continued their dance in the yard. The clarinet-player seated himself on the steps of the storehouse — very much in the way of the busy women — and went on playing. But unfortunately he was a very mediocre musician, and a number of the young people collected by the door of the parlour and danced quite different dances to the music of the fiddle, which could be heard through the open door.

All the afternoon both Vilhelm and Claus had been circling round Tora, the girl who was related to the Sheriff, trying to get a dance as often as they could catch her. As far as Vilhelm was concerned this was due to her being the only girl he knew, and at first he was bashful about asking those girls who were strangers. And then Tora was so charming and friendly. But soon Vilhelm made the discovery that he was really a good dancer — the music seemed to course through his whole frame and guide his limbs; even the country dances which he had never tried before offered no difficulty. From that moment his bashfulness was gone, and whenever Tora had to fly away and attend to her household duties he confidently turned to the prettiest girl who happened to be free. And it was not long before he noticed to his intense gratification that the girls were very willing to dance with him. This was not only because he was a nephew of the bridegroom, for Claus was that too. And Claus was much better looking. Indeed the girls were very willing to take the floor with him too, but they very soon broke off — the fact was, Claus could not dance at all.

Vilhelm saw this with a touch of malicious satisfaction. This would serve the silly boy right. Ever since last Christmas he had made fun of Vilhelm for hopping about with his arm round a girl " just to get in practice so that you can curry favour with Tilla Hauss." Claus himself had an altogether childish contempt both for girls and for antics, as he called them. Now he could stand and look on like a poor beggarman.

But after this Claus too had his eyes on Tora. She was

far too good-natured to let him feel she regarded him as a clumsy bungler; on the contrary, she guided him kindly and patiently — like this and this, and not like that; there, now that's much better; oh, he would soon learn to dance.

So the end of it was that the brothers nearly came to fighting for Tora whenever she showed herself in the room. She tried in her gentle way to be fair and dance with them turn and turn about, and Vilhelm would have fallen in with this, if Claus had not proved cantankerous. He tried to push in and get a dance with Tora out of his turn, and when the girl gently pushed him aside and gave her hands to Vilhelm he stood glaring at them — till someone shoved him aside for getting in his way. And every time this happened it obviously made him angrier — so he went out, and when he turned up again in the room Vilhelm could see that he had had something to drink; he was already fairly drunk.

He was by no means the only one as the afternoon wore on, and several times the young men were on the point of getting in each other's hair. But until now the women and the older men had always succeeded in separating them before it came to a regular fight. And towards evening many of these doughty swains had been compelled to surrender to the forces of beer and spirits. Some of the older men too had disappeared to bedrooms and other recesses. And along the outside walls, where the grass was high and soft, were young men sitting or lying; some were still bravely resisting the assaults of Morpheus, while others lay at full length snoring loudly. There were others again whom nature forced to surrender what they had taken in excess; through all the noise of music and dancing there could be heard the miserable gulps of retching.

The sun had gone down behind the hills. The long shadows of houses and trees seemed suddenly to shrink into a queer little darkness under walls or foliage, now that the soft white light from the vault of heaven had sucked as it were all the strength out of the colours of daytime. The green meadows paled, and the brown log-houses turned grey, as their windows reflected the evening light. Vilhelm was dancing with a big brown-haired girl — she was a good head taller and twice his weight, but her legs worked like drumsticks and she whirled round as lightly as a top; they danced so well together that they were laughing in each other's faces. Neither of them had any thought of stopping while there was breath in their bodies.

Then came the procession to supper in the old house — with the drummer at its head, accompanied by the fiddler and the master of ceremonies with his staff. Ole and Inge-björg then led the way, hand in hand.

"Well, now you'll have to go in too, you and your brother," said the girl Vilhelm was dancing with — Anne was her name and she was the daughter of one of the Herberg farms. "Seeing that you're groomsmen" — she herself slipped into her place among the bridesmaids.

Claus was hanging about by the grindstone — he did not look fit to go anywhere. He had lost his hat; his brown curls fell in disorder about his flushed forehead. He had unbuttoned both waistcoat and shirt, as though to let his bare chest cool down.

At that moment someone touched Vilhelm's sleeve — Tora. "You must go in too, as you're a groomsman," she said like Anne Herberg, looking at him with her charming, rather indolent smile.

" If nobody forces me? Oh no, I know what's good
manners! " Vilhelm laughed ecstatically and flung his
arm round Tora's shoulders. " Well, but — perhaps you
ought to go in? "

" No, the likes of us have to wait. It's only for the
farmer folk to sit down first."

" Oh, but that's splendid! Come along, Tora, we'll
have a dance! "

" I think you're crazy, Vilhelm." She laughed softly and
tried to free herself from his embrace, when he butted his
forehead against her bosom. Her red-striped jacket was
made of stiff material and it was fastened with little metal
hooks which pressed coldly against his hot skin, but he
could feel her soft bosom within the jacket. " No, let go,
boy, I'm tired, I can't dance any more."

" Well, but then we can go and sit down somewhere —
Tora, my little darling — we can go and find a place to sit
and take a rest."

A lad had taken over the clarinet — he played it much
better than the professional. And all the unoccupied
young people together with some of their elders, cottagers
and the like, who had to wait till the second supper, kept
up the dance. The yard was well trampled by this time
and parts of it were quite bare.

With a sigh and a shake of the head Tora gave in and
allowed Vilhelm to lead her along the wall outside the
dancers. As they passed the grindstone Claus straightened
himself and made a grab at the girl: " 'Shmy turn now,"
he babbled; " you owesh me this — this dance — yesh
you do."

" No, I can't dance any more, I'm tired! " She looked
at him with a little tolerant smile: " I don't know — I

almost think you can't dance any more this evening either,
Claus! " He was not very steady on his legs; every time
he reached out and tried to catch hold of her he nearly
overbalanced. Tora gave him a friendly little push which
nearly upset him. Then she let Vilhelm lead her past.
" He looks as if he'd had enough too, Claus does," she said
with a little laugh.

" Yes, poor fellow, he's fit for bed now," Vilhelm
laughed back.

They turned into a grass-grown path that led away from
the farm between cornfields fringed by high balks. The
fresh shoots of corn were already thick enough to shroud
the brown mould in a fine shimmer of green. " Some rain
would be a good thing now," remarked Vilhelm.

" Oh, we'll have rain for Botalfi, sure. 'Tis always bad
weather the day we move up to the sæter."

St. Botolph's Day — that was less than a week from now,
Vilhelm reflected with disappointment. It was intended
that they should stay here with their mother for a week
or more after the wedding festivities. But now he thought
there could not be much to wait for, if Tora was to go to
the sæter.

Here and there people were lying in the tall grass of the
balk. It was much lighter here than among the houses;
they had the whole open sky above them, and it seemed as
though the broad valley below them also sent back light.
The evening was so bright that they could clearly see every
house and every fence below, and little dark specks moved
where the people had let their cattle stay out in the fields.
It grew quieter and quieter as they walked away from the
house, and all the noises of the wedding were merged into

a monotonous hum where only an occasional loud cry sounded above the rest. The murmur of the river was hushed, but they were coming nearer and nearer to the roar of the millstream.

Vilhelm noticed that a figure was staggering after them on the path. He was surprised to find that after all it was not so light as he thought, and stopped to see who it was. Then he recognized Claus Hartvig.

Claus came up: " I want to dance with Tora — you'll have to come with me now, Tora! "

The girl pushed Vilhelm a little to one side and placed herself between the brothers. She looked so pretty and so grown up and full of authority in her holiday attire: the plaits which she had twisted round her head were decorated with rosettes of silver and ribbons, her red-striped jacket was embroidered with a pattern of little flowers and fitted so closely as to accentuate the charming forms of her shoulders and breast, but from the waist it was cut into basques which the stiff skirt held out over the rounding of the hips. She tried to calm down Claus, asked him if he would not go and lie down for a little — there would be time enough to dance later.

" I'm coming with you — where are you two going to hide yourselves? "

" That's no business of yours," said Vilhelm.

As Claus leaned forward — he looked exactly like a butting bull-calf — he pitched into Tora, making her trip lightly to one side. Vilhelm gave his brother a well-aimed right-hander, landing on his ribs, and with that he collapsed and was left lying on the grassy edge of the path as Tora and Vilhelm walked on.

" You were rather rough with your brother," said Tora, looking back over her shoulder. " He's lying there yet, poor fellow."

" Well, that will do him no harm," said Vilhelm lightly. " He's only a raw youngster."

" Isn't he the elder of you two then? "

" Indeed he is not. He's long for his age, that's all."

They had reached the end of the fields and now the path made a fairly steep descent into the gorge where the mill-stream came roaring down from the mountain with one little waterfall after another. A solitary sheep fled down the path, baaing in terror, and disappeared in the bushes that grew luxuriantly at the bottom of the gorge. Farther down a smooth sheet of water could be glimpsed through the leaves — the pool by the mill-house.

" Huff, it's good and cool here — I'm so hot — ain't you hot? " She wiped her face with a corner of her apron.

" But it's raw — feel, the grass is quite wet."

The steep grass slope was sprinkled pale with cowslips. Here by the side of the stream there was a fresh and acrid scent from the leaves of bird-cherry and birch. Moisture dripped upon their faces as they passed under the trees.

Arrived at the little mill-pool they were suddenly out in the light again, and the air felt quite mild and calm after the raw cold of the thicket. Here too the grass was wet, but they caught sight of an old sledge lying close to the path, and on it they sat down.

All they could see of the Dale from here was a little of the dark blue ridge on the other side, but it was as though they could also see the great space of air which lay between them and the opposite slope. The pond below them was smooth and pale — once some rings appeared on the surface, a little fish. And when they had been sitting a little while Vilhelm could feel that the old sledge still held some of the sun's warmth, and a faint good smell of flour or hay hung about the spintered old wood.

Tora unhooked her jacket and turned it back, showing the top of her white linen under-garment and the red braces of her bodice: " Huff, I'm sweating so it bites my skin — " she scratched herself between the shoulder-blades.

" That's bad! " Vilhelm ventured to feel her throat. " You must have had a deal of hard work today."

" Oh yes! We've been hard at work all of us, you may be sure." She looked him in the eyes with her frank smile, made no show of withdrawing from his warm hand, and Vilhelm let it slip down her throat till it enclosed one of her soft little breasts —

— I'm touching her breast, he thought, and remembered how comic it had sounded when one of Father Holberg's characters said it: may I feel your breast, my pretty maid? Oh, it was so good to sit like this caressing Tora's sweet little girlish breasts. He drew closer to her on the sledge and put his other arm round her waist. Her armpits exhaled a fragrance — just the same smell that came from the wet half-opened leaves of the wild cherry — only that was a cold smell, but Tora's was a lovely smell of warmth — for a moment he withdrew his hand and sniffed at his fingers. They smelt of black-currant leaves, as when one has been stealing black-currants in the garden on a sunny day. And again he put his hand in under the linen on her bosom and let it rest there.

" Oh, Tora — you are so pretty! I believe you are the loveliest girl in all the wedding! You are much prettier than the bride."

" Ho no, not that! I'm only the daughter of a poor widow, I am, even if Mother is a cousin of the Sheriff. But Ömbjör is the only daughter at Gullaug."

" Yes, but you may be just as beautiful for not being rich."

" There's not many that think so," she said with a smile, but the glance of her lovely dark eyes was serious as it swept the blue sky over the valley.

" Tora, dear Tora — I am so immensely fond of you! "

" Yes, I almost think I've noticed that " — she laughed softly, with a touch of mockery.

Vilhelm pressed her to him — little voluptuous thrills rippled down his spine. " Will you let me kiss you? "

" No, indeed I will not," she replied good-temperedly; but she made no sign of releasing herself from his arms, and so he took hold of her head and turned it towards him. Her cheek was so cool and smooth and soft, and when his lips found hers they parted slightly, so that he was kissing into the girl's open mouth — giddy with rapture he went on kissing and kissing —

Till suddenly she gave a little jerk — Vilhelm's last kiss barely grazed her cheek-bone. " Give over now, boy, that'll do now — " she said, shaking with suppressed laughter. " You're something of a forward young fellow, Vilhelm."

The boy too collapsed in laughter, with his head in the many folds of her lap: " Well but, Tora, you do like me — you like me to kiss you, don't you? "

She smiled mysteriously: " You think so — " and then

she buried her fingers in his mop of red hair, ruffling it mercilessly. " Ah, you Vilhelm — " and she began to untie the ribbon of his queue, letting down his hair till it flowed about his face, then she filled her hands with it and pulled with a will: " did anyone see the like of his red hair — he's ugly too, is Vilhelm." It sounded like a playful caress.

He took hold of her ankle above the buckled shoe — how fine and slender it was! — and her calf in the rough knitted stocking so round and firm. But when his hand had strayed up under the many petticoats, as far as the warm naked skin above the knee, she gave a sudden start: " No, Vilhelm — now you must behave yourself — you're not to do that, no."

The boy had a feeling that her protest was perhaps not to be taken too seriously, and went on carressing her under all these skirts. Then the girl gave a harder tug at his hair and pushed him away: " Behave yourself now, rude boy."

He sat up, disconcerted for a moment — but she did not look angry; she smiled slily, pulled her jacket on again and began to hook it up: " We'd better be going home soon, hadn't we? "

" Do you think it's getting cold? — look here — " he pulled off his coat and threw it round her shoulders. He had no objection to disclosing that his black silk waistcoat had long sleeves and that there were lace frills to his shirt.

" Now *you* will be cold," she said; but she stayed where she was, fingering the polished steel buttons of his coat and examining them. Vilhelm got his arm round her waist again and arranged his coat so that it covered them both.

Fancy his imagining he loved Mathilde Hauss — that

saucy person! He had been so afraid she might laugh at him that his heart had often throbbed when he ventured to speak to her. Tora here — when she laughed at him it was in such a lovable and pleasant way that his only desire was to coax out more and more of that sweet girlish laughter. Ah, how lovely she was. He chanced to remember that he had kissed Tilken once at Christmas when they were playing forfeits — what a great to-do she had made.

Tora said neither yes nor no, but now Vilhelm thought he knew what *that* meant. So they kissed each other for a while. Till Tora gave the signal that that was enough — she turned her head away, and then began to talk about the move to the sæter.

" Are you comfortable here at Lunde? Is not my grandmother a terribly hard taskmistress? "

" Oh, you know." It was now so dark that he could only *hear* that she smiled. " She got the prize from that Agricultural Society for weaving a thousand ells of different kinds of cloth from wool and linen from the farm. You can be sure the maids were kept hard at it at Lunde that time. Well, I won't say but what she's straight and kind in many ways too, is Elisabeth."

" Has Grandmother taken prizes? I never heard that. I know the Sheriff got a silver medal for ditching and reclaiming the bog here a few years ago."

" Yes, it's nothing but prize-taking here. When they have such a sight of servants in the place as Haakon has, then it goes fine. My father, he didn't get so far as clearing his home fields, what was left of the land after the landslide and the flood, before he died, he'd strained himself carrying stones, you see."

It was now the middle of the night, the darkest hour of

the twenty-four. Wrapt in the twilight Tora told Vilhelm
about her home, in reply to his sympathetic questions.
Synstevoll had been a large and well-kept farm when her
mother was married, but the next year — when Tora's
eldest brother was just born — was the flood year, '72.
Most of the home fields were buried under rocks and
gravel, and almost all the houses on the farm were damaged. Tora was born and brought up at Synstevollhaga,
the croft to which her parents had moved, while her father
toiled at clearing his land after the disaster. But he had
not gone very far with this when he died — Tora was then
five years old — and it was hard enough for her mother,
whose health was not strong, to carry on the farm, small as
it was. So the younger children were sent to kinsfolk. The
eldest brother had just taken over Synstevoll, and he
meant to go on clearing it where his father had had to give
up. But then came the Great Flood of '89 and destroyed
it all again. Tora did not know whether she would ever
be able to go home to her own people.

Vilhelm sat with her hand in his, pressing it now and
again, as she told her story, simply and calmly. She was
just as enchanting, he thought, now that she was serious.

It was hunger that finally made them get up — it occurred to them that they had had no supper! But Tora
assured him that she would be able to manage that.

Vilhelm saw that it was already growing lighter as hand
in hand they walked by the field path back to the farm. It
lay deserted and still in the light of the moon, which could
hardly be said to shine, so light was the sky already.

They had almost reached the farm when they came on
signs of life: two young lads lying asleep at the edge of the
path.

"What about Claus — oughtn't you to look for your brother, I wonder?" asked Tora anxiously.

"Oh, he must have got home somehow — since he's not lying in the ditch anywhere," said Vilhelm lightly.

When they were among the houses Tora led him towards a little one-storeyed cottage which lay squeezed in among the bigger buildings. She confided to him in a whisper that she knew Madame Elisabeth had here treated a few chosen ones among the guests to coffee — she would look if there might be a drop left in the pot.

It was dark inside the old house — it had an open hearth in the middle of the floor and a smoke-hole in the roof. Thin blue smoke from the dying embers floated up to the open hole, from which blades of grass peeped down in the morning light. From the benches along the wall and from the dark corners came sounds of breathing and snoring — and Vilhelm remembered with a sharp sense of embarrassment that he had shirked his duty as a grooms-man; of course he ought to have accompanied Uncle Ole to the bridal chamber. But Ingebjörg and Ole must have gone to bed long ago. Well, perhaps he was not the only one — in any case he had recognized one of his colleagues on the field path.

Tora had found a big bowl — and she contrived to conjure a little coffee, mostly grounds, out of the pot that stood on the edge of the hearth. It was stuffy in the room and there was a rank smell of human bodies and tobacco-smoke — a tankard full of clay pipes, broken and whole, stood on the table together with baskets and trays containing the remains of cakes. Tora collected what looked most appetizing, filled the bowl with milk and stuck a piece of brown sugar between her lips: "Come along."

There was a porch outside the door, and there they stood and ate their meal. She bit the lump of sugar in two and gave him half; they drank in turn from the bowl and swallowed waffles and bits of wafer and cream bun, sniggering and giggling at nothing the while.

It was broad daylight when at last they agreed that now they *must* go to bed. " Do I get a good-night kiss, Tora? " Nobody could see them here in the porch. And now Vilhelm knew that he was not to wait for an answer. It was a long and a good kiss, and she put her arms round his neck in such heartfelt confidence. But in the middle of it she yawned so that her jaws cracked.

That made them both laugh — but then she tore herself away and fled across the yard. Vilhelm was about to set off after her, but suddenly found that he was himself fearfully sleepy. So he shuffled off in the other direction to find the room in which he had slept the night before.

10

THE WEDDING took its course. On the evening of the third day some of the guests went home, but the greater part were to remain until the sixth day.

Vilhelm was so much occupied with thoughts of Tora that he paid little attention to what was going on around him. He had quickly made up his mind to become engaged to her. Why should he not be able to marry a peasant girl? Such a thing was not unheard-of; there were many merchants in Christiania who had taken wives from the country, and now he had decided to adopt a commercial career.

In tales and comedies it frequently happened that the hero — he was usually a young baron or something of the sort — fell in love with a beautiful peasant girl and pro-

posed to her. To be sure, it turned out in most cases that
the girl was the very young lady of fortune whom his
father would have forced him to marry. She had fled into
the country and was living there in disguise, because her
cruel father was going to give her to a bridegroom whom
she had never seen and detested in advance. Anyhow, the
main point was that the baron or whatever he was paid his
suit to the fair one in the belief that she *was* a peasant
girl.

More than once the thought occurred to him that if his
father had been alive perhaps it would not have been such
plain sailing to obtain his permission to betroth himself to Tora Synstevoll. But Vilhelm put the thought behind him. His grief for his father was genuine and sincere.
But now his loss seemed so long ago — so much had happened since. He preferred to look at it in this way: that
as he had lost his father so early in life he must take steps
to become self-supporting as quickly as he could. And as
he was thus compelled to regard himself as a grown-up
person, why should he not secure as his companion for
life the girl of whom he was so immensely fond?

Of course he would never go against his mother or
marry without her blessing. But when she came to know
Tora his mother would certainly appreciate her amiable
qualities and be charmed to embrace her as a daughter.
Why, had not his mother joined in the chorus of admiration when his grandmother had exhibited to the assembled matrons her stores of woollen and linen articles, spun
and woven here at Lunde? And they were the fruit of
Tora's skill and industry, some of them in any case.

He would get Tora to go into service in town, when they
moved to Christiania. In a house where she could acquire

a certain polish. Not but what she was good enough as she was; it was quite impossible that she could be sweeter or more attractive. But as they were to live in town it would be more fitting for her to adapt herself to townish ways.

When all was said and done — without giving offence to her mother and her stepfather and her brother Ole, his mother could not oppose a marriage between him and a near relative of Sheriff Lunde.

Meanwhile Vilhelm had not yet had opportunity — or courage — to initiate Tora into his dreams of their common future. She was always so taken up with household duties that he was not able to see very much of her. A swing round at odd times in the afternoon. She knew all the modern dances to perfection — had learnt them from her uncle. He had served in a Holstein regiment, she told him, and he happened to be the fiddler who played at the wedding. But only on one evening had Vilhelm had a chance of stealing away from the farm with her. They had sat in a hollow below the King's lodge, and he had been allowed to kiss her and to hold his hand over her breast. But she dared not stay out so long as the first evening.

For the rest, they lived here at Lunde in a profusion of food and drink. On the morning of the second day they were even brought drams and waffles before they got up. Vilhelm was now rather cautious with strong drink — he had no desire to find himself incapable as on that terrible night in the spring, when he had been drinking at Sandtangen. Besides, to tell the truth he did not think brandy tasted so very good.

Claus, on the other hand, did; one could not avoid noticing it. For that matter, Vilhelm had not seen much of his brother during these days; he had not been in their bed when Vilhelm got up on the morning of the first — or rather, the second day of the wedding. Claus must have found other sleeping quarters and kept to them, for now Vilhelm shared his bed with a hearty young peasant, a relation of Ingebjörg Gullaug.

Whether Claus remembered that his brother had knocked him down the first evening, Vilhelm could not tell. But he had the impression that Claus was not getting much fun out of the festivities. The other young lads had arranged wrestling matches, and they had also shot at a target fixed on the wall of the smithy. Claus took part in the shooting, but was far from distinguishing himself — he was more or less fuddled the whole time, so he did not shoot nearly so well as usual. Vilhelm came off much better, though as a rule he was not such a good shot as Claus Hartvig.

Claus had quite given up dancing. When the others danced he hung about looking on. And after Tora had once decisively rejected his somewhat drunken advances, he contented himself with glaring sullenly when he saw her dancing with Vilhelm.

Vilhelm could not help feeling something besides pity for Claus. He was quite pleased to be able to assert himself as the elder, the grown-up who knew how to deport himself among other young people of his age; and he had found a sweetheart. Tora could not conceal the fact that she had taken a fancy to him. If only he had a chance of talking things over with her, he felt sure the dear girl would not send him about his business.

And Claus, poor boy, was neither fish, flesh nor fowl. He was no longer a child, but it was abundantly clear that he was far from being grown up.

It was with his new bedfellow, the cousin of Ole's wife, and two other lads, that Vilhelm went up into the hills on the seventh day after the wedding. They had to see to something at the sæter, and they took with them a dog, guns and fishing-tackle. The peasant lads had also provided themselves with pocket pistols of spirits.

So when they had been out early and got a few hares — Vilhelm was rather proud of having shot one of them — and afterwards netted the sæter stream, they made for the sæter, ate and drank and went to sleep. And the afternoon was far advanced before they thought of leaving. The sun had already disappeared behind the ridge when the sportsmen came strolling down through the copse just above the farm.

There was an enclosed pasture here, with alder scrub and osiers, and the ground was soggy and well-trodden — the wedding guests had turned out their horses here during the past week. They were just at the gate of the home field — the stakes had been pulled up and it stood open — when a half-smothered female voice was heard shrieking: " Let me be, I say — you *mustn't* — " and the thick tones of a boy: " Don't make a fuss, girl."

The dog tore itself out of Per Vold's hands and dashed into the alder-bushes, barking loudly, till its leash caught in something. Per ran after it, with Vilhelm at his heels. Beyond the thicket, on a little patch of green by the fence, lay two dark bodies struggling — the boy was wrestling to get the other down — and now Vilhelm recognized the voices.

Per seized his arm and held it: " No, let be, boy, this is nothing to do with us — " he whispered hotly. But he stood bending forward, with one hand in the collar of the dog, which was struggling to get at the two.

Vilhelm had a glimpse of something white — Tora's knee and a bit of thigh — she lay with her petticoats thrown back. He tore himself free of Per's hand. With a stifled cry of rage and his gun raised like a club he rushed towards the couple.

Claus was already halfway over the fence. Vilhelm struck at him with the butt of his gun, hit his brother between the shoulder-blades with some effect. The next instant the heel of Claus's shoe caught him in the face, as the other swung himself over the fence and set off at a run across the field.

Vilhelm looked round for Tora — she was standing straight up, shaking with suppressed sobs. The dog had got free and was jumping at her, barking and wagging its tail; she answered absently with little pats.

" Tora — Tora — has he done anything to you — Tora — was he horrid to you? " He tried to catch her, support her.

" Let me go — let me go! " With a loud heart-rending cry she turned and fled along the fence so that the bushes swished as they closed behind her. They could hear her stumble over the stakes lying by the gate.

Per Vold led Vilhelm back the way they had come. He was as silent as a stone, but he did not relax his grasp of the other's arm. Vilhelm had fished out his hankerchief and was trying to check the flow of blood from his nose — it was so nasty, running into his mouth — and now his face began to hurt him horribly from the kick he had received.

On reaching the gate Vilhelm saw that Tora was standing still a little way down the path across the field. The tawny body of the dog jumped and tugged and wanted to go on, yelping impatiently — Tora held her by the collar. Vilhelm wanted to follow, but Per's hand gripped his arm tighter: " No, bide here."

Vilhelm raised his gun and shook it: " If this had been loaded — by God, I'd have — ! "

" You shouldn't have mixed yourself up in this," said Per. The young peasant's whole being radiated a strong disapproval.

Far below them the other two lads were making for the farm. When they had disappeared under the slope Tora looked back over her shoulder. Vilhelm tried to dash forward, but Per Vold held him as in a vice.

" But let me go, man — I must speak to Tora."

" Stand still, I say! Don't you think you've brought disgrace enough on the poor girl? "

" Have I — ? " Vilhelm snuffled, with his nose full of blood.

" You should never have meddled with this, Vilhelm," said Per firmly, but rather more calmly. But he still kept a tight hold on the younger lad, while Tora walked slowly down towards the farm.

" But good God, man! He was just going to defile her! "

" Oh — oh." Per spoke slowly and reluctantly. " It wasn't so bad as all that. If only you hadn't raised such a rumpus."

It dawned on Vilhelm that his companion took another view of the matter — one which to him was unknown and incomprehensible. Nor was it easy to talk with his nose bleeding as it did — and his face was painful and his upper lip felt thick and stiff.

Not till Tora's form had disappeared did Per release him and set up the stakes again. And then at last he too began to walk slowly down.

Misfortunes never come singly. For years afterwards Vilhelm was to remember this saying whenever the unhappy ending of Ole Haagensen's wedding feast occurred to his mind.

On entering the yard he turned his steps at once to the watering trough by the stable. But hardly had he ducked his damaged face in the dark and ice-cold water than someone touched him on the shoulder:

" But dear goodness — what's this! "

It was Madame Dabbelsteen — in the pale evening light the big white cap shone around her ugly horse's face.

" It's nothing, Madame Aleth — I've given my nose a knock, that's all." Vilhelm quickly ducked into the water again and blew it into bubbles.

" But it is shocking the way you have damaged your face, little Vilhelm. Do let me help — I can stop bleeding."

" I can manage quite well — many thanks all the same."

Madame Dabbelsteen put her hands on her hips and shook her head: " Ah, these feastings, these feastings! " She sighed with a smile. " There is *something* in what he says, Pastor Struwe — ay, and poor Dabbelsteen said the same many a time — the intemperance of their ways here in the Dale, with their brandy and beer, on festive occasions. And where the drink goes in, the wits fly out — and it ends in fighting and rioting, and worse things than that. Here comes pretty little Tora running as if something was the matter, with the tears streaming down her cheeks —

and now Vilhelm — " she stopped short. Then she clapped her hands together, with a sly smile: " Oh, Vilhelm — surely it wasn't with Tora Ommundsdatter you've been at fisticuffs? "

" What is that about Vilhelm? — has Vilhelm been at fisticuffs with somebody? — but heavens, boy, what a sight you are! "

Vilhelm had turned round, boiling with rage, to answer Madame Dabbelsteen. When he saw that his mother and grandmother had also arrived on the scene, he was completely nonplussed. Fright, shame and bewilderment jostled one another in his soul — then a new feeling, compounded of exasperation and dread, obtained the mastery — was *he* to be given the blame for his brother's misdeed?

He did not know what he dared say. Appeal to Per Vold's evidence of what they had seen — and compromise the poor girl? He began to realize that perhaps there was much to be said for the young peasant's attitude. But surely in God's name he could not have let Claus ruin the girl at his ease — only he saw that, if anything came out about that scene by the fence, it would be Tora who would suffer most. If he said that he was only defending his betrothed — but that was just the horrible difficulty; she was not his betrothed, he had not even been able to declare his love to her — and he vaguely sensed that now he could not do her a worse turn than speaking of his passion for her. And beneath all the rest was the feeling, deeply rooted from his childhood: one does not tell tales about one's brother.

Aloud he replied: " Nothing — it's nothing. I just stumbled and fell and made my nose bleed."

" But there! Let me take a look at you — you had better come in with me."

Madame Aleth repeated her offers to " stop the bleeding." But now his grandmother interposed: " Dear me, Dorthea, you need not make such a fuss about this grown-up lad for getting a scratch on his nose and losing a few drops of blood. Go upstairs and lie down flat on your back, my boy, that will stop it. I think it is time too that we all went to bed; we must see about getting into regular ways again after all this stir and bustle. Haakon went to bed a while ago. But have you had supper? " she turned to Per and Vilhelm.

Per mumbled something about their having had a meal before leaving the sæter. Madame Dabbelsteen exclaimed with officious zeal that that was many hours ago, they must be hungry again by now, " — but I can send Tora up to you with some food, I'm sure she is still up, she cannot possibly have finished washing up, coming in so late."

" You need not trouble about that, Aleth," said Madame Elisabeth. " And there is no need for you to take so much upon yourself without being asked " — and Vilhelm recognized in his grandmother's manner a threatening note which he knew he had heard before.

The three women said good-night. " Good-night, my boy," said his mother in a low voice. She had stood perfectly still, hardly saying anything, but this very silence of hers told the boy how uneasy she was. She guessed there was something the matter.

" Ay, 'twould have been better had you listened to me," said Per Vold when they reached their garret. " And now this Dabbelsteina — if she's going to poke her long snout into it, why — " his air was so gloomy that Vilhelm did not venture to say anything. Nor was he in any mood to discuss the affair. Per pulled off his boots; he thoughtfully divested himself of his outer garments and rolled into bed.

The room in which they lay was really nothing but a kind of passage between the two rooms in the upper storey of the dower house — the opening to the balcony had no door. It was delightfully airy, Vilhelm thought — and he reflected that when Tora brought them their food he could easily slip down after her. He *must* have a talk with Tora; even this Per must surely be able to see that.

He flung himself down on the bed outside Per Vold; his heart was beating furiously as he lay waiting for Tora to appear. His nose and his whole face were cursedly painful too — the pulses throbbed and the strain of the swelling flesh became unbearable. It was no use trying to lie still — and his least movement was enough to shake the whole bed as if it was about to fall into its separate component parts. It was a rickety patched-up concern that had been placed in the passage for him and Claus; in the ordinary way there could not have been any furniture here beyond the heavy iron-bound chests along the wall.

He could not lie quiet — his excitement and his fear grew by degrees into an unendurable torture. But *he* had done nothing wrong — and at the same time he knew it was not altogether absurd that he should be lying here with the feeling that the disapproval of which he was sensible was not entirely baseless. Every time he thought of Claus his fury knew no bounds — and the thought of Tora Synstevoll plunged him into a bewilderingly painful sense of shame — and then the image of his mother presented itself, and his conscience pricked him terribly. It was only with distaste that he looked back upon the sweet intoxication of love in which he had floated during the whole week of the wedding — it seemed he was now suffering from the most distressing after-effects of this indulgence. But at all costs he must have a long talk with Tora.

At last there was a step on the stairs. And then it was not Tora. An elderly, quiet-mannered maid whom he had seen flitting about among the houses during the festivities set down a bowl of milk and a wooden platter of buttered bannocks on the floor by the bed, invited them to help themselves — and disappeared.

But Per Vold was already asleep. And Vilhelm had no inclination to wake him. The cool sweet milk was extraordinarily grateful, before he knew it he had almost emptied the bowl. He also ventured on a bannock — there was some grand salt sausage inside it. Insensibly life took on a brighter aspect.

Nevertheless he was prepared to lie awake with his sad and anxious thoughts — and with his throbbing face and aching head — when he crept back under the skin rug. But before he knew it everything sank into the mists of sleep and he was off.

Next day was sermon Sunday at Herberg church and the immediate family — no others were now left at Lunde — were to accompany the young couple to morning service.

Ole, sedately attired as a newly married man, drove his Ingebjörg with the black matron's cap, Per Vold sitting behind. Next, in the big carriage, came the Sheriff and his madam, their mother and Madame Dabbelsteen, with one of the serving lads on the box. A saddled horse was waiting for Vilhelm — a few men and women from the farm were to ride. And among these he caught sight of his brother; Claus held himself erect on the Junker's back as though nothing had happened. As Vilhelm came up he turned aside, and a moment later he and some of the other riders moved off.

Tora was nowhere to be seen.

The sky was overcast and the sunshine gone when they came out of church. And before they were back at Lunde it began to rain. For the rest of the day it poured quietly and steadily, dripping from all the roofs and trees. And the Dale was half-hidden in the mist. But although in reality it was fairly bleak and cold, Vilhelm on looking back always had the impression that it had been a sultry day.

His head was burning and he felt unwell — his stiff and swollen face affected him unpleasantly both physically and mentally. All he recollected of the church service was that he had hidden himself as far back as he could in the gallery where the young lads sat. Somebody smuggled a pocket pistol over to him, and it made him horribly embarrassed — was his morning-after appearance so evident? But for once he really had a burning desire for a stiffener. The dram did him good — and he saw with relief that the flask continued to circulate from man to man — so it was not because he looked so bad that it had been offered.

When they went in to dinner he and Claus could no

longer avoid each other — they had to sit side by side. But they did not exchange a word, and they scarcely looked at each other — and the feeling of close proximity to his brother's dense corporeal mass, which also enveloped he knew not what thoughts, though they were certainly occupied with the same subject as his own, intensified the tingling unrest within him till it became almost unbearable.

After dinner he plucked up courage and went out to seek for news of Tora. Forlorn and wet he wandered about the farm in the pouring rain — looked in at the old house where he and she had found food and coffee on the first evening of the wedding. There was a grand fire burning on the hearth. At the end of the long table some young fellows sat playing cards, others stood about looking on. Vilhelm felt tempted to go in and rest awhile — the fire was so bright and cosy. Then he discovered that Claus was there, and stole out again.

He humped his shoulders, ran across the yard and down to the bake-house. But there the door was bolted and barred. The middle-aged maid who had brought him food on the evening before happened to be passing; she had a ragged sack over her head and back to protect her from the rain and was carrying two buckets on a yoke. She was more than ready to have a chat with him: they never used the bake-house in the ordinary way, only when they were baking or had killed a pig; well yes, they had cooked there for the wedding feast. But now that all the guests were gone they did the cooking in the kitchen of course.

He had been in the kitchen several times already and had seen nothing of her: " You couldn't tell me where to find Tora, could you? — Tora Ommundsdatter — I should like to have a few words with her."

"Tora? she must be home at Synstevoll by now, I should say. She went off early this morning." It seemed to Vilhelm that the maid glanced at him in an oddly knowing way.

And again he was assailed by this sense of bewilderment and terror, as when one walks in pitchy darkness, afraid of stumbling over invisible obstacles, plunging into invisible pitfalls. His mother had looked so oddly, he thought — silent and moody. By the same token he had not ventured to look at her very often today.

In the end he stole back into the main building. In the parlour his mother and Madame Dabbelsteen were engaged in packing crockery and other borrowed articles in big baskets, while Madame Elisabeth sat at the end of the table superintending: " From Holen — there should be one pewter dish and seven pewter plates — let me look, they have their mark on all their things — and four silver spoons."

Vilhelm slipped into the bedroom beyond. The Sheriff lay on the bed sleeping peacefully, his long pipe still hung from his mouth, the bowl resting on the floor.

In front of the little window stood a table and an armchair; on the shelf above were several books. A mythology in French — that must have accompanied his grandmother from some earlier phase of her existence. Bible and hymn books. A manuscript book of remedies for the ailments of domestic animals. A German book of homilies inscribed with Haagen Halvorsen's name: " This book was acquired by me for 1 speciedaler and twain mark in Altona ano D. 1769." At last he found a volume: " Essays in Belles Lettres and Useful Knowledge, collected by a Patriotic Society." He settled himself in the armchair and began to read a tale about " Sigrid, or Love, the Reward of Valour."

Truth to tell he had never before cared very much for love stories. But today it was different — and then the tale dealt with the old heathen times when people believed in Freya and Thor and Odin, and all the heroes were either noble champions or savage and bloodthirsty villains. And the lovely Sigrid Syvald's daughter took on the form of Tora — and he himself was Othar. The Hunding warrior, who fell upon the princess in the wood and tried to ravish her, he instinctively imagined in the shape of Claus, but the treacherous Ragnhild bore some resemblance to Madame Aleth.

The farther he read the more thrilled he was. Darkness came early that day, but Vilhelm held the book close to the yellowish green window-pane, which to make matters worse was freely splashed with muddy water from the eaves above. He paid no attention to the pain in his swollen bloodshot eye — only strained his sight to make out the letters which were beginning to run into each other.

He started up as his grandmother entered the closet — by the last remnant of daylight he had been trying to get to the end of Othar's pretended marriage to Insegunde, with Sigrid's agony of mind as she held the candle for them. It was immensely exciting — and the description of Earl Ebbe's home seemed to merge itself into this great farm here. He had jumped up and offered the chair to his grandmother, but was only waiting to be allowed to take his book somewhere else.

" Stay a moment, Vilhelm," said Madame Elisabeth. " I have something to say to you. You may go and find your brother though — it concerns you both."

Vilhelm felt his face turn pale and cold. Now it was coming, what he had been afraid of all day — he did not quite know what it was.

" Ah, but do ye think this is wise, Lisabeth? " came the voice of Haagen Lunde from the darkness of the bed.

" That cursed hag Aleth has coaxed the whole story out of Tora! " Madame Elisabeth had seated herself in the armchair — her face shone like a great yellow patch in the twilight. She drummed with her finger-tips on the table before her. " One must get these people to understand they have only to hold their tongues. And not take it so tragically as poor Dorthea. You must leave me to clear this up, Haakon."

" Ay ay, so be it." The Sheriff swung himself into a sitting position and felt for his boots. " Ye ken your own folk best — I leave it to you." He drew a deep sigh.

It was much lighter out of doors than in. Vilhelm shivered in his wet clothes as he hurried across the yard. And as he opened the door of the old house he was met by a warm air thick with smoke and the odour of human bodies. The fire glowed on the hearth, warm and red. Around the rushlight on the long table the faces of the card-players became visible, shrouded in the bluish smoke of their clay pipes. Vilhelm thought he would have given a great deal to be able to hide in a corner here in the warmth and the shadows. But he went up to Claus, who stood behind one of the players looking over his cards. He touched his brother on the shoulder:

" Grandmother wants to speak to you. You are to come to her in the closet."

Claus Hartvig turned abruptly, dark-red in the face, and went out quickly, followed by Vilhelm. No sooner were they under the open sky than Claus turned round in a fury:

" I see! You've been blabbing! Well, I might have guessed that."

" Oh, you miserable blockhead! *I* haven't breathed a blessed syllable — haven't you sense enough to see that? Don't you understand it's Tora? You've frightened her so she daren't stay in the same house with you, you — you — And I suppose she had to give some reason for not wanting to stay here as long as you were at Lunde."

Claus Hartvig's expression became strangely childlike all at once — Vilhelm guessed he was afraid too. But he tried to brazen it out: " Oh — I don't think I was the only one she had to be afraid of." All the same he looked very down in the mouth as he followed Vilhelm into the parlour.

Someone had revived the fire in the hearth. In its flickering light Madame Dabbelsteen was sorting linen at the table. Their mother was not there.

Their mother was in the closet. She was standing by their grandmother's armchair. The lighted candle on the table before Madame Elisabeth showed up her mourning dress with all the white over the black, and black borders again on the white, so that her face seemed almost as yellow as the old lady's, and her eyelids were red. She looked taller than she really was in this low-ceilinged room, and there was something in his mother's whole appearance which made Vilhelm think of profaned sanctuaries —

virtue, filial duty and everything of that sort. Although *he* had done nothing wrong — as far as he could see, at any rate — but he had never seen her like this before. The mother to whom it had always been so easy to go, with whom he had always felt so entirely at his ease — he had a sudden feeling that it would be the worst thing that could happen if this business of Tora were to be laid open to her sorrowful and serious eyes.

His grandmother sat drumming with the pointed fingers of her fat little hand on the leather binding of the book he had laid down. Her queer bullet-eyes travelled from one boy to the other, and her snuff-stained nostrils dilated, sniffing. But Vilhelm felt at once that she did not take this affair in the same way as their mother; he was aware of a certain benevolence emanating from the old woman, in spite of her annoyance with the boys.

She looked stately, almost handsome, in her Sunday attire, with a fine lace-bordered head-band under the black silk cap and a light brown silk shawl crossed over her breast, above her linsey-woolsey gown, which was of a shiny dark green and almost townish in style.

" Sit down, Dorthea — sit down, my girl," she said rather impatiently to their mother.

Madame Dorthea seated herself in the little chair on the other side of the table. But she turned it a little, so as to face her sons.

" It is a tiresome affair, this, little Vilhelm," his grandmother began, still drumming on the book. " It is not the custom in the country for young people — lads and girls — to mix so freely as is the habit in your circles. It is not considered becoming for them to be seen together or to converse with one another in the sight of their elders. Of

course, on festive occasions where there is a good deal of
dancing and drinking, the tone may easily become less
constrained. We know that, and we let it pass. But it is
nevertheless very, *very* unfortunate for a young girl to be
surprised in a friendly tête à tête with a lad. So decent
people, if by an unhappy accident they come across a
young couple in a tender situation, pass by and take no
notice. Oh yes, I know you meant no harm, you are un-
familiar with our customs here, I am willing to believe.
But it is bad for poor Tora — she feels she is disgraced,
her reputation in the neighbourhood has received a stain,
a very regrettable stain."

Vilhelm's face had turned red as fire during his grandmother's harangue. This was surely turning things
upside down — and he dared not say anything for
Tora's sake, and it was equally impossible to blab about
Claus.

Claus appeared to feel greatly relieved. And Vilhelm
was already thinking with exasperation that in addition to
all the rest he would have to put up with this devil of a
boy crowing over him as soon as they were alone. But he
did not intend to take this altogether submissively.

"Well, Claus has not behaved as he should either,"
Madame Elisabeth continued. "It appears you were trying to act in the highest degree indelicately, and that with
a good, modest girl."

"Yes, that's just it," Vilhelm interrupted hotly. "I
can assure Grandmother, I really did nothing but try to
help Tora. So that she might be free from his — dastardly
— aggressiveness." Dastardly — that was the very word
he had come across several times in the story of Sigrid with
the Veil, and it was the right one — the whole affair was

so dastardly that he felt he could have cried with rage.

" Oh, it was not so bad as all that," said Madame Elisabeth. She looked at Claus with the faintest smile of compassion. " The boy there would scarcely have succeeded in doing the lass any great harm — Tora knows how to defend herself. And I am sure Claus has not much experience."

" But Mamma! " Madame Dorthea turned abruptly to the old lady, painfully scandalized. Claus stood looking angrily at his grandmother, dark red in the face, but she met them both with a deprecating gesture. " Yes, yes, Dorthea, I have told you, I am sorry about this. Of course the Sheriff and I can see that it is not discussed openly in the neighbourhood. But no one can stop people whispering in corners."

" Then I think the best thing would be for Tora to go away." Vilhelm felt himself going white in the face underneath all the bruises and freckles — how would his boldness be received! " I had thought of asking her to do so anyhow. And to go into service — in a gentleman's house — or in Christiania. To wait for me — that is, if she will have me."

Now it was his turn to receive his grandmother's compassionate smile. " That is not the custom either among peasants, my friend. They do not allow their daughters to be betrothed until the wooer is in a position to marry. And I must say that is very sensible. Before you reach that stage, my poor boy, both your love and hers — if she is *in* love with you — will long ago have faded away."

" Oh, I have no great fear of that." Vilhelm met his grandmother's eyes with a glance which he hoped might be called proud. But Madame Elisabeth continued to smile — till she suddenly looked at the door and said in a tone of irritation:

" What do you want here, Aleth? — no one has sent for *you.*"

" No? " Madame Dabbelsteen slipped inside the room and stood leaning against the door-post. " I just came to tell you that I have packed everything you wanted to send away tomorrow."

" Well well, I will come and see to it directly. What are you standing there for? " she added impatiently, as the other made no move to go.

" Oh yes. Aleth was good enough, I dare say, to find out for you what your grandsons had been up to — that has always been your way, Elisabeth, I was just good enough to do your dirty work, when there was anything you wanted to know. But there was one thing I was never to be told, and that was what Elisabeth had in her mind."

" I think you're wandering. Here you come flying as if the devil was after you and serve up a story about Dorthea's sons and the daughter of Haakon's cousin; did anyone ask you to do *that?* Haven't I told you a thousand times — don't poke your nose into what doesn't concern you, my dear Aleth, it might be the worse for you one day, I have always said. But you are as inquisitive as a monkey, you are indeed! " Madame Elisabeth gave a little grating laugh. " God knows what you imagine you ought to be told this time — did you think I was going to flog these great boys, perhaps? For I'm sure you would have enjoyed seeing that."

" I am used to your spite. But that you should be spiteful to your own grandchildren! I heard what Vilhelm said — "

" That was well done — listening at the door."

" — and there may be *much* in it. It would certainly be best for poor Tora to go away from here. And if she and Vilhelm are fond of one another — for I could see she was *very* fond of Vilhelm Adolf — "

Madame Elisabeth chuckled:

" Oh, you romantic old fairy, is your head still full of that sort of thing! It is strange, though, that you have not learnt wisdom from experience even now," she said sharply. " Poor Margit, she was in any case the heiress of a nice little farm — and that good-for-nothing son of yours could never have been either parson or curate, he might have been glad to be sexton or school-teacher. But now you have seen what her waiting for your Gusten led to — oh, God have mercy on us all! "

" You could have helped them, Elisabeth, as Augustin begged you."

" Claus and Vilhelm, you may go now," said Madame Elisabeth. " No — you stay, Aleth, I have a bone to pick with you yet."

Claus did not wait to be told twice; he darted out of the door and through the parlour as if his tail was on fire. Vilhelm followed, at a considerably slower pace.

The parlour was now almost completely in darkness, with a red glow of embers on the hearth. Vilhelm could not tell why he stopped. He was annoyed at his grand-mother having driven him out just when Madame Dab-belsteen was getting exciting. He would have liked to know whether she had any more to say about himself and Tora. Besides, there was that book he wanted to get hold of.

" As far as I am aware, Aleth, I have helped you from

the very first day you entered our house, Eckelöff's and mine — as to the relationship that is supposed to exist between us, I do not know what truth there may be in that."

" The Major *was* my uncle."

" Yes, I dare say that is quite possible. My brother-in-law Joachim was a gentleman of somewhat extensive gallantry, though he may sometimes have been credited with more than he had actually performed. But be that as it may, you were given a home in my house, not only during Eckelöff's lifetime, but even after I had been left a widow for the second time — and God knows my circumstances were straitened enough with my three children. However, I kept you with me, I shared what I had with you — no, no, don't interrupt me now — I shared my bread with you in the years of poverty. And when I was married to Sören Theilemann you had a generous share of our abundance."

" Did I not make ample return for the food and clothing you gave me, Elisabeth? "

" You know very well, little Aleth — you were never very capable. At any time *I* should have been better off with a strong and active servant girl than with a — fantastical — and high-flown companion — "

" — And then you were afraid of me! " Madame Dabbelsteen's voice grew shrill. " You were afraid I should disclose what I knew of your secret ways, Elisabeth! "

" I was *not* afraid. All that wild farrago of rubbish you invented when — David was dead " — Vilhelm noticed that his grandmother paused for the twinkling of an eye before mentioning his grandfather's name — " who do you *think* would give credence to that, in a place where everyone knew you well enough to put you down as nothing but a poor half-crazy moonstruck creature? Rumours you could certainly set going — there were rumours enough about Eckelöff's death in any case, and I have never doubted that some of them came from you. I never cared to call you to account for that. You had proof " — the old lady's voice took on a curiously deep tone of exultation — " that they did *me* no harm. I married David Frazer and let them talk."

For an instant there was silence in the little room. And then someone began to sob — it must have been Madame Dabbelsteen.

" Yes — I had not failed to see that you — I guessed what hopes you had cherished. The clerk and the house-keeper, that would have been quite natural. If only you had not been what you were, incapable and unattractive, wild and impetuous, with your head quite turned by novel-reading and poetry and all sorts of trash — poor Aleth, I am sure I never wished to make things any worse for you than you made them yourself. And as you were so set upon staying with me and David, I had not the heart to show you the door."

Madame Dabbelsteen wept and wept.

" And all your flights of fancy after David's death — I took them for nothing more than the delusions of a demented woman. And when you came once more and begged to be allowed to stay with the children and me — she was really very fond of you all, especially of you, Dorthea — well, then I took pity on her again, she had nowhere else to go, people were afraid of her, she was down-right touched in the head at times.

" Then when I married de Theilemann — it was chiefly

for the sake of you children that I did it — yes, little Dorthea, I know very well you thought I was not so fond of you as I ought to have been, but it was nevertheless your future that was uppermost in my mind, that you should grow up in easy circumstances. And I was still a young woman — well, Theilemann was a good man, but with the cares of a big house I had no time to see very much of you. But I thought I could depend upon Aleth, that she would take good care of you at least, for your father's sake. And indeed she did so. But when Theilemann's good friend Pastor Thue became a widow, we obtained for Aleth the situation of his housekeeper. I had a hope that this might lead to her marrying him; I thought, if only she could be landed in a marriage-bed she might be less distracted.

" No, Aleth, I can truthfully say I have never done you any harm. And when I heard that your husband was a curate at Mo and that you had a son, I was sincerely glad for your sake, even though I cannot exactly say that I longed to meet you again. And yet I did so, after you were left a widow — I paid you a visit, I invited you to my house, I assisted you and your boy in many ways."

" You dared do nothing else," screamed Madame Dabbelsteen with tears in her voice. " And if your Sheriff had found out, you would not be sitting in the parlour of his house, if there's any justice in the world — in the little room with the barred window, that was the place for you, Elisabeth Eckelöff! "

There was a bang on the table. " Hold your tongue," said the grandmother threateningly. " We are coming to that too — I could see by that crazy boy of yours, Augustin, that you have filled his head with some of these old

— fables — of yours. What an imagination you have! It will soon be half a century since Eckelöff died. Do you think *you* can injure *me,* with any tattle you may carry? — oh no, my good woman! But now I have had enough of it, I have done with you, Aleth Svensdatter. First I just want to know how much you — or your son — have told Dorthea here and her boys about these old fables."

" Nothing, nothing," whined Madame Dabbelsteen. " But now Dorette shall hear what sort of a one you are."

A chair was knocked over in the little room. Vilhelm had just time to squeeze into the wood-corner behind the fireplace when the door of the bedroom opened and Madame Dabbelsteen came out backwards knocking her head with a crack against the lintel. Madame Elisabeth was pushing her into the parlour, but she screamed wildly:

" God will take vengeance! God will take vengeance! Do you remember what they said about Eckelöff, when David brought him back on a peasant's sledge? — they said he had done it himself, because his money was short, he'd gambled away the Crown's money — and that's what they're saying of your son-in-law today! Is there anyone who knows what happened that evening my uncle was shot by the Ensrud lake? — no more than they know what's become of Dorthea's husband. An accident it was called — David Frazer took his oath on it — you got him to do it, when you saw the Major didn't trust either of you any longer. That other man with a gun that he said he'd seen there in the scree by the shore, he was never seen nor heard of after. And five months later you were married to David."

" Help me to get her out." But Vilhelm had a glimpse

of his mother's form standing motionless at the bedroom door.

" Nothing have I said. But now, now I need no longer think of Augustin's future, him too you have snatched from me. Now I say what I will! That you are a whore, a murderess, an adulteress."

" Then say it, say what you will — but out you shall go! " The old woman puffed and panted as she pushed the shrieking, sprawling creature towards the outer door foot by foot. " Open the door at least, Dorthea — don't stand there like a block."

At last his mother moved. She crossed the room and opened the door to the rain outside. As far as Vilhelm could see she took one of Aleth Dabbelsteen's arms and loosened her hold on the doorpost, but that seemed to be all the help she gave in getting the crazy woman out of doors.

The other two stood at the door for a moment. Then Madame Elisabeth said: " You must go after her, Dorthea, get her upstairs and to bed. Otherwise she'll run round screaming all over the place."

His mother made some reply which Vilhelm could not catch. " No, no," said his grandmother, " then I'll go myself." Aleth Dabbelsteen continued her ravings just outside — but just as Madame Elisabeth went out the Sheriff's voice was heard. There was a good deal of parleying by the doorstep.

His mother crossed the floor of the dark parlour. She seemed to be wiping her face again and again with her apron. " Now Haakon will take her in hand. So no doubt he will bring her to her senses. She has these fits — everyone knows that. Perhaps it will be best if you go up to

her presently — but you must be prepared for her din-
ning into your ears."

"I cannot face it — I really cannot see that person ever
again. Mother must understand that!"

Madame Elisabeth paused for a moment:

"Is it really possible that you have never heard of these
old — rumours?"

"Never a word!" Dorthea's voice trembled in desperation.

"Well, in that case it was bad that you should happen
to. It was bad that Aleth should have taken one of her
fits this evening," his grandmother repeated, in a voice
that sounded a little more withered.

Dorthea flung her hands to her face and wept.

"There, there, child. You can see very well that it is
all the fabrication of a crazy woman."

"All — ?" asked Dorthea tonelessly.

Madame Elisabeth seemed to consider for a moment.
Then she said:

"All — except that my first husband was jealous of
your father. He was that. And Aleth was also in love with
him."

"And then?"

"Well," said the old lady thoughtfully. "Good heavens, Dorette, you will soon be an old woman yourself —
can all this affect you so terribly? That your mother was
young herself once — more than forty years ago. Yes, we
were both in love with David Frazer." A strange note of
gratification came into her voice.

"And that is what Aleth has embroidered upon — out
of her own jealousy. All the rest of it. That your father
was not a treacherous — you may well imagine for your-

self, when you look at his handsome features — you have
that little pastel portrait of him, have you not? "

"It is so indistinct." Dorthea swallowed once or twice.
"Some water got in under the glass."

Madame Elisabeth said nothing.

"But how have you been able to bear it! " Dorthea
exclaimed. "To live — all these years, when you knew
people were saying these — frightful things about you,
behind your back! Mamma! "

"Dear me, child, what people say — " she laughed
quietly, but it was not a happy laugh. "One does not
trouble so much about that, when all one's time is taken
up with living! "

"But — but," faltered Dorthea, "what about your —
your present husband — if he were to hear of this? "

"Haakon — " again the old lady's voice had that
strangely satisfied tone. "He is no greenhorn either, you
must remember. An old soldier like Haakon has heard
worse things than that.

"But now I think you'd better go to bed, my girl,"
said the grandmother after a pause. "When you have
slept on it you won't think it so dreadful."

"I will *not* go up to her," whispered Dorthea impul-
sively.

"No no, if you won't, you won't. There's the little
room over at Ole's — the bed there is empty tonight. I
will go across with you, in case the young people have
gone to bed already. And I fancy Haakon will make Aleth
understand that it is unwise of her to carry on as if she was
ripe for the madhouse."

His mother seemed to totter, and the old lady supported
her. "O Mother, Mother, Mother," cried Dorthea, as she

allowed herself to be led out. Vilhelm noticed that she said Mother and not Mamma.

He stole out of his corner, peered from the door into the rainy darkness of the yard to see if the coast was clear. Then he ran along the wall, under the eaves, to find a hiding-place. Slowly some threads of thought began to release themselves from the tangled skein in his head.

11

It was a somewhat depressed company that drove out through the gate of Lunde on the second morning after that disastrous evening.

The Sheriff had decided to accompany his stepdaughter in order to help her in arranging the formalities that had to be gone through before she could leave Brovold. Therefore they drove in the fine big carriage which Haagen Halvorsen had had made on the pattern of some he had seen abroad. The body was hung on great S-springs, so that it rocked very agreeably, and there were stuffed leather cushions on both seats, and a hood over the after-part of the carriage. The fact that he was driving in such style gave Vilhelm a certain self-confidence. And he needed it.

He sat on the front seat facing the Sheriff and his

mother, who were leaning back in their corners. That Claus was not in the carriage was some consolation — he drove their own gig with the Junker. Their mother had decided this: " *You* drive with *us,* Vilhelm." He had the impression that she purposely avoided Claus. And indeed she had good reason to be displeased with his behaviour during the wedding at Lunde. The only thing was, Vilhelm could not help thinking all the time, how much worse *he* had behaved himself. If his mother only knew of his eavesdropping in the corner! Every time he thought of it he had a nasty drawn feeling at the pit of his stomach and his heart seemed to contract. He did not understand how he could have done such a thing. But while he was doing it he had not thought for a moment that it was disgraceful.

Nor could he tell why he had done it. Perhaps he had expected to hear the grown-ups say more about him and Tora — Aleth repeated some words of hers which made it clear that Tora was not angry with him, she saw that his attentions had not been dishonourable, they were quite different from Claus's dastardly attack. Or he had hoped that some words from his mother might wash his poor soiled little adventure clean.

He felt he could not bear to think about it now — and then he could not help thinking about it all the time. It was horrible to have to feel ashamed of himself for having been so simple and so happy — and to have them all letting him know, some with silent disapproval, some with words that were like a box on the ears, how frightfully wrong his behaviour had been — stupid, indelicate, disastrous for Tora, like that of a silly boy and a person entirely without good manners. He was certain he would never forget those evening hours they had passed together so innocently and enjoyably — he would always remember her sweet little breast which he had held in his hand, so lovely and warm it felt as they sat in the raw, cold dingle by the mill-dam, with the hills opposite such a dark blue and so far away. And her kisses seemed as it were more full-flavoured and better from the desolation around them, which would have been eerie if there had not been two of them. Henceforth, whenever he smelt the strong scent of fresh young leaves of the wild cherry, it would remind him of her moist linen shirt and of the little river foaming behind the cherry-bushes below them. And always these memories would be inseparable from that of his humiliation — that he had dreamt he was a grown-up young man, and had then been rudely flung back into the world of striplings, where one is constantly in danger of making a fool of oneself and of having to eat humble pie.

His mother's face was so pale and tired. She sat huddled in her corner under the hood and had wound the rug closely about her, as though feeling the cold. It was in fact a fairly cold day — the rain had ceased, but the sky was overcast and the air was raw. After a while his mother's eyes closed; Vilhelm guessed that she had gone to sleep. Soon after Sheriff Lunde also fell asleep.

Vilhelm could not sleep in his front seat; it was pretty narrow, and the back rose straight up to the coach-box. When the carriage swayed more than usual he was nearly thrown out of his seat. Once or twice he tried to turn around and ask the lad who was driving about things he saw along the road, but it was so difficult to talk in that position, and he was also afraid of waking the other two.

It was better to let them sleep — he had no wish to be spoken to by them.

He shrank from thinking of it, but he could not help wondering — what must it feel like to know that such terrible rumours had been afloat about one's own parents? When Madame Dabbelsteen began to scream and shout the implication of her words had scarcely made any impression on him — he merely thought it was shocking and disgusting of the crazy creature to rage like this, and of the two old women to fight — for they were positively fighting, she and his grandmother. Not till afterwards did he realize what she had actually said. Of course it was not true; he had not the slightest belief in Madame Aleth's stories. Why, it was almost half a century since this was supposed to have happened. And Vilhelm somehow could not imagine that anything so far back could be real. If it had not been for Herr Dabbelsteen. But he now recollected the desperate scene the tutor had raised on the night they had lost themselves and turned up at Lunde — he remembered the big threatening face of his grandmother as she stood there in her night attire, the green silk gown that made her look like a mountain. " Bathsheba, Bathsheba, David's wife," Dabbelsteen had shrieked, and his grandmother had towered above him, enormous and sinister. Now of course he could say to himself that Herr Dabbelsteen had referred to something he had heard from his mother. But even if it were only gibberish, most of it! The memory of his grandmother's massive bulk and of his own foreboding fear of something, he knew not what — these grew painfully distinct. Whatever might be the truth of it — the ponderous old woman seemed full of secrets. The fact alone that she had been married four times and to men who came from widely diverse spheres of existence to let their life-strings converge in her hand — this must have filled her massive person with so much knowledge and such singular thoughts that Vilhelm felt he would never again be able to think of his grandmother without an oppressive sense of insecurity.

Every now and then he could not help stealing a glance at his mother as she slept. Surely *she* could never believe it was *true?* For if so she would be the daughter of an assassin and an adulteress — no, it would never do to think of such things! And again the anxious dread flashed through him, giving him a pain across his diaphragm — fancy if she came to know that he had been listening in the wood-corner. She would never hear of it — but so long as they lived he would carry within him the knowledge that she harboured thoughts, not knowing that he was aware of them.

He looked out on the wall of rock, glistening with moisture, under which they were passing. Tufts of moss and wild flowers, with jets of water spurting down the rock, which looked brittle, eaten up by brownish red rust — it was the sort of rock one amused oneself by pulling to pieces with one's fingers as a child. The wheels bumped and slewed over stones, sank deep in miry patches, the horses had hard collar-work and the carriage rocked and swayed, and the two in their corners under the hood stirred in their sleep. Vilhelm was beginning to feel cold.

He had never thought of it before — of course he had always known that his parents and all other grown-ups had a world of their own of which only a small outer fringe was revealed to the children. Just as the latter kept a good many things to themselves — had he not read in books of " the children's world "? — the grown-ups were outside this, and indeed it was clear enough there would have been the devil to pay if Mother or Father had found out one or two things about it! But this state of affairs had been perfectly natural. He was certain that Bertel and Birgitte, for instance, never gave it a thought; it did not prevent their taking refuge in happy confidence with their mother and the grown-ups, who surrounded them with comfort and security. Just as he had had a sense of warm protecting wings whenever he thought of his mother and his father. Even when his father suddenly disappeared and the lives of them all became full of uncertainty and fear and sorrow, it had not occurred to him that there could be more in it than his father's fate on that disastrous journey, more than his end, obscure and uncanny as it was. He knew of course that people were talking and guessing all sorts of things, but he had thought that only natural — it was an unusual and startling event for a man to vanish completely in this way. Now he could not help thinking — well, he did not think it *was* so, but it was present as a sort of possibility — there might be other things in his father's life of which no one had any knowledge. Or their mother might know about them, but no one else. And whichever way it was, *he* would never find out.

Their mother had been married once before — this too appeared to him now in a new light. Vilhelm Adolf Bisgaard, after whom he had been named — he was represented merely by two big chests in the attic, full of books and many bundles of elegantly written manuscript to which their mother forbad them to help themselves when they were hunting for paper to make kites or squibs. Portfolios with charming watercolours of butterflies and moths, each with its caterpillar and grub beside it. A Horace bound in white vellum which they were allowed to use at school, but it was frightfully easy to get it stained with ink, and then their mother scolded so annoyingly. An amethyst necklace and charms — the case containing them was at the top of her jewel-box, and when the children were shown it their mother said it had been Bisgaard's wedding-present to her. He now reflected that Bisgaard too had been a living person, and their mother had lived with him for seven years, he thought it was; but that was before they came into the world, and only their mother knew anything of that time and that man.

It was as though he had made the sudden discovery that all human beings were enclosed each in his own invisible shell — invisible, but no less impenetrable for all that. He himself stored up so many things which he had experienced, which he would always remember, and which his mother must never know about. And his mother, his grandmother, the Sheriff there, and everyone else, they had masses and masses of secrets which they hid away within their shells. It was really terrible to think of, for in this way one was always alone in a sense, no matter who might be present.

They did not make very rapid progress with the heavy carriage on the road which had been washed out by the rain. Several times they were delayed by meeting cattle on their way to the sæters. And at the first stage where they stopped to rest the Sheriff met acquaintances and sat a long time talking to them — several hours it seemed.

Meanwhile his mother and he sat by the fire, but they scarcely exchanged a word. Vilhelm envied Claus, who was independent — he drove on ahead as soon as they had had something to eat and the Junker was rested.

They had to pass the night at the stage which lay about halfway between Lunde and the glassworks, and they did not arrive there until late in the evening — it was past nine o'clock. Claus had supped and was already in bed in a kind of passage, which the boys were to occupy. He was asleep when Vilhelm turned in.

There was a fearful draught in this passage, but not enough to overcome the smell of old tainted food on a shelf above the bed. It was altogether an uninviting stage, this one. The woman had just tumbled out of bed as they came and received them as she was, with hardly anything on. Her legs under the ragged smock were dirty and flecked with swollen blue veins; her shift was so open at the throat that it kept dropping to show her skinny collar-bones and sometimes her flat dangling breasts. For some reason or other it affected him in a new and painful way to see so much of an old body's misery. Especially as she must have been pretty once, as could be seen by her face: it was brown and puckered, and her hair was matted, greenish white and stiff with dirt under the black cap, but although her mouth had fallen in there was something handsome about it, especially when she turned her side-face.

He had not been long in bed before the fleas began to torment him, and evidently they were not the only vermin here. And Claus took up an impudently excessive amount of room and slept like the good conscience itself.

Finally he began to repeat to himself his long evening

prayer. It had happened somehow this spring that he had got out of the habit of saying his daily prayers on getting up and going to bed. He knew this was not as it should be — and if he did it now, that was not quite right either. For experience told him that if he began his prayers after he was in bed, he usually fell asleep in the middle. And he did so now.

Madame Dorthea lay on the narrow bench in the parlour and had no great hope of getting any sleep to speak of. For one reason, because she had slept during a great part of the drive. And her couch was extremely uncomfortable, in spite of the Sheriff's having brought in the carriage cushions and spread them on the bench; as a coverlet he lent her his own fur rug which he always took with him when travelling. And it was indeed kind of him to do so, while he himself slept with the driver in the only available bed, which was even shorter and more uncomfortable than peasants' beds usually are, and which looked moreover extremely unappetizing.

Dorthea lay with a hand under her cheek, turned towards the fire, where the heap of embers grew darker and darker, flared up again in a little flicker only to grow darker than before, while the burnt wood rustled and subsided with a faint shuffling sound.

Yes, he was a good man, Sheriff Lunde. And the strange thing was, she felt in spite of all that she had come nearer to her mother than ever before. Perhaps because they were now two old women. When one has oneself retired from the dance, the feelings which once gave rise to such sharp antagonisms are apt to lose their intensity.

As if by a mutual tacit agreement they had allowed the

abominable scene of that evening to be buried in silence. On the following day her mother had taken her aside and spoken to her about her future. There was really nothing to prevent her coming to Lunde with the younger children; they had houseroom and food enough, thank God. Vilhelm had already an occupation in the book-keeping at the glassworks, and Claus could no doubt be placed in some office to learn commercial ways — possibly with the assistance of Antonette Bisgaard? She herself and the Sheriff, and she was sure she could speak for Ole, would be glad to have her. There was only one drawback — the Gullaug folk might perhaps look on it with disfavour. They were already rather displeased that Haakon and she were not disposed to hand over the farm to Ole and Inge-björg at once on their marriage. But if Dorthea would send some of the youngest children there, they would be very well looked after at their grandparents' — she herself would be delighted to have a couple of little toddlers in the house, and Haakon was fond of children — he had never really got over the sorrow of losing their little Halvor. So it would be best if they took Rikke and Christen — it would not be so long before Ole and Inge-björg had some little ones, and a few little children more or less about the place would make no difference. " Well, you can think it over, my girl. If you should find as time goes on that your whole flock is too much for you, then you can send some of them up to us whenever you like — they will be welcome."

Dorthea clearly saw that her mother meant it sincerely. Nor would it have been like her to make any self-sacrifice unless she was really glad to do so. Although — in her dealings with Aleth Svensdatter she must have shown her-

self charitable and patient. For that she should have kept
Aleth on simply from fear of what rumours the other
might circulate — that was not very probable. No doubt
it was only too true that her mother had never cared very
much for what people said. So it was more reasonable to
suppose that she had taken pity on the girl for being hope-
lessly in love with a man whose heart she herself had cap-
tured. Dorthea kept wishing she could remember her
father more clearly — but she did remember that he had
been young and handsome, gentle and kind. It was absurd to think of him in connection with any kind of deeds
of darkness. Well, for that matter she could not credit her
mother with downright criminal actions. But the fair
young father who played the flute in the evening twilight
— never!

All at once it came back to her that she had seen him in
a dream one night that spring. He — and the Major —
had entered a room where Jörgen was also present —
they had come to fetch him.

No. She tried to change her position on the bench,
with the result that the leather cushions under her slid
away and the fur rug was on the point of falling on to the
floor. Dorthea got up, arranged her couch again and lay
down with her face turned to the wall. She must try to
get a little doze in any case — if she shut her eyes and
tried to think of something less alarming. Rikke and
Christen — no, of course she could never send them away
from her — how delighted Rikke would be with all the
lovely cakes in grandmother's basket.

No — give way to a belief in dreams and omens, *that* by
all the powers she could not do. However seriously her
nerves had been shaken by recent events. It was bad

enough to have let herself be taken in by that gypsy
woman the other night. And even though her feelings
had been further harrowed since that time — for God
knew Aleth Dabbelsteen's demented behaviour had been
harrowing enough —

That she and her mother had never understood each
other — that had been clear to her ever since she was
a child. But that she should credit her on that account
with — no, *that* exceeded all reasonable bounds. In her
own way no doubt her mother had meant well by her
children — better at any rate than Dorthea had understood when she was younger. Her kindness however had
appeared so cordial when they parted that morning —
and the fifty speciedalers and all the lovely linen and
woollen things her mother had bestowed on her had been
given with hearty good-will — and were extremely welcome —

— But as to handing over any of her children to her
charge — no, that she would not do. She had none to
spare, however hard it might be to provide for them.

Vilhelm *could* of course stay at the glassworks — but
no, not under these people who were to have the sway
there — it was no future for the boy to spend his life there
as a clerk or a warehouseman.

Perhaps after all she ought to have considered Captain
Cold's offer to help Claus. Officers as a class always enjoyed a certain distinction, and it was true that many of
them were also worthy of the highest respect as men. But
no — now less than ever did she dare to think of letting
that boy choose a career which was so beset with danger
in a moral sense. The slight drowsiness that had begun to
steal over Dorthea gave place again to wakeful terror.

Claus was far too fond of drinking when he had the chance — that was the naked fact and she could not shut her eyes to it. And then there was that horrible business with the girl. The thought of it oppressed her like a nightmare.

Even though Aleth of course exaggerated egregiously in making out that he had actually tried to ravish Tora, he must in any case have behaved rudely and aggressively, since it had made the child really afraid of him. And this was a boy who had not yet completed his fifteenth year. No, my friend, your mother is not going to send you out at large among the young warriors in King's Copenhagen.

Vilhelm — he had been quite touching, poor boy, as he assured them in all innocence that he would have asked this Tora to wait for him. Yes, he was a good child, her little Vilhelm. She had no anxiety about him. Even if possibly he had an inflammable heart. This was his second flame already. Well, that being so it would not be so long before he found a new object for his dreams of the future. Thank God, she need not take *his* little affairs to heart. Dorthea smiled fondly in the dark — for the present at any rate she could smile at Vilhelm's love affairs. And she lay thinking of her pet child till rest came upon her and she fell asleep.

Next morning, when Vilhelm came out with his arms full of the Sheriff's carriage cushions, Claus was there, examining the construction of the vehicle. Vilhelm affected to take no notice of him: " — oh, can you move a little? " He arranged the cushions and went back for the other things that were to go in the carriage. But when he returned his brother was still in the same place.

They had scarcely exchanged a word since that evening.

And now this morning, when they awoke, muzzy after a cold and miserable night, Vilhelm at any rate did not care to utter a word more than he was obliged to. Even a generous portion of the beer-posset which his mother made for the party was not sufficient to thaw him to any great extent.

" I say, Ville — " Claus began in a half whisper, as he turned to go indoors again.

" Yes. Was there anything? " he enquired in a chilly tone, as Claus said no more for the moment.

" No, it doesn't matter — I only wanted to tell you something." Claus blushed slightly and fixed his handsome eyes on his brother, in some embarrassment: " I'm sorry that — that I happened to kick you in the face."

Vilhelm felt himself go quite pale with anger. The swelling had gone down, but he knew he was still a fairly ugly sight, mottled blue and green and brown on one side of his face, and the eye was bloodshot. " Fancy — are you really sorry about it? Well, you are a nice one! "

" You can understand, Ville — if I had known that — known that you and she — that you were good friends, why — But I thought it was nothing but — I didn't think you meant any more than just fooling with her either."

It took Vilhelm a little time to find words: " — that I didn't either! And *that's* your idea of fooling."

" Well, yes." Claus stamped his foot, but he continued to look the other in the face. Vilhelm was quite aware that Claus wanted to beg his pardon, and also that he did not find it easy to do so. " You know, I had seen that she let you — and I thought it was just frolicking. And that made me wild — that she should be so prudish with me."

" Well, if you aren't possessed by seven devils! Will you never understand there are things you *can* say and things you *can't?* Now will you be so kind as to shut your jaw! "

Claus looked at him for an instant longer, biting his under lip — then he dropped his eyes. Vilhelm felt with intense satisfaction that he had given his younger brother a dressing-down and that Claus felt it too. The boy turned abruptly, went across to where their gig stood, with the Junker already in the shafts. Claus whistled a few notes as he found something to do to the harness.

A minute later, when Vilhelm was in the parlour telling the Sheriff that the carriage was ready, he heard Claus drive out of the yard.

Again it was late in the evening before they reached Brovold.

Bertel rushed out, followed by Claus, who helped his mother down from the carriage — and then Bertel threw himself into her arms and clung to her, as he burst into a violent fit of weeping.

" But my dearest — this is quite wrong — are you up at this time of night? " But Gunhild the nursemaid explained that it had been utterly impossible to get him to bed. Ever since Claus came home that afternoon and brought the news that the others were to be expected in the course of the evening, Bertel and Birgitte and Elisabeth had been wild with joy; it was not much more than an hour since the little girls had at last given up struggling against their sleepiness and allowed her to put them to bed.

Dorthea went through her house, still wrapped in her hooded cloak. Everything was in order, clean and tidy: the table was laid ready in the bedroom, and candles were alight in the candlesticks in front of the mirror; her own good bed had the curtains drawn and stood waiting with the sheet turned down, clean and inviting. Looking into the nursery she could see that the maids had tidied it up with extra care. Little Christen slept sweetly in the arm of the sleeping Johanne, and over in the children's bed all three little girls were asleep, lovely and warm, the baby half locked in the limbs of her bigger sisters — and the coverlet had slipped on to the floor as usual.

She went upstairs to see about the spare room where the Sheriff was to sleep; there too everything was as it should be — a pair of the best sheets on the bed and nothing forgotten.

In the kitchen Ragnhild was busy heating and pouring out the cream porridge, and Finchen Wagner was just coming up from the cellar with a bottle of her finest cherry syrup. They greeted her with a hearty welcome and Finchen kissed her hand — her dark eyes vied with her lips in smiling as the squat little woman declared in reply to Dorthea's enquiry that the children had been " as good as gold " — and all was well in her own home, thank you for asking.

Welcome home — ah, never had it been such a blessing to be home again. How cosy this house was, how good it was to be here. And now she had only come home in order to break it up; it was not to be grasped or imagined.

Next morning she had received her maids' report of everything that had happened during her absence, Elen

the dairymaid had given an account of her department.
" And Carl Cold? " she asked Gunhild, " what day did he
go home? "

The evening before last he had been sent for. The
Captain wished to have him home — and indeed it was
strange enough that he should wish it now — for just
think of it! poor Jomfru Langseth, it was to be death after
all! And the Captain was getting ready to leave; he was
to go to Denmark as soon as the funeral was over, on
Monday. And it was last Friday that the housekeeper
died.

" Oh, God have mercy on us! So that was the end after
all."

Yes, Gunhild would have told her the evening before,
only the Sheriff came in just then. Ah yes, it was last
Friday it happened. She was almost well again, it seemed
— the Captain had got a doctor up from Christiania, and
he said too that Jomfru Langseth was going on well. But
then they were to move up to the sæter on the Saturday,
and on the Friday afternoon Jomfru Langseth took it into
her head that she simply must go downstairs a moment
to see that everything was in order for the move. Well,
then they helped her to get some clothes on, and they had
to lead her, the dairymaid and Magnille, for she was so
weak, she could hardly stand on her feet. And just as
she was going down the stairs she fell in a swoon, and then
it was all over in a moment almost.

" O my God, how awful! "

" Yes, poor woman. Even if you can't help saying she
had a hand in it herself — it's a great pity all the same.
Such a kind and brisk and bonny woman she was, Marie
Langseth." Gunhild guessed that her mistress was not

in a mood to hear more of the disaster at Fenstad, and so she withdrew.

On the stairs, on the stairs — but it must be a coincidence. One heard sometimes of people who had gone through a long illness with severe loss of blood being snatched away suddenly like this, just when it was believed that the danger was past — indeed so far as she knew it happened not infrequently that death came upon them quite suddenly the first time they were on their feet again. On account of their brain being emptied of blood, she had heard — other doctors said it was because all the tainted blood had not been got rid of, with the result that a clot was formed, and if this went to the heart it was fatal.

That being so, the gypsy might easily have had some knowledge of cases of this sort and have foreseen that it might happen to Marie. Poor girl, poor girl — and poor Cold, both his heart and his conscience must be torturing him now, his nature was far from unfeeling. He was not a bad man.

O God, what did it serve her now that she had always hated superstition and mysticism — no, not hated, she had rather despised everything of that kind, treating it with a scornful smile. It was only now that she hated — now that she felt this abominable thing was trying to force its way into her soul, to poison it with the loathsome fumes of imposture.

Yes, for all this oracular business — it was poison! Sorrows and misfortunes, O God, be they never so heavy — one was given increase of strength with which to bear the increase of burdens. If only one could see one's way clearly, face one's misfortunes with open eyes, then reason helped one to preserve one's balance. But once one began to speculate whether mysterious forces, beyond the bounds of reason, lay behind the blows of fate, to search for obscure meanings within the impenetrable darkness — well, then life became unbearable! Darkness is always evil, it makes one unsteady of foot, afraid of shadows, irresolute, weak.

And moreover, what loathsome, vulgar tools they made use of, these powers of darkness postulated by superstition! A supernatural world which published its pronouncements through disgusting quacks or half-crazy hags, greasy playing-cards and low-minded gossip! Horrible! it was as though their mere contact infected everything — sorrows and passions, anxieties and disasters assumed the hideous discoloration and formlessness of corruption — no! O God, I am indeed weak, much weaker than I thought. But preserve me from being weak enough to put my faith in soothsaying and omens — for in thine own words thou dost call these things an abomination in the eyes of the Lord.

Dorthea decided to go to church this Sunday and to take with her the five elder children. The Sheriff accompanied them. So today their pew was quite full. And in the gallery the servants from Brovold were present in full force.

Perhaps it would be the last time she sat in this pew, thought Madame Dorthea; it was in the nature of a farewell, and therefore solemn, in spite of the fact that Pastor Muus as usual preached a very long and tedious sermon. But he had a good voice when he intoned. And the sight

of all the familiar faces round her, to which she bade
farewell in her heart, the music of the organ and the singing of the hymns, all this caused her deep emotion. Several times her eyes filled with hot tears as she sat wrapt
in her own thoughts during the sermon, holding on to
Birgitte, who nodded again and again. Little Elisabeth
slept peacefully on Haagen Lunde's lap — she and Rikke
had taken confidingly to the kindly giant, who with
these two entirely filled the part of benevolent grandfather.

The sun shone with Sunday brightness as they came out
of church. While Madame Dorthea moved slowly towards the church-yard gate, greeting one after another of
the groups that wandered among the graves to see to the
resting-places of their dear ones, she thought sadly —
here her Jörgen should be lying. Ah, in reality it could
not mean very much whether we committed the dust of
our friends to the earth or the Lord alone knew where a
person's mortal remains mouldered in the depths of the
forest or at the bottom of the sea. And yet she wished so
bitterly that it had been granted her to lay Thestrup in a
grave into which she herself could be lowered one day by
his side. Would his body never be found?

And it was so beautiful here by the old church, when
as now the sun shone upon the thick foliage of lime and
maple along the wall and the bells rang out over the summer scene. Oh, it was sinful that she should think of it
even for a moment — think of it while she was leading
her two little girls and her three boys were walking before
her on the path. But all the recent shocks had left behind
a weariness in her heart so deep that she could not help it.
But of course she did not mean it in earnest — and yet the

desire passed like a breath through her soul — if only she could have stayed here, been allowed to stretch her weary limbs beside the loved one, in the earth over there under the green lime-trees.

Her mournful reflections were interrupted by Pastor Muus coming up to greet her. He would be so glad if Madame Thestrup and her party would come over to the parsonage and take a little refreshment. Then Sheriff Lunde would have an opportunity of inspecting the alterations he was making — and would not Lise and Gitta like to meet his little girls and play with their fine new doll's house? He gave Elisabeth and Birgitte a friendly pat on the head.

Dorthea was obliged to reply that she had no time, while thanking him for the invitation. But she had to go home and make wreaths — she was driving to Fenstad this afternoon to pay her last respects to Jomfru Langseth, as the funeral was tomorrow.

It was so, replied the parson peevishly. It was well known that Pastor Muus was rather lazy, except where the work of improving his parsonage was actually concerned — to be obliged to visit his chapels of ease at odd times was not much to his liking. But Captain von Cold had expressly desired that his housekeeper should be interred on a week-day — he wished to show her all possible honour. Well, in that case Pastor Muus would not detain Madame Thestrup any longer. There was only one thing: he had heard that she intended to hold an auction before leaving the glassworks. And the pastor had thought of asking whether she would not sell him privately some of the furniture which he might need for the new rooms at the parsonage. There was in particular the large and handsome four-post bed that stood in the room she used daily — he and his wife would be glad to acquire that for the bishop's bedroom.

Painfully moved, Dorthea answered that the pastor might call at Brovold one day, then they could talk about it.

She could not take it with her. But nevertheless — it had been their marriage bed, the pavilion that had hedged about their tenderest bliss, in which their children had received the gift of life. And in which she had thought that at last they would close their eyes — the one not too long after the other, if God willed. But she could not take it with her — and for a lonely widow it was only a tragic monument.

Nevertheless, a bishop's bed — She was not very fond of bishops and bishops' ladies, from what she had seen of them while wedded to a clergyman. On the whole, her childhood in one deanery and her youth in another had given her a certain distaste for the clergy.

" It will be best for you to drive me," said Dorthea to Claus. She glanced with satisfaction at her work lying in the basket, the great wreath of all the finest roses and summer flowers in the garden, before folding the cloth over it and closing the lid of the basket. " The Captain has shown you so much kindness that you ought to pay the last respects to Jomfru Langseth. And you and Vilhelm are too young to attend the funeral tomorrow."

Claus looked down. " Cannot someone else drive Mother? I — I have such a pain in my stomach today."

" Have you, Claus? I saw no sign of it while we were having dinner."

" No, it has come on afterwards. And I'm sure I shall be ill — it will make me sick."

" O-oh — is it as bad as that? "

" Yes, if I have to look at her now," said Claus hotly. " She has lain there over a week already. And they never let you off that in the country — viewing the corpse."

Dorthea herself dreaded viewing the corpse. So she nodded: " Well well, then you shall be let off." But she could not refrain from adding, rather sarcastically: " It is a very natural feeling. But I thought you wanted to be a soldier."

" That's quite another matter," Claus began fiercely. But his mother handed him the basket and he hurried out with it.

So she drove herself. No, she had no desire either to see Marie's body or to meet the Captain again, she thought, as she emerged from the wood and saw the old house standing on the slope above the bog. The little water-holes twinkled so blue, and the leaves of the osiers gleamed smooth and oily — the whole bog was now rich with wild luxuriance and a wealth of flowers, forget-me-not, buttercups, gauze-like clouds of some kind of little white flower, gleaming tufts of bog-cotton. Yes, it was summer.

The cattle were at pasture in the meadow beside the bog, so they had not yet been taken to the sæter after all. Perhaps the Captain had decided to keep them at home as they were to be sold, and she would have to do the same with hers.

At Fenstad itself there were signs of activity, but it was not the Captain who came out to receive her. A strange woman in town clothes appeared at the door and invited her in. Her resemblance to Marie Langseth was striking, though this one was older and not so good-looking. It was in fact the dead woman's sister, and her name was Madame Kaxrud. They exchanged the customary greetings, and Madame Thestrup expressed her condolence.

" Unfortunately I cannot ask you to see my sister — the Captain had the coffin nailed down some days ago. But I dare say you would like to see *that,* and to lay your lovely wreath upon it with your own hand."

Dorthea drew a sigh of relief and accompanied Madame Kaxrud into the parlour.

There stood the black shell, resting on two trestles — how small it looked in that great room. The parlour seemed even more desolate than usual in the restricted sunlight that found its way through the sheet-covered windows. It had also been cleared of the Captain's things which usually littered the place — books, weapons, musical instruments. The clavichord was gone. And the portrait over the couch — a space on the wall which was less faded and dusty than the rest was all that was left to remind one of Fru von Cold. And here in the coffin his mistress's body had already begun to decompose — the smell was quite unpleasant, and Dorthea could see that someone had just wiped the floor under the coffin with a wet cloth.

It was not difficult for her to yield the appropriate tribute of tears to Marie's dust as she added her wreath to the others which decked the coffin. They were not so very few — six, and it was not a general custom for peasants to send wreaths. Jomfru Langseth had still enjoyed

the friendly consideration of her neighbours in spite of
what was irregular in her way of life. Dorthea wept un-
constrainedly with her handkerchief to her eyes — and
nose: the dead woman had been kind, handsome, industrious, faithful to her task — and for what was immoral
in her conduct she had atoned with her life, so it must
have been forgiven her by a merciful Heaven.

Afterwards she had to sit down and allow Madame
Kaxrud to wait on her with cake and a glass of wine. The
woman's husband joined them — he was tall, with a thin,
sharp-featured, florid face and he wore his hair in military
fashion, with a long pigtail tied with black ribbon. His
person exhaled an unpleasantly rank odour, which com-
bined with the smell of the corpse and of dust and withered flowers in the close air of the room. The mouthfuls
of cake were hard to get down and the wine went to her
head, even the first glass. But she was obliged to sit a
little while and to drink another half glass before she
could take her leave of the mourners with propriety.

The Captain was keeping his room, said Madame Kaxrud; he was unwell.

She fancied she caught a glimpse of a face at the window
upstairs as she went out to her gig. No doubt he was trying to drown his pangs of conscience in Norway's Lethe.
But at any rate everything had been done to give Marie
a becoming funeral. She had caught the smell of roasting
and baking as she passed the kitchen, and the death
chamber had been arranged very neatly — with wreaths
of heather on the sheets over the windows and mirrors,
candlesticks on the coffin and juniper strewed on the floor.
Well, Madame Kaxrud looked as if it could safely be left
to her.

She had not been able to bring herself to enquire about the children — what the Captain intended to do about Margrethe.

Then, as she drove past the goose-pond, she discovered the child standing out on the little pier which ran out into the water. An old wash-tub was floating just by it, and Grethe was trying to reach it with one litttle bare foot, singing loudly and merrily to herself the while.

Dorthea called out to her, but the little one pretended at any rate that she did not hear. She had to get down from the gig and go round the pond to stop the child playing in such a dangerous place. Now she could hear what Margrethe was singing:

> So off we must send, as fast as we can,
> To fetch Inger here on the morrow,
> And bid her to make as much haste as she can
> To help in our mistress's sorrow.
> For now is our pussy-cat dead dead dead,
> The mice are in the larder
> Stealing the butter and stealing the bread —
>
> First came the rats all dressed in crape
> And the mice came tumbling after —

" Come here to me, Grethe dear," Dorthea called. There was something so painful in her singing the gay nursery ditty, evidently inspired by the events at home of which she understood nothing. " Won't you come and say good-day? "

" Those are my ducklings," said Grethe beaming, as she pointed to the family which furrowed the muddy grey water in its flight to the opposite bank.

" Are they? But come over to me — shall we go round so that you can show me your ducklings better? "

Margrethe left the little pier. That she was barefoot did not necessarily mean that she was neglected — Dorthea knew from experience that little children love to run about barefoot in summer; Rikke pulled off her shoes and stockings whenever she was left alone for a moment.

She was a charming little girl, with smooth light-brown hair which fell about a delicate, healthy face. She reminded one a little of a Chinese porcelain figure, for her eyes were set a trifle aslant, and she half closed them in a curiously roguish way when she laughed. And she was laughing now, as she put her hand into Madame Dorthea's and confided to her: " Auntie Marie, do you know what she is? — she's gone dead! " Her little face beamed with pride.

It could be of no use to explain to the poor mite — better for her not to know what she had lost for the present. So Dorthea said merely: " I know that, my lamb — but now go up to Magnille, she will change your wet clothes."

" And so there'll be a funeral — a funeral at our place, with Auntie Marie."

" Oh yes — and they're making cakes now for the funeral. If you run up to the kitchen I'm sure they'll let you have a taste."

Not till she had seen Grethe safely inside the front door did Dorthea get back into the gig and drive on.

As she turned into the forest road a dog barked and a figure rose from the heather by the roadside. He approached her with his hat in his hand — in his green shooting-coat, with his gun on his shoulder, he looked younger and healthier than usual; she thought too he seemed less corpulent, and his face had lost its puffy look.

" I have been sitting here waiting for you, Madame Thestrup." He laid a hand on the side of the gig and looked up at her. " I was in doubt whether to pay you a farewell visit — or shirk a duty which inspired me with dread " — he gave a laugh of self-irony — " and write to you instead when I had arrived in Copenhagen. But then I saw you drive up to the house. And so I decided to look out for you on your way back."

Well, at any rate this was better than lying dead-drunk in his room. " I see — then perhaps we meet today for the last time, Captain Cold."

" That is indeed very probable. And do you know what, Dorthea — the thought brings me infinite melancholy! You occupy a greater space than perhaps you are aware of, in my too capacious heart." Again he laughed sadly. " But however that may be, I wish to thank you, dear friend, to thank you cordially, for all you have been to me during these years. Not least," he added in a low voice, " for what you did for my poor Marie. I am sensible of your brave struggle to wrest his prey from Death. But it was to be in vain."

" Yes."

" You have been weeping — your eyes are red. Ah well, Dorthea — I suppose you think I am a monster."

" I know very well that you are *not* one, Cold." She shrugged her shoulders. " You are no different from most men. But it is not a pretty picture, that is sure."

" No, you may be right there. But let me remind you of a maxim of your own which you once quoted to me: *L'amour c'est un plaisir, l'honneur c'est le devoir.*"

" It proved a costly plaisir for Marie Langseth, Cold."

" Ah, but — in reality we all pay dearly for that plaisir, in one way or another; you know that too, Dorthea! "

" Perhaps. But it depends upon whether the love we gained was *worth* a heavy price or not — "

" — and you consider Marie paid too high a price for what she got? Well, I don't know. You saw her sister, did you not? and the husband, Kaxrud is his name, a tanner. Do you not think that Marie was happier in her — illegitimate life here than if she had become the respectable wedded wife of some Kaxrud or other? "

" Perhaps. But from what you have yourself told me, you thought otherwise when you proposed to her a *mariage de convenance* — the first time she was with child by you."

" I did so. But as always Marie was the wiser of us two."

" And the result of all her wisdom is that tomorrow she is to be laid under the sod."

" Ah, Dorthea! Do you think I would have regretted it if it were myself that was to be laid in the earth tomorrow? — but for only one thing: to me *le devoir,* duty — *my* duty, you understand, as a man of action — has always been dearer to me than the joys of love. *Always,*" he said in a low voice, as though talking to himself. " The active service of my profession was life to me — more even than my wife — and yet I worshipped her! "

" Well then, Captain Cold — I hope you may recover your peace of mind in busy activity. You have my every good wish, you know that, I am sure."

" I do believe it, Dorthea." He seized her hand and kissed it warmly.

"And Carl?" asked Madame Thestrup. "How does he like the idea of going to Denmark?"

"He does *not* like it!" The Captain gave a little laugh. "He has really surprised me. I had no idea the boy was so passionately attached to Fenstad and everything here. I picture the future at Aunsögaard to him as attractively as I can, but upon my soul he seems to have no appetite for the life of a country gentleman in Denmark."

"Yet it is his native land."

"Oh, as far as that goes — he was such a tiny mite when we came here, he remembers nothing of home."

"Carl will soon accustom himself to the new life. And then you may be sure he will not wish to exchange it for the life here. And what of Margrethe?" she then asked. "Have you come to any decision as to where your daughter is to go?"

"The Kaxruds will take her in," said Cold, and his air became markedly gloomier. "In the circumstances that is the best I could do for Grethe. They are comfortably off. And in any case her aunt is an excellent and capable woman. She resembles Marie a good deal, I think?"

"Let us hope so. And now, farewell, and good luck to you, Captain Cold."

"Farewell!" Again he kissed her hand warmly and lingeringly. "Farewell. You amiable creature — "

"And my remembrances to the children, my friends Claus and Bertel above all," he cried after her as she drove away. He was standing in the road waving his green sportsman's hat when she looked back for the last time, as the road turned sharply into the wood.

12

HAAGEN LUNDE proved to be a good support to Madame Dorthea. He arranged all the legal formalities that had to be gone through before Thestrup's estate could be wound up — even undertaking a journey to Christiania to negotiate with those concerned; and he put Dorthea in communication with a lawyer of his acquaintance whom he considered trustworthy.

With his competent knowledge he valued the stock at Brovold and informed Dorthea of the lowest offers she ought to accept. If she was unable to obtain these prices for some of the cattle, he promised to take them off her hands; he would know how to dispose of them to advantage.

Jörgen Thestrup had always got on well with Sheriff

Lunde when they met. But it was not to be denied — a certain feeling of strangeness had prevailed between the manager and the farmer — both were men of pronounced self-confidence, and the consciousness that they belonged to different classes of society caused them both to maintain a certain distance. This was spanned however by plenty of bridges on which they could meet in friendly understanding — both were zealous patriots, active in their support of all undertakings tending to further the common weal, though each had his own sphere of activity.

The situation changed of itself now that Thestrup was no more. Haagen Lunde took charge of Dorthea's affairs with a truly paternal hand, and she now felt herself united to her mother's consort by a genuine bond of kinship. And in her house he soon assumed the position of a grandfather.

Vilhelm and Claus, it is true, continued to address him as " Sheriff," and Bertel was so shy with strangers that he never said a word to the visitor unless spoken to. But the three little girls had entirely surrendered their hearts to their new-found " Grandpa Haakon." They trotted after him wherever he went, while he was at Brovold; they fought for the privilege of holding his hand — and afterwards they related to their mother the most extraordinary stories which " Grandpa " had told them — jocular fairy tales, amusing fables about animals, but other things too of which Dorthea was less inclined to approve: she discovered with astonishment that even this very enlightened and enterprising representative of the peasant class believed in such beings as gnomes, fairies and ghosts of people who while alive had removed their neighbours' landmarks.

This was one of the reasons which made her hesitate to let him take little Elisabeth home to her mother's. Otherwise there was much to induce her acceptance of the offer. It was true, as Haagen Halvorsen said, that the child was "skinny and pale," it would undoubtedly do her good to go to Lunde and eat all the butter and cream she could manage. And Dorthea had often remarked that mothers who had shown themselves excessively harsh or indifferent towards their own children made up for it by becoming the tenderest and weakest grandmothers. It was not improbable that her mother would receive her little namesake with affection, indeed she might vie with the Sheriff in spoiling her. For Haagen Lunde and Elisabeth were as thick as thieves.

She was really a very pretty child — the one who resembled Dorthea most — blue-eyed, with the fairest silky hair and charming features. But although she had never been sickly like Bertel, she remained thin and was always extremely pale. She had also grown a good deal too fast; she was almost as tall as the sister, two years older than herself, who was the picture of health. Among grown-ups she was usually very quiet, but she could be boisterous enough when romping with the children from the glassworks or with the dogs in the yard. She got on badly at school, but then she was no more than five — it was fairly certain however that she would never have much aptitude for book-learning. On the other hand she was very quick at needlework and knitting, and showed great skill for her age at weaving and carding wool.

And she herself was so set upon going with Feierfax and "Grandpa Haakon" when they left. When Elisabeth found that all the animals were to be sold — even her own sheep and lambs — she wept bitterly. But Haagen Halvorsen consoled her: when she came to Lunde he would not only give her a sheep but a calf too, and a " little, little silver spoon " — and he would turn pretty cups and other nice things for her on his lathe, so that she could make herself a playroom as fine as that of the parson's daughters. Not only she but Birgitte and Rikke already had whole collections of the neatest little wooden spoons, rollers and other toys which " Grandpa " had made for them as they sat by the wood-shed in the evening — he was astonishingly dexterous in this way. But most of the things were for Elisabeth.

Little Christen was not really ailing, but he did not seem about to thrive properly. Perhaps Hanne's milk was too old; she had nursed Rikke before him. Dorthea was occupied more and more with the question of handing over Elisabeth to her grandparents. Her own future was so uncertain — as yet she had received no definite information as to the amount of the pension that would be allowed her. And although several old acquaintances of Thestrup and herself in the coast-town wrote encouragingly of her prospects of making a certain, though modest living if she were to open a dame's school there, this too was still very much in the clouds. And she had no doubt that at Lunde Elisabeth would live like a " pig in clover."

Then one mail-day Vilhelm came in with a bulky letter for her. With glad surprise she saw from the address that it was from Lauridz Winther. She had not expected so prompt an answer to the letter in which she had informed him of Thestrup's fate. With deep emotion Dorthea broke the seals.

Randrup Parsonage, the 28th June 1793.

My dear beloved Dorothea!

With the deepest Pain and Horror I have just learned from letters to my Wife from her Cousins in Christiania of the terrible blow of Fate which has fallen upon you: our Thestrup is no more! Three months have already elapsed since that disastrous evening when he left you and his house, and only now do we learn of it here in our quiet Corner of Denmark. Ah, dear Dorothea, how shall I be able to interpret to you my Sympathy, the Anguish it occasions me to think upon your wounded Heart, your Anxiety, your Loss, your Loneliness! You know, I am sure, how intensely I share your Grief. For to me too Thestrup's departure signifies the loss of the dearest Friend I ever possessed, the only one of my young Days. You know how steadfast was the bond of Kinship and Friendship wherewith from my earliest Childhood I was bound to my Cousin Jörgen. Yes, from those distant days of Childhood in our native Town I preserve the precious, now so sacred Memory of my playfellow Jörgen. Indeed it is all I recall of those years in Trondhjem, how Jörgen and I beguiled the fine Summer afternoons, while my Father conducted Evensong in the Cathedral. We then passed happy hours, playing together in the ruined part of the same, situated in front of the Church. Delightfully the sunbeams played upon the fresh greensward which clothes the soil among fallen piers of masonry. We two little Boys plucked the ripe raspberries which grew upon the heaps of shattered Stonework and played Hide-and-seek in and out of the openings in the venerable Remains of the ancient Church wall. With what unspeakable Longing did I await my Cousin Jörgen's arrival, when

Mother had informed me of Uncle Thestrup's decision that he should complete his Schooling with us. How happy were the years of Youth we spent together as Students in Copenhagen, how my Heart leapt with Joy in my Bosom, when I sailed back to Norway in order to enter upon my Calling as Curate to your first Husband, since I knew that thereby I should again be living in my dear Friend's vicinity.

Forgive me, dear Dorothea, if in the presence of your Grief I enlarge upon these Memories of him, but he was in truth so beloved by us both! Nor is it entirely for selfish reasons that I here rehearse the Remembrance of the Life we shared in Childhood and in Youth; this you will understand when I now lay before you my Proposal concerning the Future of your elder Sons.

As you will recollect, Jörgen and I had agreed that Vilhelm Adolf and Claus should complete their schooling at the Metropolitan School and should at the same time live in our Home, an Arrangement which both Christence and I would have been most happy to carry out. Now however, as you doubtless know, circumstances have altered, in that I occupy a Living in a remote country Parish of North Jutland. But, dear Dorothea, this need not necessarily involve any complete change in the Agreement arrived at between Thestrup and myself. In short, my Petition to you is, that you nevertheless send the Boys hither to Randrup Parsonage. My Wife and I would receive them with open arms, and with the ample time which is here at my disposal (only one Chapel of ease is attached to Randrup, namely Gliim), and with my many years of Experience as a School Teacher, I think I may venture to promise you that your Sons' Studies would be attended to no less sedulously than if they had been entered at the Metropolitan School. That our Neighbourhood is somewhat secluded is not to be denied; nevertheless we frequently enjoy the society of the neighbouring Clergy and of the amiable Family at Ravnsbjerg, the only Mansion in the Parish. Its owner, Counsellor Verner, is moreover a distant Relative of mine, since his Grandmother was a Winther, my Grandfather's Sister. However, it may not be an unmitigated misfortune that your young people should spend the last years before their Matriculation in rural Tranquillity, not exposed to too many disturbing impressions. The Shooting is good in the neighbouring tracts of Heath, and I assume that my Jörgen's Sons have acquired at an early age their Father's taste for the delights of Sport, as well as a familiarity with Dog and Gun.

Meanwhile, " That thou doest, do quickly." These Words of Our Lord and Saviour I permit myself to adopt, though in another and a more profane sense. The most advantageous plan would be if your Boys could arrive here and commence their Studies before the expiration of this Summer. And now I learn that the most favourable opportunity offers for their coming here in an easy and unusually inexpensive way. I must tell you that a number of my Parishioners add to their earnings from the niggardly soil, little suited for cultivation, by the fabrication of the famous black earthen Pots, which, after Bullocks for fattening, are doubtless the most widely known of North Jutland's Articles of Export. And it happens most fortunately that a Son of the most considerable Farmer here, Seier Andersen Quistgaard, is sailing immediately to Norway with a cargo of Jutish Pots, of which he disposes yearly in Christiania, from whence they are retailed in the surrounding country districts. Now if the two young men could present themselves in Christiania about the first of August, they would be met there by my Skipper, Anders Quistgaard, of the Schooner " Else Marie " of Mariager. He has promised me to await the Boys' arrival until 15. August and to make diligent enquiry for them at the house of Frue Bisgaard, where I assume they will be able to lodge until Skipper Quistgaard is ready to sail. He will then put them ashore on Danish Soil at Mariager, from whence they can drive by carrier's cart to Viborg, where without difficulty they will find a conveyance to bring them hither to Randrup. Should the weather conditions necessitate Quistgaard's putting into another Harbour, a thing of which however there is little probability at this Season, then Quistgaard has promised me that he will assist them in finding means of conveyance to Randrup. The excellent Quistgaard has declared his willingness to carry them both for the modest price of 8 Speciedalers (they must however bring their own provisions). If you furnish them with a sum of 20 Spd., it should be ample to cover all expenses, even such as may be entirely unforeseen, on their voyage hither.

And now, dear Dorothea, farewell, a heartfelt farewell. May God strengthen and comfort you in your grievous Sorrow. May He, who is Father of the fatherless, hold His Hand over your great flock of Children and grant you abundant Blessing and Joy in the progressing Lives of your Offspring and Jörgen's. This is the Prayer, from a full, sympathetic Heart, of your ever devoted Friend

Lauridz Th. Winther.

P.S. Christence unites her Greetings and warm good Wishes with mine. She too bids Vilhelm Adolf and Claus a hearty welcome to our quiet Home. Our little Mine looks forward with eager anticipation to making the acquaintance of the two hearty Lads from Norway and sends Greetings and Kisses to her Aunt Dorothea!

L. Th. W.

Madame Dorthea instinctively pressed Winther's letter to her bosom; her eyes filled with tears of relief. Here then was the solution of the question which had harassed and disturbed her more than any other — the immediate future of her two elder sons.

They were children no longer — alas, she reflected, only last winter she had still regarded them as such. But neither were they so grown-up as they themselves imagined. They were at the dangerous age when the youth has most need of being guided by a man's sure hand. Yes, this was in truth the direction of a benevolent Providence. If for the next two years she could know them to be safe in the good Winther's charge — he was a high-minded and judicious man, an experienced director of youth, and above all steadfastly devoted to their father's memory — oh, then something would be found later, when once they had taken their examination. Already she would see if she could set aside a sum against that time — if the proceeds of the auction were sufficient. And she could work — pinch and save. It would be easier now that on this point at least she had a definite goal on which to fix her eyes. And as students the boys themselves would have a chance of contributing to their own support — they could give lessons or take posts as tutors. Ah, then perhaps

Vilhelm after all would have an opportunity of following his bent, studying natural history; perhaps he might be a doctor. And Claus would have leisure to discover how his capabilities, of which the Captain had spoken, might be applied in a productive way.

She had scarcely dared to admit to herself how shockingly that business of the girl at Lunde had affected her. Claus's share in it was ugly. And the brothers had not been really good friends since it occurred. At times she said to herself that in reality it was only childish pranks — the desire of playing the grown-up had doubtless been the chief motive in the whole episode. And many of the other little things which caused her anxiety were really trifles — but they affected her so unpleasantly.

As for instance the other day when they arrived at home with their hair cut — without asking her leave, without even mentioning the matter beforehand. They simply appeared one day, and there it was. It was the schoolmaster at the works who earned a little extra money as hairdresser to the work-people; in his young days he had been in service as a valet in Copenhagen. Vilhelm had taken him a message from Thommesen, and then it had occurred to him that he would get rid of the pigtail which gave him so much trouble every morning. On his way home he met Claus, told him what he had done — and off went Claus to do likewise. And now both of them went about with heads à la sansculotte.

It could not be denied that this suited Claus; his hair fell naturally in graceful waves. But poor Vilhelm was a less pleasing sight — his unruly red mop was impossible to keep tidy. It bristled above his forehead worse than ever, reminding one of the flame of a candle. She had to present him with a whole pot of her own pomade, but that only made it look dark and straggling — besides greasing his coat-collar.

Thestrup had hated this new fashion of short hair — he thought it looked so slovenly. She could not refrain from laughing at him, of course, but he had replied with indignant protests: for if he had not much time to devote to it in the ordinary way, he *could* arrange his hair on occasion so as to look like a well-dressed gentleman. And that was true — he had always presented a courtly and elegant appearance when dressed in his best.

Well, that in itself was a trifle. But by degrees so many trifles of this kind accumulated that she passed her days in a perpetual feeling of insecurity: she had too little power over the two young lads to be able to guide their lives into safe channels; in attempting to do so she would scarcely achieve anything but making them impatient — or in the worst case disingenuous towards her.

They said very little when she informed them of their Uncle Winther's invitation. In the beginning neither of them showed any enthusiasm, but they concealed their lack of it under an air of sympathy: would it not be too much for Mother in present circumstances to let them both go to the university?

To which Dorthea replied earnestly, no, these very conditions made it a stroke of good luck for them to be given the groundwork of a more advanced education than she would otherwise have been able to provide for them.

" Ah — then is it Mother's intention that either of us ought to study for the Church, for instance? " Vilhelm asked anxiously — he was speaking for them both.

No, she did not intend that, if neither of them felt a call. Little by little, by pointing out the many possibilities that would be open to them, she got the two boys to take a more cheerful view of their forthcoming journey to Denmark.

In the evening, when she went to the kitchen to give an order, she was surprised to hear loud peals of laughter from the servants assembled at supper. She opened the door and discovered the young gentlemen marching up and down the long room, each crowned with a Jutish pot as with a helmet. Claus had got hold of the deep soup-cauldron which was so narrow in the mouth that it towered high above his head. Vilhelm had found a saucepan — it came down right over his ears and the handle stuck out coquettishly to one side. They were considerably abashed on catching sight of their mother.

Thank God, now and again they were still only children.

The auction was fixed for the third of August and the following days. So it was impossible for Dorthea to go with them all the way to Antonette's, to speak to the pot skipper herself and to see them aboard the schooner. She had to content herself with accompanying them part of the way and saying good-bye to them at one of the posting-stations on the road.

Haagen Lunde went home, but he was only allowed to take Feierfax with him, not little Elisabeth. After all, it was more than Dorthea could bear to see her flock reduced at a stroke from seven to four. She would have to keep the children together now, she thought, and this would be easier for her when the two elder boys were disposed of for the time being.

Already during the preceding winter she had sewn and knitted things for their journey to Copenhagen, so that they were now sufficiently supplied with underclothes and stockings, strong and made to allow for their growing. And she had gone through their wardrobe before the wedding, so luckily they required nothing new but a couple of thick great-coats. For these the good duffel cloth her mother had given her was the very thing. This was fortunate, for she had not much time to complete their outfit.

So Mikkel the tailor took up his post in the boys' room, and Dorthea sewed day and night. And it was a blessing to be so fully occupied; it kept her from thinking of anything but the work she had in hand, and it made her sit up so late that when at last she could go to bed and close her smarting eyes she fell into a deep and dreamless sleep, almost before her head had settled itself comfortably on the pillow.

A friendly letter from Christence had been enclosed with Winther's. Thank God. As her mother had said of Aleth, perhaps the effect of a marriage-bed — perhaps Christence had become more settled and sensible from having to fulfil the duties of a wife and mother.

The day of the boys' departure broke cool and misty. It was one of those mornings of late summer when one feels that the year has already begun to decline: the foliage looms dark-green at the edge of the meadow, where the darkening hay-cocks bear witness that Mary Slops has been true to her nickname, has been followed by James Wet Hat and finally by Olav Soaker.[1]

With a heavy heart Dorthea witnessed the farewell scenes in the yard, as Vilhelm and Claus were about to get into the gig. The little sisters clung screaming to their brothers, Bertel stood by the gig pale and shaken with emotion, the maids wept, and Lars and the other farm servants pressed the boys' hands with a solemn air and bade them farewell. No wonder Claus and Vilhelm looked pale and overcome as they glanced around for the last time at the dear familiar buildings which surrounded the pleasant grass-grown yard.

Just as they were driving off a magpie made its grating voice heard from one of the great ash-trees in front of the main building. So loud was the sound of its curiously wooden screech that everyone gave a start, and poor Bertel was utterly staggered.

They drove through the buildings of the works. Everywhere the work-people came out, men and boys, waving and shouting their greetings to the travellers. Hans Wagner in his leather apron, with rolled-up shirt-sleeves, swung his reddened arm with a loud cry of " Grüss Gott! "

Then their road took them over the old wooden bridge, where the wheels rumbled with a dull, hollow sound over the well-worn planks. The boys looked back over their shoulders.

" Well, perhaps we shall never be back here in our lives," said Claus in a hushed voice.

" We cannot tell. The only thing we know for certain

[1] These Saints' Days have the same reputation as the English St. Swithin's. — Tr.

is that the rest of us will soon be leaving here too, little
Claus. When all is said and done this only means that you
two are leaving a few weeks earlier than we should all have
been going away together."

" Yes, but that's just *it,* Mother! Had it been so we
might have thought that after all our home was here at
Brovold. Then it would not have been so."

" No. But now, you see, it has turned out like this, dear
child." Dorthea stroked his hand affectionately. " So we
must try to face the future with cheerful courage, shall we
not, Claus? "

Claus took her hand rather awkwardly and pressed it
significantly.

As it turned out they did not say much to one another
after all during the drive. Dorthea's heart was too full of
all the things she would have liked to say to her boys —
she positively shrank from beginning. If she were unable
to master her emotion — but that would be unfair to the
two lads, and not good for them either, if she herself
should appear too deeply moved: it could only serve to
make them faint-hearted and depressed. For at their age
it was natural that they should regard a journey like this
as an alluring adventure — the sooner they arrived at that
frame of mind the better.

But there was nevertheless one thing of which she must
speak to them.

However, she did not bring herself to say anything
about it until the very last moment — next morning, just
before they left Raaholt, the posting-station at which they
had passed the night.

Madame Dorthea was sitting with her sons on the bench

under the big elm in the yard, watching the busy life displayed before their eyes. The main road ran between the
houses of Raaholt. Two young gentlemen, each driving
his high-wheeled English dog-cart and followed by a
groom on horseback, had just attracted the boys' attention. Over by the coach-house some men were harnessing
four horses to the heavy chariot in which a clergyman's
numerous family were migrating from a living in Hedemarken to Laurvig — Dorthea had talked to the lady and
the elder children on the previous evening. And now
Hans appeared with one of the postmaster's lads carrying
Claus's chest — Vilhelm's was already stowed in the post-
chaise which was to take them on their journey to Christiania.

" Well — then it will soon be our turn to make a start."
Vilhelm turned quite pale under his freckles as he said it.
" I expect Mother will be home early this evening, as
there will only be you and Hans and no baggage in the
gig."

" I hope so. I don't like leaving the little ones alone
at home — with so many strangers about. I'm sure Johanne will not be able to resist having many a long chat
with them, and it will not do for her to trail little Christen
about too much in this chilly weather."

" Mother," said Claus bashfully. " I know that Mother
— that Mother has been displeased with me — several
times — this summer. Yes, and I know you had cause to
be so. And so — well, I wanted to ask Mother's pardon
for it all, before we say good-bye."

" God bless you, my boy — you have my forgiveness
already; for I know that at heart you are still our own
good, kind Claus. But I was glad to hear you say it.

" But still there is *one* thing I wish to speak to you both about, before we have to take leave of each other in a few moments." Their mother made a little pause. " You see, I have noticed that there has existed a certain, what shall I call it, a certain resentment between you brothers lately. Since your quarrel at Ole's wedding, to be precise.

" And this is what I beg of you earnestly. You must not allow this ill humour to take root in your minds — oh, for God's sake, dear children, do not let a quarrel, an outburst of passion, spoil the good brotherly relations that have existed between you two ever since you were quite little boys. You are so young, you do not yet know how easy it is for one person to wound another. Even those who are bound together by the bond of blood — oh, it is not to be avoided, even brothers and sisters, nay, even children and parents, even loving friends, may be led to do each other harm, from thoughtlessness, or in the heat of passion — often indeed unintentionally. And yet, with all its imperfection, the bond of blood, of kinship, is the most sacred, the strongest, the most beautiful of those which bind us human beings together in this imperfect world —

" And you are destined to help and support each other even more than most brothers. On whom should you rely, if you cannot rely on each other? Dear Vilhelm, dear Claus — you are now so alone in the world, you have hardly anyone but me, and I am able to do so distressingly little for you. If God will this may be changed, it may become easier for us all, easier for me to be a refuge and a support to you — but at this moment we know so little."

She ceased speaking, overcome by her emotion. Claus

had laid his head upon her shoulder and was weeping audibly; Vilhelm sat erect and pale, but he took his mother's hand and squeezed it spasmodically.

" Dear, dear children — be friends always, keep together! "

" Beg pardon, Ville," Claus sobbed against his mother's sleeve. " I didn't mean it the way you think either. You know that though, I told you one day."

Vilhelm nodded: " I remember. And I was — I was cross and stiff and sour, I know that. You mustn't — you mustn't be angry with me any more."

Dorthea embraced and kissed them time after time. The hour of parting had come; she had to release them — their post-chaise stood ready horsed a little way off, and old Hans was waiting to say the last farewell to his young friends. Dorthea felt as if her heart must break — but it was some consolation to see her boys reconciled to each other as they set out, waving affectionately to her as they went.

She waved back with her handkerchief, till she saw the chaise disappear at the bottom of the hill. Then she drew her veil over her tear-stained face and returned to the yard, where Hans stood waiting with her own conveyance.

The weather cleared up in the course of the day. And the summer evening was fine and calm as she neared home. In the vast expanse of sky there still floated the last masses of swelling dark clouds, which the sunset tinged with gold and purple. But it looked as if the rain intended to give over for the present. Dorthea saw the advantage of this: more people would attend the auction, and if it could be held in the open, out in the yard, the bidding was always brisker than indoors.

There was some bustle at the dragoon's as she drove by — Else no doubt counted rightly on doing business while the auction was on. This tavern, which occupied a sort of enclave on the glassworks' land, had always been an offence to Thestrup. But it was nevertheless convenient that on a day like tomorrow the people attending the auction could get beer and a dram to go with the food they brought.

Ragnhild the cook, Gunhild and Johanne hurried out to meet her as she drove up to the front door of Brovold. They wanted to hear about the boys' journey.

Dorthea looked in at the nursery to see to the little ones. Rikke lay fast asleep in the sisters' bed, but over in the other bed little Christen was awake — he hoisted himself into a sitting posture, stretched out his tiny arms to his mother, crowing and gurgling with joy at seeing her again and babbling his plaintive " moa, moa, moa."

Dorthea lifted up her youngest — the wet little mite — and pressed him to her. He had shuffled off his cap; the sweaty down on his head was rumpled and reddish — he was going to be a red-haired boy like Vilhelm.

" But the others, Johanne, where are the big ones? " Bertel, Birgitte and Elisabeth would hereafter be known as " the big ones."

They were down at the Scharlachs', Johanne explained. Finchen Wagner had been up to fetch the things that Madame had said she and Mother Scharlach were to have as souvenirs. And when she went home the children had gone down with her. Should she run down and bring them back?

" Oh no — I should like to go down myself. Just you go to bed, Hanne — you have had a busy day. You can go to bed, all three; I will help the little girls to get undressed — if Gunhild will first lay the table for us in the bedroom. The children and I can have supper together. But listen, Ragnhild, you can find something good for us — rusks, and a cream cheese, one of the fresh ones with caraway seeds. And milk for the children."

The sky was clear with a greenish light in the north and west and the last drifting banks of cloud were now black, but the east was dark and blue, and everywhere star after star pierced the darkness, already bright with the radiance of autumn. A belated corncrake could be heard grating in the field.

The corn now stood high on both sides of the road, as Dorthea with a shawl over her head and shoulders hurried down the slope towards the river, the bend of which gave a paler reflection of the light in the sky. She recalled that evening of late winter when she had hurried down here in the storm and the ghostly moonlight to seek advice and comfort with the old German. It seemed an eternity since then. What a good thing one cannot look into the future — had she then guessed how they were to become the sport of destiny — oh, then she could not have found the reassurance which good old Scharlach had nevertheless been able to impart to her on that unhappy night.

The work-people's quarters also looked quite different in summer-time. Against the red-painted walls, which glimmered softly in the last of the evening light, stood high hollyhocks with bunches of pale flowers, and the porches were surmounted by the dark mass of hop-vines.

" *Herein!* " came the answer, as she knocked at Scharlach's door. But no one was in the kitchen except Master
Wagner; he sat in the chimney-corner cleaning his gun
by the light of the embers and a solitary tallow candle,
while whistling softly and musically one of those strangely
moving melodies of which these Germans knew so many.

The others were in the garden, he explained in reply to
Madame's question. He pointed to the little door at the
back; Madame Thestrup could go out that way.

A short flight of steps led down to the narrow garden
path bordered with bright flowering plants which trav-
ersed Scharlach's garden and ran in a straight line down
to the arbour near the river bank. Here a strong and
pleasant scent of aromatic herbs came from the beds —
dill, celery, chives. The potato-beds were luxuriant with
dark-green leaves, interspersed with the starry clusters of
pale blooms. The moist evening air was cleft by the flight
of bats, and from the arbour at the bottom of the garden
Dorthea caught the intoxicating perfume of honeysuckle
— " *das Blümlein Je-länger-je-lieber* " Mother Scharlach
called it.

They had a candle on the table inside the arbour — it
stood in a tall glass shade against which hovering night-
moths beat their sombre wings. It showed up the old
man's face — he was sitting with a book before him,
reading aloud; it was a German prayer-book, Dorthea
gathered. And by the benches surrounding the table
knelt not only Mother Scharlach and Gottlieb, their
youngest son, Finchen Wagner with her little boy, but
also her own three children.

Now Scharlach closed the book, clasped his hands upon
it and bent his head. In his deep voice he recited the

words of the Requiem in his native German, and his kneeling companions uttered the responses.

" *Die ewige Ruhe gieb Ihnen, o Herr, und das ewige Licht leuchte Ihnen!* "

" *Dich ziemt Lobgesang auf Sion, o Herr,*" responded Mother Scharlach and Finchen, " *und dir soll man Gelübde zahlen in Jerusalem, erhöre mein Gebet. . . .*"

" *Sie mögen ruhen im Frieden. Amen.*"

Dorthea paused, hesitating. There was something finely patriachal about these quiet family devotions in the arbour which impressed her, but at the same time it jarred on her that the Scharlachs should allow her children to take part in an alien act of worship such as this.

Scharlach continued in Norwegian:

" We also pray Thee, dear Lord God, to have mercy on the soul of Thy servant Jörgen Thestrup, that Thou mayest cleanse it from all sins and graciously confer on him Thine absolution, so that he may enter into Thy heavenly bliss! Grant him eternal rest, O Lord "

" and let eternal light shine upon him," replied the clear voice of Bertel. " May he rest in peace. Amen."

Dorthea stepped abruptly into the arbour: " Good evening," she greeted them, but could not repress a note of irritation in her voice.

The whole company rose. Birgitte and Elisabeth looked bashful for a moment, as though they had been caught doing something naughty — but then they darted to their mother with little cries of joy and embraced her round the waist. " Mother — has Mother come home! " But Bertel regarded her with a strangely irresolute glance and seemed to shrink away in the direction of the little brown Mother Scharlach.

Dorthea exchanged the customary greetings with the foreman and his family and delivered messages from the boys. Then Scharlach blew out the candle, put his book in his pocket and showed the way round the houses and out on to the road. Without too many words they said good-night outside Scharlach's door — the embarrassment on both sides was very apparent.

The children said nothing as they began to mount the slope with their mother. But then Dorthea roused herself; she gave the little ones greetings from Vilhelm and Claus, told them about her journey and found amusing little incidents to describe to them. About the parson from Hedemarken who had to have four horses to draw his coach because he had so many children: " they were twice as many as you — don't you think it must be great fun for them to be so many brothers and sisters? "

" Yes, but if they are as small as Christen many of them? Then they can't have much fun with them," remarked Elisabeth sententiously.

" That is all rubbish, Lisbeth — don't *you* have plenty of fun with dear little Christen — when you sing to him and play with him, then you make him laugh, don't you? "

" *I* can play with Christen, and that makes him laugh. But *he* cannot play with me," said Elisabeth decisively.

Birgitte and Elisabeth were simply in ecstasies on seeing the dainty meal laid out for them in their mother's bedroom. Not many times in their lives had they been allowed to have supper with the grown-ups — a bowl of oatmeal porridge or bread and milk in the kitchen was their daily fare. And here were biscuits and cream cheese, together with other delicacies usually reserved strictly for the grown-ups.

Only Bertel was silent. His couch had now been moved into this room. The boys' room upstairs had been cleared and stood empty, none of these brothers would ever use it again.

And Dorthea was still feeling greatly depressed, though she chatted and joked with her little girls. The room looked so strange and poverty-stricken since the great four-post bed had been taken away. It had been replaced by a simple wooden bed — the one that had been in Dabbelsteen's room. It looked bare-legged, thought Birgitte, who was used to her parents' canopy bed with curtains falling right down to the floor. It was really a very apt description of the unpretending piece of furniture which stood there on its four thin legs. And Dorthea had not yet been able to accustom herself to the absence of curtains around her bed — she did not sleep so well at night.

But to the two little girls it was quite a treat to be allowed to undress in here, helped by their mother herself. They did what they could to prolong the scene, but at last Dorthea managed to get them safely tucked up in their bed in the nursery.

Bertel lay on his couch with his face to the wall when she returned to her room. The feeling that this room had suffered grievous impoverishment overcame her again — the light on the supper table was reflected in the window-panes, on which the darkness outside seemed to be pressing inward. In summer she was not in the habit of closing the shutters — whenever she woke up she liked to see how far the night was advanced, and what the weather promised. But now she felt a sudden desire to shut out the night. But as she opened the first window to stretch out for the shutter, she started back in alarm — a dark figure was standing beneath the window.

" It is only me, Madame Thestrup."

" But heavens, Scharlach, what are you doing in the garden at this time? "

" I was just thinking whether I should knock — if it is not too inconvenient for me to come in and speak to you a moment."

" It is late, but — " Dorthea hesitated an instant. " I think I understand what you wish to speak to me about — I will come round now and open the door for you." Just as well to get it over. If he himself wished to talk about it, she would have no objection to letting him hear her opinion.

Scharlach followed her into the bedroom. He paused in the shadows by the door, with his cap held against his chest. Dorthea seated herself in the armchair by the table: " Come over here, Scharlach, and take a seat, if you have something to say to me."

" Yes, Madame Thestrup." The old man lowered himself on to the stool opposite her. " I could see that you were displeased at Mutter and I allowing the children to be present this evening when we were saying our prayers."

" Displeased — well, we can call it that. You know, Scharlach, the religion which you and your wife profess is quite a different one from ours."

" *Quite* a different religion it is not, I think? "

" Well, a different confession then."

" That it is, undoubtedly. But still we sometimes go to

your church, Madame Thestrup — because we have no other up here. Finchen's children were baptized by Pastor Muus."

" I know *you* go to church now and again, and the Wagners too. But I am sure Mother Scharlach has never set foot there."

" No. No. But, you see, Mutter does not understand Norwegian very well."

" Is that the reason? I see."

" Well, so I was thinking, Madame Thestrup, as we have prayed to Our Lord in your church — I thought there could be no harm in it if the children of this house said their evening prayer to the dear God together with us."

Dorthea thought for a while before answering:

" Well, Scharlach — they say everyone is blessed in his faith. It is far from being my desire to take your faith from you. But you know me well enough to understand that I dislike any kind of — extravagance. Also religious extravagance — I will not on any account have my children infected with that."

" Extravagance — " repeated Scharlach thoughtfully.

" Yes — I heard it, quite accidentally, as I came up — you were praying for the dead."

" But we always conclude our evening devotions with the prayer for the poor souls, Madame Thestrup."

" You said just now, Scharlach, that you had allowed the children to be present while you said your evening prayers. But that is not quite true, my good man — it was more than that. I heard with my own ears that you prayed specially for my husband's soul — and so did Bertel; it is obviously not the first time *he* has taken part in your prayers for his father. Eh, Scharlach? "

Scharlach looked up at her with that curious dark gleam his eyes had under their hoods of bushy grey eyebrows.

" Eh, Scharlach? "

" No," he said quietly. " The first time it came about by chance — Bertel happened to hear that Mutter and I were praying for the repose of the manager's soul. When he asked me, I told him in Norwegian what we had been saying — and then he wished to join us. And that I *could* not refuse him, Madame Thestrup — I had not the heart to do it! For it is such a miserable thing, madam, to think of a poor soul whom no one remembers in his prayers — and this was his own child."

" But how can you say, Scharlach, that no one remembers! And that Thestrup should be a poor soul, as you call it — who stands in need of others' supplications. Why is that — because he is a heretic, I suppose — ? " she asked caustically.

" Ach du lieber Gott, Madame Thestrup — are we not all poor souls? When we reflect " — he flung out his hand, fixing his dark eyes upon her with a strangely sorrowful look — " that one day we shall be plucked out of this our mortal frame and stand naked as we were born, face to face with Eternal Perfection! "

Dorthea was silent for a moment. Then she tried to shake off the disturbing impression: " Eternal Perfection — yes, that may be all very well. But we mortals cannot come up to that — and I am sure Heaven does not demand that of us."

" And yet Our Lord Jesus says that we shall be perfect, even as our heavenly Father is perfect. Yes — it is really terrible to think of, I have often felt that. But He actu-ally does demand as much of us."

" O-oh. I cannot remember having read that. I did not think, by the way, that you Papists were so well read in the Bible? "

Scharlach smiled. " Unfortunately no; I have never possessed a Bible. I must content myself with those por-tions to be found in my old Goffine. But he gives us the lessons and the gospels for every Sunday and holy day in the year."

" But at any rate there is nothing in it about our having to pray for the dead — that is a purely human device and nothing else."

" Oh yes, there is, madame — it says in the Book of Maccabees that it is a holy and wholesome thought to pray for the dead. It is the lesson for All Souls' Day. Per-haps it was a human device, as you call it, in the first in-stance, when Judas Maccabeus prayed for the fallen among his people and offered sacrifice for them. But then God has approved his solicitude for the dead, since it is to be found unchallenged in holy Scripture that it *is* a holy and wholesome thought to pray for them."

Dorthea shook her head impetuously:

" No, no — that is what I call extravagance. And if Jesus really said that we are to be perfect, it can only have been an exaggerated expression, intended to incite us to greater zeal in our efforts to act up to the lofty and bene-ficial principles He has left us in His testament. To show due reverence to the Origin of all goodness and to serve our neighbour according to our ability — if we do this I do not think we need have any fear for our eternal welfare.

"And, my good Scharlach, I do not think you will dispute the fact that your manager was a sincerely good man who always endeavoured to do right by everyone and to be useful to his fellow-men. If you can really hold that at this moment Thestrup's spirit is — poor and homeless — so that you and the children have to implore God as a favour to admit his soul to eternal rest in Heaven — oh no, Scharlach, who could then stand the test? Then no living person would dare to face death with an easy mind."

"Ah, dear madam, we also pray that He will cleanse us from all sins and let us be partakers in His redemption."

Dorthea shivered involuntarily. Cleansing from sins, redemption and the blood of the Lamb — oh yes, these were the things her stepfather had constantly preached about. And yet he himself, in spite of his unquestionably good points, was an avaricious, gluttonous and ambitious man. Whereas Bisgaard, who had not the slightest belief in all this mystical side of the Christian religion, worshipped God's exalted majesty in pious humility and sincerely admired the Lord Jesus as the originator of the most beautiful and excellent moral principles, which he himself did his best to follow. That she had felt bitter repugnance to becoming his wife, that she had been forced to waste her youth with him when he was no more than an ailing and exacting old man — these considerations had never blinded her to the fact that Bisgaard was at the same time a generous and charitable man, a true philanthropist, whose guidance in the formation of the mind and heart she would do well to follow.

" Scharlach, Scharlach — all that is fanaticism and morbid flights of imagination. A dark superstition which leads to nothing, except to prevent the clear and lofty light of religion from penetrating our understanding and ennobling it."

" Dear madam! " Scharlach's face wore a melancholy smile. " Indeed you have a wise and kind disposition, and that had Herr Thestrup too, God bless him. But that is not *enough*, madam — that religion enlightens our understanding. Our understanding is good to have and to use, but it is only a part of our spirit — just as the day is good and blessed — but it is only a part of the twenty-four hours."

" It is *that* part of the twenty-four hours, Scharlach, which is given us to turn to account and to work in. Darkness is evil and ugly — that is why we give the name of powers of darkness to all the hideous mummeries conjured up by human cowardice and stupidity and malice. No, the night is the friend of no man! "

Scharlach looked at her for a moment. Then he burst into a laugh, a quiet laugh of amusement: " The night is the friend of no man — but my dear good madam, how can you say such a thing! You who yourself have had seven delightful children."

Dorthea blushed with annoyance. But the old man's smile was so disarmingly innocent — and so she had to smile too. But this was not a thing to which one could make reply — that she had not meant it in that way when expressing her hatred of night.

" Ach ja, Madame Thestrup — no doubt God's blessed sun and the fair light of reason are given us for our good.

But nevertheless the sun must go down every evening, to let us see how many stars there are in the heavens — each of them a sun, just as great and beautiful as our own, so I have been told. No doubt there are dangers and many an evil thing threatening us in the darkness — but it also brings coolness, refreshment, rest to everything that grows and lives here upon earth. And the good sleep — and it is only the night which truly brings together those who love one another, the night it is which breeds new lives."

Dorthea's eyes suddenly filled with tears. It was so true, what the old man was saying — only she had never thought of it in this way. That the night might also have claims on our gratitude for the good gifts it brought.

" Nor is the sun able to light up its part of this world for us, except by concealing what lies farther off — for the stars are there above us just the same all day long — except by masking all that lies farther off, by the very power of its light. Just as everything that is out and about at night — birds and beasts and all the sounds which we do not hear except in the stillness of night — they are just as much alive, even when they have crept away to hide from the strong sunshine. And it is not true either that the daylight is serviceable only to that which is good, unfortunately for us sinful creatures. Think of all those to whom the day means only toil and trouble and anxiety — and of all those who use their day and their intelligence to torment and cheat and fleece their neighbours. Ah no, Madame Thestrup — we can just as readily use our intelligence for evil as for good."

"You are wrong, Scharlach," said Madame Dorthea hotly. " It only appears so! To do evil, that can never be really sensible. Genuine intelligence, that is the same as goodness! "

"God bless you, Madame Thestrup! " Scharlach regarded her with sympathy. " That everyone is blessed in his faith, as you said, is not my opinion. There are plenty of those who believe that wickedness is the true sagacity — even if you will not acknowledge that this is so. Well, but I dare say you are right there. And I am sure of one thing: that with your faith you will at any rate never be *altogether* unhappy."

He got up: " — but it is getting late. I am keeping you up — and you have a tiring day before you tomorrow."

"Yes." She shuddered. " Tomorrow it begins. Well — there may be a good deal of truth in your extravagant notions, Scharlach — for extravagant they are. And in spite of all you can say they are related to all those monstrous beliefs in ghosts and fairies and signs and omens, all the things with which human imagination has peopled the darkness."

" But I would never deny that there is both good and evil in the darkness as in the light. No doubt the Devil and his angels are abroad both by night and by day, they never rest nor sleep."

"Ah, then do you believe in the Devil too — with horns and hoofs and bat's wings and all the rest of his masquerading? "

" I believe he is a liar and the father of lies — as to the deceptions and mummeries he may assume to scare us into his toils, I can say nothing. But behind all these — superstitious trappings which you despise so heartily — and rightly abhor, there may lurk worse powers than are suspected by your honest soul, Madame Thestrup."

The old man was now on his feet, and Dorthea also rose. " Upon my word, you have no small opinion of your own view of these things, my good Scharlach," she said with a little laugh. " However — what I wanted to say was, that you must not fill the children's heads with this kind of ideas and curious speculations. But now, more's the pity, there will be no more chance of it. Soon our ways will part for ever — Scharlach, my good friend! "

" That is not so sure, Madame Thestrup. Whether you like it or not, Mutter and I will continue to pray the good God to bless you and your children, dear madam," he said in a low voice, squeezing her hand so that it hurt.

Dorthea let him out and walked a few steps with him. As she emerged from the dark screen of the ash-trees she saw that the sky was studded with a profusion of stars. They flickered and flared in the faint night breeze that had sprung up and set the foliage quivering restlessly.

" Well well, good night then, Scharlach — and give my love to Mother Scharlach, and Finchen and Wagner and the little ones."

It looked as if there might be more wind in the course of the night. Should she go round and close the shutters of the bedroom windows from outside? — inside it was impossible to get them properly fastened so that they would not spring open and clatter if the wind got up. But honestly she had to confess she dared not; no, after all she was not very brave in the dark.

Those flaming masses of stars high up in the dark, velvety and boundless vault of heaven — no, to her they seemed inhospitable, they inspired anxiety. Suns, said Scharlach — well, they might be that, but they were not her dear familiar sun, any of them. A cold breath came from empty space, where they wandered on their appointed paths. She went in, carefully bolting the front door after her.

True enough, the night meant also gentle sleep, it was the protector of the sweet raptures of faithful lovers, of their life-giving embraces on the couch of love. But, but, but — were not these the things to which one ought to abandon oneself without deliberation? Close one's eyes, not look into the Janus-face of Night, too full of things both evil and good.

Day — ah well, that too existed both for evil and for good. But still it was our home — an island, situated in the ocean of the unknown, but lighted by the sun and by human reason. It was exposed to breaths both from the vulgar mouths of witches and from the starry sky of the pious old visionary. In effect both the one and the other gave her a feeling of discomfort.

She gave up fastening the shutters. It was now so late — and she was tired; she felt she would fall asleep as soon as she lay down. And when she awoke it would be getting light already; the nights were still short, thank God!

With quiet, rapid movements Dorthea began to undress. On the dressing-table lay an open book, turned face downward — it was the rebus Bible. She had lent it to the girls while she was away.

She picked it up to replace it in the drawer of the escritoire. It was opened at the page which contained this passage: He that followeth after righteousness and mercy findeth —

And then came the picture of the child blowing soap-bubbles, sitting astraddle on a death's-head. Life, it was intended to represent.

Quickly she dropped the book into the drawer and shut it with a bang. Then she blew out the candle, crept on bare feet to her bed and drew the coverlet over her head, barring out the darkness of night by the darkness under the bedclothes.

A NOTE ON THE TYPE

THIS BOOK is set on the Linotype in Baskerville. The punches for this face were cut under the supervision of George W. Jones, the eminent English printer and the designer of Granjon and Estienne. Linotype Baskerville is a facsimile cutting from type cast from the original matrices of a face designed by John Baskerville, a writing-master of Birmingham, for his own private press. The original face was the forerunner of the " modern " group of type faces, known today as Scotch, Bodoni, etc. After his death in 1775, Baskerville's punches and matrices were sold in France and were used to produce the sumptuous Kehl edition of Voltaire's works.

This book was composed, printed, and bound by The Plimpton Press, Norwood, Mass. The paper was made by S. D. Warren Co., Boston. The typography and binding are based on designs by W. A. Dwiggins.